# THIS WILL NOT BREAK ME

- ANGELA M. GREEN -

# DEDICATION

I dedicate this book to anyone who has ever had a dream. Keep Dreaming. Keep Hoping. Keep Believing.

# TABLE OF CONTENTS

# PROLOGUE

"You are way past your time." Cindy rolled her eyes in frustration. She hated when her johns tried to steal time.

"I'll pay you for your time. Just let me finish. Turnover. Maybe that'll work."

Cindy reluctantly rolled onto her stomach and pushed up on her knees. She stole a glance at the closet. Everything seemed to still be ok. A couple of minutes later... Eureka! Finally, he was finished and Cindy could move on to her favorite person of the day.

"Don't forget to pay me for my extra time." Cindy recited as she got up from the bed and pulled on her robe.

The john continued to dress without saying a word. Then he grabbed his wallet as if to pay her, but put it in his back pocket instead.

Cindy took a step toward him. "I said you need to pay me."

"Believe me, it's not even worth the extra money." The john headed for the door and swung it open hoping to make a quick exit.

"We got a problem here playa?" A tall, dark, scary looking fellow, with dreads down his back blocked the john's path.

The john took a step back. "No... no there's no problem."

"Seems as if you have overstayed your welcome. Did you pay the lady for her extra time?"

"I was going to."

"Don't look like you was to me."

The big scary fellow pulled up his shirt to reveal an all silver 9mm. The

John took a step back.

"Look. I don't want any problems." The john's voice was trembling.

"Neither do I said the dreaded guy with his hand on his 9."

"Look, I'm going to pull out my wallet from my back pocket and pay the lady."

"How about you hand that wallet over to me instead."

The john reluctantly obliged.

"Not much here. He sifted through the wallet. I'll be taking all of this."

"Tha… that's fine." The john stuttered. He was just trying to make it out alive.

The dreaded guy handed him back his wallet and the john took off as fast as his legs would take him.

"Thanks." Cindy muttered. She hated looking weak in front of Daryl, her pimp.

"I don't see why you're thanking me. This money belongs to me."

"Daryl? You know I need that money." Cindy tried not to sound threatening.

"Oh really. For what?"

"You know for what." Barely speaking above a whisper. She didn't want to bring it up.

"Oh yeah." Daryl took a step inside the room with a smile plastered on his evil face. "So how is your little special project going anyway?"

"It's fine. I appreciate you again for allowing me to take on the project." Cindy emphasized project, not really wanting to call her daughter a project.

Cindy glared toward the closet trying to imagine what her sweet little girl was doing in there. She hated raising her in a whore house, but this was all she had right now. She was just lucky Daryl was letting her keep her little girl.

"Do I have any more clients?" Cindy asked. Even though she was hoping to be done for the day she was willing to try anything to get Daryl to turn around and leave.

"So, where is she?" Daryl asked totally ignoring Cindy's question.

"She's sleeping." Cindy lied. She actually didn't know what her little girl was doing. All she knew is that she didn't want her around Daryl.

"Well?" Daryl stepped even closer to Cindy.

"Well, what?"

"I want to see the girl."

Cindy took a deep breath. There was nothing she could do but oblige Daryl. After all, it was his house.

She walked toward the closet, opened it, and looked into the two most beautiful eyes she had ever seen.

"Mommy." Michelle exclaimed pulling off her headphones.

Cindy had set up a little oasis in her walk-in closet full of fun things for Michelle to do while she entertained company. She even brought her some noise-cancelling headphones and told her she had to keep them on no matter what. She hated for Michelle to hear what was happening on the other side of the door. But Michelle always did what she was told. She called the closet her enchanted forest. She would tell Cindy all the adventures she had at the end of the day or early in the morning when she woke up. Michelle's getaway was equipped with a sleeping bag in case Cindy's night ran well over into the next day.

"Is it time to come out now mommy?"

"Yes, baby. It's time to come out. I want to hear all about your adventures!"

"I was sleepy. I didn't have any adventures. I just woke up." Michelle wiped her little eyes. She grabbed her favorite blanket and stepped out of the closet.

"She has really grown up." Daryl smirked staring Michelle up and down. "She almost makes me want to start providing my clients with some special services." Daryl laughed as if something was amusing about what he was suggesting.

"I tell you what. Let me make some calls and I'll get back to you. I think it's about time your little girl started earning her keep too. Nobody lives here for free."

A chill went down Cindy's spine.

After a quick shower with Michelle, Cindy headed to the McDonald's down the street. She had to catch herself when she realized she was practically dragging Michelle beside her.

"Mommy are we racing?" Michelle had asked.

"Yes baby, let's run, let's run as fast as we can."

Cindy ordered Michelle something to eat and got her situated. Cindy pulled out her cellphone and pulled up the number for Ms. Sims, the midwife who came to the house and delivered Michelle. Ms. Sims also came to give Michelle all her checkups and kept her shots up to date. She came across the number. Dialed.

"Hello."

"Hi. I'm looking for Mrs. Sims."

"Who is this?"

"A friend."

"Ms. Sims moved out of the country a couple of months ago."

"Oh, okay. Thanks."

Cindy's heart began to beat out of her chest. She didn't know what she was going to do. She had to get Michelle out of the house and quick. She was not going to let Daryl violate her little girl. She would die before she let him hurt her. Cindy couldn't believe what she was about to do, but she felt she was out of options. She scrolled through her phone and pulled up another number.

"Hello."

"Hey mom. It's me Cindy."

"Cindy, I thought you were dead."

"Well, as you can see, I'm not mom."

"Well, what do you want? I told you I never wanted to speak to you again."

"I need your help."

"What makes you think I would help you after what you put me through."

"It's not for me mom. It's for my daughter."

"You have a daughter? You stopped prostituting?"

"No mom. Look, I need you to keep my little girl until I can get a safe place for her."

"I am not about to keep no babies Cindy. You got knocked up; you take care of your own responsibility."

"Mom, I have been taking care of her, but my pimp just noticed Michelle and now he wants to adopt her into the business. Mom, she's only six years old, please."

There was silence on the other end of the phone. "Tell me where you are."

Cindy grabbed Michelle's hand and walked her outside to her mother's car. “Michelle this is your grandma. Can you say hi to grandma?”

“Hi grandma.”

“You are going to stay with your grandma for a little while and then I'll come back and see you later okay.”

“No, I wanna stay with you.”

“I know baby, but mommy is going to work. Grandma will buy you some ice cream. Lots of it.”

“Yes. Ice cream. I'm in.”

“Always remember I love you, Michelle.”

“I love you too mommy.”

“Get in the car babe.” Cindy stood up and looked at Michelle sitting in the backseat unaware of what was going on. She was such a happy child. Cindy went into her pocket and pulled out some cash. “Use this to get her some clothes or whatever you need. I can’t risk taking her back to the house to pack her bags.”

“I don’t want your money. I got money.”

“Look, I'll call you and check on Michelle as much as I can. Please take good care of her.”

“She'll be fine. Just don't bring your trash to my house. If there is ever a conflict, I promise you I will turn this little girl over to child services faster than you can blink.”

“I won't mom. Just please take care of her.”

The car sped off. Cindy broke down crying. Did she make the right choice? Would Michelle really be safe with her mom? She could only pray that her mom would do the right by Michelle. Lord knows she never did right by Cindy. *God, please take care of my baby. God, please.*

Cindy finally got the courage to go back home. She had walked around the park for what seemed like hours. She didn't know how Daryl would react to knowing that Michelle was gone and he wasn't going to be able to fulfill his plans with her. But right now, she didn't care. As long as Michelle was safe, she didn't care what Daryl did to her.

"Well, she finally returns." Daryl was sitting in the recliner in Cindy's room.

"Yeah, I had a lot to do."

"I bet you did. Where's the kid?"

"I don't have her anymore."

"What do you mean you don't have her anymore?" Daryl stood up.

"I thought she would be better off somewhere else."

"You need to go get her right now."

"I can't. She's with… she's with child services." Cindy lied.

"Child services!" Daryl screamed as he began to approach Cindy. "Do you know how many clients I had lined up for her? Now I'm gonna be losing money because of you!"

Cindy started backing up. "You are so sick! She is only six! How could you do something so terrible!"

"Oh, now you have a conscious. You think you are a real mother now?"

"I'm the closest thing that little girl had to one."

"You are going to pay big time for this Cindy, big time."

# CHAPTER ONE

Michelle closed her eyes and held her breath. Here she was bent over Principal Nelson's desk once again. She couldn't believe he would do this in his office, at school, during school hours. Michelle just tried to focus on anything other than her principal, Drew Nelson, and so-called adoptive father, raping her once again. Everything started out so nicely. Mr. and Mrs. Nelson gave her everything she wanted and of course they still do, but a month ago, Mr. Nelson thought it was time she gave back.

"What do you mean?" Michelle asked.

"I mean, I give you everything and now I need something from you." Mr. Nelson eyed Michelle from head to toe.

"Wha...What do you need from me?" Michelle was hesitant to ask. She didn't like the look in Mr. Nelson's eyes.

Michelle stood in Mr. Nelson's office just before first bell awaiting his next words.

"Unbutton your shirt."

Michelle's eyes widened. "Excuse me?"

"Unbutton your shirt and let me see." Mr. Nelson repeated.

"Why?"

"Because I said so and if you want to keep living under my roof and receiving all of those nice things that you have, you'll do it. And if you tell anyone, I promise I will make your life a living hell."

Michelle didn't know what to do. She didn't want to get put out on the street. Where would she go? Would she be forced into prostitution like her mom? There were so many scenarios that swirled around in Michelle's head and none of them were good. Reluctantly she unbuttoned her shirt. Mr. Nelson walked over to her and begin to fondle her breast. Michelle wanted to throw up right in his face. But she thought she'd better not. Instead, she just looked away and focused on the plaque that hung on Mr. Nelson's wall. Principal of the Year. What a joke she thought. Is this what the principal of the year does? Would they have given him that plaque if they knew what he did behind these closed doors? Michelle felt tears welling up in her eyes. She still couldn't believe her granny hand given her away.

Michelle woke up to the smell of pancakes. Sitting straight up in her bed she thought to herself, *I can't even remember the last time my grammy fixed me breakfast. I wonder what I've done to deserve this.* Michelle threw her legs over the bed and slipped her feet into her fluffy pink slippers. After she managed to get up from her bed, she walked into her bathroom. She wanted to take a shower but her curiosity about breakfast over took her. She washed her face and brushed her teeth and headed to the kitchen. She walked through the curtain separating the kitchen from the dining room. *Why do people even do this?* She wondered. *Just get some French doors or something.* But she would never say that out loud to her grandmother. Her grammy was old school and she didn't tolerate back talk. Michelle also was afraid that if she said anything to her grandmother out of the way, she would kick her out of the house. Michelle knew her grandmother wasn't her real grandmother and there wasn't a day that went by she didn't remind Michelle of it.

"You cooking pancakes grammy?"

"Yeah child. Today is a special day."

"What do you mean? What's special about it?" Michelle thought maybe her luck was about to change. Maybe her grandmother was finally going to start giving her the love she desperately wanted. Or maybe this was the day her grandmother would tell her about her mom or rather the woman who was raising her before she gave her up, maybe she would get to meet her.

"Today is the day I finally get rid of you." Sadie Jemison glared at Michelle with a sinister look in her eyes, brandishing a devilish smile as she flipped a pancake.

"Wha... what do you mean by that?" Fear gripped Michelle's entire being. As soon as Sadie looked back at the pancakes she was cooking, Michelle looked around the room for her best exit strategy. If she's going to kill me, I need a way out. She thought to herself.

"Don't worry, I'm not going to kill you." Sadie said almost as if she had read Michelle's thoughts. "I found somebody else to take you in."

"Why can't I stay here?"

"I'm tired of raising a child that ain't mine."

"But I'm no trouble."

"You will be. You are turning out just like your mother."

"Which one?" Michelle immediately regretted her words. Good thing Sadie kept her cool.

"Your birth mother. What my daughter told me about her, she had an exquisite beauty and a body to match. Every day I look at you and I can tell you belong to whoever that was. My daughter was not nearly as beautiful and well built as you're turning out to be and your only fourteen. Anyway, I found a nice couple that doesn't have any children and they are excited to take you in. The husband is a principal of a high school, so naturally you'll attend his high school. All you need to know is that you will be well taken care of. All I need to know is that I will no longer be responsible for you."

Michelle sat down at the kitchen table. She couldn't believe what she was hearing. She knew her grammy didn't like her, let alone love her, but she never imagined she would give her away. Even though Sadie wasn't the best grandmother she ever had, she was the only one she knew. The closest she had to family. Without Sadie she had nothing. No connection to who she was or where she came from. Tears began to roll down her face drop by drop and then in floods.

"Don't waste your tears, Michelle. You're a big girl. You will be able to handle anything that comes your way." Sadie placed two pancakes on Michelle's plate.

Michelle just stared at the pancakes. The news Sadie had lain on her made her lose her appetite. Michelle didn't want to eat. She wanted to throw up. What was she going to do?

"Grammy please." Michelle begged. That was all she could come up with. Beg and hope her grandmother changed her mind.

"I would say I'm sorry, but I'm not. I just hate I didn't think about this earlier, but when I heard about what my daughter's pimp had planned for you. I couldn't allow that, although now you're old enough. So, you tell me. You want to go back and live with your mother in a whore house or you want to go live with these nice people?"

"Where's my mom? Your daughter?"

"My daughter died shortly after she gave you to me. That's what I was told anyway. Her pimp beat her to death for getting rid of you and messing up his plans. So, as you can see, it's your fault she's dead. She didn't have to take you in. She didn't have to rescue you. And she surely didn't have to give her life for you. I have decided I'm not giving my life for you. I have taken care of you long enough. It's time for you to make your own way now. I've done my part and now I'm done. The family will be by to pick you up later on this evening. So, eat up and then go pack your things."

That was the last time Michelle ever saw Sadie Jemison

Michelle heard Mr. Nelson grunt a couple of more times and then he was done. Michelle felt relief that she didn't have to worry about getting pregnant. Mr. Nelson made sure of that. Not long after she moved in with him and his wife, he convinced his wife that she needed to be on birth control. Something about the possibility of her turning out like her mom and them not wanting any extra responsibilities. Michelle should have known something was up then, but she was just so used to people prejudging her based on her mother, whom she still did not know. *How does this keep following me around?* Michelle would think to herself. *I don't even know my mother. How am I going to become like someone I don't even know and why do I keep having to pay for the mistakes she made?*

"Go get yourself cleaned up." The sound of Mr. Nelson's voice brought Michelle back to reality. She raised up from lying over his desk and let her dress fall back and place. She walked to his in- office restroom and washed herself like she had done so many times before. Michelle stared in the mirror. She was getting to the point she hated wearing dresses, but lately it was all Mr. Nelson would let her wear. Easy access he would say. Michelle walked out of the restroom. Mr. Nelson had already gotten back to work on his computer.

"I'll see you after school." Mr. Nelson didn't even look up from his computer. Michelle would never respond she just kept right on out of the office, hoping no one could see the shame that covered her from her head to her feet.

*24-36-48. No that's not it.* Michelle turned her locker back to zero. *48-24-36. No. What is wrong with me.* Michelle looked at her hands. They were shaking. *Why am I shaking? I've been through this enough times to be used to it. Used to it? How can I get used to being raped? I can't get used to it.* A tear threatened to roll down Michelle's cheek, but she couldn't let herself cry. She couldn't let anyone know that her life was a mess. *Breathe Michelle. You're fine. You can do this. You only have one more year and then you'll be out of here. 36-24-48. Yes.* Michelle switched out her books. *Late again. Ms. Ross is going to be so mad. Please God, let her let me in today.* Michelle walked reluctantly to Ms. Ross's class. The door was still open. Maybe she had a chance. Michelle slowly approached the doors opening. Ms. Ross was turned toward the board. Maybe she could sneak in without being seen. Michelle walked quietly and quickly to a seat in the back.

"Girl, you fine!" J.T. Turner yelled out as soon as Michelle reached her seat.

The entire class erupted with laughter.

Ms. Ross turned around searching the room for Michelle. "Why are you late again?"

"You know her dad's the principal Ms. Ross, she can do whatever she wants. Come to class late, leave early. Pass without trying."

Once again laugher filled the classroom.

"I pass because I'm smart." Michelle knew she should have kept her mouth closed but she didn't like J.T. hinting that she was stupid and the only reason she passed her classes was because her "dad" was the principal.

"Michelle stop playing. You know you need to be in the special class." The class erupted in laughter.

Michelle bit her tongue this time. She knew it was useless to argue with him. She pulled out her notebook and text and begin to take down the notes from the board.

"You think writing down the notes is going to help you? Cause I'm pretty sure it's not. But go ahead, I know you have to pretend to be smart. I applaud you Michelle for at least trying." J.T clapped his hands and the rest of the class joined in.

Michelle just kept staring at the board. She had become an expert in tuning out all the bad and hurtful things that she dealt with on a daily basis. Fighting back tears and anger she just kept on writing.

Ms. Ross turned back to the board. Michelle let out a sigh of relief until she heard her name.

"Michelle, this is the absolute last time I'm going to let you in my class late. Unless your daddy gives you a pass, don't even bother coming this way."

Michelle was relieved she at least made it through this time. She would worry about next time when it came.

# CHAPTER TWO

Autumn Dance paced around her office, full of pure electric energy. Auditions were her favorite part of the creative process. Picking the perfect people for the perfect video. This was what it was all about for Autumn. Giving a never heard of dancer a chance to fulfill a lifelong dream. That made her heart flip more than a hit song. Autumn allowed her mind to journey back to the time she entered the music business. Running from her past had caused a head first collision with her destiny. She found herself on the doorstep of Fight of Your Life Productions where she met billion-dollar record producer and legend Axel Smith. The rest was history. For the past seven years this means of escape had turned into an adventure that was always blossoming into something she had never experienced before. Every time she thought she had identified the flower, it transformed into something else. All she could do at this point was keep her eyes open and take in the beauty of it all.

Day three of auditions really got the butterflies jumping inside her belly. Just the thought of seeing the dancers for the first time since auditions started and dancing with them sent her emotions into overdrive.

Autumn began her daily affirmations:

"You are talented and creative."

"You are the best dancer."

"You are strong, confident and full of energy."

"You are exactly who you are supposed to be and doing exactly what you are supposed to be doing."

"You cannot fail."

*Wait a minute.* Autumn thought back. "You are exactly who you are supposed to be," she repeated. That felt different coming out for some reason. She didn't know why but it did. Lately she didn't feel much like she was exactly who she was supposed to be. She felt as if something was missing. Was it a friend, significant other, what was it? She felt like she was fulfilling her wildest dreams, but yet something was missing.

*Turn to me.*

There was that voice again. Lately Autumn had been hearing a still small voice. As if it were giving her direction. Leading her to something bigger than herself. She believed it to be God, but she hadn't talked to God in such a long time. She was sure He had forgotten all about her.

"God, if this is you talking to me. You are going to have to lead me. Cause I don't exactly know what it is that you want me to do. But I want to. If you could ever forgive me for walking away, I will do what you want me to do."

*I love you and I have never left you.*

Autumn didn't know if she had made that part up herself or not, but she believed she heard God speak it to her and she was willing to take it at face value. Tears began to fill her eyes. For the first time in a long time, she believed God was with her.

Autumn continued her affirmations. She had to get her emotions back under control. Even though she was having some doubts about the direction of her life since God started speaking to her, she still had a job to do.

"You are a leader and a trendsetter."

"You are beautiful."

"No one can outshine you when you do what you do."

Autumn made a habit of keeping herself encouraged. In this business there was always someone trying to put you down and make you feel lesser than. She was determined to rise above it all and do what she knew she was created to do. For now, anyway. Autumn took a deep breath and exited her office. She walked down the hall and around the corner to her favorite dance studio. Axel had named it simply "The Dance Studio." He thought it was a perfect play on her name and yet reflect the simplicity and the humility of her character. At least that's what he told her when she gave him the Rock eyebrow upon his revealing the name to her. She stood outside the secret entrance to the back of the room. A little something Autumn asked to have installed for this very moment. The moment she would sneak in the room and surprise the other dancers. She loved her "Dance Studio." It was small and intimate. Just the way she liked it. She never liked a lot of dancers. She liked to keep things simple but creative. All she needed was a few great bodies that moved like the waves and hearts that shined like the sun. She would take care of the rest.

Autumn took another deep breath. Counted to ten. Flashed a big smile while bouncing up and down. Then ran in just in time to catch the rhythm of the next beat of her first big single.  Some of the dancers were too stunned to continue. Some didn't know what to do but keep dancing.  Then there where those who tried to match Autumn's energy. It was those that she liked the most. After about thirty seconds of dancing amongst the newbies, Autumn took her place in front of the dancers and continued dancing enjoying seeing the fire in the dancer's eyes; all the while sizing them up. Seeing if anyone jumped out at her. If they jumped out at her, she knew they would jump out to anyone watching her video.

"Way to go guys!" Autumn exclaimed once the dance came to its conclusion. "I'm sorry if I startled you. This is my absolute favorite part of the process. Dancing with new people. Feeling their energy. Thank you for this experience! My lead dancers are going to get you all started on the second choreography that you were taught. This is the one that you will be judged on. Let's go!"

The lead dancers immediately stepped in and began to condition, encourage and prepare the dancers for the next phase. Five minutes later the music began. The dance started and in walks Axel Smith. Some dancers were thrown off and missed steps. Others took their energy to the next level. Some, women mostly, became overly sexual to get his attention. One such dancer was a high yellow, fake boobed wannabe with a pink shirt that read, *Wanna taste?* Autumn wanted to throw up in her mouth, but she decided against it seeing how it might look unprofessional. Autumn had noticed Ms. Pinktop rolling her eyes at her multiple times since she entered the auditions. Did this stupid girl forget that she had the power to veto her behind right off this dance team? Autumn studied her a bit longer, just to make sure she was being fair. The girl was pretty with plenty of sex appeal but significantly lacked in dance skills. You would think she would have used a bit of her plastic surgery money to buy her some dance classes. But judging by the extent of that plastic surgery she probably ran out of money before she got around to it. Either way, little missy would be the first one to go. Autumn flashed her a big smile. *You have no idea you are about to slaughter your last dance on my floor.* Autumn thought to herself.

When the dance was over, several smaller groups of dancers began to form. It was apparent they were out of their mind excited over the presence of Axel Smith and couldn't wait to talk about it. Even if he wasn't the owner of this label, he still was the kind of man who could walk in a room and demand the attention of everyone present. The chatter immediately subsided at the sound of Axel's deep baritone. To tell the truth, Autumn herself almost went weak in the knees.

"Good morning, ladies and gentlemen." Axel was always such a gentleman, that is until he wasn't.

Giggles resonated throughout the dance room. Head nods went up from the men.

"So, what do we owe the pleasure?" Autumn thought she would break the ice.

"Just wanted to see what your dance team was looking like. I see you still haven't made any cuts."

Heads dropped. They knew they all wouldn't be able to stay.

"No I haven't. They are all just so great!" She exclaimed, trying to lift their spirits. "But, unfortunately I will be making the final decision on tomorrow. Thank you all for coming. I will see you bright and early on tomorrow."

Everyone waved and exited the room after retrieving their belongings.

"So, you're going to bring them all back just to kick some off?"

"No. I'm going to make the calls tonight. The ones who show up tomorrow will be my new team."

"That's cool. I hope you make good choices." Axel stared at Autumn. The more he stared the more he realized how beautiful she was. He was also thinking if he was making the biggest mistake of his life not pursuing her.

"What are you looking at?"

"The most beautiful woman I've ever seen in my life."

Autumn couldn't help but blush, but her joy quickly turned to frustration. She was tired of Axel giving her all these mixed signals. They were best friends. They were never supposed to be anything else but something had changed in the last two years. Things were getting weird. She had fallen in love. Axel didn't know and she would never tell him. She wanted him to make the first move, but he never would. He just flirted. The end result was always him walking away.

"Axel, get out of my dance room."

"What? Did I say something wrong?"

"You always say something wrong. Now just leave me alone. I got a lot of thinking to do."

"Why don't you walk with me to my office pretty girl and you can think in there."

# CHAPTER THREE

Autumn paced back and forth in Axel's office. She looked at the top contenders for her dance team. One girl, River was the truth. It seemed like she had been studying every video Autumn had ever put out. She did every dance move the way she did it on her video. She admired her dedication. River also had a seduction about her when she danced. Almost as if she had been a stripper in a previous life. But it wasn't on her resume. Most girls thought by putting that they were strippers, it would actually help them get the dancing gig. Many times, it did. But stripping was nowhere on hers. Maybe she has something to hide? Or maybe unlike other girls she wasn't proud of her stripping days? River looked like she had had a good bit of plastic surgery. Autumn knew of girls who invested in plastic surgery just to get men in the industry. Part of their get rich quick plan so they never have to work a day in their lives. Maybe that was her goal. Become a backup dancer and get a chance to jump in bed with as many male artists as she could until she finds one that will commit. Autumn didn't like being used, but to River's credit she was an amazing dancer and a quick learner.

Then there was Jaylah. Jaylah was barely 18 and a cutie. She always had a smile on her face; like she was just happy about everything. Autumn didn't know about her sex appeal but she could dance. She was proficient in every style of dance. Couldn't walk away from that. That was a very good skill to have. The downside was that she was a little bit creepy. She kept staring at Autumn the whole time. She never looked away. Even when she left the dance room, Autumn noticed her look back and stare for a moment longer. She hoped she wasn't about to hire a crazy single black female.

Then there were the twins. Skye and Faith. They weren't really good dancers but they had plenty of personality and sex appeal that would work great for her videos and on stage.

"Why don't you let me help you?" Axel's deep voice knocked her from her thoughts.

Autumn turned and faced Axel, knowing he didn't have a clue about what was going on with her auditions. "So, Axel, tell me, who do you think I should pick?" She rolled her neck and folded her arms.

"To be honest with you Autumn..." he started scratching his head.

*Here goes*, she thought. *He doesn't have a clue*. She flipped her head to the other side waiting on an excuse.

"I think you should definitely pick Jaylah, her dance background is impressive. River is the bomb dancer. I would swear I've seen her strip before but her face doesn't look familiar. The twins are more eye candy but they can hold their own. I would choose those four, one more and let the rest go. Now when you pick your mouth up off the floor, we can discuss my last and final pick."

Autumn humbly obeyed. She couldn't believe he actually followed the auditions. Autumn was now even more confused than ever.

"So, who's your final pick Mr. Smith?" Autumn plopped down on the couch.

"Harmony". He said rubbing his hands and obviously reminiscing in his mind.

"Who is that?"

Axel flipped through Autumn's stack of headshots and bios and handed it to Autumn.

Autumn almost fell on the floor. "Oh no, not Ms. Pinktop. I don't like her at all and she can barely dance."

"Ms. Pinktop?" Axel couldn't help but laugh. "Autumn do you even know who she is?"

Autumn looked back at the folder. "Harmony Ellis. So what?"

"The name Ellis doesn't mean anything to you?"

"No. Should it?"

"Yes. Her mom was Miss California like 25 years ago. And her dad is the presiding ADA. Plus, she has such a wonderful body." Axel leaned back in his seat with his hands behind his head brandishing a boyish smile.

Autumn rolled her eyes. "I'm pretty sure every part of her body was bought with her mommy and daddy's money."

"Doesn't matter to me."

"Whatever."

"For real Autumn. This could really work out in my favor."

"Oh, you mean for all your illegal stuff?"

"Really Autumn?"

"I'm just saying. I don't like her Axel and she is going to cause trouble."

"Not if I play my cards right and you know I always play my cards right."

"I can't with you Axel."

"Plus, don't you think it's time for me to have a high-profile relationship?"

Autumn could have died right then and there. She had no response. She didn't even like this Harmony girl and right here before her eyes she was about to steal the only man she has ever loved. Her blood was boiling like a pot of grits.

"Autumn." Axel knew he had hit a nerve with her and he was on fix it mode. "Please trust me here. I know you don't want to do this. But please do this for me." He turned toward Autumn with his bottom lip poked out.

"Whatever Axel." Autumn stood up. "I'm going to consult with Ashley and Layla and see if they found me some dancers who can actually dance."

"I want you to pick the best dance team Autumn, you know that, just make sure Harmony is on it."

Autumn opened the door and slammed it without responding. She hated Axel. She was ready to end their friendship on the spot, but then she would lose him in her life forever. To be honest. Was it really worth it?

Autumn walked back into the dance room.

So ladies, what do you think?

Ashley handed her a list:

Jayla

River

Skye

Faith

Autumn rolled her eyes. "And Harmony. Add Harmony to the list please."

"What? Layla spoke up. "She can't even dance. She just has a body."

"Same thing I said but her daddy is the ADA and Axel wants to get in good with the family."

"Figures. I'm sure that's not all he wants her for." Layla and Ashley burst into laughter.

"Ya'll are regular comedians."

"I'm just saying." Ashley responded.

What Autumn really wanted to say was, *oh the same way he wanted you two and don't mention, got.* But she kept her thoughts to herself. She hated the fact that she even wanted someone who had slept with everybody she knew and probably a whole lot of others she didn't know. But Autumn was living her dream life and she wasn't about to let Axel, Ashley, Layla or Harmony for that matter mess it up.

"Ok. Well, I can't deal with this right now. I am truly pissed so you guys can handle the dancers and I will see them in rehearsal. Thanks a lot."

"We got you Autumn. It's gonna be ok. Don't worry. Just get some rest."

Autumn threw them a peace sign and she headed out the door.

# CHAPTER FOUR

Mitchell walked through the doors of Windbusch High School. He hated that he had to move from his hometown of Atlanta, Georgia to the cold eventless area of Longcreek, South Carolina. But what choice did he have. Either he could change schools or face a sexual assault charge. Mitchell's anger boiled within him as he thought about it. *Clarissa Scott. She wanted it. But she got scared when we got caught in the boy's locker room. When I find out who told, it doesn't matter how long it takes. I will pay them back right along with Clarissa. She should've had my back. But it's ok. I got her. I got all of them.*

*Well, well, well, what do we have here.* Mitchell saw the most beautiful girl he had ever laid eyes on standing next to her locker. She was shifting her weight back and forth, from one foot to the other. She looked nervous. She looked insecure. *Seems like she needs a friend. Seems strange that probably the prettiest girl in the school would need a friend or feel insecure, but this is about to work out perfectly for me.* Mitchell approached the girl who was still trying to figure out her locker combination. *She must be new too.* He thought.

"Hey."

Michelle looked up briefly. "Hey."

"Looks like you might need some help." Mitchell smiled at her. Hoping to gain her trust. Step one in his plan.

"Ummm… I'm good." Michelle frustratingly rolled the combination back to 0.

"You must be new here?"

"Nope, been here 3 years. I have anxiety. When I've had a rough morning, I seem to struggle with this stupid combination. That's all. It's just gonna take me a minute." Michelle tried to pop the lock once again only to have it stubbornly rebel.

"Hey." Mitchell grabbed Michelle's shoulders and turned her toward him. "Look at me."

Michelle allowed Mitchell to guide her away from her locker. She looked into his eyes. And she was immediately mesmerized. She hadn't really paid him any attention until she was looking at him face to face. His eyes were… grey. She didn't think that she had ever seen a black guy with grey eyes. But she liked it. Maybe he was mixed with something, like she was. Michelle didn't know her father or her mother so she didn't know what she was mixed with. But when she looked in the mirror, she knew she wasn't all black. Anytime anyone asked, she would always tell them she was all black. After all, the closest thing to a parent she ever had, her grandmother, was all black, so why shouldn't she be.

"You need to take a deep breath. Go ahead take one."

Michelle closed her eyes and breathed in and out. Then she looked back into Mitchell's eyes.

"Everything is going to be okay. Stop worrying. I'm sure you're all of 14 or 15…" Mitchell was searching, just to make sure she wasn't too young.

"I'm sixteen."

Mitchell's left eyebrow raised. Pleased with Michelle's answer. "Okay, sixteen. Life can't be so bad that you can't even open your locker?"

Michelle lowered her eyes. "You don't know anything about my life."

"Why don't you tell me beautiful?"

Michelle looked up. She didn't think she ever had anyone tell her she was beautiful. Fine, sexy, maybe, but never beautiful. Her eyes lit up.

Mitchell knew he had her... hook, line and sinker.

"I... I can't. I mean it's nothing. Don't worry about it." Michelle tried to pull away from Mitchell, but he held on to her. Michelle just stared at him.

"What's your name?"

"Michelle."

"It's nice to meet you, Michelle. I'm Mitchell."

"Nice to meet you as well." Michelle responded.

"What class are you headed to?"

Michelle's eyes widened. She had totally forgot about class. "Oh no. Ms. Ross is going to kill me!" Michelle turned and continued to struggle with her locker with no success. "Just open!" Michelle hit the locker, frustrated beyond what she could handle.

"What's your combination Michelle?" Mitchell asked, gently sliding Michelle away from the locker.

Michelle gave it to him. He opened it with ease.

Michelle gathered the things she needed out of the locker. "It doesn't matter now. She's never going to let me in the classroom."

"Are you always late?"

"I've been late a couple of times."

"How many is a couple?"

Michelle squinted her eyes with irritation at the many questions Mitchell was asking.

"Wait a minute. That name sounds familiar." Mitchell pulled his schedule from his back pocket. "Ms. Ross. Calculus. I am actually headed to that class too."

"Well, she'll probably let you in but she's not going to let me in, I can promise you that."

"How much you wanna bet?"

"What do you mean?"

"How much do you want to bet that Ms. Ross will let you in?"

"I'm not betting you anything."

"You have to. Unless you're afraid I'm right?"

"What do you want to bet?"

"If I'm right and she let's you in, you gotta give me your number."

"And what do I get if I'm right?"

"I'll leave you alone for the rest of the year." Mitchell glared into Michelle's eyes.

Michelle remained silent. She wanted to be right, but she wasn't sure she wanted Mitchell never to talk to her again. "Deal." She finally managed to say. She wasn't about to let Mitchell know how she felt about him, plus she was kind of hoping he could get her into class. If not, she would have to go to Mr. Nelson's office and she already knew what would happen if that were the case.

"Well, you're going to have to lead the way, because I don't know where I'm going."

Michelle reluctantly walked past Mitchell and headed towards Ms. Ross's class. Mitchell obediently followed behind her, watching her every move and enjoying every curve of her body. *I gotta have her.* He thought to himself. *I sure hope I can get her into this classroom or else I'm really going to have my work cut out for me.*

Michelle arrived at Ms. Ross's door. It was open and she could hear Ms. Ross already in the middle of her lesson. Michelle stepped into the opening of the door.

"Absolutely not. Don't even think about coming into my class. Go to your daddy's office." Ms. Ross said that last part with disgust.

Michelle always shuddered when someone mentioned that Mr. Nelson was her daddy. She was sure that daddies didn't do to their daughters what Mr. Nelson did to her on a regular basis.

Mitchell stepped through the opening. "Hello Ms. Ross. I'm Mitchell and this is my first day."

Ms. Ross looked Mitchell up and down like he was a full meal ready to be devoured.

"Michelle was helping me find my locker and then for some reason I was having the hardest time with my combination. She told me she couldn't be late, but I begged her to help me. I apologize. "

Ms. Ross's eyes softened. "Mitchell, right?"

"Yes ma'am."

"Okay Mitchell, you saved her this time, but let me tell you, the next time that little girl is late, she can't come in, no matter what."

"Yes ma'am. I'll make it my personal responsibility to see that she gets here on time."

Mrs. Ross slowly sashayed over to Mitchell. Making sure he understood why she was unofficially named the finest teacher in school. "Mitchell, you seem like a good kid. But let me give you a word of warning, if you want to remain a good kid, you might want to stay away from that one." Ms. Ross motioned toward Michelle. "I can assure you, she's nothing but trouble." She gritted her teeth with every word that came out of her mouth.

Michelle hung her head in shame. She didn't know what made her so bad and detestable, but she knew she was. She knew that with everything that had happened to her and everything that she was, there couldn't be any good in her or to her. She resigned to just be thankful that she was allowed to get to class. Now with Mitchell taking personal responsibility for her, she might just make it every day. Michelle looked up at Mitchell and nodded her appreciation and headed to her seat. Mitchell took the seat right beside her and smiled at her as he slid in and opened his textbook.

Michelle curved her lips up and rolled her eyes. *What does he want from me?* She thought to herself. *Why is he being so nice to me?* Ms. Ross's voice shook Michelle from her thoughts.

"Okay, the pages you need to finish by the end of class are on the board along with the pages for your homework. Make sure you write them down. Mitchell, you can partner with someone so they can explain the lesson to you."

"Yes ma'am. I'll partner with Michelle."

"I guess you don't hear very well." Ms. Ross wasn't shy about showing her disapproval about Mitchell's choice of partners. "If you want to pass this class, you're going to want to partner with someone who is in class long enough to know what we've been talking about." Ms. Ross finished her statement with a roll of her eyes.

"I trust her Ms. Ross. She seems to be real smart." Mitchell picked up his seat and slid it over to Michelle's.

"I'm pretty sure it's not her brain you're after." The class snickered. "But let me tell you this," Ms. Ross continued. "Don't let all that booty and breasts fool you. Michelle is not good company, unless you're just looking for a good time."

Michelle's eyes widened. She couldn't believe what she was hearing. Her teacher, the person that should be building her up, was tearing her down with no remorse. Water began to well up in Michelle 's eyes. She dropped her head so no one would notice. But someone did notice. Michelle felt Mitchell rub his hand over her back and then she heard his voice in her ear. "Don't pay any attention to her. It sounds like she's jealous to me." Michelle looked up at Mitchell as he smirked his approval at her change in posture.

Michelle didn't know why Mitchell had taken an interest in her, but she hoped it wasn't just for her body. She really wanted someone to genuinely like her for her. Maybe Mitchell was that someone. But what could really happen good in her life? After all, nothing had ever happened good in her life before. Why should it start now? Michelle looked in Mitchell's eyes trying to detect maybe a hint of deception, but she didn't see any. I guess only time would tell. Michelle thought it better to just focus on her work and she began to teach Mitchell the lesson like a scholar.

CHAPTER

# FIVE

Autumn walked out the massive doors of Axel's label and into the pool area. Girls were definitely on the menu. There were girls by the pool, in the pool, dancing under the pavilion. She was pretty sure they were wearing bathing suits. They were just too small for her to see them. The guys showed up too. Six packs were closing in on her from all direction. Autumn started not to come but she knew Axel wouldn't let her hear the end of it if she didn't. Autumn sat on the side of the pool and put her feet in. She was not about to jump in today. Her hair was done to perfection and nothing was going to mess it up. Not even a relaxing dip in the pool. Which was looking better and better by the minute. She imagined just swimming all her problems away. She felt things just couldn't get any worse for her. And right on cue as if they had heard her thoughts, out walks Axel and Harmony. Holding hands. Looking like the perfect couple. *I see he didn't waste anyntime.* Autumn didn't know whether to run and hide or drown herself in the pool. She tried to act like she didn't see them.

"Hey."

Autumn was so relieved to see Jaylah sit down next to her. She wouldn't feel so awkward sitting with someone. It would look as if she had a life outside of Axel... which she knew she didn't.

"Hey Jaylah. What are you up to?"

So far Jaylah hadn't been as creepy as she thought she would be. Even though she still stared at her more often than she thought was normal. She seemed to be pretty sweet. *Maybe she just really admires me,* Autumn would say to herself.

"Nothing. Just trying to find something to do. These guys are all over me. I guess I'm the new booty."

Autumn laughed a bit louder than she expected to. Although she knew Jaylah was right. "Why aren't you enjoying them like the rest of the girls?"

Jaylah leaned over to whisper to Autumn. "I'm a virgin and I'm scared." She backed away from Autumn taking in the glance she was now giving her. "What? You think I'm crazy now too, don't you? The only virgin left in the world." Jaylah dropped her head.

"Actually, I don't think you're crazy." Autumn replied stunned by Jaylah's revelation. "I'm proud of you and I am very jealous of you right now."

"Jealous? Of me? Why?"

"Jaylah, don't let people fool you. All this that you see around you is so overrated. You see all these girls?"

Jaylah nodded her head.

"These girls get laid by these guys on a regular basis and these guys ain't ever going to marry them. So, what have they gained? Most girls want a guy to be attracted to them. But what's the end game? To sleep with them. Then what? They are just another notch on their belt and they're left brokenhearted and used. They may say they are just having fun but trust me, they are not. You don't want this life baby. Please stay a virgin as long as you can. Until you find that special someone."

"Wow. That was pretty deep. Thanks." Jaylah looked around the party and then back at Autumn. "You sound like you are tired of this life."

Autumn was doing everything in her power to keep her attention on what Jaylah was saying but Axel and Harmony's PDA was really distracting her.

"What? I mean yeah. I have been thinking about going in a different direction, maybe even changing my genre and singing some inspirational music." Now it was Autumn's turn to check out the expression on Jaylah's face.

"Inspirational? You mean like Gospel?"

"Not really gospel, just inspirational. I don't know. I just have been struggling getting into it lately."

"Well, I would say go with your heart, except your heart may lose you your job."

Autumn couldn't help but giggle. Jaylah joined in. "I'm just saying. Axel might not want you going all inspirational on him."

"It was just a thought." Autumn sighed still eyeing Axel and Harmony.

Jaylah followed Autumn's gaze. "What do you think about Axel and Harmony's relationship?"

Autumn looked at Jaylah. "I don't think anything about it. They are both grown and they can do what they want."

"Doesn't sound like you're too happy about it."

"I am perfectly happy about it. Axel is my best friend."

"So, there has never been anything between you two?"

Autumn wanted to tell Jaylah that her personal life was none of her business, but as she rolled Jaylah's words around in her head, she secretly found herself wishing there was something that she could say had transpired between them. But there was nothing. Not even a kiss.

She exhaled. "Nope. Nothing. We are just friends." Autumn sadly admitted. "Look I gotta go Jaylah. It was nice talking to you. We should do this more often." She patted her slightly on the shoulder. "And don't forget what I said. Keep your legs closed."

Jaylah grinned. "I promise."

"Good girl." Autumn got up and made her way to the entrance of the building, but not before stealing one last look at Axel. She froze. Axel was staring back. *What to do?* After a moment longer, Autumn did the only thing that felt normal. She retreated. Away from the pain. Away from the hurt. Away from Axel's beautiful eyes. She wanted to stand there and stare at them forever. But she just couldn't stand it. She had to get away? She couldn't keep this charade up any longer.

# CHAPTER SIX

Michelle sat at the top of the bleachers peering down at the football game that was taking place on the field. Mitchell, her boyfriend was the starting quarterback, with five touchdowns and eight tackles to his name as the game ended. Switching out between offense and defense, there was nothing this guy couldn't do. Even the opposing team's fans had to cheer at some of the moves he was making on the field.

Michelle made her way down the bleachers to go and congratulate her man. If she could make it through the crowd of adoring fans who relished at the chance to make contact with the All-Star player. Just as she made her way to the last bleacher her heart almost stopped beating. Her breath caught in her chest. There was her boyfriend of three months standing with his arm around two girls. She shook her head, recovering from the initial shock. It's nothing she told herself. Just fan-fare. He knows who his girl is. Michelle made her way onto the field. She pushed her way through the boisterous crowd. Just a few feet away and she would take hold of her prize from these thirsty girls who were pawing her man. Michelle stopped in her tracks as her eyes met his. She could've sworn she'd seen a smirk on Mitchel's face. He pulled one of the girls toward him in a full body hug and planted several kisses on her cheek. After one last look at Michelle, he turned and walked towards the gym, with one arm still draped around the girl's shoulders.

Michelle could barely take in what was happening. *What is he doing? Why is he doing this?* She didn't think they were having problems. Michelle turned around and headed for the exit. She kept her head low and her feet moving fast. She stopped abruptly at the exit of the field when she remembered Mitchell was her ride home. She had one of two choices. She could wait on Mitchell or she could call Mr. Nelson. She dared not call him her dad. As she thought of the consequences of calling Mr. Nelson, she thought better of it. He would ask her to pay him back for rescuing her in one form or another. Besides she really wanted to have a conversation with Mitchell and find out why he was acting the way he was. She made her way to the gym which was across the street from the parking lot where others who had gotten dropped off were waiting on their rides. She pulled her jacket tighter around her as she paced back and forth. October had already started to bring in a chill.

Michelle checked the time on her phone. It was almost 10:00. Mitchell still hadn't made his way over to pick her up as he usually did after the game. Michelle turned around when the lights turned off in the gym. *Where is Mitchell?* Michelle's eyes darted back and forth around the lobby. Her heart began to race. She pulled at the door, thankful it was still open.

"You got a ride home?" The assistant principal walked up to Michelle with keys jingling in her hand.

"I.. I was waiting on Mitchell." She stammered.

"I'm pretty sure Mitchell already left. I saw him leaving the parking lot and heading in the opposite direction."

Michelle dropped her head. How could Mitchell just leave her?

"Look. Let me lock up this gym and then I'll drop you off at home. It's not far from where I stay. That okay with you?"

"That would be great. Thank you." Michelle opened the door and stood outside grateful she didn't have to call Mr. Nelson, but she would definitely be having a conversation with Mitchell when she got home.

Michelle stood at Mitchell's locker the way she did every morning. She checked both ends of the hall anticipating his arrival. She did a double take when she saw him finally coming down the hall. Again, a smirk was plastered on his face. An ambush at his locker seemed to be the only way to talk to him seeing how he was ignoring her calls.

"Can I get to my locker please?" Was the first thing out of Mitchell's mouth.

"What is wrong with you Mitchell?"

"What do you mean?"

"You were hugging and kissing on another girl and then you had the nerve to leave me last night."

"I didn't think you would want to ride with me and Ashley."

Michelle's mouth formed a perfect O. "I thought we were together. Who is Ashley?"

"Look Michelle what we had has ran its course. If you still want to come over and let me hit it, I'm down with that, but Ashley is my girl and that's that."

"Mitchell you can't be serious. I mean, what did I do? Just tell me, I'm sure I can fix it." A tear threatened to roll down Michelle's cheek.

"Michelle look, find you something else to do and leave me alone."

Mitchell pushed Michelle aside with the back of his hand. She stumbled, caught off guard by his gesture. Mitchell snickered and continued to open his locker. He placed his backpack in his locker after removing his first period books and notebook and then turned around and walked away as if Michelle wasn't still standing there. She watched him walk down the hall and into Ms. Ross's class and then she remembered. She better hurry and get there herself. Without Mitchell she didn't have a prayer in the world of getting into her class late.

## CHAPTER
# SEVEN

Axel sat down at his keyboard. Looking around the room; he couldn't remember the last time he entered the Money Maker. It was the room he retreated to when he was inspired to write. It was where he wrote all his number one hits when he first started the label. But he was rich now. He had made it to the place of success that he always dreamed of. He didn't need to write songs anymore. He paid people very good money to do that for him. Besides, who needs continual hits when you already hold the record for most #1 hits with no one even close to being in reach to compete. Axel had created the multi-billion-dollar corporation that he wanted. Work was the last thing on his mind. Axel ran his fingers across the keys; enjoying the solitude. He began to feel the same rush he used to feel when he was preparing to write a hit song. Axel drew his hands back. *What if I can't do this anymore?* He thought to himself. Axel couldn't remember the last time he doubted his ability to write. I must've really been out of the game for too long. Axel placed his fingers back onto the keys. His fingers began to move and a melody began to take form. Like riding a bike. *Whoa, this is fye!* Axel thought to himself. Words start coming to his mind and just as they came to his mind, they came out of his mouth. Axel hadn't sung like this since he first started the company ten years ago. But he was feeling it today. He was singing like he had never sung before.

Feeling every stroke of the keys in his very soul and letting whatever came out of his mouth to come.

Suddenly the door cracked open and Axel immediately stopped when he heard footsteps. I thought I locked that door? Axel was hoping no one heard him playing. The next thing that came to his mind was who was he going to fire for coming into his private room. Everyone who worked for him knew this room was off limits. And then she walked in. A smile crept across Axel's face. Autumn Dance. Autumn was Axel's best friend, but when she bent that corner it had him thinking about Usher's song Lovers and Friends. Autumn was wearing a black fitted, Cat woman suit for the Halloween party and those thighs were speaking to him as she sashayed over to him in those thigh high black stiletto boots. Axel found himself imagining undressing her right here, right now; in the Money Maker, on top of his favorite keyboard. Had she always been this fine? He must've been stuck in the friend zone too long to notice. Even though being in the friend zone was his choice.

"You haven't been in here in a while." Autumn's eyes twinkled as if she knew exactly what he was thinking.

"I needed the distraction." Axel decided to play it cool. *Don't say anything out of the way Ax. She's your best friend.*

"Seems like you have enough distractions."

"You don't say."

"I do say."

"How about you just say what you came in here to say. We're cool like that. At least I thought we were."

"What's going on with you and Harmony?" Autumn folded her arms as she shifted her weight. Her thighs jiggling just enough to command Axel's attention.

"What you mean?" Axel would never just give up the goods. He was going to play stupid as long as he could.

"I see you all have started to take your relationship public."

"That was the plan right." Axel's eyes finally left Autumn's body as he met her gaze.

"I just didn't know you were truly serious about it. I mean you know you are not the relationship type. So why are you even doing this?"

"So that's what we're doing now?"

"What do you mean by that?" Autumn arms came undone and found their way to her hips.

"You act like you're my girl." Axel deflected.

Autumn was not only Axel's best friend but she was the only female in his crew he hadn't slept with. He just couldn't. From the time he met her, she was always like a little sister to him. Axel could still remember the sweet little girl who he found on his label's doorstep. Back in the day when he was the one who did the opening and the closing. She stood up when she saw him open the door. She promised that if he would just give her a chance, she would prove to him that she would be the artist he needed and wanted for his label. Axel had all kind of crazies come up to him but there was something different about this girl. She was 18 and obviously running from something.

*"You got a place to stay?" he asked. It looked as if she had slept on his doorstep.*

*"No, but I'll find somewhere. I just need a chance." Autumn looked desperate.*

From that moment on, he and Autumn were inseparable. He took Autumn in and gave her a whole wing of his house.  And she kept her word. With a little work Autumn had become the star that he needed. The star he wanted. Autumn eventually became his ride or die. Always bright-eyed and bushy-tailed, eager to learn the music game. As she got older, she became a great sounding board for his problems in the company. She had great ideas too. It was like she was born to do this. Now as he looked at her, that whole best friend, little sister thing was flying out the window fast. Autumn had let her hair grow out and curled it. She looked more like a woman than anything else to him right now. So of course, he wanted to see where her mind was at concerning himself.

"You're actually lucky I'm not your girl. Because if I was your girl, this whole encounter would be going a different way right now."

"Is that right?"

"It is."

Axel stared at Autumn, trying to figure out if he should cross that line or not.

"I ain't gonna even lie. You looking real good in that outfit. And if you weren't who you are to me, you would not even be wearing that outfit right now. Those heels, he tilted his head to the right to get a better look, you can keep those on."

Autumn tried not to blush, but how could she not.

Axel noticed. He started to say forget it but he would regret it for the rest of his life if he killed what they had. So, he decided against it. He knew he would have to be the one with the restraint because the vibes Autumn was giving him was telling him he had that in the bag.

"Look. Let's just move on from that. And I'll be straight with you. I am seeing Harmony. We've been seeing each other privately for some time now. I told you that was my goal. I don't know why you tripping. I think she might be the one. Time to go very public." Axel turned back to his keyboard and began to play a melody. Hoping it would distract him from that I could kill you look that Autumn was giving him.

Autumn couldn't help but feel a sharp pain through her chest. She thought this conversation was going another way and just like that, stuck back in friend mode. Autumn didn't even want to entertain the fact that Axel wanted to marry someone else. She always thought she would be the one. That was her whole purpose for coming to the studio. She wanted Axel to see her in her new outfit and hoped he would see her as a woman that could be his wife and not just a girl that was his best friend. But it hadn't worked. He didn't want her. He wanted Harmony. What did Harmony have that she didn't? After all this time she had invested in him and he just walks off to someone who she didn't even think was worthy of him. She decided to change the subject.

"I heard you in here."

"Aw man Autumn. I was hoping you didn't." Axel turned back toward Autumn relieved she had changed the subject unprompted.

Autumn gave him a half smile. She had gone into full fledge friend mode. "I did and it was beautiful. I can't believe you don't write anymore."

"I don't have any need to."

"Why is that?"

"I have people to do it for me. I'm rich. I already made it. Why should I be in here working?"

"Because it's what you love. You should never stop doing what you love."

Axel couldn't look at Autumn. Had she read his mind? How did she know that is what he was thinking just moments before she entered? That was one thing he loved and hated about Autumn. She knew him all too well. Nevertheless, he knew she was right. He had given up his love and gotten lost in the benefits of his money.

"You remember when we used to write together?"

Axel closed his eyes and allowed his mind to reminisce. "I sure do."

Autumn sat on the keyboard next to him. "Those were the days. When everything was so simple."

"Yeah. But growth is always the goal right."

"I guess so. Play me something." Autumn insisted.

Axel scrunched his nose up at her but his fingers seemed to have a mind of their own and dutifully obeyed. Autumn closed her eyes and began to sing lyrics of one of Axel's old songs. One of the few he had never released.

Axel stopped playing. "You still remember that?"

"Yep. It was actually one of my favorites. Always hated you never released it."

"I don't know Autumn. I feel like I've hit my peek in this business. I want to do something else."

Autumn threw her head back. "And what would that be?"

Axel hesitated. He hadn't mentioned his idea to anyone else. But if he was going to tell anybody, it would definitely be Autumn. He took a deep breath, hoping Autumn wouldn't think his idea was stupid. "I want to start my own NBA team."

Autumn turned and just stared at Axel. She could tell by the nervous look in his eyes he wasn't joking. "You're serious?"

"I knew you would think it was stupid. Never mind. Forget I brought it up."

"Actually, I don't."

Now it was Axel's turn to stare at her. "Really?"

"Really." Autumn stood up to leave. "You've always been amazing Axel. No need to stop now. I know that whatever it is that you put your mind to, you are absolutely destined to succeed."

Axel watched her as she sashayed away. Autumn's genuine heart never ceased to amaze him.

Before she exited the room, she heard Axel's voice. "Hey Autumn."

She turned to look at him.

"I hate to see you leave, but I love to see you walk away."

"I can't stand you." Autumn exited the room and slammed the door behind her. Autumn decided to skip the Halloween party. She had too many thoughts running through her mind. She was upset that Axel wanted Harmony but this new side of him, the side that she fell in love with was making her crazy for him. *How do I break away from this man?*

# CHAPTER EIGHT

Michelle stood at the closed gym door peering in through the bottom section of the rectangular glass. She hated being so short. *Maybe that's why people think they can take advantage of me.* Michelle thought to herself. Her thoughts went to Mitchell and she had to fight back tears. She couldn't believe how he just dumped her without saying anything. Shaking the thoughts from her head she focused on the veteran dance members putting the finishing touches on the dance moves that the newbies would eventually have to emulate. She was determined to get Mitchell off her mind and out of her heart and joining the dance team would be perfect. As she continued to watch the girls, she couldn't help wondering if watching was considered cheating or not, but as she stood there, something else crossed her mind. *I can do better.* Michelle's thoughts surprised even her. *Why would I want to outdo anyone on the dance team?* Clearing the thoughts from her head once again Michelle watched intensely as Ava Long, dance captain, was effortlessly flowing through a routine which Michelle could tell by the look on her cohorts' faces was supposedly difficult.

"The new girls will never be able to get this choreography Ava." Serena snapped.

"That's the point Serena." Ava snapped back.

"What do you mean?"

"I want the routine to be hard enough that they want to quit. We don't need any weak links on the team. I'm trying to win state this year. Maybe even get a shot at nationals. And I'm not going to let weak girls stop me. So, tell me Serena, do you want to win or do I need to replace you as well?"

Serena glared at Ava. She hated how she always backed down to Ava's intimidation. But she knew she wasn't a better dancer than Ava and she felt lucky just to be a part of the team.

"I guess I want to win." Serena reluctantly submitted.

"Good. So just stand back and watch me make all these little girls cry." Ava's lips curled in a satisfying smile.

"Hey, you going in?"

Michelle jumped to see a tall, slender girl standing behind her. "Oh, I guess. Just nervous that's all."

"Well, I'm going to tell you this, so you'll be prepared. You are a little thick and short. Ava doesn't like that so, get ready for the ridicule. Other than that. Good luck."

Michelle stepped back to let the girl pass. Her chest felt like a percussion session was taking place inside her. After seeing several other girls enter at the opposite side of the gym and begin to stretch, she took a couple of deep breaths and forced her shaking legs to take her on in.

Michelle found a space away from the other girls and began to stretch.

Ava walked over to Serena. "Is that Michelle? The little weird girl who lives with the principal?"

"Looks like it."

"She is too thick to be on this team. She needs a whole diet. As a matter of fact, she needs to just stop eating. And she's way too short. I would have to keep her in the front and I don't want her in the front, period. Naw, she's a hard pass."

"Ava, you don't even know if she can dance or not."

"I really don't care. I don't want her on my team."

"Alright girls, bring it in." Coach Philips loud voice silenced the gym.

"Ok. Just in case you ladies don't know who I am, I'm Coach Phillips. Standing next to me is Ava Long." She pointed Ava's way with four fingers. "She is your captain and she will be conducting your try-out. I will be sitting over here on the bleachers observing. So good luck. Ava."

Ava stepped forward as if she were about to be crowned Miss America. "Thanks Coach. Ok ladies. I'm going to be very blunt with you. I demand perfection and hard work. This is not going to be a walk in the park. If you feel like you can't handle it, you can leave now."

None of the girls budged.

"Ok. Great. So, I'm going to start with something simple. Spread out and watch closely. I'm going to be nice today and actually show you the dance twice before I turn on the music and watch you perform it to see how much you can remember. If you can't get it after two times, you really shouldn't be here, but we'll see."

Ava gave a nod to the coach and the music filled the gym. 5,6,7,8 and Ava began to twist and turn. It was a simple eight count.

Michelle could see the girls felt confident they could get it and she was right. Each girl executed the dance perfectly.

"Ok. Good. Let's move on."

After 30 minutes of simple choreography, Michelle saw Ava give a wink to Serena. She guessed this was when the hard part began.

Ava nodded at her coach and the music blasted once again. Once Ava counted in, she lit up. Michelle had to give her credit. After seeing the entire routine, it was pretty good. But not Nationals worthy. Michelle knew she could have come up with something simpler; more creative and still rocked Nationals. Michelle relished at the thought. Michelle looked at the other dancers. You would have thought they were watching a horror movie instead of a dance routine by the twisted expressions on their faces.

After the routine two girls grabbed their bags and left. To Ava's amusement of course.

"Anyone else want to leave?"

None of the other girls said a word.

"Ok let's do it!" Ava exclaimed.

One girl finally raised her hand.

"What?" Ave sighed. Aggravated by the interruption.

"I thought you said you would show us twice?"

"I'm actually going to run through it again. If you would have waited a second before you rudely interrupted me you would have known that." Ava responded with an eye roll.

"What if we don't need to see it again?" Michelle's words jumped out of her mouth like a deer emerging from the woods. Quick and unexpected.

"Speak for yourself." The one who raised her hand folded her arms in aggravation as if she were two.

If looks could kill, Michelle would have been dead. Execution style.

"So, you're telling me you don't need to see it again fat girl?"

Snickers circulated amongst the dancers.

"I'm surprised you've survived this long without passing out."

Michelle walked to the front of the line ignoring Ava's disrespectful comments. She stood directly in front of Ava anticipating shoving those words right back down her throat.

"I don't need to be anorexic in order to be in shape." She looked passed Ava at the Coach. "Can you play it back please?"

The coach obliged.

Once she counted herself in, Michelle executed with precision every step mocking Ava the entire way through. Once she finished, she stepped a little closer to Ava and spoke her words clearly and loudly enough for all to hear.

"You call that difficult? To be honest I could have done it better with a lot less steps. What you came up with was overkill and it won't win you Nationals."

Michelle did an about face, walked to the bleachers, grabbed her bag and left the room, leaving the entire room of dancers speechless. She wished she could have seen Ava up there trying to pick her face up off the floor but she couldn't risk ruining her epic walk out.

Michelle had more adrenaline than she had blood racing through her veins. *Did I really just do that?* She didn't need any more enemies, but something just kept pushing her. As quickly as the thought ran through her mind, the afterthought responded. Michelle knew if she didn't know anything else she knew dance and she hated when arrogant people disrespected the craft that she had grown to love. Living in a house with a bipolar grandmother, Michelle had spent countless hours in her room with nothing but her thoughts to keep her company. Eventually music and dancing became her escape. She could break out of the prison of silence that engulfed her as she lost herself in the music and every move of her body. Then it hit her. *What did I just do? I shouldn't have walked out. I need that team.*

Michelle paced the floor. Should she go back in and apologize and beg for a position on the team? Michelle continued to pace, back and forth, back and forth.

"Michelle."

Michelle turned to see Coach Philips walking towards her.

Michelle just knew she was in trouble. She halfway thought about running out of the front door, but maybe this was her chance to beg the coach instead.

"Hey, I'm glad I caught you. Have you had professional dance classes?"

Michelle looked down at her feet and then back up at Coach. "No." She responded just above a whisper. "I taught myself."

"Well, you did one heck of a job doing so."

Michelle responded with a nod returning her gaze back towards the floor.

"Look, do me a favor. Please don't quit. We need you if we are going to have any shot at State let alone Nationals."

Michelle looked around the foyer contemplating how she should play this. She was so relieved she was on the team, but since the coach was begging her, she might as well use it to her advantage. She decided a direct approach would be the best approach.

Michelle shifted her gaze upward and looked the coach directly in her eyes. "Under one condition."

"What's that?"

"I want to be captain."

Coach Philips's mouth fell into a perfect circle. You would have thought Michelle punched her in the stomach. "Michelle, I can't make you captain." She finally said.

"Why not?"

"Ava's the captain and she's earned it."

"How?" Michelle decided not to let up.

"She's been on the team since her freshman year and she's the best dancer on the team. Not to mention the only one who can come up with her own choreography."

"Until now."

"That's true, I guess, but..."

"Look if you want to win State or even have a chance at Nationals, you need to make me the captain."

The coach thought about it. She paced the hallway. Through her hands into the air every now and then. Then she came back to Michelle. "What if I make you co-captain?"

Now it was Michelle's turn to think. She knew she was putting Coach in an impossible situation so she decided to fold. "That's fine. But I need Ava to know that we are on equal ground."

"Fine. Done. So, you're back?"

"Sure. Whatever." Truth be told, Michelle would have taken any position.

"Ok. Let's head back in. I'll tell everyone now."

Michelle followed Coach back into the gym.

"Ok girls. Let's try to sort this out. I believe Michelle has something we need."

"I disagree." Ava barked.

"So, what I'm going to do is make Michelle co-captain."

"What?" Ava shrieked. "You can't be serious?"

"I'm dead serious. If we want a shot in the big leagues, I'm going to need you and Michelle working together on this one."

"If she's co-captain I quit!"

"If that's what you want to do Ava, be my guest. If you want to waste the time you put into this, then it's fine with me. This is your senior year, not mine." Coach looked at Ava hoping to get through.

Ava threw darts straight through Michelle's face with her eyes. "She can have it. And I bet you don't make it to Nationals and you will regret this decision." Ava grabbed her things and stormed out of the gym.

Coach looked at Michelle. "Well, it's on you now. I hope you have a plan."

Michelle smiled. "I'll see you guys tomorrow."

# CHAPTER NINE

Autumn fired up her laptop, excited to hear the new music her writers sent over. She wanted a new song to sing on tour and she had hit a creative roadblock. She couldn't come up with anything. She rarely used writers, but she had to make money. She clicked on her email. There it was. A list of five songs for her to choose from. Just below that email she saw the words Contract Renewal. It had been sitting in her inbox for weeks. Autumn just stared at it. She never took this long to resign her contract. She just didn't feel like it was the best thing for her right now. Not when she was having doubts. She decided to ignore it once and again and move on to more pressing issues. Her song list. Just as she was about to open the first song her phone rang. It was Axel. She put him on speaker.

"What do you want? You're interrupting my creative flow session."

"You ain't in there creating nothing."

"Wait til I hit you with what I got. You're going to be picking your face up off the floor."

"Whatever you say sexy girl."

Autumn almost caught whiplash as she swept her head around to stare at the phone. *Did he just call me sexy girl? What in the world brought this on? Was he still thinking about the Halloween party. Maybe my outfit achieved its goal after all. No Autumn. Don't go there. Leave it alone. Don't allow your mind to go there. He's dating Harmony.* Autumn made a mocking face as she thought Harmony's name.

"Autumn, I need you."

Axel's voice shook Autumn from her thoughts. *What did he just say? If this man don't stop playing with me.* "What did you say?"

"I need you. Come to my office."

"For what, cause I don't like your tone."

"What you scared?"

"Scared of what?"

"What might happen in my office."

"You mean like a whole bunch of hot sweaty nothing.

Axel laughed. "Why don't you come to my office and find out."

Autumn wanted to kick her heals off and run to his office, but she had to play it cool.

"I think I'll decline."

"You do me so wrong?"

"I think I do you just about what you deserve."

"I think I deserve better."

"I'll let you know when you deserve better."

"Who is this and what have you done with my best friend."

"This is your best friend. The 2.0 version."

Axel laughed a bit harder this time. Autumn loved to hear him laugh. It always warmed her heart. She just wished she could be the one making him laugh for life.

"For real Autumn. I need you to come by my office right away if you can. I need to run something by you."

"On my way Friend."

Autumn disconnected the line. She wondered what Axel wanted. She also wanted to know what was going on with this playful sexual banter he was indulging in. *Well, I can't worry about that.* She thought to herself. *I must stay professional. Can't let him get to me.*

Autumn got up and checked herself in the mirror before she left her office. Axel's office was down the hall to the left of hers. She opened the door and tried to calm herself. *What did Axel want?* The more she tried to relax the more anxious she got.

She finally arrived at Axel's office. She took a deep breath and knocked.

"Come on in here girl." She heard Axel say from the other side.

Autumn wasn't quite ready to go in but she had no other choice. She reluctantly opened the door intent on having a good attitude.

Heyyy… Autumn stopped in her tracks as she took in the scenery.

Axel was sitting behind his desk and a light skinned big booty girl was standing way to close to him.

"You guys always flirt with each other or is there some pint up sexual frustration going on?" Asked the big booty girl.

Autumn was still too stunned for words.

Axel, feeling Autumn's tongue-tied anxiety decided to answer for her." We always play. As you heard me say. Autumn here is my best friend. We play all the time. Please Autumn, have a seat."

Autumn had to will her legs to move. *Who was this chick?* She already had to deal with Harmony, now this.

Autumn sat in the chair in front of Axel's desk. Axel mentioned for his companion to take the seat adjacent to Autumn. The girl reluctantly obliged and sashayed around the desk, making sure she gave Axel something to look at the whole way.

Autumn rolled her eyes as she moved behind her and then to her seat.

"Autumn, I would like you to meet Charlie. Charlie you already know who Autumn is but now you have officially met her." Axel began. "Autumn, Charlie is my new artist. I just offered her a deal yesterday."

Autumn's eyes flew towards Axel. But before she could tear into him, he spoke what she was thinking.

"I know. I know. Axel started as he held up both hands in hopes of fending her off. We usually talk about these things together but I was hanging out with Fred and we went to this club that had local talent performing. I saw Charlie and offered her a deal on the spot. We haven't officially signed a contract yet but those are just formalities. But yet and still I wanted you to meet her. Maybe you can show her the ropes."

Charlie spoke first. "No disrespect to your BFF boss, but I don't need her to show me the ropes. I got this."

Axel nodded. "Okay. I'm loving the confidence."

Autumn still didn't speak. She was burning up on the inside. She was tired of having to compete with every female artist Axel signed. They all knew she was his number one artist and they all came in gunning for her. This one was no different. Autumn was pretty sick of it herself. Maybe she was right to be wanting to get out of the business. This wasn't the life she had signed up for, but she wasn't the one to back down from a challenge. It was the vicious cycle that kept her in this business.

"Well, looks like you all got this covered, so you don't really need me." Autumn began.

"You got that right." Charlie chimed in.

Autumn bit her tongue. "It was nice to meet you Charlie" She got up and headed for the door.

"Autumn." Axel called behind her.

Autumn didn't stop, neither did she look back. She shut the door. Went to her office. Grabbed her purse. And went home. She had had enough.

# CHAPTER TEN

Axel glared at Charlie.

"What," Charlie said innocently.

"I haven't even signed you and you're already making trouble with my artist. My artist that is my best friend I might add."

"I get what you're saying Mr. Smith, but to be honest with you, I have never been the type to mince words. What you see is what you get. I don't like Autumn as an artist and I believe I'm better than her and I'm going to prove it. So, if you want to make some money, you are going to have to look over my disapproval of your best friend and sign me."

Axel stared at Charlie trying to read her. He was usually very good at reading people but for some reason he couldn't get a grip on why Charlie had it out for Autumn on this level. He understood competition but this sounded personal.

"First off before we even go any further. I need you to know that I don't need you at all. Must I remind you. I'm already rich. The only one benefiting from this deal is you. You are the one who needs the money. You are the one who wants the fame. I already have it. Secondly, I love your competitive, aggressive nature, but there is a limit to all things. And you are coming dangerously close to stepping over that line. Actually, if you have such a problem with Autumn that door over there will let you out the same way it let you in." Axel stood and motioned toward the door.

Charlie swallowed hard. She wasn't expecting this at all. She pretty much thought she would walk in and start running things. But not here. Not when it came to overshadowing Autumn. Whatever they had going on, it was pretty serious. She didn't know if this was a battle she could win. But she couldn't lose this opportunity. She did the only thing she could. She submitted.

"I mean, what's your deal with Autumn anyway?" He asked her. "I get your determined and you want to be the best, but this thing with Autumn seems more than that."

Charlie looked uncomfortable for the first time since she stepped into Axel's office. She knew exactly why she had it out for Autumn but she wasn't about to let Axel know the truth. She had to come up with something that would be close to the truth but not reveal all of the details. Charlie took a deep breath before uttering her next words. "Let's just say Autumn has rubbed me the wrong way in ways you couldn't even imagine and I want to expose her for who she truly is. A fraud."

"You're gonna have to be more specific than that." Axel was getting frustrated with Charlie. He was almost at the point he didn't want to even sign her.

"That's all I can tell you." Charlie stared at her lap avoiding Axel's intense gaze.

Axel knew a decision had to be made.

"I'm not going to sign you Charlie."

"What!" Charlie flew up from her seat. "What do you mean you're not going to sign me. Just because I don't like your little girlfriend."

"Sit down and lower your voice in my office!" Axel was the one standing now.

Charlie quickly took her seat. She hadn't expected Axel to respond like this. "Please Axel, whatever I have to do I'll do it. Please, just don't take this opportunity away from me. I've been waiting on this moment my entire life. Look, I'll be nicer to Autumn. I promise. I just want to be the best that's all. You can understand that right?"

Axel sat back down at his desk and leaned forward placing his forearms on his desk. He thought about his next words very carefully hoping he wasn't making a huge mistake and putting Autumn in danger.

"I'll give you one shot and one shot only. Like I told you. I like your ambition and I do believe you will be a money maker. But I will warn you. Autumn is a pro. There's nothing fake about her. Many artists have come for her and failed. You may find yourself in that same category all though I'm sure you don't think so." Axel added when he saw Charlie about to protest. "'m down with a little healthy competition and it doesn't make Autumn anything but better. But I will let you know this. Even though I still don't understand what your personal beef with Autumn is, Autumn is my ride or die for life. Any harm comes to her from you outside of healthy competition and I will end your contract faster than you can sign it. I don't play when it comes to my family. And Autumn is my family. Do you understand that?"

Charlie couldn't even find a comeback. She realized Autumn's place in Axel's life was a little more fortified than she thought. She definitely had her work cut out for her. But if she wanted to save her contract, at this time, she figured, it was best for her to keep her mouth shut.

"Yes sir." Was the only reply Charlie let part her lips.

Axel sat back in his chair satisfied that he was still in control of the situation and that he had everything handled. But he had shocked himself. He is usually protective over Autumn, but never had he let it be terms of ending someone's contract. What had come over him? He hadn't been able to get Autumn off his mind since the Halloween party. This was getting very difficult. He needed to see her. To make sure she was ok. Or at least that's what he was telling himself. *What if I can't control myself? What if we cross the line? No, we can't cross the line. I've controlled myself before. Tonight, will be no different. I got this.*

# CHAPTER ELEVEN

Axel sat in Autumn's driveway. He hoped he hadn't lost his best friend. "Man, if I don't get it together, I'm going to lose her for real one day. I've had too many close calls."

"What are you doing here Axel? What is your real motive?" He asked himself feeling very nervous all of a sudden. *You've been here a million times. Why is this time making you feel a way?* Axel let out a huge sigh. He didn't know what he was doing. All he did know is that he couldn't get Autumn off his mind. He wanted to make sure she was okay following the day's events with Charlie especially after he found out she went home early. Right after the meeting as a matter of fact. But even more than that, he just wanted to see her. To spend some uninterrupted time with her. Axel confessed. He didn't just want to see her. He needed to see her. This can't be good. Or could it? Axel finally got up his courage, exited his car, walked up to Autumn's door and rang the bell. It was no turning back now.

It took a few minutes, but she finally answered the door. Truth be told, he would have stood there all night if he had to.

"Hey there stranger. I didn't know you knew who I was let alone the way to my house." Autumn answered the door without the smile he had grown so accustomed to.

But it wasn't her lack of a smile that had caught and held his attention. It was the Mauve Chalk button-front sleepshirt she was wearing. Had to be Victoria Secret. He could tell she had the matching lingerie underneath since only two of the buttons were fastened.

"You expecting company?"

"I was thinking about it, but now that I have been so rudely interrupted. I guess not."

Axel looked Autumn over again. He didn't know how he felt about her giving all that away to someone else. "You gonna invite me in or let me stand on the porch?"

"I should let you stand out there all night."

"Oh, it's like that now?"

"Yeah." Autumn replied with a roll of her eyes. She reluctantly opened the door to let him in. "Come on in boy."

"Bout time you learned some manners."

"Whatever. What do you want?" Autumn asked as she led the way into the den and onto the Circle Italian leather sofa. It was her favorite place to chill.

As much as Axel tried, he couldn't seem to take his eyes off all the curves of her body.

"I don't know why you are staring me down my friend. This ain't for you."

"I can't tell friend, cause you flaunting it."

"I can flaunt it all day. You are the one who came over to my home unannounced remind you. And like I told you before, I was thinking about having company anyway. Besides, you act like you've never seen me in my good stuff before, so stop trippin." Autumn plopped down on the couch.

"It's different this time." Axel locked eyes with Autumn. He knew he had her full attention. "Look I'm sorry about today. Charlie was wrong and I told her so. I told her if she came for you outside of healthy competition, I would end her contract."

"You can't do that Axel." Autumn responded although feeling very touched that he even bothered to say it.

"I can and did. Already had the contract reprinted to say as much."

"Axel. You really shouldn't do that."

"I know, but I don't know what has come over me this last month. To tell you the truth, I haven't been able to stop thinking about you since the Halloween party and I don't know what to do with that."

The struggle was back. Cross the line or not. Axel didn't think he could make the right decision this time because the look in her eyes was lighting a fire in him that could not be extinguished.

"What do you want to do with that?"

He reached across the couch and grabbed her leg pulling her to his side of the couch. Before she could protest Axel's tongue was down her throat. He could tell Autumn was still somewhat resistant. Her body remained tense, but as he rubbed his hand back and forth on her thigh, she slowly began to relax. He knew then he could take her all the way.

Axel had never made love before, but tonight he had. And enjoyed every minute of it. As he looked over at Autumn sound asleep, he realized she had given him something he never had before and was sure he would never have again. He just wasn't cut from that cloth. But he was glad he got to experience it and he was glad to have experienced it with Autumn. He couldn't think of a better person. And he would always love her and respect her for that. He just hoped he hadn't ruined what friendship they had left. He didn't know what he would do without her.

# CHAPTER TWELVE

Michelle sat next to Hunter on the first bleacher at the gym. Basketball season had finally arrived. Practice had just ended and again Mitchell left the gym and drove off leaving Michelle sitting there once again. This was the third day she sat there waiting and hoping that he would at least look her way. She had no idea why she continued to let Mitchell treat her this way. He had offered to take her home several times and like an idiot she had let him. Funny how the only days he took her home were the days he knew the Nelson's would be away from the house conveniently giving him an opportunity to sleep with her. Hunter, who worked out running the bleachers after practice, had noticed her waiting and offered to give her a ride home on the first day and then again on the second day. On the third day it may have appeared that she was waiting on Mitchell, but she was actually waiting on Hunter.

"So, you still crushing on Mitchell?"

"Not really. It still hurts a bit, but you are definitely helping with that." She smiled.

"Hopefully I can make you forget about him altogether."

"I just might be up for that."

"How about we get out of here and get something to eat."

"Lead the way, after all, you're the one driving."

"So you're saying you trust me?"

Michelle stopped in her tracks. She thought back to the time when she trusted Mitchell and she began to have doubts about Hunter. Was she just an easy target for him. Were they trying to pass her around?

Hunter noticed that Michelle was no longer following him and turned back to face her. "You ok?"

"Why are you being so nice to me?"

"Can I not be nice to you?"

I" don't know. Mitchell was nice to me too and look how that turned out?"

"So, you think I'm going to do you just like Mitchell?"

Michelle immediately regretted telling him the things she did about her relationship with Mitchell. "I guess."

"Michelle, what is it that you think I want from you, because I haven't asked you for anything."

"Not yet. Of course, that's not how it works. You earn my trust and then we sleep together and then you dump me. And then what, the next athlete is going to be my knight in shining armor after you only to do the same thing."

"Michelle. I realize you've been hurt, but if you always think someone's out to get you, you're never going to find anybody, besides, seems to me that the remedy to that plan is to keep your legs closed. I'm going to be real with you, of course I would like to sleep with you, but I don't need to sleep with you. I'm just looking for a friend and I figured you could use one as well, so once we get in the car, I can either drive you home and we can be done with this or we can get a bite to eat and get to know each other, your choice."

Michelle thought about all that Hunter had said and figured he had a point. She didn't have to sleep with him and that would protect her. So she figured, she might as well enjoy his company while getting a bite to eat. "So, where are we going to eat?"

Hunter smiled. Reached out and grabbed Michelle's hand and led her out of the gym.

# CHAPTER THIRTEEN

Charlie sat inside her new office. She had finally arrived. She was Axel's newest artist. Now she had to be his top artist. The person currently holding that position was no other than Autumn. Autumn Dance. Charlie spoke out loud with disdain falling from her lips. She briefly thought back on the day Axel had come for her because of Autumn. She couldn't make that mistake again, but she was in no way about to back down. She just had to play the game smarter. She breathed in deeply taking in the smell of a thousand wishes. It was one of the few requests she made when asked about specifics of her office. She loved a thousand wishes because that's what she had, a thousand wishes and she was determined to make all of them come true. As a matter of fact, Charlie began to spin around in her swiveled desk chair, that could be the name of her first single. Her mind began to travel all over the place. Ideas were hitting her left and right.

Yeah, this was going to be nice. She would solidify herself as the sexiest girl in the business. Funny twist would be, she would be every man's dream but a man was the last thing she would want. The female flavor was more of her taste. She licked her lips as the thought crossed her mind. All the females she was about to get her hands on was making her feel some type of way.

Charlie thought it was time she took a little tour around her new label. She might just make her way to the dance studios. Autumn was sure to be in one of them. She got up from her seat and exited the office. She looked to her right and then to the left. She saw the sign on her left that pointed toward the dance studios. She turned left and strolled slowly down the hall running her hand over the beautiful graffiti that graced the walls. Musical notes and lyrics were the theme. It was like a tribute to the artists. That's one thing she could say about Axel, he really valued his artists and he took very good care of them as well. She was going to love this gig. She had put in a lot of work to get here. She even had to lower herself to sleeping with a guy. Charlie almost vomited at the thought. She knew a guy that could get Axel to the club where she was going to be performing. It worked like a charm. It was worth every miserable minute she spent with her hookup.

Charlie rounded another corner and was finally at the dance studios. She would have to look in each window since the rooms were sound proof. She took her time looking in each one. She noticed some of the artist. Some she didn't.

Bingo. She found her. She saw Autumn with her head pressed up against the wall. She was clearly frustrated. Charlie smiled. She couldn't have come at a more perfect time. Seeing Autumn at her lowest was going to be great. And if she could sow a couple more seeds of doubt into her, she would have No. 1 artist in the bag. It wouldn't go against what she had promised Axel. It was just a little healthy competition. She wasn't going to hurt Autumn. Yet. She smiled to herself.

Charlie opened the door and closed it quietly. Autumn hadn't heard her enter. Charlie just stared at her for a moment taking in the sight. She studied Autumn from her beautiful curly brown hair down to her toned caramel-colored legs. If it wasn't for the fact that she wanted to humiliate Autumn in order to take her place, she would definitely take a shot at getting her into bed. Charlie stood there for a second longer debating the thought in her head. She eventually shook the thought from her head realizing being top artist meant more.

I'll find someone else to conquer. Autumn was going down a different way. Charlie opened the door and slammed it shut causing Autumn to jump and turn in her direction.

Autumn rolled her eyes at seeing Charlie. She walked over to grab her phone and turned off the music.

"What do you want Charlie? I'm trying to work."

"Didn't look like you were working to me?"

"Doesn't matter what it looked like to you. You're not important."

"Not now maybe. But just you wait. When my first single hits No. 1 and stays there, I'm going to leave you and all the other artist on this label in the dust. I think I'll be more important to you then."

"Charlie, we don't operate like that here. We are all friends and we support each other. We aren't in any type of competition. We are just her to make great music."

"Sounds exactly like what a loser would say. Anyway, I'm different. I'm here to kill the game not fit in and play nice."

"Why don't you just get out Charlie. I'm done talking to you. I could be doing so many other things with the air that I'm breathing besides wasting it on you."

"Testy are we. No problem. I'll leave. Unlike you I have actual work to do. But let me leave you with a bit of advice. From what I've seen, you've been working on this dance for a minute. From what I hear, that's not your usual. Supposedly you're a beast when it comes to dance routines and it doesn't take you long at all. But I'm going to tell you what the problem is, since you clearly haven't figured it out yet. The reason you can't come up with any good dance steps is because the song is trash."

Autumn's eyes widened in surprise. She couldn't believe Charlie's audacity.

"I'm actually surprised that Axel didn't tell you. He should have. I'm pretty sure his friendship with you is blinding him from true talent. Or lack thereof I should say."

Autumn was getting angrier with every word that came from Charlie's mouth. "Look, Charlie, you just got into this business! You don't know anything about this business, about me or about Axel, so don't assume you do!" Autumn's voice was shaking with anger.

"That may be true, but I do know music and that song you came up with is trash at its best." Charlie couldn't help but laugh as the words left her lips.

She turned and exited the room before Autumn could think of a comeback. Charlie walked down the hall relishing in her victory. She knew she had rattled Autumn's cage. This was going to make it that much easier to take her throne.

Autumn leaned back on the wall and slid down until her butt hit the floor and her elbows rested on her knees. She could feel the anger rising in her chest. But she wasn't mad at Charlie. She didn't like Charlie but she wasn't angry with her. She was angry at herself for being so naïve. She knew in her heart her song wasn't good. She had even seen it in Axel's eyes when he listened to it but she had grown complacent. She was the top artist and Axel's best friend. She had it made in the shade. But now here was

Charlie. Challenging her. Maybe it was just what she needed to get back focused. Autumn couldn't help but let out an evil laugh. Charlie thought she was hurting Autumn but she may have just delivered her own death blow. *Stupid girl,* she thought to herself. *I told you, you didn't know the business. But I'm going to show you just how much.*

## CHAPTER
# FOURTEEN

Axel stared across the table at Harmony. Her slanted green eyes, with those long thick eyelashes seemed to pierce his very soul. He enjoyed looking at them and for whatever reason he couldn't take his eyes off hers. It was only when her eyes left his that he could finally break away. He looked down at his plate. He was a steak and potatoes man if there ever was one. Well done always. The potatoes, he could change up. Sometimes he ate them baked and loaded, sometimes smashed and loaded, other times grilled and loaded. It didn't really matter, as long as they were potatoes and loaded. His choice of vegetables, were a no change just like his steak. Broccoli steamed. No variations. Harmony had chosen to order Cajun jumbo shrimp on Pesto zoodles with sliced lemons on top. It looked pretty good but Axel rarely strayed from his usual.

He and Harmony had been publicly dating for a while now, he guessed it was time to take the next step, but could he? After what he and Autumn had just experienced just weeks ago? How could he just forget about the most amazing night of his life and just move on? He tried to forget it many times. Tried continuously to push the memories from his mind. But he couldn't. If he was being honest with himself, he didn't really want to. He wanted to think about it all day every day. As a matter of fact, he wanted to experience it again and again and again.

"Axel." Harmony's soft voice beckoned him from his fantasy land. "You ok?"

"Yeah. I was actually just thinking about you." Axel lied.

"Oh really." A smile began to spread across her beautiful face.

"Really. I was thinking it might be time to take our relationship to the next level."

Harmony's eyes grew wide. "Are you serious?"

Axel hesitated. He was and he wasn't. But all these stupid words just kept falling out of his mouth before he had a chance to stop himself. And he knew once he said them, he couldn't take them back. Why was he being such an idiot. This was the worst possible time to take his relationship to the next level, especially when he really wanted it to end. Because... Because... because he really wanted Autumn. Did he just finally admit that to himself? Axel felt in his jacket pocket as he thought about Autumn and then something hit the floor.

*Please don't let that be what I think it was.* Axel looked down and for sure it was. This is about to be awkward. Axel bent down and picked it up and sure enough when Harmony saw it, she shrieked.

"Yes!!! I'll marry you!"

Axel looked confused. "What?"

"I said yes. Isn't that a ring for me?"

Axel looked down at his hand. He was still holding the ring box he picked up off the floor. He couldn't believe what he had just done. Did he just propose? He didn't think so? But how could he convince her that he didn't? All he really wanted to ask Harmony was to move in with him, but now he was stuck.

He looked back down at the ring box. This was not for Harmony, it was for... Axel felt sick to his stomach. A lump began to form in his throat so big, he could have sworn he had just swallowed a fat midget.

"I had no idea you were going to propose? Oh Axel. I promise you. You will not regret this."

Harmony made her way over to Axel's side of the table and held her hand out. Axel just stared for a moment. He slowly opened the box. And another shriek escaped Harmony's throat. To Axel's dismay, he slid the ring onto her finger. He had no idea how he was going to get out of this. But what he did know is that he was a dead man. Autumn was definitely going to kill him. And he deserved it.

## CHAPTER
# FIFTEEN

Michelle walked out onto the balcony of the condominium that she shared with the Nelson's. She never felt settled in. She felt like a stranger in these people's home. All she ever wanted was a family that loved her. Someone who would really be there for her and not judge her for something she had no control over. She braced her arms looking over the side. She often walked out there and battled with thoughts of jumping over, but it wasn't high enough. The fall would never kill her. Just injure her and make matters worse. She had decided that if she was going to do it, she would do it right. No mistakes. No regrets. But today wasn't that day. She had met Hunter and Hunter had given her hope.

Michelle jumped as the sliding door to the balcony opened. It was Ms. Nelson or Janet is what she had told her she could call her. But she never did.

"Hey Michelle."

"Hey Mrs. Nelson."

"I guess you will never call me Janet huh?" She propped her arms on the balcony alongside Michelle.

"It just doesn't seem like the respectful thing to do."

"So, you do respect me?"

Michelle turned to look at Mrs. Nelson. The statement had caught her totally off guard.

"You don't think I respect you?"

"Well, when you first came here. I wasn't so sure. But you have always been very respectable and sweet. But there is just something that I cannot get off my mind."

"What's that?" Michelle asked almost afraid to even breath.

"The fact that you might be sleeping with my husband." She turned and stared daggers into Michelle.

Michelle wanted to definitely throw herself over the balcony at that very moment. She didn't know how to respond. Should she tell her or should she just keep her mouth shut? What did she have to lose? Maybe if she was lucky Mrs. Nelson would throw her off the balcony and save her the trouble.

Michelle looked down at the grass that was three floors down. It had just been cut and she could smell the freshness of it. There was a flower garden that she loved to sit next to, admiring all the beautiful colors, wishing she was somewhere else, anywhere else.

She took a deep breath and decided, she didn't care any longer. How much worse could her life get? If she had any chance at having a normal relationship with Hunter and getting away from this sick life. She had to deal with the craziness. So, she decided.

"I'm not sleeping with Mr. Nelson."

Mrs. Nelson closed her eyes and allowed a tear to fall from her right eye.

"He's raping me."

Mrs. Nelson's eyes flew open and her head swiveled around to look at Michelle. "What did you say?"

Michelle contemplated repeating herself, but she had stepped in it now. She had to go all the way.

"I said your husband is raping me." Michelle said more harshly than she had intended, but now rage had filled her chest and tears began to flow down her face. "I would never sleep with your husband. I am not like that. I don't' care what anyone thinks, but your husband is raping me almost every single day, so instead of coming out here accusing me of sleeping with your husband, make your filthy, disgusting husband keep his hands off of me!" Michelle was almost screaming.

Mrs. Nelson looked around to see if there were any bystanders that might have heard, but there were none. She didn't know whether to slap Michelle or hug her. So, there she stood, trying to digest what Michelle was saying to her. She figured her husband was cheating on her, but was he so sick that he would rape someone, a teenager at that?

"When, when did this start?"

"A couple of months after I moved in."

Mrs. Nelson tried to hold back the bile she felt rising in her stomach. "That is almost three years."

"Yeah, it is," Michelle responded through gritted teeth and tear-filled eyes.

"Did you say no?"

"Of course, I said no! but he threatened me. What did..."

"Stop Michelle, please, I'm sorry for asking, just please stop yelling. Look. I am so sorry for what my husband did to you and I'll take care of it."

"What are you going to do?"

"I don't know, but I'll let you know." She placed her hand on Michelle's shoulder and returned into the house.

Michelle didn't really know what to do or what to say. What was Mrs. Nelson going to do? Would she confront her husband? Would he lie? Would she take his side? Would they put her out? So many thoughts were swirling around her mind like a tornado. What was she supposed to do? What could she do?

CHAPTER

# SIXTEEN

Michelle stuck her head into the opening of the gym. The day had finally come. The first dance of the season. She had been tossing and turning all night going over every dance move. Wondering was it perfect enough? Was the music right? Were the girls ready? Was she ready? Now here she stood more confident than the night before but still nervous. She couldn't wait for it to be over and everything be a success, but she hadn't reached that point yet. Her mind was a bit distracted from the altercation she had with Mrs. Nelson two weeks ago and she hadn't seen her since. *I guess she's not going to do anything.* Michelle thought to herself. The game still had three minutes left until half time. Michelle took in the sight of the gym. The building was packed for the first game of the season. *Why did it have to be packed?* Michelle's stomach began to turn flips. Could she really pull this off? Could she really lead this team to a state championship. Michelle tried to shake all the crazy thoughts that were running rampant in her head. She had to focus. She had to make it successfully through this dance. She couldn't let anything distract her. She turned her attention to the final two minutes of the second quarter. She watched Mitchell as he effortlessly made a beautiful NBA range three-point shot. He really was amazing. She couldn't help but feel a sting of pain over losing him, but then she saw Hunter. He was sitting on the bench. His eyes met hers and he gave her a wink. Michelle smiled as her thoughts took her back to two days ago. They were walking around the track talking about their hopes and dreams. Their plans for after graduation. Hunter was already being scouted by some of the top Division 1 teams. He wanted to play the entire four years so he could really enjoy college life and then his plan was to go pro. Michelle couldn't believe that she hadn't noticed him before. Hunter came to Windbusch the year after she had and this was his second year, yet she didn't know him. But to her credit Mr. Nelson had kept her on a short leash when she first started at the school. Maybe he was afraid his secret would come out. But as he became more comfortable that he was covered he start letting her have a bit more freedom.

"So, what do you want?" Hunter had asked her.

Michelle looked at him. She truly didn't know the answer to his question. Her only hope and dream was to survive the day. She couldn't tell Hunter that. So she just shrugged her shoulders. "I haven't really thought about it I guess."

"Well, can I tell you what I think?"

Michelle blushed. She had never had anyone take this much interest in her life. Her hopes and dreams. It was weird and refreshing all at the same time.

"I guess."

He looked into her eyes, making sure he had her full attention. "I think you're going to be famous."

Michelle's eyes grew wide. How did he know about the secret desire she had buried so deep inside of her until she often forgot it was there.

"I think that you are going to be a professional dancer one day. Speaking of dancing, I can't wait to see your first dance of the season."

Hunter stopped walking and pulled her in for a hug. And kissed her gently on the forehead. “I don’t know what you have been through but it has seriously scarred you. But I want you to know I’m here for you. I want to love all your pain away. And I hope that one day you will feel comfortable enough to tell me about it.”

Michelle just hugged him back and buried her head into his stomach. There was no way she could ever tell him the about the hell that was her everyday life.

One minute and thirty seconds left in the game and the coach calls for Hunter to reenter the game. The same butterflies began to flutter around in her stomach but for a totally different reason this time. A smile spread across her face as Hunter entered the game. The game was tied. Everyone waited in anticipation to see who would take the lead at the end of the first half. So far, the lead had bounced back and forth in this hard-fought game against rivals.

Windbusch was on defense, fighting harder than ever. They were determined not to let their opponents score. As the last twenty seconds of the game played out the team was in a fierce battle of keep away, but Hunter anticipated a pass and stole the ball. With 10 seconds remaining Hunter exploded from one end of the court to the other and did a windmill dunk just as the buzzer went off. The crowd went wild. Hunter stood in front of Michelle flexing his muscles and blew her a kiss before heading back to celebrate with his team. Everyone except Mitchell who had a scowl on his face. When the team finally stopped celebrating, they came rushing toward the door where Michelle was still standing. Hunter stopped and wrapped his arms around Michelle.

"I can tell by the look on your face your nervous, but you got this. Just do what you do."

Hunter kissed Michelle and ran off with the rest of the team to the locker room. Michelle watched as the cheerleaders took the floor for their routine. Michelle's group would be up next. She took the time to return to her squad and prepare to hit the floor.

"You guys ready to set this building on fire!" Michelle exclaimed to her team. The girls screamed and cheered. They were obviously just as pumped as she was to get out there. Michelle smiled. She was ready. Her squad was ready. Now they just had to go out there and show this school that they were the dance team to take them not only to the state championship, but all the way to nationals.

"You guys are up." Coach Philips said.

It was go time. Now or never. Go big or go home. Michelle knew they were definitely not going home. The girls lined up. Michelle moved to the back of the line in order to make her grand entrance.

When the dance came to a conclusion. The gym went wild. Even the people who were at the concession stand were fighting their way back into the gym to catch the routine once they heard the reaction of the crowd. Michelle couldn't believe it. They had done it. And everyone loved it. She turned to look at the girls. The smiles and tears told her they were just as proud. They were definitely well on their way. She stood at attention to take command of the girls and led them off the court.

Once in the back hallway, the girls exploded in cheers. Michelle noticed the basketball team coming out of the locker room. As soon as she saw Hunter exiting, she sprinted toward him and jumped into his arms. He spun her around.

"I told you, you could do it." He finally placed her back on her feet. He grabbed her face in his hands. "Michelle Moore you are absolutely amazing at what you do. You are going to be a star one day. Mark my words beautiful. You will be a star, I promise."

## CHAPTER
# SEVENTEEN

"That was an amazing routine! I knew it was going to be good, but actually seeing it was more than I could imagine." Hunter took Michelle's hand in his as he drove her home.

"How in the world did you see my routine?" Michelle blushed.

"I have my ways. And I don't tell my secrets."

"Oh really."

"Yep. Trying to be more like you."

Michelle frowned. "So that's how it is?"

"Until you tell me. I'm not going to let it go. Just so you know."

"Duly noted." She grinned.

Hunter looked in his rear-view mirror.

Michelle noticed. "You have looked in that mirror so many times, what's going on? And you missed our turn."

"Someone is following us and I didn't want to lead them directly to your house. I'm going to circle around a bit and see if I can lose them."

Michelle looked in the side mirror. She didn't notice the car and she hadn't noticed it following them. She tried not think too much into it, but when she looked in her side mirror again it seemed as if the car was speeding up. She felt the speed accelerate in the car. She looked at Hunter.

A look of worry crossed his face. He obviously noticed the car speed up as well.

"What's going on? Who is that?"

"I don't know, but hold on. This ride might get a little bumpy."

Hunter sped up just as the car was about to ram them.

"What is this guy's problem?" Michelle's voice was shaking with terror.

Hunter hit a quick turn but the car was right on their bumper. Before Michelle could catch her breathe the car rammed into the back of Hunter's car. Michelle screamed.

The car rammed them again. Hunter tried to speed up but it was no use. The car pursuing them was fast. The car then came up beside them and rammed them on the side and until he pushed them down the hill. The car was out of control. He couldn't stop it. Hunter tried his best to steer the car and miss the trees but the car slid and came up off the ground. Once it landed, it slammed into a massive tree. Michelle flew out of the front window shield and landed into the lake that was a few feet away. She was in pain but she was alive. She swam back towards the car. She had to see if Hunter was okay.

"Please be ok Hunter. Please be ok."

Michelle managed to crawl her way back to the car. She came up to driver's side. And she pulled herself up so she could see inside.

Michelle shrieked and fell back to the ground. Hunter's head was smashed in. She looked up at the tree. He must've flown out the car as well only to hit the tree and the force must've thrown him back into the car. Michelle turned over and began to vomit. She crawled around to the passenger side. She had to find her phone. Once she reached the door, she braced herself. She had to focus on anything besides Hunter. She couldn't bear to see him like that again. She took a deep breath and pulled the passenger side door open. She saw her purse on the floor where she had left it. She pulled it out, closed the door back and dialed 911.

## CHAPTER
# EIGHTEEN

Autumn was stretching in her own personal dance studio. The first thing Autumn made sure she put in her new million-dollar home was a dance studio. This is where all the magic took place. The T.V. she hung up in her studio was perfect for her to watch Entertainment Television or BET. Whichever one had the hottest news concerning the music industry. She had to stay current on what everyone was doing. That's how she stayed original. She made sure she knew what others were doing and then did something completely different. Today as she watched the news feed, it was on mute. She wanted to work on her vocals as well. Autumn was determined to take Charlie down a notch. Plus, she needed to clear her head from the events that had taken place with Axel. She still couldn't believe they had slept together. That was the one thing she promised herself she would never do, but it was too late. The line had been crossed and all Autumn could do was pray that she hadn't ruined any chance she may have had with Axel. As she was lost in her thoughts something caught her eye. A picture of Axel and Harmony flashed on the screen. With the heading.. Engaged!!!

"Alexa, turn up the volume."

She heard how Axel had been seen proposing to Harmony and there was a picture of Axel and Harmony leaving the restaurant and you better believe she made sure that every photographer that was trying to steal shots could see her engagement ring without any guessing. Autumn sunk down to the floor. She couldn't believe it. *How could he do this to me? How could he sleep with me and then ask Harmony to marry him just weeks later?* Autumn was beyond furious. *I was right. I have totally messed this up. How could I let this happen? I swore I would not get caught up in Axel's foolishness. I was the only person he had never slept with. Now I'm just another one of his girls.* Autumn's shoulders began to shake as her tears responded to the anguish that was seeping out of her soul. Is this why Axel hadn't contacted her? She thought it was because he felt awkward about sleeping with her as had she. She just figured they would take some time and then he would contact her and they would solidify their relationship. But here he was proposing to Harmony. Harmony, her dancer. Someone she would have to see every single day. How could he? Anger interrupted her hurt once again. Autumn grabbed her phone to call Axel and give him a piece of her mind. The rumbling of the phone startled her and caused her to drop the phone. Had Axel beaten her to the punch and called her first? Autumn picked up her phone and flipped it over. Her eyes widened, her palms grew clammy and her heart skipped a beat. It was Phoenix. Her ex-boyfriend. The same ex who had cheated on her and made her look like a fool in front of everyone she knew. Had he seen the news too? Did he call to gloat? Memories came rushing over her like a tidal wave. Autumn couldn't face him. She let the phone go to voicemail. A minute later her phone buzzed letting her know she had a new voicemail. *That was quick.*

Autumn closed her eyes momentarily as a single tear escaped down her cheek. She opened them once again as if staring at Phoenix's name would make it disappear, but there it remained. Staring back at her. Haunting every fiber of her being. Should she check it? Could she check it? She dropped the phone as she noticed her hands were shaking. After everything he had put her through, yet she still felt as if she was in the last round of a hard-fought boxing match and she was about to tap out.

Autumn rubbed her fingers across her hairline. She must have a death wish, because between Phoenix and Axel, they were both killing her slowly. How much of this torture could she endure? Finally, as if something or someone else, clearly deranged had taken over her body, she pushed her voicemail icon to find out what had possessed Phoenix to ever think about dialing her number.

*Hey Autumn. I just saw the news. I don't know if you've seen it or not so I'm not going to say anything, but I just wanted you to know I'm here if you want to talk. I know we didn't end on good terms but I still love you and I hope we are still friends. So yeah, anyway, call me. Ummm... I hope to hear from you Autumn. Ok. Bye.*

*I can't believe he was civil about it. And did he say he still loved me? No, Autumn do not get caught back up in his charm.* Autumn dropped her head in her hands. She was definitely going to call him. Not because she thought he really cared, but because she was hurting and she wanted to believe him anyway. She needed this. She needed to hear a man's soothing voice letting her know she was still loved and wanted. Autumn picked up the phone and hit the call back button.

"Autumn." Was the first thing she heard when Phoenix picked up the phone. "I must admit, I didn't think you were going to answer let alone call me back. But I'm glad you did."

"Hey Phoenix." Autumn tried her best not to sound hurt and disappointed but she knew her tone gave her away.

"From the sound of your voice, as sweet as it is, I see you saw the news as well. Or did you already know?"

Autumn didn't really know if she should reveal to Phoenix that Axel kept her in the dark about his engagement to Harmony. But the words just seemed to fall from her lips. "I didn't know. I found out the same way the rest of the world did."

"I am not in the I told you so business Autumn, but I tried to tell you that Axel was just a heartless selfish man, who doesn't care about the people who he hurts. You must have tried to move on from him. That's the only way I can see him doing something like that without telling you."

Autumn was silent trying to figure out how she would respond to Phoenix.

"Autumn… you there. I'm sorry. I shouldn't have said that."

"No Phoenix. You don't have to apologize." Autumn decided to go with his version of the story. She wasn't about to tell Phoenix that she had allowed Axel to make the ultimate fool of her. "I was breaking away. I guess you're right."

"What are you going to do?"

"I think I need a bit of a getaway. I want to just get out of California for a while."

"I think that's a great idea. How do you feel about Paris?"

"Paris? Why do you ask that?"

"That's where I am. And I would love for you to come and spend Thanksgiving with me. Maybe even stay for Christmas. I can show you how sorry I really am for all of the foolishness I put you through."

"Phoenix, it would take you a lifetime to make that up."

"Well at least you can let me start on the rest of our lives."

Autumn didn't really know what Phoenix meant by that statement, but if he was talking about marrying her, she was definitely open to the idea. If Axel was going to be married, she would too. He would not flaunt another woman in her face without her having someone on her arm as well. "I would love to come see you, Phoenix. I think I could use a trip to the love capital of the world."

"And I will make sure it will be just that for you. I promise. I'll send you my info and you let me know when you're packed and ready to go. I have to go and get some things ready for your arrival."

"Like what kind of things?"

"That's something you will have to find out for yourself my love."

Autumn couldn't help but blush. She was sure Phoenix was planning a proposal and she was absolutely going to accept. "Ok. I'll talk to you later."

"Looking forward."

Autumn jumped up and did a little victory dance. "Look out Axel. Two can play this game."

# CHAPTER NINETEEN

Phoenix hung up the phone with Autumn. He couldn't believe that everything was working out the way it was. Axel's engagement couldn't have come at a better time. Phoenix looked around his lavish apartment. The one Josiah was paying for. Josiah was a doctor in Paris whom he met. Phoenix always knew he liked men, but it wasn't something that was acceptable in the music business. So, he hid how he felt and only dated women. He had to leave California just to hook up with guys. When he met Josiah, he had stolen his heart in an instant. Everything moved fast after that. Josiah was still in the closet too so it all worked out. No one knew about their relationship and Josiah took very good care of Phoenix as well. That was until two weeks ago when Josiah caught Phoenix with another man. Josiah had paid up the rent on the apartment and because he still cared about Phoenix, he told him he could stay until the lease ran out and then he had to find somewhere else to stay. Thankfully, Phoenix had until the new year. He could entertain Autumn for a couple of months and then propose to her on New Years or maybe Christmas. He didn't want to risk Josiah coming back to make sure he had moved out. So he would propose on Christmas and leave before the new year and then he would be back on top. Phoenix hadn't had to work since he left California being a dancer for Autumn and he didn't plan on having to ever work again. When he saw the news, he knew Axel had probably hurt Autumn and he saw his ticket back in the game. *Poor Autumn. She's so desperate right now. She is going to forget all about my transgressions and still say yes to my proposal. The best part will be that she will probably be so vulnerable that she won't even make me sign a prenup.* At least that is what he was hoping for just in case Autumn ever tried to divorce him and she would when she catches him cheating. Phoenix had no plan on being faithful for long. Autumn would surely divorce him and he would be paid for life. Phoenix smiled at his ingenious plan. The universe had smiled on him once again. How could life get any better than this? Phoenix rose up off the couch feeling exceedingly confident and began to devise the perfect visit for Autumn that would prove to her that he was a changed man and he knew without a doubt, she would marry him in a heartbeat.

# CHAPTER TWENTY

Axel followed Harmony into her parent's house. She had been making a fuss about her parents being upset that he never asked their permission to marry their daughter. What he really wanted to tell them is that he never meant to ask their daughter to marry him and really had no plans on following through with it. For right now, he would just ride it out. If he played his cards right, he could have her parents in his pocket and still break things off with Harmony. And he always played his cards right. After all, he was Axel Smith, a man who was used to getting his way. He knew he could make it work somehow... Well, he should say that he would find a way to make it work out with her dad. He already had Harmony's mom on lock. All he had to do was send her some flowers and a message to her private studio, inviting her to his hotel room. A studio her husband didn't even know about. She took the bait immediately. Before he knew it, she was walking through his hotel room door wearing a chain detail plunging neck slit hem bodycon dress. He couldn't do anything but admire her beauty. At the tender age of 53 she was still a stunning woman, who was leaving very little to the imagination. There was barely any talking when she arrived. He just picked her up, took her to the bedroom and had his way with her. After he was done. He politely let her know that the whole encounter had been recorded. Her mouth fell to the ground. She had slapped him hard.

"What do you want?" She folded her arms across her ample bosom.

"When I break it off with your daughter, don't come for me. I know you have friends in very high places and if or when I should need your services or your connections, I expect to receive them. Understood?"

Her chest rose and fell and she was contemplating her options, but as she came to the realization that she was backed into a corner she just whispered. "Understood."

"Oh by the way," he spoke before he left. "You were pretty good back there for an older woman. If you want to keep this going, you know how to reach me."

"How about right now?" She figured she might as well take advantage. "Besides she hadn't been with anyone who made her feel like this man just made her feel in a long time."

"Oh, you down for round two?" Axel asked a bit surprised.

"You already got me on camera, I might as well get something out of this whole deal."

Axel turned around and started removing his clothing. "You ain't said nothing but a word."

Now he just had to get the dad. Luckily, he remembered something Harmony once said during one of her drunken stupors. One thing about Harmony, if you ever wanted to know anything, just get a little alcohol in her and she will sing like a bird. He thought back to a cozy night they had spent by the fireplace, drinking wine and exploring each other's bodies.

"I'm so glad to be marrying you Axel." Harmony had said.

"I'm glad to be marrying you as well." Axel had lied.

"I want us to be happier than my mom and my dad. They are never happy."

"Really. Why is that?"

"He can't keep it in his pants. And just between you and me..." Harmony put her finger in front of her lips like she was shushing someone. "What my mom doesn't know is that my dad has a whole other family just 30 miles away from where we live. He also doesn't know that I know. But I followed him one day. 107 Greencircle Way. He thought he was sneaking away but I followed him." She giggled. "And that's when I saw it. He walked up the steps, kissed his wife and two kids and then walked in the house. I was so stunned. I just sat there down the block, staring. Then they emerged from the house. They got into her SUV. The kids were calling him daddy and before they could take off, he got out the car and went back to the house. The woman yelled out for him to get something she forgot. He responded. 'Yes, my loving wife.' And I almost threw up, right there in the car. Speaking of throwing up." Harmony took off and headed for the restroom.

Axel lay there thinking. *This information has got to be useful someday.*

Axel looked around the huge family room off the foyer, as he thought to himself. *This is that day.* A smile crept across his face. He thought about Harmony's mom. He had a little something for her as well. But she would get that later on tonight. He would have both of them eating out of the palm of his hands. And when he dumped their daughter, they wouldn't dare open their mouths or oppose him.

"Axel, how are you doing, son." Harmony's dad was the first to make an appearance.

“I’m fine sir.” Axel said offering the man his hand.

“I’m glad you came by. My wife is out by the pool. Shall we?”

“After you sir.”

Axel and Harmony followed her dad through the kitchen and out the back door. Their home was impressive. But Axel just smirked, knowing it still couldn’t hold a candle to his house.

He looked over at Harmony’s mom, who was obviously awaiting their arrival, trying to close her wrap-around after giving the man she intended a full view of the merchandise. Axel just smiled. *This was too easy.*

Harmony’s dad walked over to his wife with Axel and Harmony in tow and kissed her on the cheek. “I’m going to let you two ladies catch up while Axel and I step inside and talk, man to man.”

“But I want to talk with him as well. He’s marrying my daughter too you know.”

“Honey, you will have your turn over dinner. Right now, this is a man thing. “

“Excuse us ladies.” Axel nodded his head at the women and followed Harmony’s dad inside the kitchen. After closing the sliding door, they took their seats at the island.

“So, you want to marry my daughter?”

Axel didn’t really know how to play this, but in his experience getting the upper hand was always the best route. “Not really.” He replied. Axel almost burst out laughing at the ghastly expression that fell over her dad’s face.

“What kind of sick game or you playing?”

Axel had done some digging on his own. He verified everything Harmony had said and more. He knew he would have his back against the ropes.

"Harmony found a ring I had and she mistakenly thought it was for her. I didn't have the heart to tell her that I would never marry her, but here we are."

"Well, you are not going to embarrass my daughter, whether you meant to or not, you will marry her and you will treat her well."

"You mean like you treat your wife well?"

Axel watched his face fall to the floor.

"I treat my wife very well. What are you trying to insinuate son?"

"First of all, I ain't your son. Secondly, with all your extracurricular activities, you can't possibly tell me you treat your wife well."

"I'm a man. She knows that. As long as I come home, she's fine."

"Home? Which home are you referring to?"

Harmony's dad almost fell out of his seat. "What are you talking about?"

Axel could hear the confidence deflate from Harmony's dad's chest.

"I'm talking about 107 Greencricle Way."

"No." A gasp lept from his throat. "How did you find out about that?"

"I have my ways. So, tell me, how does it feel to have a new bundle of joy on the way?"

The sick look on his face told Axel that if I wasn't before, he was in the driver's seat now.

"Look, you cannot tell my wife this. She will destroy me."

"I don't plan on it. As long as you play your part."

"What part?"

"If I need something covered up or if I need the cops to look the other way or if I need a heads up on some kind of raid. I need you to be my man. And further more when I finally do get rid of your daughter, you nor your wife or going to give me any problems about it."

If Harmony's dad was white, he would be red right now. He was so angry you could boil an egg on that bald spot he was sporting.

"You are not gonna get away with this Axel."

"Is that a threat?"

He hung his head in defeat, knowing he was in no position to challenge Axel.

"That's what I thought. So, get your demeanor straight and let's enjoy this wonderful dinner your wife is having catered because we both know she ain't cooked nothing." He laughed and made his way back outside. Leaving Harmony's dad to rush off to the restroom. No doubt to throw some water on his face after he threw up.

CHAPTER

# TWENTY-ONE

Autumn stood on the balcony of Phoenix's luxury apartment as the sun rose. She couldn't believe how beautiful the view of Paris was from here. She tried to make sure she stood in this exact same spot every day since she arrived almost two months ago. That is except the days when Phoenix woke her up with a little something special. Life with Phoenix had picked back up where they had left off. She didn't realize how much she missed him. His smile. His charm. His corny jokes. She loved feeling his arms wrapped around her. He made her feel so safe. And as if he had read her mind, Phoenix appeared behind her and wrapped his arms around her and kissed her several times on her neck and cheek. Autumn leaned her head back against his chest. She wished she never had to leave Paris. Never had to leave Phoenix. She turned around to face him. "This is the most amazing time I've had in a long time."

"Well, I'm glad I could make that happen for you."

"I want to stay here forever."

"What about your music career?" Phoenix rocked Autumn back and forth as if they were slow dancing to music only they could hear.

"I'll leave it all behind. Stay here with you."

"Do you really think Axel will let you do that?"

Autumn pushed away from Phoenix. "Axel doesn't control my life."

"I see he still hasn't contacted you."

Autumn turned away from Phoenix. She didn't want him to see the tears that were threatening to run down her face.

Phoenix knew it was now or never. He went into his pocket and pulled out the ring he had bought for Autumn. Phoenix got down on one knee.

"Autumn, I don't want you to forget about your career, but I also don't want you to go back to California alone."

Autumn turned around and almost lost her balance when she saw Phoenix on one knee with an engagement ring. "Phoenix are you serious?"

"As serious as I can be. I don't want you in California alone having to put up with Axel. He has Harmony now. He doesn't need you. Now we can move on and have a life together and you can still do what you love. Except this time, I will be there to love you and protect you, never to hurt you or take you for granted again. Autumn Dance, will you do me the honor of becoming my wife forever?"

Autumn couldn't believe what she was hearing. Phoenix wanted to marry her. She figured he would but it had been tow months and she was starting to think that she was the one that was going to have to propose to him. Either way she didn't plan on returning to Cali empty handed. "Yes Phoenix! Yes! I'll marry you!"

# CHAPTER TWENTY-TWO

*How did I end up back in this position again? Bent over another desk in another room.* Michelle stared at the dry erase board in the chemistry lab, which was conveniently in the basement of the school. Edward Brooks, chemistry teacher, married father of two was standing behind her pounding away. It was bad enough she was being raped by Mr. Nelson, but now, Mr. Brooks too. And who would've thought this new venture was set up by none other than Mitchell Bennett, her ex-boyfriend. Just when she thought her life couldn't get any worse, it had. It was the day of Hunter's funeral. Michelle had been so distraught. She had eaten anything in days. The only good part about all of this, was that Mr. Nelson hadn't touched her. He was actually being nice to her. Making sure she was ok. After the funeral she was sitting in a swing across the street. Mitchell had walked over to her and that's when her extended hell began.

Mitchell sat on the swing besides Michelle.

"You ok?"

Michelle wiped the tears from her eyes with the back of her hand. "No, I'm not. I can't believe he's gone."

"Well, I can't say I feel the same way."

Michelle didn't even look up. She knew Mitchell didn't care for Hunter, especially since they had started dating.

"As a matter of fact, I'm glad he's dead."

Michelle did look up this time. The audacity of this guy was really pissing her off. "I know you didn't like him but that was really uncalled for. The least you can do is respect his memory."

"I see Hunter has given you a little more courage than you need. I think you should watch how you talk to me before you end up like Hunter."

Michelle's eyes grew wide. "What do you mean by that? Did you have something to do with Hunter's death?"

"Let's just say this," Mitchell stared hard into Michelle's eyes, "you were never supposed to be in the car. But I can assure you other arraignments can be made."

Michelle's breath caught in her throat. She had totally forgotten how to breath at this point. It wasn't until she started to feel light headed that she realized she needed to exhale.

"How could you!" She stood up.

Mitchell stood as well. "You better sit back down and shut up for I knock you down."

Michelle thought better than to challenge Mitchell. After all he had hit her before. She instinctively touched her cheek remembering the pain.

*"Did you just hit me?" Michelle asked for lack of anything else better to say.*

*"So not only are you disrespectful but you're stupid too." Mitchell paced back and forth staring at Michelle.*

*"I'm not stupid." Michelle stated as she picked herself up off the floor.*

*"It sounds like it to me." Mitchell walked over to where Michelle was now standing. Michelle tried to take a step back, but Mitchell grabbed her arm. "Don't you dare back away from me!"*

*"I'm not. I was just..."*

*"Just shut up Michelle. You know why I came over here, so just take off your clothes."*

Michelle eased back down into the swing feeling defeated.

"Now, first off you are not going to repeat anything you just heard, second, you are going to have to start paying me to keep your little secret."

"What are you talking about? What secret?"

"I know all about you and Mr. Nelson. I know he's been banging you probably ever since you moved in with him. Don't really know when it started but I know it's happening. I actually have proof." Mitchell sat back down in his swing. He knew he had her full attention.

Michelle could have died right then and there. She didn't know whether to deny it and call his bluff or just submit. She couldn't risk calling his bluff and her secret get out. She would be humiliated and she might as well be dead.

"How much do I have to pay you?"

"Oh, I don't want your money. I have another idea."

Michelle looked at Mitchell. A shiver ran down her spine. She could only imagine what was going on in his twisted mind.

"Hurry up and put your clothes on." Mr. Brooks voiced echoed in her ear. "Did you hear what I said little girl?" Mr. Brooks voice got a bit louder.

Michelle stood up and looked around to find where Mr. Brooks had tossed her panties. When she located them, she put them on and looked in the full-length mirror that was stationed near the front of the classroom. Every girl in her class would try to make it to the chemistry room first so they could get the seat right next to the mirror. They would spend the entire time checking themselves out and taking pictures. That is until Mr. Brooks banned any girl from sitting there a week ago.

Mr. Brooks made a slight rap on the front door. Mitchell walked in. "You guys all done in here?"

"Yeah. You can take your girl out of here. I'll let you know when I'll be needing her services again." Mr. Brooks walked over to the board and begin writing out the next day's notes. "I'll see you in class tomorrow, Michelle. Have a great day." Mr. Brooks talked to Michelle as if they had just finished a study session.

"Sure thing Mr. B." Mitchell wrapped his hands around the back of Michelle's neck and escorted her out of the class.

Michelle dropped her head and made the journey back upstairs to the main part of the building. It was time to go home. Mitchell had told Mr. Nelson that he was tutoring Michelle and that it would only take about thirty minutes. Mr. Nelson always waited for them in his office, oblivious that Mitchell was really pimping her out.

"You ready to go home Michelle?" Mr. Nelson asked when they reached his office.

"I guess." Michelle responded without ever looking up at him.

"Your mom is still out of town. So, it's just me and you tonight."

Michelle's head jerked up. When was Mrs. Nelson going to get back. The rape and abuse had grown more frequent. She guessed he was making up for lost time because of the two weeks he hadn't touched her after Hunter died, but now she realized with Mrs. Nelson's absence there was just more opportunity. Michelle held back the scream that was threatening to escape her lips. She knew by his words she would be at his mercy all night. She didn't know how much more of this she could take. One horrible thing after the other just kept interrupting the great things in her life. She had found hope in Hunter, but now he was gone. She also found hope on the dance team. They were doing so well and it kept her mind off of Hunter, if only for a little while, but that all changed once Ave convinced Mrs. Ross to take over the team and the first rule of business was to kick Michelle off the team. It's like she couldn't catch a break.

"Maybe we could order some pizza and watch a movie."

Michelle could've thrown up at his fake suggestion. She shrugged her shoulders. She could already feel the spaghetti they had for lunch coming back up.

*I just want to die.* Michelle thought to herself. *Why can't I just die?* Michelle slowly walked out of Mr. Nelson's office, out of the building and to the car where she stood without saying a word.

"Thank you for tutoring Michelle." Mr. Nelson told Mitchell after Michelle was gone. "But I know there is more between you and my daughter. Even though I don't have a problem with you seeing her, I do have a problem with you putting your hands on her."

"What are you talking about sir?" Mitchell tried to play innocent.

"I'm not stupid son. I can see the bruises on my daughter."

"Which ones? Cause there aren't any on her arms. I'm not that stupid. I put them where no one can see them. That is unless you're looking some where you're not supposed to be."

"What are you trying to insinuate Mr. Bennett? And be careful what you say. Your next words could possibly be very detrimental to your education and athletic career."

"We'll see about that. I know your secret." Mitchell's smile got bigger with every word.

Mr. Nelson's eyes grew twice as big as they normally were. His mouth dropped open slightly.

"What secret are you talking about?" Mr. Nelson's voice was cracking like an egg.

"I know you be bending Michelle over your desk when she's late for Ms. Ross's class. You also are the reason that she is late for Ms. Ross's class, because she has to go clean herself after you're done."

"It's all a lie! Did Michelle tell you this? Michelle is a really troubled girl."

"Is that birthmark on your Johnson, all the way down to the reddish-brown color all a lie as well?"

Mr. Nelson remained silent.

"So, look. This is how it's going to be. You're not going to say anything else to me about Michelle and what I do with her or to her and I'll keep your former secret just that, a secret. Notice I said former secret. Because if you ever put your hands on her again, like you plan on doing tonight; which by the way is officially cancelled, or if you tell her anything we have discussed, I will ruin you. Do we have an understanding?"

Mr. Nelson could have fried chicken on his bald head from the heat. "Whatever."

"I don't think I understand what whatever means."

"We have an understanding." Mr. Nelson responded through flared nostrils and gritted teeth.

"Great. Well, you have a great evening Mr. Nelson and don't forget that pizza and a movie for Michelle and I'll see you tomorrow." Mitchell walked out of Mr. Nelson's office satisfied that he had shut Mr. Nelson down. Normally he wouldn't have a problem with Mr. Nelson sleeping with Michelle, but he wasn't getting paid for it. He wasn't about to allow Mr. Nelson to get away with any freebies.

Michelle sat in her room applying her lotion. She had relished showering all of Mr. Brooks filth off of her. But what awaited her would only make her feel even more dirty. She knew this was just the first shower of the night.

Mr. Nelson knocked on Michelle's door. Michelle almost didn't know how to respond. Mr. Nelson never knocked on the door. He just walked right in, hoping to find her in a vulnerable position.

"Come in." She finally managed to say.

Mr. Nelson walked in with a medium pizza and a bag. "Here's your pizza. There is a drink and a movie in the bag. Enjoy your night." And with that, Mr. Nelson left out of the room leaving Michelle in silence.

## CHAPTER
# TWENTY-THREE

Autumn walked into rehearsal with a new attitude in the New Year. She was engaged to Phoenix. They had come back to California and now she was ready to face Axel without feeling shame and embarrassment because of his engagement to Harmony.

"Ok guys, let's get this show on the road!" She exclaimed as she placed her bags by the full wall length mirror. As she stood up and turned around to face her dancers, she noticed they were all huddled around Harmony. I guess they were checking out the new ring. This was probably the first time they had gotten back together since her departure to Paris. Autumn walked over to the huddle, determined not to pass out on the way. *Just act normal. Remember, you're engaged too. You don't need or want Axel anymore. He is your best friend. Nothing more.* The more Autumn tried to convince herself the less she believed it.

"Ok, ok. What's going on over here?" Autumn tried to act as if she didn't know or care because her life was too exciting all on its own.

The circle of dancers split like the Red Sea and there stood Harmony with her hand outstretched, brandishing the biggest, prettiest ring she had ever laid eyes on, in person that was.

"Oh my, congratulations! So, who's the lucky guy?" Autumn tried with every fiber of her being to sound genuinely excited.

"Where have you been, under a rock? Did you not see the news?" Harmony asked.

"I have actually been in Paris for the past two months, so no I haven't seen any news." Autumn seen the air slightly deflate from Harmony's face, but she must've gained second wind since she burst out...

"Axel asked me to marry him!" She shrieked.

And so did everyone else. Including Autumn.

"That is so exciting! Congratulations!" Autumn was losing her ability to be fake by the minute, she just wanted to get this over with. "Well, let's get started."

"What's the rush Autumn? I kinda wanted to celebrate a little more. After all, this is the first time I have been able to share this news with my team."

Autumn didn't like the way Harmony emphasized the word "my". What was she trying to insinuate? She didn't have to wonder for too long. Harmony's next words made it very clear.

"Since I'm basically Axel's wife now. I guess that technically makes me..." she paused for emphasis... "your boss." She finished with a smirk. The dancers began to walk away and stretch. They too knew Harmony had overstepped.

Autumn's blood immediately began to boil and she knew that this was not going to work out at all. "You know what Harmony you're probably right." Autumn finally reputed after calming herself the best she could. "Ok, I will let you, um... celebrate. I will be back and then we'll get started. Yeah. Ok."

Autumn turned on her heels and it took everything in her not to sprint out the door. As soon as she exited the room, she hit her speed walk like she had calories to burn and steps to make up for. She bent the corner and headed straight for Axel's office. She didn't even knock. She busted in his office like the police on a drug raid. Axel jumped and instinctively reached for his 45 he kept underneath his desk. Autumn forgot about the gun, but quickly remembered when she walked through Axel's door and it was pointed directly at her head. Her heart stopped, knowing she could have lost her life.

"Girl, what is wrong with you! Do you know I could've killed you!"

Autumn stood there, blinking rapidly trying to grasp a hold of reality and the fact that she was still alive.

"Autumn?" Axel realizing the answer to his last question came around his desk and hugged Autumn. "I'm so sorry Autumn, but you can't be busting in my office without warning like that."

Autumn wanted to relish in the embrace of Axel's arms but then she remembered why she had burst into his office in the first place. She pushed back from Axel.

"What's wrong with you? I said I'm sorry."

"So, you weren't going to tell me?" Autumn got straight to the point.

"Tell you what?"

Autumn took a deep breath. Frustration was beginning to set in. Axel was being his normal self. Playing dumb until you caught him dead to rights with undeniable proof. Autumn tried to stay as calm as she possibly could. "You weren't going to tell me you proposed to Harmony?"

Axel backed up even further from Autumn. He expected the fallout but, not this soon. He was hoping she would just let it slide as she had done so many times when he had crossed her the wrong way, but he could tell this had hit a nerve. This indiscretion had hurt her. And even though he had hurt her before, he knew this was the worst thing that he had ever done to her. He shouldn't have slept with her. He just couldn't help himself. He finally gave in to his desire for Autumn. He looked into her eyes and their entire passionate night flashed in his mind.

Axel made himself snap back into reality. He walked to his floor to ceiling window and looked out over the lake.

"Can I be honest with you?" Axel knew the only way he was going to salvage his friendship with Autumn was to open his heart, let her in by truly being honest with her. Axel turned and faced Autumn after she remained silent for what seemed like an eternity.

Autumn met his gaze. "By all means. I think you owe me at least that much."

Axel walked over to his desk and began to straighten some papers that were disheveled. He felt so vulnerable. He needed to distract himself as he poured his soul out before Autumn.

"Honestly, I don't know what I'm doing. I messed up big time. Not with Harmony. That was just part two. I should have never slept with you. I'm not saying it wasn't one of the best experiences of my life and I don't regret it at all, but you are my best friend and I need you in my life. I knew as soon as we did it that a line had been crossed that never should have been." Axel finally looked up at Autumn. He caught a glimpse of a tear rolling down her cheek and his heart broke.

"Autumn, I am not the man you need in your life. All I would do is hurt you and I don't want to do that. I don't want us to lose the friendship we have. You are the only person I can be real with. The only person who I can be myself with. You don't want anything from me and you let me be me. I can't lose that. So, after we slept together, I panicked. I had to do something to make sure we didn't get together. Although, I could have done something other than propose to Harmony, huh?"

Autumn didn't answer. She just stared at him. Axel let her. He needed to give her all the time she needed and he was willing to do whatever it took not to lose Autumn. So, he waited.

Autumn took in everything that Axel said. She realized he respected her and that was more than he had given to anybody, especially a female. More than that, she had his heart. If Axel wasn't the womaning, woman-user that he was, they would make the perfect couple. But that was not who he was or who he wanted to be. She guessed being his best friend would have to do.

"I understand, but you did hurt me and it might take a minute for us to... for me to get over that." Autumn dropped her head.

Axel could tell she was searching for words. He walked around to where Autumn was standing. He lifted her chin and grabbed her by her waist and pulled her closer to him as he sat back on the edge of his desk. He stared her in the eyes. "Autumn, I love you. I love you more than anybody on this planet."

Autumn's eyes widened in amazement. Axel had never said anything like that to her before.

"You mean the absolute world to me. The last thing that I ever would want to do is hurt you. I promise you, if I have to, I will spend the rest of my life trying to gain back your trust and friendship. Because it's worth it and I need it. I need you in my life Autumn. I can't say that enough. I don't want to lose my best friend, but I totally understand if you want to walk away."

"So, what are you going to do?" Autumn tried her best to move past her hurt.

"You mean with Harmony?"

Autumn was so thankful he didn't play stupid that time.

"I don't know man. I can't marry her. I don't want to marry her. I thought I needed a wife, but I really don't want one." Axel wasn't about to fess up that he had accidently proposed to Harmony. "You know what? I blame you!"

"Blame me!" Autumn tried to step back and pull away from Axel but he wouldn't let her. He held her waist tight and pulled her closer.

"Yes, I blame you. You made me feel all these gushy feelings. You made me want to have a special someone. But you will always be my special someone. No matter what. I'm good with that. Even when you get married, your husband gonna have to understand... you're my special someone too. He's gonna have to share you. And what we have he will never have. Non-negotiable."

Autumn smiled. "You're crazy."

"On the real. Are we at least cool again?"

"Yeah, I guess."

Axel was so thankful Autumn hadn't strung him up by his testicles.

"So, since we're cool; help me figure out a way to drop Harmony."

"No! You are on your own with that buddy. Now let me go. I have a rehearsal to return to."

"I'm sorry I didn't tell you. I just didn't know how to tell you. But don't worry. I'll find a way to pay you back."

"Oh, don't bother because I'm going to tell you how you can pay me back right now."

"Ok, shoot."

"Tell your future wife or whatever she is. She doesn't run me."

"What do you mean by that?"

"Your girl basically told me she was my boss in rehearsal!" Autumn took a deep breath when she realized how elevated her voice had become.

"You're kidding me, right?"

"Does it look like I'm kidding?" Autumn frowned folding her arms.

"That's something you never have to worry about again after today. I will definitely put an end to that."

Axel pulled Autumn even closer and tried to kiss her.

"Don't even think about it. The vault is locked to you. Now let me go." Autumn pulled away but again Axel wouldn't let her go. He pulled her in and this time he put his arms around her and kissed her on the forehead. "I love you Autumn."

Autumn pushed Axel playfully. Axel grabbed her hand after catching a glimpse of her ring. "What is this?"

Autumn had been so angry over her exchange with Harmony she totally forgot about the engagement ring. She wasn't ready for this exchange. But whether she was ready or not. It was happening.

"I... I got engaged."

"When?"

"In Paris."

"So that's where you were?"

"Yes."

"So, who's this dude I need to get right?"

Autumn was a bit hesitant to tell Axel. She knew Phoenix was not his favorite person.

She took a step back. "Phoenix." She said just above a whisper.

Axel stood up and walked closer to Autumn.

A surge of fear shot through her with Axel's full frame standing over her.

"What did you just say?"

"I said Phoenix." Autumn looked up at Axel and held his gaze.

"Really? Phoenix?"

"You don't want me Axel, so why is it such a big deal if I'm with Phoenix?"

"Let me ask you something? Because if you answer yes, I will do it in a heartbeat. Are you willing to marry me, be my main girl and be okay with me having girls on the side, even in our house from time to time? If you are Autumn, I will marry you today, because that is how much I do want you!"

"Of course, I wouldn't be okay with that!" Autumn finally admitted to herself. She knew that no matter how she felt about Axel he would only bring her heartache. Plus, it would kill their friendship.

"Ok, I love being around you because you're my friend and I am protective of who you spend your time with because I don't want anybody doing you wrong. Like Phoenix."

"What do you mean like Phoenix?"

"Did you forget what Phoenix did?"

"No, but he apologized and he has been really great."

"Great? You mean for two months. Unless you have been talking to him before now."

"No. Just the two months." Autumn walked away from Axel realizing how stupid she sounded. "Look I always support you. Can you just support me for once?"

"No, I can't just support you, now that I think about it. You spent the holidays with that nigga when you normally spend them with me."

"So you wanted me to spend the holiday with you and your fiancé?"

"Of course not. I would have kicked her to the curb just for you."

"Whatever Axel. But I am serious. I need you to just support me on this, for once, please."

"Okay, okay. I'll support you, but if he hurts you, he will have to answer to me. Just letting you know."

Autumn shook her head.

"I'm not playing Autumn, if he crosses you wrong, his life will be in danger."

"I hear you." Autumn tried to ignore the chill that went down her spine. She hoped Axel was just playing, but something in her gut told her he was dead serious.

"So, we cool? Or are you gonna keep giving me the stiff arm?"

"We're cool. I'm sorry for acting so crazy."

"It's all good. Now go make me some money." Axel slapped Autumn on her backside.

As she strolled back toward the dance room, she allowed everything that just transpired to replay in her mind. She paused right outside the studio door. Was she really blind to who Phoenix was? Was she crazy for overlooking all the things he put her through? Autumn didn't know. All she did know was that she couldn't be solo while Axel was engaged. Then it hit her. What if Axel really didn't go through with his marriage to

Harmony? What if there was still and chance for her and Axel and she was stuck in a marriage to Phoenix? Autumn felt sick to her stomach. Had she moved to fast? Did she even want to marry Phoenix? Autumn looked down at the ring on her finger. She pulled it off and slid it in her pocket. She didn't want anyone to know. Just in case.

Autumn took a deep breath and entered the dance room. She looked over at Harmony. Part of her felt sorry for her.

"You guys done celebrating cause we have a lot of work to do." Autumn tried to get back to business as usual.

"Autumn, didn't think you were coming back. You good?" Harmony asked with a hint of arrogance.

Immediately the empathy Autumn had for Harmony slipped through the door. She couldn't wait for Axel to crush her heart and then she would be the one picking her face up off the floor.

"Well, you know I had to go congratulate my BFF."

Harmony sneered. She hated that Autumn was Axel's best friend.

"So, your best friend didn't tell you?" Harmony fired back.

"If you remember, I was out of the country and couldn't be reached." Autumn shot back.

Harmony couldn't say anything else. She didn't know that Axel had tried to tell Autumn. She was hoping he had left her in the dark and she would have one up on her.

"So, let's get started!" Autumn exclaimed. Feeling satisfied she had won.

# CHAPTER TWENTY-FOUR

Several months had passed and Mr. Nelson had not laid a finger on Michelle. He didn't even look her way. When she got sent out of Ms. Ross's class, he would write her a pass compelling Ms. Ross to let her in. He even made time for her to make up work that she missed. Michelle thought it odd, but she was glad Ms. Ross was no longer a threat to her GPA. But still Michelle didn't know if Mr. Nelson was setting her up for a greater punishment later or had he truly moved on and left her alone. Meanwhile Mitchell was on to bigger and better deals. He had arranged for another teacher to visit with Michelle after school along with two other basketball players. Mitchell seemed to have started his own little business... on Michelle's back.

Michelle dressed herself as she serviced the second client of the evening, Alex Turner. Alex was the second star of the team, behind Mitchell, but was dumber than he looked. All the teachers let him pass because they wanted him to remain on the team. Michelle was sure he couldn't even read. And according to the three minutes that passed before he released himself, he wasn't too good at much else either. Michelle was grateful for it anyway. The shorter, the better.

*I have got to find a way to get out of this mess. I can't take this anymore. I can't keep letting him do this to me.* Michelle thought as Mitchell walked into the room to announce that she was free to go. Michelle walked past him without saying a word or even looking in his direction. She didn't want to give him the satisfaction of seeing the hurt and pain that filled her eyes.

Michelle walked to the door of Mr. Nelson's office and alerted him that she was ready to go. She walked out to his car and waited on him to meet her there. Then they road home in silence. Michelle exited the car and entered the house through the garage door. The door led into a cook's dream kitchen. It had double ovens. A huge pantry. State of the art refrigerator and an island that a whole family could dine at.

"Mrs. Nelson?" Michelle called out looking around the massive kitchen, hoping the woman had returned.

"She's still not here." Mr. Nelson responded as he entered the house behind her.

"When is she coming back. Is everything okay?"

"She filed for divorce. If you must know."

"Why didn't she tell me anything? Is it because of me?" Michelle didn't know if Mrs. Nelson had confronted him or not. All she knew is that she left without helping her at all.

"Not really. You know your mom really was excited when we first agreed to take you in. But then it started to become too much. But I guess it didn't help that she found out I was cheating on her."

"With me?" Michelle asked startled.

"No. She doesn't know anything about that."

I guess she hadn't said anything to him. Michelle decided not to say anything about their conversation either.

"It was Ms. Ross. I was sleeping with Ms. Ross."

"Is that why she doesn't like me?"

"Absolutely not. She's probably just jealous of your looks. Ms. Ross hates anyone who she perceives is a threat. Right now, you're the only one."

Michelle looked at his face. It seemed as if he had aged ten years. She guessed all his bad deeds were finally catching up with him. Either way, it seemed like he wanted to get some things off his chest and she was more than willing to take advantage of the situation.

Michelle pulled out another bar stool and hoisted herself up. "Do you mind if I ask you another question?" Michelle asked cautiously hoping she wasn't going too far.

Mr. Nelson shrugged his shoulders.

"Why... why did you..." Michelle's voice trailed off. She thought she could ask but her words kept getting caught in her throat.

"Why did I violate you? Is that what you want to know?" Mr. Nelson held his head up for the first time and held her gaze.

Michelle could do nothing but nod.

"It really wasn't what I had in mind. My wife and I have always wanted a daughter. When your grandmother came to us, she initially met with your mom and I and..." Mr. Nelson's voice trailed off for a second. "She made it seem like she was in a bad financial spot and could no longer take care of you. She said she wanted you to get a good education. Your mom and I jumped at the chance. Even though we initially wanted someone much younger, your mom was desperate and she just really wanted a child. But then your grandmother called me and asked me to meet her alone and I did. I thought something was wrong and I definitely didn't want to tell your mom that the deal fell through. So, I went. When I met her, she told me that you were the daughter of a prostitute and that you were interested in following in her footsteps. She told me you were discreet and to enjoy myself. At that moment I knew I needed to save you from this terrible woman..." again his voice trailed off, but this time Michelle could see tears well up in his eyes. "When your grandmother dropped you off, she definitely had you dressed the part."

Michelle thought back to the day she was left with the Nelson's. Her grandmother had gone to the store to buy her something special to wear to meet her new parents. Michelle had gotten her hopes up. She figured these were nice people and they would take really good care of her and everything would be fine. She would never have to deal with Sadie or her past ever again. But when Sadie came home, she began to pull clothing out of her bag, that no fourteen-year-old should wear, especially if they wanted to make a good impression on her new parents. She felt like a tramp in the mini skirt and halter top Sadie bought her, complete with a pair of stilettos. She had sat her down and fixed her hair and applied more make-up than she had ever worn in her life. In her opinion, more than she would ever need in two life times. When she looked in the mirror, she thought to herself. *These people are going to think this is a scam. There is no way they are going to believe I'm fourteen.* Michelle didn't even believe that she was fourteen. She actually could pass for twenty-five. She thought as she looked herself over and over.

"When you and your grandmother arrived at our house, we were expecting a sweet innocent little fourteen-year-old, not someone who could pass for a grown woman."

The sound of Mr. Nelson's voice snapped Michelle out of her memories.

"My wife and I didn't want to turn you away but I could tell from the look on my wife's face, she didn't want you. And me. Well, looking at your body. I thought about what your grandmother said and my mind went to wandering. I thought to myself. What if this girl is actually older than what she says she is? I wouldn't really be doing anything wrong would I? Your mom and I hadn't been intimate in a while. And following that day, things just got worst. Your mom grew to like you, after seeing through the façade that your grandmother portrayed. She started seeing you as a really sweet girl. For me. I couldn't get that image out of my head. I knew you may truly be fourteen, but your body was not and your grandmother's words kept coming back to me and... I know it's no excuse but I wanted you so badly, I just went for it and it was the best feeling in the world, but it was wrong. Michelle, I'm so sorry. I never meant to hurt you, but I was really messed up. Who am I kidding; I'm still messed up!" Mr. Nelson dropped his head into his hands and the tears that he had been holding back came out like a flood.

Michelle didn't know what to do. Should she comfort him? Feel sorry for him? Instead, she just sat there staring at him in silence.

After a while Mr. Nelson's head popped back up. And he stood up directly across the counter from Michelle. Michelle flinched thinking he was about to do something to her. But he just looked for a second like he was calculating his next move.

"I know what Mitchell is doing to you. I know he is pimping you out after school and I'm sorry about that too. But you told him! You told him about us!"

"I didn't tell him! I didn't tell him anything." Michelle began to tremble with fear. She knew she might need to run. Should she stand, to give herself more of an advantage or would he take that as a threat and come for her?

She decided to remain seated. She wanted him to remain as calm as possible.

"If you didn't. I wonder how he found out? Anyway, he threatened to ruin me if I said anything about what he was doing and he told me I could never touch you again."

"That's why you stopped. I couldn't understand why."

"You didn't want me to?"

Michelle didn't want to anger him but she wanted to be truthful. So, she took a gamble. "Yes. I wanted you to stop." She said as calmly as possible. "I was just curious to what made you stop."

Mr. Nelson took a deep breath and wiped the tears from his eyes. And his next words shocked Michelle to the point she almost fell out of her seat.

"I am going to help you get away from Mitchell. I have some money stashed away. Is there someplace you would like to go?"

Michelle was still stunned by his statement and found herself lost for words.

"Well, is there?" Mr. Nelson demanded.

"Umm... I always wanted to go to California. Maybe Los Angeles. Just far away from here."

"Deal. Pack all your things. You're taking a sick day tomorrow. I'm going to give you my car. It's paid for. You do know how to drive, right?"

"Yes sir. Sadie, my grandmother, she taught me."

"Ok. I will put you on a flight and have the car delivered to you."

"Are you sure Mr. Nelson?"

"Yeah. I'll set you up an account and put you some money in it to last you a bit until you can find you a job or something. And I will have you a house ready when you arrive. A real nice one. You deserve a real nice one.

With the rent paid up for six months in advance. I know some people. I can set all this up rather quickly."

Michelle couldn't believe what was happening. Could she really be about to leave this life of pain and struggle and bad breaks. Would she be able to start a new life; a better life?

Michelle didn't care if it sounded crazy or not. She wanted to believe it and so she would. She immediately ran upstairs. "I'm going to pack!" She shouted from the top floor.

"Great."

Michelle shut her room door behind her and pressed her back against it. Her heart was racing. She would never have to have sex with Mitchell or any of his "clients" ever again. Michelle wanted to break down and cry. But she didn't have time for that. *I have to pack. I am going to Los Angeles.* Michelle could barely contain her excitement. She would have Mr. Nelson's brand-new Mercedes Benz. Life couldn't get any sweeter. Then it hit her. What was Mr. Nelson going to do? She shook the thought from her mind. It didn't matter. As long as she was safe and far away from this place. Michelle began to pack. She grabbed the suitcases she came with and the ones her mom bought her for when they went out of town on family vacations. It should be just enough to fit all her things. Whatever couldn't fit. She would leave. It didn't matter. She just wanted out of there. She decided she should pack what she really wanted first.

"California here I come!"

# CHAPTER TWENTY-FIVE

"I see you're not wearing your engagement ring." Phoenix blocked Autumn from walking out of the front door.

"Umm.. I... I just thought that we could take it slow before we announce it to the world. You know this is all so very new to me."

"It wasn't new to you when we were in London. You couldn't wait to tell everyone. If I recall correctly, it was I who said we should take it slow."

"Well, now I agree. I was just excited about being engaged that I wanted to shout it from the rooftops. I wasn't thinking."

"So, you were just excited about being engaged, not necessarily excited about being engaged to me?"

"Why would you say that? Why would I not be excited about being engaged to you?"

"I'm just repeating what you said."

"You know what I meant."

"No, I don't. It seems like ever since we've been back or should I say ever since you've been back with Axel, things have been different. It's like you don't want him to know. But I'm not surprised. I expected it. Axel has always wanted you all to himself. And you gladly oblige."

"Phoenix, that is the furthest thing from the truth."

"Prove it."

"What?"

"Prove it. Let's announce our engagement."

"I told you, I'm not ready and that's the end of that!" Autumn pushed past Phoenix and stormed to her Jeep.

Phoenix watched Autumn as she got into her car and slammed the door behind her. He knew Autumn was having second thoughts. He knew it would be a problem as soon as they got back to Cali and she was in Axel's presence once again. How stupid could she be? Axel was engaged and she still couldn't move on.

*I know how to set her straight tho. I'm just gonna get the word out myself.* Phoenix let a smile creep across his lips. *There is no way she's taking my security from me. And if she tries to fight me on it, well, I'll take a nice settlement.* Phoenix burst into laughter at his thoughts. "Now I just need a plan." He said aloud.

## CHAPTER
# TWENTY-SIX

"Axel do you like the last song I put out?" Autumn sat across from Axel as they played around with beats on the mixer.

Autumn turned his chair as if he was really into what he was doing.

"Really Axel." Autumn scooted her chair up so she could punch him in the arm. "Tell me what you think for real. You are supposed to be my best friend. Why wouldn't you be honest with me?"

Axel turned to look at Autumn. He could see the tears that threatened to burst from her eyes. He knew she was being serious.

"Autumn, what's wrong? What brought this on?" He grabbed her hand. He looked down at her hand and noticed she wasn't wearing her engagement ring. "Don't tell me homeboy already out the door?"

Autumn couldn't help but laugh. "I hate you and you're stupid." She said between giggles and sniffles. "I don't want to talk about it."

"I'm for real tho. What's going on?"

She let out a deep breath. "Your new artist, Charlie."

"That's it. I'm getting rid of her. I told her if she came at you..."

"It's ok Ax. She actually helped me. Maybe I need her here to keep me on my toes. I don't like her attitude and I don't know why she's gunning for me, but if she can keep me motivated to go harder then I need her here. But don't think I'm going to let you off that easy. Stop deflecting and tell me why you didn't tell me the song wasn't good?" She pulled her hand back and folded her arms waiting patiently for an answer.

"Autumn. I didn't want to hurt your feelings. You were so excited about the song. I didn't want to break your spirit."

"Axel you can't do that!" Autumn almost shouted as she scooted to the edge of her seat. "I know we are best friends, but you have to tell me the truth. You always have to tell me the truth. Do you understand that?"

"Yeah. Calm down."

"I'm serious Axel. My music is my life. I can't jeopardize that by getting complacent."

"I get it Autumn and I promise, never again. You are absolutely right. I should have told you it was bad."

"You think it was bad?" Autumn almost whined.

"I mean, not bad, but..."

"Axel." Autumn's arms reverted to their folded position.

"I mean yeah it was bad. I'm sorry Autumn. It wasn't good at all. As a matter of fact..."

Autumn put up her hand. "I get it. You can stop now."

Autumn looked up at the ceiling. Not wanting the words, she was about to say to find their way past her lips." I didn't feel it like I normally do but I have been struggling so bad. I had to put something out so I convinced myself it was good enough and then when you signed on I just left it at that. Now I can't find the right dance moves for the song because the song is terrible." Autumn dropped her head into her hands.

"Autumn. Autumn." Axel repeated. "Look at me."

Autumn slowly lifted her head.

"You are a great artist. You are the most original, creative artist I have. That is not by accident. It's in you. It's who you are. You have just become distracted. Find out what's distracting you and then you'll get your mojo back."

"My mojo Axel."

"Yeah. That's what they call it." They both began to laugh.

"But on the real Autumn, because you haven't given me a set list that I can sink my teeth into. I'm going to have to put your tour on hold."

"On hold!" Autumn jumped out of her seat. She never wanted to hit Axel so bad in all her life.

"Autumn calm down! You told me to be honest with you and I am! Can you respect that or not?"

"Did I interrupt something?"

Autumn and Axel looked behind them to see Charlie standing at the door.

"Charlie." Axel gave her stern look.

"I just came in here to give you a copy of the song that I want to use for my first single."

"You're finished already?" Axel's whole demeanor changed.

"Yep. It was a breeze. I knew exactly what I wanted to say. I just needed a hot beat to go with it. The engineer you hooked me up with hit the nail on the head. That's when magic was made. You ready to listen to it."

Axel looked over at Autumn, who was slowly taking her seat.

"Let's hear it." Autumn said reluctantly, her breathing slowly returning to normal.

Charlie pulled up the file and handed her phone to Axel. He plugged it into the sound system and hit play.

Autumn couldn't help but feel jealous. The beat was sick. This was sure to be a hit. Autumn wanted to throw up.

Axel was clearly feeling it. Autumn let a smirk slide across her face as she watched him bob his head like a silly teenager.

"What's the name of this?" Axel asked after the song had ended.

"A Thousand Wishes."

"I like it." He replied.

"I think it's going to be a hit. Congratulations Charlie, you're about to release your first single."

Charlie smiled. "The first of many."

"Ok. I like the way that sounds." He handed her back her phone. "Come see me in my office first thing and we'll get this ball rolling."

"Sure thing." Charlie glanced at Autumn before she about faced and walked out the door.

Autumn looked at Axel. "I'm in trouble huh?"

"Big trouble." Axel honestly replied.

# CHAPTER TWENTY-SEVEN

"What is wrong with me?" Michelle sat thinking to herself. She had just popped a bag of popcorn and was sitting in front of the television like she did every day. She had pretty much dropped out of school. She claimed to be homeschooling but she hadn't done any work the entire year. *Pretty sure they will find out eventually,* she thought to herself. Six months had passed and Michelle got by the best way she knew how. She only went out to go to the Wal-Mart up the street, and even then, she went out in heavy disguise. People often mistook her for a hobo, but she was fine with that, because it meant no one would bother her. All she had to do was look like an adult hobo, a homeless child would cause too much attention.

Michelle dropped her bag of popcorn down next to her on the couch and retrieved her phone off the old coffee table that was full of all the junk she had eaten in the last week. "I need to find a job, I'm seventeen now, I need to get out of this house and do something with my life." As good as that sounded, Michelle was terrified of the outside world. Every experience so far had been tragic. She typed in a familiar job sight she had been frequenting every now and then. She scrolled and scrolled until she came upon one for exotic dancers. Dancing was something Michelle did very well. To pass the time she would turn on the radio and begin to move her body however the rhythm inspired her. She watched videos like an addict and learned as many dance numbers as possible. She figured she probably knew enough to be in every music video that was made in the last year. Michelle laughed at the thought. She took a look back at the ad for dancers. Could she? Would she? *Will they hire me, could I pass for eighteen, and even if I could where would I get a fake I.D. from?* Well, I can find that on the internet as well.

Michelle stood in front of the club. She was shaking all over. *Why couldn't I just get a job at McDonalds like a normal seventeen-year-old.* It was her first day or I guess you could say first night since the time was 10:00pm. The manager barely looked at her I.D. as his eyes were on her body. Hired her on the spot. He didn't even ask her to dance. He just said be here tomorrow at 10.

Michelle thought she might start making her way into the club. It was bad enough she had become a stripper; she didn't want people thinking she was standing on the corner prostituting. Michelle's stomach began to turn just thinking about a bunch of strange men on top of her. She quickly shook the thought and escaped to the loud music gracing the club. It was so dark and solemn. Many people often came here to drown out their sorrows, but walking in that place just added at least seven to ten more sorrows to her life.

She headed to the back where the girls got dressed. Another strange world that awaited her. She looked around at all the mirrors. There were already several girls their practicing their routine for the night. They must be the big entertainers. The money makers.

"Girl, what are you doing here?"

Michelle turned to see a blond staring her down. Pretty sure it was a wig. Never really seen a black woman with natural born blonde hair. It was really hard to focus on her hair or anything else for that matter because her boobs were almost hitting her in the face. She almost wanted to put her hands out just in case the melons fell out of the bag but she didn't know if the woman would take it the wrong way. Michelle definitely did not like women. She didn't want a man right now but she was absolutely sure she didn't want a woman.

"I, I work here. I guess you can say I'm the new girl." Michelle gave a nervous giggle.

The tall dark blonde grabbed Michelle by the arm and escorted her to the far part of the room where she knew she wouldn't be heard.

"Sit down." Michelle didn't have any other choice seeing how she basically pushed her down in the chair. Weightlifting must be a requirement for dancing, cause this chick was strong, Michelle was thinking to herself. She wanted to adjust herself in the seat, but she wasn't about to move and get choke slammed back down.

"How old are you?"

"Twenty-one, you wanna see my I.D.?" Michele took the chance to adjust in her seat so her butt wouldn't go numb, but just as she was moving, the blonde pushed her back down again. Luckily this time she was in a better seating position.

"I don't want to see your fake I.D. Now tell me how old you are? And don't lie, because as you should know by now, I can read you like a book."

Michelle was shaking by this time. "Are you gonna tell?"

"Am I gonna tell? Am I gonna tell? You must be about sixteen. Cause that's something a sixteen-year-old would say."

"Seventeen." Michelle finally confessed.

"Look, I'm going to take the night off and get you outta here, cause believe me, the manager didn't hire you because he thought you were twenty-one, he hired you because he knows you're not twenty-one and he knows he can use you up and make a fool out of you. I've seen it happen too many times. So, you wanna leave or you wanna stay?"

"I need the money."

"Not this money, you don't." The blonde tilted her head up to the ceiling and closed her eyes as if she was contemplating doing something she didn't want to do. After a few seconds she blew out a long sigh. "I can't believe I'm doing this. Look little girl, if you promise to leave this place now, I will help you figure something out, but this is not the life you want. The man who owns this club is evil and I promise you, you are biting off way more than you can chew. Trust me little girl, this is not the life you want."

"You're here. It must be doable."

"Trust me, please. Look I will explain everything to you and answer every question you have. All I ask is that we leave now before the boss comes in looking for you."

Now it was Michelle's turn to let out a long sigh. "Ok, ok."

Before Michelle could take another breathe the blonde grabbed her by the arm again and almost dragged her out the back door. Michelle started wishing she was a bit taller cause her short legs could not keep up with the long legs of the blonde. She almost thought of kicking her legs up and letting the girl pull her along as if she were a flag waving in the wind, but she thought against it. Might be inappropriate. She had already proved her age. She was pretty sure that gesture would surely demote her from seventeen to seven.

# CHAPTER TWENTY-EIGHT

Axel rolled off Harmony and onto his back. He let out an exasperated sigh. He was tired of having sex with Harmony. It wasn't that she was terrible in bed, although he'd had better. He just needed some variety. He wasn't down with sleeping with one person for the rest of his life, especially if she didn't pick up her game in the bedroom. At this point he could take it or leave it.

"Did I wear you out?" Harmony rolled over on her side and propped herself up on her forearm in order to get a better view of her man. She ran her hand over his bare chest, rippled with muscles. She still couldn't believe he was all hers.

Axel remained silent.

Harmony then began to trace her hand across imaginary lines all around his chest, trying to fill the void she felt in Axel's unspoken words. She enjoyed her time spent with Axel. She had been at his house for the last six months, even though she thought it strange he had yet to give her a key. Plus, every time she brought up the subject of moving in completely, he always changed the subject and they would end up where they were now. In bed. She was tired of living out of her Louis Vuitton Bandouliere. What was his deal? He was the one who asked her to marry him, but still had not set a date. He wouldn't even discuss it with her. She was starting to feel stupid every time someone asked her if they had set a date. She would always tell them they were taking it slow and enjoying their engagement and new found love. It seemed to be working so far, but this had gone on too long. It took her four months to convince him that staying at his house was better for her since she was the one always having to make the drive back from his house to hers.

Eventually he agreed to let her bring a couple of things but not much. Only what she could fit in her Louis. She thought that it could just be him adjusting to having a stable girlfriend for a change but she was starting to wonder if marrying Axel was ever going to happen. But for now, she had the ring, which meant maybe she had his heart. She couldn't decide yet. She lived in his house even if it wasn't completely, that would just have to do for now. Besides, it was better than the alternative which was losing him altogether. She didn't want that. So, she kept her mouth shut and played his game.

Axel didn't even look at Harmony. He wished she would go back home. The more time he spent with here on a normal everyday basis the more he knew this is not what he wanted. He had to get rid of her somehow. And he had to do it fast.

Axel jumped at the sound of his phone. Saved by the bell. He sat up and grabbed his phone off the nightstand. He didn't too much care who was calling him at this point. He would answer it and play like he had somewhere to be even if he didn't. Axel looked at the caller ID. It was the manager of his strip club.

"I gotta take this." Axel jumped up and left the room, not even waiting for Harmony's response.

"What's up man? Everything good?"

"Great. Axel's manager, Demetrius, of seven years responded. I actually have some good news for you."

"I could use some good news." Axel looked back towards the room where he left Harmony.

"There's this girl. She started tonight. She gave me a fake ID. I believe she may be 16 or 17. Not sure. But Ax. She is the finest thing I have ever seen. A rare jewel. I think you would love her. Her name's Michelle."

"She there now?"

"That's the one problem?"

"What do you mean?"

"She bolted."

"What do you mean she bolted? She get scared?"

"I thought that at first but when I looked back at the security cameras, I saw her leave with your girl. She must've said something to her."

"What girl?"

"Destiny."

"Good ole Destiny. I don't even know why I keep her around."

"Good to keep your enemies close boss."

"I hear that. Ok. I think I'll just go pay Destiny a little visit. You haven't said anything have you?"

"No. Called you first."

"Good thinking. Ok. Just go back to business as usual. I'll handle the rest."

"Bet."

Axel hung up the phone and made a call to his most loyal sidekick.

# CHAPTER TWENTY-NINE

Phoenix knew this was the only way to get Autumn to sign on fully to their engagement. He had to get it out to the public. Autumn would no doubt hit the roof but he was determined not to let her string him along until Axel finally made up his mind if he wanted her or not. He had set up an interview with Cedric Johnson. An entertainment journalist that covered a lot of what the stars where up to in their personal lives. Cedric knew exactly who he was an was very interested in what he had to say.

"So, tell me Phoenix, what is that you have to tell me?"

Phoenix reclined back in his seat. He looked around Cedric's nice penthouse condo. He would love to live in a place like this. Phoenix was sorta surprised when Cedric suggested they meet at his place. He said he had an area in the back where he had interviewed countless number of celebrities. Phoenix quickly agreed after hearing that. It made him feel more important. As he looked out the massive windows in the sunroom he anticipated if he really should do this or not. This could cause him to lose Autumn for good or it could propel their relationship forward. Phoenix wasn't sure, but he had to do something.

"I'm engaged to Autumn Dance." Phoenix watched as Cedric's eyes grew twice as big as they had been.

"You are engaged to Autumn Dance?" He recited.

"Yep, we have been engaged for six months now. We got engaged in Paris. It was like a pre-marriage honeymoon."

"So, why isn't Autumn here with you sharing this amazing news?"

"She is just so busy and we've already been putting it off trying to wait until she had time, but with her new album dropping and her possibly going on tour, she absolutely has no time. So she asked if I would be okay doing it without her. She didn't want to do it without me but she didn't want to prolong telling her fans her fantastic news. She'll probably try to put something on Facebook live later on."

"Well, we will be anxiously awaiting her confirmation."

"But what about Autumn?" Cedric leaned back in his seat and held Phoenix's gaze.

Phoenix stared back trying to figure out where he was going with this question. He didn't come on here to be embarrassed.

"What do you mean by that?"

"Well, I was just sitting here thinking that there are so many rumors out about Autumn and Axel Smith. Is there any truth to the rumors? Could this be why she's not here with you making this announcement? I mean could she be with Axel right now?"

"Okay, this interview is over." Phoenix got up and begin to remove his microphone. "I didn't come here to be embarrassed. I tried to help you get an inside scoop. I am now taking back my permission for you to air this story and if you air it, I will sue."

Phoenix began to walk away.

"Phoenix wait." Cedric stopped the recording and ran after Phoenix.

"What do you want?" Phoenix stopped but kept his back turned towards Cedric.

"I went too far. I apologize. I was actually just asking that part for myself. I would not have aired it."

"Why do you want to know about Autumn and Axel?"

"To tell you the truth I was hoping they weren't just rumors and maybe you would be more inclined to stray."

Phoenix turned and faced Cedric. "Stray how?" He asked raising his eyebrow.

"With me. I wanted to know if you would be inclined to stray with me."

Phoenix looked at Cedric. "How did he know?"

"When you called me, I really wasn't interested in your story about you and Autumn. I just wanted to see you. I used to see you on Autumn's videos and fell in love with you over time; always wanted to meet you. I actually tried to get an interview with you and Autumn when you guys dated the first time. I must admit I became a bit obsessed and trolled you for a while, found out where you would be and started following you, but never had the courage to actually engage you in conversation. Imagine me, the journalist, afraid of conversation. So I went to a gay bar one night and who do I see but the man of my dreams walking in checking out the scene. I started to introduce myself then but I could tell you were trying to be incognito and if I were to recognize you it would probably scare you off. Didn't want to do that, so I have been waiting and waiting and waiting hoping for an opportunity like this to come along so I can get you alone."

Phoenix couldn't believe his ears. He didn't know if this was some kind of game to out him or what? All he knew is that he had been thinking the same thing about Cedric since he walked in the door. He wanted to snatch him out of that turquoise V-neck he was wearing and have his way with him. Could he trust him or would this be the biggest mistake of his life?

"I didn't know you were gay." Phoenix tried to play it cool.

"I'm not out with it. I keep my private life private until a time when I'm comfortable to take it public, now isn't that time."

Phoenix liked the way that sounded. "Well then what you waiting on. Give me a tour of the bedroom."

Cedric walked over to Phoenix and grabbed his hand. "I'd be much obliged."

# CHAPTER THIRTY

"So, how did you get into this business?" Michelle asked as she walked around Destiny's living room. She was amazed at her apartment. She halfway expected there to be a stripper pole and exotic pictures. But it wasn't like that. It was real homey. There were pictures on the mantel and drawings on the fridge. The kitchen was right off the living room and Michelle couldn't help but peek in. By the looks of the pictures on the mantle she had a child. A little girl. But why would someone with a child do something like this? Does she still have her child? What is going on with this girl? Michelle had so many questions, but she figured she would find out in time.

"Have a seat, Michelle. Look I can tell that you are very interested in this line of work, but even though I'm in it, I don't recommend it."

"I just want to know why?"

"You see that little girl up there?" Destiny pointed to one of the pictures on the mantle. The beautiful dark-skinned girl with pigtails was smiling from ear to ear while she swung on a swing.

"She is why I got into the business. Her daddy beat me every day. I needed quick money to get out. I made what I needed in two nights and I got out of there as quick as I could. I know it may not have been the best choice but I needed quick cash. Those were the longest two nights of my life."

"So, why keep doing it?"

"Michelle, that's the down side, most of these girls in these strip clubs say, I'm just gonna do this until I can get on my feet, but truth is, the money starts to pull them in and before you know it, they get lost in the business. They feel like there's no getting out."

"Is that what happened to you?"

"It started off that way. Quick money. Anytime I needed something I knew where I could get a lot of cash in a little time and then it just became a habit until…" Destiny's voice trailed off.

"Until what?"

"Nothing. It's not important."

"Is there something else that you want to do?" Michelle tried to change the subject a bit.

"Michelle, I could want to do a lot of things but the reality is, there ain't a lot of options for people like me."

"Who are people like you?"

"I knew taking you in was a bad idea. Look, where can I drop you at, cause this ain't gonna work." Destiny got up and started searching for her keys.

"I'm sorry, please don't make me leave. I don't want to go home, please." Michelle thought about getting on her knees and begging. And she would have if she thought it would help.

"What's your deal anyway, why you here? Where's your momma?"

"I don't know. The only person I know is my grandma and she sold me to a man who raped me almost every day. He finally came to his senses and let me go. I have a place to stay but I need money in order to live. I'm on my own. I don't know anyone and I don't know what to do." Tears began to flow uncontrollably from Michelle's eyes. This was the first time she had ever let herself feel hurt over what had happened in her life.

"I guess I'm one of those people who don't have a lot of options. But I know how to dance so I thought that this would be the best place for me." Michelle barely got the words out between sobs.

"Man, you really do got it bad. Well look, you can stay here as long as you need to, I won't make you go home. Do you need to go by the house and get some clothes?"

"Yeah."

"Alright, I'll take you by there. Let's go."

Before Destiny could get her keys, they heard someone banging on the door like they were trying to knock it down.

BAM, BAM, BAM, BAM.

"Open the door Destiny I know you're in there. Don't make me kick this door in!" The voice on the other side of the door shouted.

"Oh no, it's Axel, he must be looking for you."

"Who's Axel? The guy who interviewed me was named Demetrius?"

"Demetrius is the manager. Axel is the owner."

"You mean the evil guy?"

"Yes, the very evil guy."

BAM, BAM, BAM, BAM

"Last chance Destiny!"

"Go in the room Michelle and lock door."

Michelle ran to the room without hesitation. Destiny walked over to the door and opened it. Axel forced his way through, slamming it closed once he cleared the doorway.

"Axel, what... what are you doing here?"

“Where is she?"

"Where is who Ax, I don't know what you're talking about?"

"I see you wanna do this the hard way."

"Axel, plea......"

Before she could get the words out of her mouth Axel began slapping her over and over again.

"Stop please, I'm right here, just please stop." Michelle emerged from the bedroom. She couldn't let Destiny take a beating for her.

"Wow, Demetrius was right. You are a pretty little thing."

"You can't touch me, I'm only 17." Michelle said feeling a bit confident.

"Feisty too. I like them like that. But I seem to have a copy of your I.D. that clearly states that you're 21."

"It's fake."

"I don't know that. Besides, do you really want me to report you for making a fake I.D.?"

"No, but I'd rather go to jail than go with you."

"I'm gonna have a lot of fun with you little lady." At that Axel pulled out his gun. “Now, we can do this the easy way or the hard way. Easy way, you come with me quietly or the hard way, you can get what Destiny got times 10 courtesy of this 45."

"Please leave her alone Axel, she's just a kid." Destiny pleaded as she tried to pick herself up off the floor.

Axel walked over to Destiny and hit her with his gun. She fell to the floor but this time she didn't get up and she didn't move.

"I could do this all night. What's it going to be Michelle?” Axel asked gently rubbing his 45 as he walked towards her.

"I'll go with you." Michelle looked down at Destiny wishing she would move or something. "I'll go with you."

"Good choice. Let's go."

# CHAPTER THIRTY-ONE

"Axel man, what are you going to do with this little girl? You can't take her home."

"Why not?" Axel asked confused.

"Did you forget about Harmony?"

Axel shook his head. He had totally forgotten about Harmony.

"I can't believe I forgot about Harmony. I guess that's why I got you here. You keep me right. I was 'sho bout to take her home."

Axel tapped the steering wheel trying to figure out what to do with Michelle until he could get Harmony out of the house. As far as he was concerned it was over between them. He thought about the girl in his trunk. Michelle. She was the most beautiful, sexiest girl he had ever seen in his life and she was only seventeen. Imagine what she would look like five years from now if she kept herself up, which he planned to make sure she did. He just couldn't pass up this opportunity. He knew that he would get flack about her being under age but he was going to have to hide her at least until she was eighteen and then she would be legal. Of course, that wasn't going to stop him from exploring that beautiful body of hers now. He was already thinking up different things he wanted to do to her and he couldn't wait.

"Autumn."

"What?"

"Autumn. I'll take the girl to Autumn's house until I get rid of Harmony."

"What do you mean get rid of? You about to marry her, right?"

"Wrong. I have been wanting to drop her since I got engaged."

"Man, I knew you weren't about to tie the knot. Everybody else thought Harmony finally broke you. But I told them just wait and see. You don't know my boy like I know my boy."

Axel smiled. He knew he could always count on his boy. His cousin Mateo was certifiable crazy, but he was cool. He knew him better than anybody and he always had his back in every crazy thing he could think of. I mean who else is going to help him go and basically kidnap a seventeen-year-old girl and not ask any questions, except what you need me to do?

# CHAPTER THIRTY-TWO

Axel walked into his house. The first thing he noticed was the smell of seafood. He placed his keys on the keyring he kept by the garage door since he was always misplacing them and headed for the dining area. There was Harmony, sitting at a candle lit dinner table with rose petals all around. On the menu; baked shrimp salmon complete with brown rice and asparagus. *Don't she know I am a steak and potatoes man?*

"That's why she couldn't be my wife. She don't pay attention." Axel thought to himself. He could see the red wine chilling in a bucket of ice. Nevertheless, she had thought of absolutely everything. He didn't know what to do. Should he sit, eat and enjoy one last night with Harmony or tell her to get out right now and forget the rest. Axel thought hard. He wanted so badly to retrieve Michelle from Autumn's house and get started on their sexcapade.

Autumn had so many questions. *Where did you find her? Did you kidnap her? How old is she? Why can't you take her to your place? Did you forget about Harmony?* Fortunately, he was able to put Autumn's mind to rest and she jumped on board. He thought he was gonna have to hem Phoenix up, but he wasn't there. Autumn told him that Phoenix had some business he had to take care of in Paris. Axel still didn't trust him, but he wasn't worried though. He was already in the process of handling Autumn's little situation. He just hoped she didn't hate him after the fact.

Axel decided it was best to play it out. He knew Harmony would be extremely hurt over the broken engagement. He didn't want to add fuel to the fire by putting her out when she had gone through so much trouble to prepare this special night for him. He wondered what was up her sleeve. Why would she be going through all of this when he hadn't given her any reason to want to be nice to him. He wouldn't let her move in. He hadn't given her a key and was never going to. He knew he would regret letting her stay there for the extended time that he had. He was perfectly fine with her going back to her place every night. Of course, when she left, the company he really wanted would come by. Two girls. Sometimes three. Willing to do whatever he wanted them to do. The best part. They would never say anything to anybody. Now with Harmony here full time, all of his fun came to an end. It was their separation that was keeping them together. He could tolerate her in short spurts, but full time was too much for him to handle.

"Give me a minute and I'll join you." Axel walked back into the foyer and dialed up Autumn.

"Hey. You on your way?"

"Naw. Change of plans."

"What do you mean change of plans? What am I supposed to do with your little package, which we will finish talking about later."

"Just keep an eye on her. Let her sleep in a spare room and I'll grab her tomorrow."

"What are you doing? Why can't you come get her tonight?"

"When I walked in the house, Harmony had this big romantic dinner set up."

"Oh. You feeling romantic tonight, are you?"

"No. I just know it's going to cause waves when I dump her. I sure don't want to make it worst by doing it when she's gone through all this trouble. I'm just going to indulge her for the night and then give her the boot tomorrow."

"You're terrible Axel. You can't make her feel like you are all in and then drop her. It may hurt her worse."

"I don't know what to do Autumn. Can you just help me out please?"

"I got you Axel, but remember, we will discuss this further. Besides, I want to know everything that happens when you dump Harmony. If you're still alive that is."

"Oh, you got jokes. It's all good. I'll be fine. Just take care of my girl."

"Your girl? Whatever Axel. Be careful."

"Whatever Autumn."

"You trying to mock me?"

"I knocked it out the ball park didn't I?"

"No. No you didn't. Bye Axel."

Axel didn't like being away from Michelle like this. It was too early. He didn't trust her not to run. He just hoped his threats were sufficient. He told her his friend would shoot her on site. Of course, he told his crazy cousin that no harm better come to the girl. If she did try to run, he was to apprehend her only. Not hurt her. He didn't want this girl dead. She was way too interesting. She was going to be fun getting to know. She was special. He wanted her. He needed her.

Axel made his way back to the dining area.

"I apologize for the wait pretty lady." Axel leaned over and kissed Harmony on the cheek. He grabbed her hand as he sat adjacent to her. "So, what is this all about?"

"I just wanted to do something special for my soon-to-be husband." Harmony gave Axel's hand a squeeze.

Axel didn't respond. Truth be told he didn't know how to respond.

"Look Axel. I know this isn't your cup of tea. But I'm willing to do whatever you need me to do to make this work. I'm just so happy you chose me. Now I just want to make you happy. Whatever that is, I just need you to tell me and I'll do it."

Axel was really feeling messed up now. He just wanted to run back out the house. How was he going to tell her he not only wanted to end their engagement but he wanted her out of the house immediately? His mind flashed back to Michelle. The look in her eyes when she came out of the room; absolute fear. And it turned him on more than anything he had ever experienced. He had to have her. He had to see that look in her eyes every day. Even when she wasn't afraid. Her eyes, her face, her mannerisms; it was just something so special about her that he couldn't deny. This girl had everything. He was in the palm of her hands, but he couldn't let her know that. The sad thing was, she was only seventeen years old. He couldn't imagine what kind of power she would have over him as a full-grown woman, especially if she ever knew that she had that power. Axel knew what he would have to do. He would have to break her. Break her spirit. Break her mind. Break her self-esteem. He couldn't ever allow her to know who she truly was and the power she actually had over men. He was pretty sure that up until now men have taken advantage of her. Poor girl didn't know she could've had anything she wanted. She could've had the world but she just didn't know it. And it was up to him to keep it that way. To take it to a whole other level and he was willing.

"Baby, you okay? Are you listening to me?"

Axel snapped back to reality. He had no idea how long he had been sitting there. He looked down at his untouched plate. Looked over at Harmony's plate and realized it was untouched too. He knew he was spoiling Harmony's special night, but he didn't care. All he wanted was Michelle. He hated to do this to Harmony, but he had to and he had to do it right now.

"Harmony. I know this is all my fault. I should have never asked you to marry me. I think I was feeling vulnerable and I thought being married was something that I needed. I am really sorry, but there is nothing that you can do for me really, except leave."

Axel felt Harmony release his hand. She began to breathe deep. He looked at her, bracing himself for her explosion, but nothing. She said nothing. She sat there for what seemed like forever. The room was so quiet you could hear the flickering of the candles. The steady drip of the faucet.

*I'm going to have to get that fixed. I make too much money for my faucet to be leaking.* Axel thought to himself. He refocused his attention on Harmony. He heard the in and out of Harmony breathing.

"Look Har..."

Before he could get the rest of his sentence out Harmony stood up from the table and walked towards the bedroom. Axel wondered what she was doing. He had every mind to follow her but he didn't think it was safe. Unless, she was back there destroying his property. Axel thought he should go and see what she was up to. He didn't want to be sitting at the table when all of a sudden, he started smelling smoke and realized his house was going up in flames. He could picture himself running out the front door, barely escaping with his life. Looking back at the house with her in the window with a wicked smile on her face. Axel shook the image from his mind. He got up from the table and almost sprinted toward the bedroom. Upon his arrival, he saw Harmony sitting on his bed in full lingerie.

Axel's brows met each other in the middle. "Harmony, what are you doing?"

"This is my house. I live here. We are getting married and that is the end of that. So, whatever you have to do to make peace with that then I suggest you start doing it, cause I am not going anywhere." Harmony stared at Axel like she could kill him.

Axel knew he had to play it cool. Harmony had crossed over from hurt to crazy in 2.5 seconds.

Axel walked over to Harmony's side of the bed or what used to be her side of the bed and sat at the edge. He grabbed Harmony by each of her arms and looked her in her eyes.

"Harmony. Look at me."

Harmony whipped her head to stare him straight in his eyes as if she were trying to burn a hole through his head.

"I am so sorry. I know this hurts. Whatever I need to tell people I will. I will take full responsibility. I will make you look like a saint and I'll make myself look like the devil. But I can't do this. I am not going to do this. So, I am going to ask you nicely to leave. I will have someone drive you home and have your car brought to you. But please understand that if you don't get out of my house right now all that goes out the window and I will make you feel like you are in a Tyler Perry movie because I will drag you out of this house kicking and screaming. So, what is it going to be?"

Harmony thought long and hard. She thought it best to abide by his terms for now. But if he thought she was going to let this go and allow him to humiliate her like this he had another thing coming.

"Take me home."

"I'll go get my keys."

"Not you!" Harmony screamed. "Anybody but you! I don't ever want to see your face again!" Harmony jumped up from the bed and pushed passed him grabbing her bag on the way out. She stood next to the front door waiting on her ride.

Axel followed her to the door. "I brought you a jacket. You can keep it or burn it. Whatever you want to do."

"You better believe I'm going to burn it." Harmony responded without looking at Axel, but grabbing the jacket.

The driver pulled around and blew the horn. Harmony stormed out before Axel could say goodbye.

Axel watched Harmony slide into the backseat of the SUV and slam the door. She didn't even give his driver a chance to close it for her. The driver instinctively put his hands in the air as if to surrender. He looked back at Axel standing at the door and shook his head before entering the vehicle himself and driving away.

Axel thought he might call her later on and make sure she got home okay, but at this point he didn't care. He was just glad to have Harmony out of the house. Now it was on to bigger and better things. Axel headed toward the dining area where the food Harmony had prepared for them was still on the table in their original position; untouched by either of them. Axel thought about eating it but there wasn't any telling what kind of voodoo she had put in it. Axel didn't trust it. He would just let the cook throw it all out when she came in the morning.

Axel looked at his watch. Autumn was going to kill him, but he was definitely going to pick up Michelle right now.

# CHAPTER THIRTY-THREE

Axel knocked on Autumn's door. He had already called her to let her know he was on the way. It took five tries but he finally got through. Needless to say, Autumn was not happy. She answered the phone as if she could have put her hands around his throat and squeezed until no life was left in him. She might as well join the club. Axel couldn't help but think that Harmony was sitting at home at that very moment still in her lingerie and the jacket he gave her planning his demise. He would deal with that later but at the moment he couldn't care less. He wanted Michelle in his possession ASAP.

Autumn answered the door with her hands on her hips, her lips frowned and an attitude that slapped him in the face harder than her hand would have. Maybe.

"What is wrong with you? First you don't want the girl, now you do. What is it? And furthermore, why do you have to drag me in it?"

"Autumn. You gonna leave me out here on the front steps again or are you going to let me in and then I can answer all of your many questions."

Autumn took a step back so he could enter. "Oh, you have no idea how many questions I have. I am just getting started, friend." She emphasized *friend.*

Axel felt the words hit him in the back of the head as he found his way to her chill room. The same room he had made passionate love to Autumn in just months ago.

She plopped down on the sofa next to him. "So..."

"What you wanna know Autumn?"

"Why you playing with me Axel? You know exactly what I want to know. Tell me everything about the girl and then tell me what happened with Harmony. Cause something had to happen for you to be so early."

"I'll start with the Harmony part first."

Autumn tilted her head to the right rolled her eyes. "Whatever Axel."

There's your favorite word. Anyway, I told her she had to leave. She had dinner fixed with candles lit and rose petals. I thought about going through with the night. That's why I called you in the first place but then, I couldn't. I had to get rid of her right then and there so I told her, in a nice way, that she had to go."

"Axel, there is no nice way to say our engagement is off now get out of my house."

"Well, I tried to say it nice. But she wouldn't leave. She went to the bedroom, got in her night clothes and refused to leave."

"Are you serious? So how did you get her to leave? Or is she still there?"

"I told her that I would take the full blame for the breakup. Make her look like the victim and I the big bad wolf. Or I could drag her out the house and make her look like a fool. It was her choice. She chose the former."

"Wow! Do you really think she's going to let it go?"

"Of course not. I'm sure she's plotting and planning as we speak. As a matter of fact, I need to put in some calls so I can beef up my security immediately."

They both laughed.

"And the girl?" Autumn was not about to let Axel get away with anything.

"The girl. Autumn the girl is beyond complicated. I don't even think you are ready to hear about the girl."

"Axel. You said we wouldn't have any secrets between us. Were you lying to me?"

"Autumn. I didn't lie. I just... it's complicated. Her name is Michelle. She doesn't have any family so I'm taking her in."

Lie. Try again.

"I'm not lying."

"If you are just taking her in, why does she need a gunman at her door?"

"That's for her protection."

"Another Lie. Try again."

"Okay. She isn't really a willing participant to the transition. But she ain't gonna tell anybody and I'm not gonna get into trouble. I got this."

"Axel. How old is she?"

"Old enough and I'm really not telling you anything else. You are just going to have to trust me on this one. Okay?"

"Okay Axel. But just so you know. I'm not covering for you if you are doing anything illegal. I promise you that."

"That's fair. I'll take that. So where is she?"

"Guest bedroom. Hurry up and get her out of here so I can go to bed. And don't expect me to be on time for work tomorrow either cause I'm not and you already know why."

"I got you. I'll make sure everything is taken care of."

"And what about Harmony? Am I about to lose a dancer too?"

"I can't answer that one for you, but you'll survive. She wasn't that good anyway remember?"

"I really can't stand you Axel."

"Am I lying?"

"Axel. Get your little girl and get out."

"Little girl?"

"Yes. I know she's underage, but like I said. I ain't covering for you, period."

"Aight Autumn. I got you."

Axel didn't wait for Autumn to take him to the spare bedroom. He didn't want her to see him have to use force if it took that. He got his mind prepared for slave driver mode. He couldn't show any weakness in front of Michelle or she would surely try him. Once he made it to the room, he relieved his cousin, opened the door and flipped on the lights. Michelle jumped and backed into a corner. She was sitting with her arms around her knees shaking like a leaf. You would've thought she was coming down off of a crack high instead of being held captive in what he considered a very nice room. She could have laid down and went to sleep.

"Get up and let's go." He pulled up his shirt so she could see his 45. "Believe me when I say, I will use this. I'm not going to kill you, but you will be in more pain than your little mind could ever imagine." Axel watched the fear well up in Michelle's eyes and he knew he had succeeded. She immediately got up off the floor and followed Axel out the room and down the stairs.

"Aight Autumn. Thank you for keeping my package for me. I appreciate you."

"Whatever Axel." And before he could say anything she continued, "And yes that is my favorite word. Just get out and don't come back."

"Oh, now I can't come back?"

"Nope. You seem to never be up to any good when you come over."

Axel smiled. Autumn had just let him know that she too still thought about their intimate night.

Autumn watched Michelle as she stood behind Axel. Tears were streaming down her face. For a moment she looked up at Autumn and all she could see was fear and dread. What had Axel done to this girl? And more so what did he have planned for her now? Autumn didn't know what to do, but she knew better then to cross Axel. She decided to wait it out. See what Axel planned to do. Right now, being his best friend meant more to her then calling him out for his shady dealings. Besides, Axel was always up to something shady. If she tried to correct him every time he did something crazy and or illegal, she would have to quit her job and follow him full time. Autumn closed the door behind them and walked back to her room. *Please God don't let Axel be into anything dangerous and illegal. I love him, but I surely didn't sign up for this.* With that she laid down and was sleep before her head even hit the pillow.

## CHAPTER
# THIRTY-FOUR

Phoenix had decided not to go public with his engagement to Autumn for right now since he was having so much fun with Cedric. He had just gotten back from Paris visiting Josiah. After Josiah realized her left he called him to apologize for kicking him out. He told him that he renewed the lease on the condo and he could come back anytime he wanted. Phoenix wasn't expecting Josiah to respond like that, but he was glad he did. Josiah was the best thing that had happened to him in a long time. He eventually broke down and told him about Harmony and he was cool with it. As long as he wasn't with another man. Phoenix didn't see the difference but obviously Josiah did. Josiah didn't know about Cedric though and he never would. He would just go back and forth from Paris to L.A., on Josaiah's dime of course. He didn't know how long he could keep this up, but he was definitely going to try to keep it going as long as he could. His first stop was Cedric's place. Cedric took very good care of him even though he knew he was with Autumn. He said he figured the time would come when Phoenix would feel comfortable enough to let that go. For right now things were good and Cedric was always decreet. He liked that about him. Even if they found themselves in the same circle Cedric acted as if he didn't even know him. Cedric played it way too well for Phoenix's taste most times and he had to call him on it, but Cedric always made it up to him the same night, letting him know that he was never forgotten.

Phoenix got out of bed and pulled on his boxers and walked downstairs. Cedric had left breakfast on the table for him as he always did when he had to be to work early. Phoenix loved being spoiled by Cedric, but he wasn't ready to switch all the way over to the other side. If he ever did, Cedric would definitely be the one. Maybe. Josiah had definitely given him something to remember before he left. Phoenix hurried to finish his breakfast, ran upstairs to shower so he could make it to rehearsal. He knew Autumn would be pissed.

*Phoenix where are you?* This was the fifth message Autumn had left for Phoenix this morning. He was late for rehearsal again and on top of that he didn't come home last night. Autumn knew what time his flight was due back and she expected to see him in her bed this morning but he wasn't. *What is wrong with him? Is he cheating? I don't know what his problem is but I'm going to find out today.*

Autumn went back to stretching. Five minutes later Phoenix walked in.

Autumn nearly burned a whole through his face with her glare. Phoenix walked over and sat in front of Autumn and began stretching.

"What's up with you momma?"

"What's up with me? You are late and you didn't come home last night. What's up with you?"

"I figured since you obviously don't want to marry me, I better get used to sleeping elsewhere."

"And exactly where is elsewhere?" Autumn stopped stretching and folded her arms.

"Just a hotel Autumn. Don't trip. You ain't feeling me no way. You too busy following up behind Axel. And I guess you'll never get it that he doesn't want you. How long you gonna keep waiting? That used to be my question, now it's how long am I gonna keep waiting cause I'm about sick of this whole charade." Phoenix got up and went over to the other dancers and started up a conversation leaving Autumn with her thoughts.

Phoenix saw Autumn get up and leave the room as he talked to Skye and Faith. He was still contemplating sleeping with them, but he wasn't sure if they would be as decreet as Cedric and he couldn't deal with that drama right now. A few minutes later Phoenix felt his phone vibrating in his pocket. He pulled it out. It was Autumn.

*Can you please handle rehearsal today? I can't do this right now. I just need some time.*

Phoenix cracked a small smile. Texted back a single word.

*Absolutely.*

Phoenix felt like this was his moment to get a little closer to Skye and Faith. See which one was best at keeping secrets. Phoenix was nothing but professional the entire time he conducted rehearsal, but he kept his eye on Faith. She seemed to be the more insecure twin. The twin that would give in to his advances and keep Autumn in the dark. Yeah, Faith would be the one.

After rehearsal ended, Phoenix kept giving Faith signals with his eyes and she was picking them up. She told her sister to go ahead to the car, while she stretched out her hamstring because it was bothering her. Phoenix stayed behind as well. When all the dancers left, he approached Faith and their lips met before anything else. When they finally caught a breath, he backed away.

"That was interesting." Phoenix finally broke the obvious tension that was between the two.

"Yeah, it was." Faith blushed.

"So, what are we doing?" Phoenix knew how to play the game.

"I don't know."

"I've just been noticing you a lot lately. I guess since you're always around. Autumn has been so absent lately. Always with Axel. Then there's the rumors. I just need a break from it all."

I might can help you out with that." Faith looked down at the ground not sure of herself.

"Don't you live with your sister?"

"No, we just ride together. But we never go over each other's house unannounced. That was mainly her decision. I think she entertains a lot of people she doesn't want me to know about."

That's cool. Maybe I can come by and see you later on tonight. Maybe watch a movie or something."

"I'd like that. I should probably go. Don't want my sister to get suspicious."

"Yeah. But I'll definitely see you later."

"Definitely."

# CHAPTER THIRTY-FIVE

Autumn sat in her Jeep contemplating whether she should go in. Axel was throwing Charlie a congratulatory party for her first single hitting number one for its sixth week in a row. She just hated it was at his strip club. *Of all the clubs and classy places he owned, why here?* Autumn wished Phoenix was here with her. She wasn't really feeling him anymore but at least he would be a distraction from Charlie and her new found success. Especially since she was stuck making a video for an old song. She felt so humiliated. That seemed to be the story of her life. Humiliated by Axel. Humiliated by Charlie. And now it seemed as if she was adding a repeat humiliation by Phoenix. *Why did I ever think it was cool to let him back into my life. After I caught him having a threesome in our bed.* Autumn could feel the anger and the hurt resurfacing all over again.

"Let it go Autumn. You are stronger than this." She encouraged herself out loud.

Autumn decided it was now or never. She knew if she sat in her jeep too long, she would eventually talk herself out of it.

Autumn stepped into the club. The music was blasting and to Autumn's dismay, girls were dancing and apparently taking it all off. Autumn tried not to look. The girls had real talent. She couldn't deny. Autumn could dance, but she did not think that she could make her body do what some of these girls were making their bodies do. She couldn't help but admire their craft.

Autumn noticed Faith and Skye putting their stripping skills to work. Dancing on top of a table for some guys she didn't recognize. They didn't even put that much energy into dancing for her. She really needed a new dance team. Autumn looked to the left. Two tables down was Charlie. She was making it rain on some blonde with a B cup and fat bottom. *Interesting.* She thought to herself. Autumn reluctantly walked over to where Charlie was enjoying herself a little too much for her taste. She needed to go ahead and congratulate her and get it over with. Charlie was not going to make this easy and she knew it.

Charlie saw Autumn coming her way. She waited a moment to see if she was going to stop or pass right by her. Charlie was pleasantly surprised to see her stop.

"Autumn."

"Charlie."

"I'm shocked to see you here."

"I don't know why. I told you we are all family here at this label." Autumn began with all the good will she could muster up. "Anyway, I just wanted to congratulate you. Your song is truly amazing."

"Wow! Very humble of you. Preciate you tho. But to be honest, I don't need your congrats nor do I want it. I told you what I was about to do and I did it. And believe me, this is just the beginning."

"Ok Charlie. Whatever you say. I just came to say congrats, I said it and now I'm done."

"That's the truest thing you've said since you started talking, cause you are definitely done. Your music career is over. Axel is engaged to someone that's clearly not you and I'm guessing your little engagement to Phoenix is just a cover up so you won't feel so stupid that Axel didn't pick you." Charlie let out a belly laugh. "Girl you are past done."

Autumn could feel her fist balling up beside her. But she wasn't about to let Charlie get the best of her. "Look, I'm not gonna stand here and listen to this BS. Wait... how did you know I was engaged?"

Charlie just laughed. "Feel free to leave whenever you want. But before you do, why don't you go say hello to your fiancé. Here I was thinking you came alone. Guess not."

"What?" Autumn realized Charlie didn't answer her question, but she couldn't understand what she was saying. Autumn knew Charlie was crazy but now she just wasn't making any sense.

Charlie pointed behind Autumn and smiled.

Autumn turned around. Her heart hit her stomach. Phoenix had joined the table of guys where Faith and Skye were dancing; filling their G-strings with money. She wanted to just chalk it up to him being in this atmosphere playing around and having some fun, that was until he took Faith by the hand and led her to the private rooms in the back. Autumn turned back towards Charlie who wasn't even trying to hide her amusement and dashed out the side exit before anyone could see her.

# CHAPTER THIRTY-SIX

River's eyes roamed around the club. She picked a table in a very dark corner. She didn't want to be recognized. She could still remember working here. The thrill of being on stage still excited her. She missed the money most of all. Autumn paid them decently for being dancers, but it wasn't nothing like that money she made when she was on stage. She can't believe Axel didn't remember her. Of course, the plastic surgery she received was the best of the best but she didn't expect it to be this good. She expected someone to figure it out by now but they didn't. No one had a clue. Not even Axel. That's how she wanted to keep it until she was able to do what she came here to do. She tried to stay away from the strip clubs. That would be the most dangerous place for her to go, but she had to show her face so no one would get suspicious. She planned on mingling a bit, which she had already done. Then she would chill for a bit, which she was doing now. Next stop, the door. She picked up her drink to finish it off and as she scooted around the booth, she spotted Jaylah heading in her direction. *Please don't let her come over here.* River didn't dislike Jaylah but she did think she was weird. And she didn't have time for this creepy girl messing up her plans.

River dropped her head as Jaylah approached her table.

"Hey River. Why you not sitting with us?"

"I don't like girls."

"I don't either but it's so fun. I have never been in a strip club before. These girls are amazing!"

"Well, be careful because if you spend too much time in this place, you might start to like girls."

"Oh, so this is not your first time here?"

River had to think quick. She didn't really know how to respond. "I have never been here, but I have been to a strip club before. You know, girl's night out type of deal."

"Why do girls like girl strip clubs?"

"I don't know Jaylah, but like I told you, be careful."

"Well, I don't think I want girls but I think I wouldn't mind being a dancer."

"No!" River shouted before she could stop herself.

"What? Why not?"

"I... I have just heard horrible stories from girls who have worked in strip clubs."

"These girls seem to be having fun."

"They have fun until you don't."

"Have you ever worked in a strip club?"

"Why do you keep asking so many questions?"

"I'm just curious."

"Ever heard the expression curiosity killed the cat?"

Jaylah's eyes grew wide. "Umm.. yeah."

"Don't be curious Jaylah. Stay innocent."

"Is there something you want to tell me?"

River knew she had said too much. "Look I gotta go. My man is waiting on me."

"Ohh... that's why you don't wanna be here. I got you. If I had a man, I wouldn't be here either."

"You're a cute girl Jaylah. Why don't you have a man."

Jaylah looked around the room and then leaned in close to River. "Because I am here for the same reason as you are. Revenge."

# CHAPTER THIRTY-SEVEN

"Dang it, dang it, dang it. How am I supposed to get a record deal if I can't even come up with a decent song? Who am I kidding, I don't need a decent song, I need a hit." Logan Bryant threw another piece of paper into the trash bin. He sat staring at the keyboard before him. "Maybe if I change the melody. AHHHHHHHHHHHHHH." He yelled out in frustration. "These lyrics are whack and this music is whack. This whole song is whack, whack, whack!" He shouted as he banged the notepad against the keyboard. "Axel is not going to listen to this crap. And if I don't bring him something real, he'll never listen to anything else that I come up with. I gotta get this right. I only got one shot. I can't blow this."

Logan stood up and walked over to the window of his third-floor apartment. He loved being up high. It made him feel like he was on top of the world. If only he could write songs like he was on top of the world, cause right now, the way he was writing, he might as well move into the basement. Logan always had dreams of being an award-winning songwriter. But up until now he had only written one song. He thought about just giving up on it, but every time he turned on the radio, it was like the songs reached out to him and he would say to himself, "I can do this!" So, he would be inspired to try writing more songs, but unfortunately success had escaped him. He didn't want to be a one hit wonder. If he was going to Axel, he wanted to show him that he had staying power. He desperately needed more songs.

Logan's cell phone began to sound off. His girls were getting off work. He almost got tired of working the switchboard. That's what he liked to call it. He was always picking up multiple calls, putting them on hold, transferring them to voice mail and only taking the calls he deemed most important at the time.

"What's going on girl?" Logan pretended to know exactly who he was talking to even though he had no idea. He knew she would eventually let him know who she was.

"Nothing much, just glad to be home from work." Said the voice on the other end of the phone.

*Here we go.* Logan thought. *I'm finally going to figure out who this is when she tells me about her work day.* He knew where all his girls worked and that's how he kept track. "So why don't you tell me about your day, maybe it will help you relieve some of that stress." Logan replied, sounding concerned.

"Logan you are so sweet, that's why I love you."

"I know you do, so come on, let me have it." Logan knew he had her.

"Well, you know how it is at the unemployment office..."

*Yes!* Logan celebrated to himself. *It's Lisa.* As she was still going on and on about her day, Logan let his mind drift back to the day he met Lisa... "Good morning, how can I help you?" Lisa recited the familiar phrase without even looking up from her computer.

"You could start by looking up so I can see how beautiful your eyes are."

Lisa looked up and before she could tell him where to go and how to get there, a smile spread across her face. Normally it would be some ugly, broke joker trying to get an easy job, but this guy was far from it. Well, she didn't really know if he was broke or not. I mean after all he was at a temp service, which meant, he had no job. But he didn't dress like it. He looked like he could've just stepped out of a magazine. She was willing to humor him until she could find out some more details. As of now, everything felt so right. As she gazed into his eyes and he gazed into hers, she could tell they were thinking the same thing: *This is going to be a good day.*

"I was wrong, not beautiful, more like amazing." Logan said without even changing his tone of voice.

"Thank you." Lisa couldn't stop blushing. "So, what can I do for you Mr...."

"Logan, just call me Logan."

"Have a seat Logan and tell me what I can do for you."

"Well, for starters, I'm looking for a secondary job." Logan lied. "I need something part-time and temporary. Just need a little extra cash so I can make some things happen." Logan knew how to lay it on thick. Talking about secondary job, he didn't even have a primary one. And extra cash, try no cash at all. But there was one thing Logan knew how to do and that was making broke look good. All he needed was women like this pretty little ray of sunshine to get captivated by him and then they will fight to pay his bills. All he needed to do was reel her in. Right about now he knew he already had her on the hook.

"I don't think we have anything like that right now. We do have some temporary jobs but they are all full time."

"Dang, I guess I'll take it, I will just have to work something out with my other job or work my butt off, it will probably be more like work my butt off."

"Well, let me see what I can do."

By the time Logan walked out of that office, he not only had an easy job with good pay, but he also had Lisa's number and a date for Saturday night. This is getting way too easy. Logan thought to himself as he left the office with a satisfied smile on his face.

"So that's pretty much how it went." Lisa finally took a breather after talking for about 20 minutes straight.

"I'm sorry you had a rough day, Lisa. Don't worry, tomorrow will be better."

"I know. I always feel better after I talk to you."

"And I like making you feel better."

"How about you make me feel better tonight?"

"Girl, you know pay day ain't till Friday. I can't be half stepping when I'm taking my baby out, especially when she's had a bad day."

"Oh boy stop, you know I got you. I just want to see you. So don't make me wait, please."

Logan loved to hear them beg. He waited a minute before he answered, seeing as how he almost couldn't contain his amusement at how that line always worked.

"Girl, you are super special. I guess I'll let you take me out this time then." More like the last five times. He couldn't remember the last time he actually paid to take a girl out.

*I guess when you got it, you just got it.* Logan thought to himself as he closed the deal with Lisa.

"Who knows maybe she'll inspire me to write a song, or not." Logan couldn't help but laugh at his own joke.

"Well, I guess I'll start getting ready, cause it don't look like I'll be writing any songs today." Logan got up from his keyboard and put his voicemail on speakerphone so he can hear all the girls he missed out on tonight. Whichever impressed him the most would be the one he would let take him out tomorrow.

"After all a man's gotta eat." Logan burst into laughter as he headed towards the shower.

# CHAPTER THIRTY-EIGHT

Lisa pushed the end icon on her cellphone. Why did she even bother with people like Logan. He was beyond cute but he was broke. She should have never believed that he just needed some extra cash. He was definitely in the unemployment office because he was just that, unemployed. But nevertheless, she had already agreed to pay for dinner so she had to keep up the appearance that she had money even though she was flat broke. The borderline nice house she was renting was taking everything she had and then some. She had to keep the lie going that she was moderately successful. Even if she was only lying to herself. After everything she had given up, it had to be worth it, right? Lisa packed her things, wasn't much. A book, her phone and her compact she kept on her desk. It was not quite quitting time but she figured no other clients would come in.

"Tiffany, I gotta go. Can you cover me?"

"You gotta go to your other job?" Tiffany joked.

Lisa regretted telling Tiffany about her other source of income.

"I'm just joking girl. You know I got you."

Lisa rolled her eyes and quickly exited the room. She decided against the elevator and made a dash for the stairs before the tears started rolling down her face. She got tired of sleeping with guys for money just to buy groceries or pay for a dinner that she shouldn't be paying for. Yet, here she was about to spread them wide once again. She almost vomited in her mouth as she trotted down the last flight of stairs. She hit the door that led to the parking structure and quickly made her way to her used Honda Accord. When she used, she meant used. It barely made it from point A to point B, but it looked good on the outside... kinda.

Lisa opened her door and sat in her car. She fiddled around to find her phone. Who would be her victim today or rather who would she allow herself to fall victim to? Which guy was the least sick? Lisa scrolled past a couple of names until she came to Eric. Eric was ok, he just wasn't as graced as she wanted him to be below the belt and she had to do a lot of faking. She didn't know if she was up for acting today. Although it's what she came to L.A to do. Just not quite like that. She continued to scroll. Andrew. Andrew wasn't a looker, twenty-five years her senior with plenty of money to spare, the bonus... he was quick and to the point. He never lasted more than five or six minutes. Perfect. *Cause I don't have a lot of time.* Lisa thought as she pushed call.

An hour later, Lisa was headed back home with $3000.00 in her pocket. Andrew was feeling very generous today. And she was thankful since Logan wanted to go an expensive restaurant. She had the mind to cancel and splurge on herself, or just save it for when she got low. So many decisions, so little time. What the heck. It would be nice to go to a nice place to eat, with someone who was actually cute and good in the bed. Might as well treat myself.

## CHAPTER
# THIRTY-NINE

Phoenix had played the game real well. He was now not only sleeping with Cedric and Faith, but he eventually slid Skye into the mix. He couldn't resist. He wanted to see if everything about them was identical. It absolutely was not. Even though he did enjoy Faith much more than Skye. Skye had been around the block and it was evident. Faith was more reserved than Skye and it was also evident. All in all, Phoenix was loving every minute of it. Autumn had become more withdrawn, especially after she asked him several times about setting a date and he put her off. She had finally jumped on board with going ahead with the marriage. But now it was he who was having second thoughts. He realized that he could just be engaged to Autumn and still have the best of both worlds. He told her he just wasn't ready yet. He told her he needed to know for sure that she and Axel weren't an issue. Something she could never answer. She continued to tell him that Axel would always be in her life because he was her best friend. Phoenix would tell her, its either him or me and that statement always bought him more time to play the field.

Jaylah and River sat at the café where the dancers usually hung out. They spotted Faith sitting at a table and phoenix sitting at another table. After a few minutes Faith got up and walked out. Phoenix waited about three minutes more and he himself exited the café.

Jaylah and River looked at each other.

"I can't believe Faith is sleeping with Phoenix. How could she do this to Autumn?" River was furious. "I suspected it but I really believe it now. I should tell Autumn."

Jaylah kept quiet. She didn't know if they should tell Autumn or not, but on the flip side of that coin it could get her closer to Autumn. She just had to get to her before River did.

"What you think?" River picked up her smoothie and took a sip.

"I don't know River. She may hate us if we say something. I definitely don't want to jeopardize my position on the team. It's only been six months."

"I guess you're right. Plus, I don't want to be the one to hurt Autumn. Somebody needs to tell her. "

"Autumn is a smart girl. She'll figure it out. I guess I can see your revenge is not on Autumn since you're trying to help her?"

River looked around. "I don't want to talk about that here. Besides I never told you I was here for revenge on anyone."

"Oh, you didn't have to. I can see the look in your eyes. You can dance. But that is not why you are here."

"Is your revenge on Autumn?" River asked trying to flip the script.

"If I told you. I might have to kill you too."

"Oh, we are on that kind of revenge."

"Naw, not really. Death only comes to those who try to stand in my way."

"Really, you ever killed anyone before?"

"That's for me to know and you hopefully not to find out."

"Whatever Jaylah." River didn't think Jaylah could possibly have killed anyone, but she was crazy and she had that crazy look in her eyes. She just might have killed someone. Even though River was here for revenge, she still didn't know if she herself was capable of pulling the trigger. Guess she would soon find out.

Jaylah was still thinking how she could share the news with Autumn. This has to be her ticket in. She would have to turn into a modern- day Sherlock Holmes and start finding clues that would be evident of the affairs. Them leaving the café around the same time wasn't definitive enough. Jaylah zoned back into River's conversation. She didn't know what she was talking about. She liked River ok, but she wasn't here to make friends with anybody except Autumn. River was just a better hang out buddy than Skye and Faith. She hated them and she was determined to take them down along with anyone else that got in her way.

# CHAPTER FORTY

"Logan this is a really nice restaurant. If only you were paying for the meal, this would be the perfect date." Lisa walked through the door as Logan held it open, just like the gentlemen she wished he was.

"I told you we could go home and just wait until payday."

"No, Logan, I'm sorry, I didn't mean to bring that up again. I am just happy to be out with you."

Logan smiled as she walked through the second set of doors that led to the waiting room. He knew this restaurant was expensive and he wouldn't have brought her here, but he heard that Axel might be here, so he just had to get there and see if he could at least get a meeting with him.

"How many in your party." A light-bright, petite woman with long hair greeted them.

Logan was almost speechless. She was absolutely beautiful. He loved light skinned women. Lisa was a little more brown than he preferred but she was good company and had a nice body, so he decided she would do.

*Why couldn't I have come here alone?* Logan thought to himself. *How am I gonna get her number while I'm out with someone else? Well, I have accomplished even more difficult things than this. I'll have her number by the end of the night.* He smiled at the thought of it.

"Two." Logan responded as he gave her his, *I know I'm with her but I want you,* smile.

"Okay. Can you give me one moment and I'll see what we have." The pretty hostess had not taken her eyes off Logan since his arrival. Lisa might as well not even been there.

"This little girl is really trying me." Lisa as always was ready to fight. Any woman who even thought about looking at Logan, she was all over them.

"Calm down girl, you know I only got eyes for you."

Lisa blushed, feeling secure again.

A few minutes later the hostess walked back to where Logan and Lisa were standing.

"Your table is ready if you will just follow me."

The hostess walked down a long walk way and then turned left down another long walkway and then to the right. Finally, they arrived at their table.

"Here we are." She proclaimed smiling as if she just accomplished some big goal.

Logan pulled out Lisa's seat for her and as she was sitting, he turned away where Lisa couldn't see what was going on and gave the hostess another once over and like clockwork, she slipped him her number as she walked off. Logan discreetly put the number in his pocket as he walked to his side of the table.

"So, what is the cheapest thing on this menu, cause I don't want my baby going broke."

"Logan, you know you can get anything you want baby. I got you." Lisa knew Logan was full of it, but what choice did she have. Nothing better had popped up so Logan is what she was stuck with.

"As long as you let me get you back."

"Definitely."

*If only she knew I wasn't talking about taking her out.* Logan thought to himself, hopeful of the end of the night activities.

Logan took a sip of his wine. He was going to need something a little stronger than this if he was going to get through this date with Lisa. She hadn't shut up since they got there. But then it happened. Logan couldn't believe his eyes. It was him. Axel Smith. He felt for the drive that contained his demo in his jacket pocket. Yes. He remembered to bring it. But just as shocked as he was to see Axel, the woman on his arm caught his attention even the more. She was gorgeous. She had a bit of a toffee tan color. She was definitely mixed with something. And that body. Logan couldn't take his eyes off of her. This girl was beyond fine. Logan knew Axel only kept the baddest chicks around him, but he had really outdone himself this time. Logan finally noticed Lisa staring at him.

"What are you at looking so hard?" She asked emphasizing every word. Logan could tell she was fire mad, but he knew how to tame the beast and get himself off the hook. "You should see for yourself."

"I don't want to look at another woman."

"It's a man and before you say something stupid, it's Axel Smith."

Lisa almost stopped breathing. Her eyes grew twice as big. Logan knew how Lisa felt about Axel Smith. "She was absolutely in love with him and always wanted to meet him."

"Are you serious?"

"Yes."

"You're not playing?"

"See for yourself."

Lisa casually turned around in her seat. "Oh my god, it is him! It's really him! Did you know he would be here?"

"Why do you think I brought you to this expensive restaurant? I wanted it to be a surprise. You know, to show my gratitude for you picking up the bill and all." Logan lied.

"You are the absolute best boyfriend ever." Lisa couldn't believe going out with Logan had been worth it after all.

Now it was Logan's eyes that grew twice their size. *Did she just say what I thought she said? Oh, I'm definitely gonna have to fall back on this one. She's getting too comfortable with me. After tonight it will be a good long minute before I call her again.*

Logan decided to let her statement ride for the time being. He allowed his attention to fall back on the beauty that graced Axel's arm. Logan could almost imagine her holding on to his arm. He wondered what it would feel like to be accompanied by this woman. He wondered what her voice sounded like. How her skin felt. He wondered how beautiful her smile was. *Her smile.* He thought again. Logan paid close attention to the girl that seemed to be in another world as Axel stopped and greeted people on the way to his seat. She had not smiled since he'd laid eyes on her. Her eyes, as beautiful as they were, were empty. She seemed like she didn't want to be with Axel. *What girl in their right mind would not want to be with Axel Smith?* This intrigued Logan and he became determined to find out why. *I have to meet with him tonight.* As much as he wanted to give Axel his demo, he wanted to get closer to that girl even more. His demo lost priority as he stared into the eyes of this broken beauty. Why was she so sad? What was her story? These were questions Logan was determined to get answers to.

"You think we could meet him?" Lisa broke Logan from his thoughts.

"I don't know. Maybe. We'll see."

As Axel came closer to their table, Logan's mind began to race. *How do I get this guy's attention?*

Logan knew he would regret this later, but he felt he had no other choice. He grabbed Lisa's hand and looked into her eyes. He talked loud enough to be noticed but not loud enough to be found out.

"You mean so much to me. I'm so glad you could finally break away from your busy schedule to go out with me." He was staring so deep into her eyes. He almost believed his own lies. "I just wanted to sing this song for you."

Logan began to sing a bit of the one song he had completed. He was thankful it was a love song. People began to stare. Logan lowered his voice, so it would seem to others as if he was trying not to draw attention. And then he accomplished his goal. Both Axel and his beauty were looking his way.

# CHAPTER FORTY-ONE

Phoenix stepped outside of the terminal and hailed a taxi. He was looking forward to spending time with Josiah. Phoenix loved being spoiled. He thought about retiring to Paris for good and just letting Josiah take care of him, but then there was Cedric. Cedric was amazing as well and just as good of a provider. He was torn between the two. Phoenix thought about Autumn. He was ready to ditch her. He liked being taken care of. He didn't want to be the one to do it. With him having Cedric and Josiah, Phoenix no longer needed Autumn. He just needed to settle on one of these guys. He couldn't risk them finding out about each other and then he would be back on the streets trying to fend for himself. That's why he was in Paris once again. He kept telling himself that this would be the trip that he made a decision, but he never could bring himself to do it. Could he? He was so conflicted. Living in Paris would be the more idea place to be. He wouldn't have to hide as much. Or he could stay in California and just come out as bisexual. I mean, he did enjoy women from time to time. But would his men be okay with him stepping out with a woman. He didn't know the answer to that. One thing Phoenix did know is that he wasn't ready to be monogamous. He wondered how much longer could he string these guys along before they gave up on him altogether. Then he finds out some other guy is living the life of his dreams. He had just had this conversation with Cedric. Cedric was ready to be exclusive. He even talked about coming out. That had made Phoenix nervous. So, he bailed. He stayed with Autumn for a night, but he could tell, that was over. That's when he got a call from Josiah and it was game on. Phoenix packed a bag and hoped a flight. He would deal with Autumn when he returned. One way or the other. Maybe. He had to be careful of Axel. Axel had stopped him in the hall a week ago and pretty much threatened his life if he hurt Autumn. He would have to find a way around his wrath.

Phoenix paid the driver once he made it to Josiah's condo. The condo that used to be his condo. The condo that could be his condo once again. Phoenix took the elevator to the top floor. He stepped off and headed to the door. He was just about to knock when the door opened and Josiah pulled him in and kissed him passionately on the lips.

"Well, you definitely know how to welcome a guy home. What else comes with those lips?"

"First, I made you something to eat and then we'll get to dessert later. "

"I like the sound of that."

Phoenix followed Josiah to the balcony where dinner was being served.

"So, how are things in L.A.?" Josiah asked as he cut his steak.

"Good. Just trying to tie up some loose ends."

"Does that mean you made up your mind to move back here permanently?"

"I have been giving it some real thought."

Josiah gently placed his fork and knife on the plate trying to control the anger he felt. "You said that last time. Are you still planning on marrying Autumn."

"Absolutely not. That's a done deal."

Josiah's eyes lit up. "Really?"

"Yes. I just need to do it in an amicable way because her best friend is crazy and he won't stand for me hurting her again."

Josiah reached over and grabbed Phoenix's hand. "Look, you don't have to even go back. Just stay here. I'll take care of you until you figure out what you want to do or you could do nothing. I got you. I've always had you. I just want us to be together for good this time. No cheating. No confusion. Just me and you. What do you say?"

"I like the way that sounds. But I do have to go back. I have to get my things and let Autumn down easy. I'll be fine. I promise."

# CHAPTER FORTY-TWO

Michelle readied herself to accompany Axel to his restaurant. The only one of seven that didn't bear his name. Most people didn't even know he owned it. Michelle hated going to any of Axel's restaurants; although it really wouldn't have mattered if he owned it or not. Any place Axel went to, he shut the place down. He took so much attention, half of the people would leave and the other half would stay only to try and catch a glimpse of the great Axel Smith. Billionaire music producer. Axel owned three different record labels; although he didn't physically manage them all himself. If you asked Michelle, she would say, Axel just wanted people to be subject to him and not be able to hold their own. Many of the would-be producers settling for being managers, under him, were glad to do so. It helped with gaining prospective clients when they told them they were affiliated with Axel Smith. The clients usually signed right after that.

Michelle prepared herself to zone out as she walked into the massive doors. You would think they were entering a five-star hotel instead of a restaurant. But that was Axel. Always doing it big. Michelle never even brandished a smile unless she was required to. Axel always gave her a what to do and what not to do speech before they exited his black-on-black Cadillac Escalade, complete with chauffeur. Michelle didn't really see the point in smiling anyways. She knew people weren't really staring at her face. She was nothing more than something to be admired for a moment, but not concentrated on for a long period of time; as if she were a necklace, a watch or a pair of diamond earrings. She was to be practically invisible, per Axel's instructions. Michelle would just hang on to Axel's arm, remaining quiet and still as he greeted his guests and then finally, they would be seated. The menu would be whatever Axel ordered. He very rarely allowed Michelle to order her own food. She was always suspicious when he did. She was sure it was a setup. Axel never gave her anything good without returning the favor with something much worse.

Michelle shifted her weight from one foot to the other. Axel was taking longer than usual to greet his guest tonight. She was also getting tired of him jerking her back and forth. He kept moving and laughing and doing whatever he wanted to do but refused to let go of her arm. Every now and then she would feel his eyes fixate on her. She would just stare straight ahead as if she didn't notice. No way was she about to look Axel in his eyes. He hated when she looked into his eyes unless he wanted her to. The few times she was made to, she would rather not. It was those times when he had his hands around her throat and he wanted to see the hopelessness in her eyes. Or the times when he was demeaning her publicly or privately, so he could see the hurt in her eyes. Or the times when he was beating her, so he could see the fear in her eyes. In either scenario she would rather not give him the satisfaction, but she knew she had no choice. This was one of those times, if she had of looked at him, he would probably begin to squeeze her arm until she would visibly let him know she was in tremendous pain and then dare her to make a scene. She wasn't in the mood to fight him tonight, so she kept her eyes forward.

Axel stopped to talk to one of his mangers that happened to be entertaining a client. He wanted to say hello to the client and make them feel a part of the Axel Smith family. The client couldn't stop smiling, from what Michelle could see out of her peripheral. As they were about to walk away Michelle exhaled, grateful that the next stop would be their table; that is until a voice caught her attention. Before she knew it, she turned and looked. She forgot about Axel. She forgot about the people around her. She forgot that at that moment she was someone else's property and that she should act accordingly. All she could think about was finding that voice. She heard a lot of singing in her short life, but this voice was unlike anything she had ever heard. If she were a record producer, she would sign this guy on the spot. To Michelle's immediate right was a table for two where a young guy and girl sat. He was holding her hand and trying to quietly serenade her. It seemed as if he didn't want to draw any attention, but his love for this girl couldn't help but spill for others to hear. She didn't even think he was aware he had just set himself up to audition for the biggest producer in California. She watched how he pronounced every word with tender love and care. She watched how he softly caressed his girlfriend's hand. She loved how his eyes locked onto hers, oblivious to everyone else in the room. She couldn't help but feel saddened. Would she ever find someone to love her like that? Would she ever get away from Axel, so she could? And the question that haunted her the most; would she live long enough to find out?

Axel didn't seem to mind that she had broken character. He was obviously just as amazed as she was at this guy's amazing voice. Axel nearly dragged Michelle over to the table were the guy sat. Seeing someone approach his table caused him to jump.

"I apologize if I startled you." Axel said taking a step back.

Michelle rolled her eyes. As if he was ever sorry about anything. If he really wanted to apologize, he could apologize for the way he was sizing up his date. Michelle had noticed that Axel had looked over this guy's lady friend from head to toe as if the guy wasn't even sitting there. Either the guy was too star struck to notice or he didn't care about this girl the way she thought he did.

"No sir. No apologies necessary. I'm honored to be interrupted by you sir." This guy was kissing butt like a pro.

"I haven't heard a voice like that in a minute. Where have you been hiding man?"

"Well sir to be honest I have been wanting to send some material to you, but it had to be right and up until now nothing was what I wanted."

"You said up until now?"

"Yes sir."

"So that means you got something ready for me?"

"I sure do sir. I just hope it's up to your standards."

"Well, if it is a demo, you don't need it. You've already passed."

"Actually, it's some original music. I'm a songwriter. That's my passion more than singing to be honest."

Michelle's eyes lit up. *A singer/songwriter.* This guy had her full attention now.

"But you are willing to sing, aren't you?" Axel asked the guy as he smiled and nodded at his girl once more. And of course, she was blushing something serious. Well, Michelle hated to say it, but this guy was not going to enjoy any postdate activities because his girl would more than likely be going home with Axel. Michelle was saddened at the thought.

Even after he just sung this beautiful love song to this girl, she would probably gladly leave him for a one-night stand with Axel.

"Why don't you and your lovely lady come and join me at my table." Axel released Michelle for the first time since they entered the restaurant. He held out his hand for the young lady to grab, which she did and began to escort her and her seemingly unfazed boyfriend to his table. Michelle knew to find her way to the table and not be too far behind. Just as she expected, as soon as he reached his table, he looked back to make sure Michelle was right by his side. This time she lifted her eyes to meet his gaze. She knew this would be one of the times she would be required to look him in the eye. It was his way of silently letting her know. *I own you.*

He wanted to look in her eyes to make sure the message was received loud and clear.

After seating his guest, he motioned for Michelle to slide in the booth where he would be seated and he then slid in right beside her, closing her in so she had nowhere to go, just in case she thought about testing him tonight. And he would no doubt go in on her mercilessly right in front of their company.

Axel wrapped his arm around Michelle all the while keeping his eye on his newest target sitting before him. She kept blushing. You would think a man having his arm around another woman would dissuade a woman from entertaining him, but now a days, it just made him that much more desirable. *If only she knew what she was about to get herself into.* Michelle thought to herself. As much as these women wanted in Axel's bed, she wanted out of it that much more. She would gladly trade places with any woman who wanted her position.

Michelle did her best to snuggle in close. She didn't want to defy Axel in front of the new people. Michelle had a slight flashback of how Axel had exerted his control over her in the past; especially in his own restaurants. If she got out of line in the slightest way, he would back hand her clear out of her seat and expect her to get up and act like nothing happened. But not Michelle. She was a fighter. She would always stay on the ground to draw more attention.

"Get up Michelle!" Axel would yell at her.

Michelle would just lay there as if she was too hurt to get up. Axel would look around trying to assure that no one saw Michelle defying him.

"Get up Michelle, if you know what's good for you!" Axel would get angrier and angrier.

Sometimes Michelle would go ahead and get up, embarrassed no doubt, but sometimes she would just lay there and wait for him to come pick her up and drag her out of the restaurant. But not today. Michelle was curious about this new guy with the voice that made her tingle all over. This was a meeting she didn't want to miss on the account of her being dragged out.

"Dude, why haven't I heard about you?" Axel asked finally taking his eyes off of new guys girl.

"Like I said, I had to come up with the perfect song."

"Yeah, I got that. Truth be told, you could've sung anything, and I would've signed you."

Michelle stared at the guy sitting across from her. Normally she would never. Her job was to keep her head down and not draw any attention to herself. But this guy made her feel a certain type of way. Was it his deep dark eyes or his nicely built physique? Was it his voice or the way he looked into his girl's eyes as he sang his song? Michelle wished she had someone to look in her eyes that way; make her feel safe and loved. Axel never made her feel that way. Every time he looked into her eyes, all she felt was fear and shame.

"Wow, wish I had of known that." The guy beamed.

"So, what's the name I'm putting on this contract man?"

"Logan. Logan Alexander."

*Logan.* Michelle repeated in her mind. She found herself longing to hear him sing just one more time.

"And what's your name pretty lady?" Axel focused his attention back on the girl.

"Lisa." She responded smiling from ear to ear as she slightly dropped her head.

"You ready to have a famous boyfriend?"

Logan's eyes darted up at Axel as if silently pleading him not to go down that road. Michelle relaxed a bit as she herself picked up the signal. Maybe he is not as dedicated to this girl as she thought. Then another thought hit her. *He played Axel. He knew he was around and had to get his attention.* Michelle smiled at the thought. She loved his initiative. She quickly straightened her face, so she wouldn't attract Axel's attention, but she kept her eyes on Logan.

"Of course. Logan knows I'm down for him no matter what." Lisa beamed as she slid in closer to Logan.

Logan sat motionless. He didn't respond to Lisa in any way. His eyes remained locked on Axel and Michelle knew they were having an entire players conversation without uttering a word. The conversation must have ended after about two minutes; they both broke out in laughter.

"I see we are going to get along very well." Axel finally spoke, nodding his head.

Axel motioned for the waitress to assist his table and she promptly excused herself and rushed right over. As Axel was leaning over whispering to the waitress, Logan found his opportunity to finally get a closer look at the beauty that was still snuggled under Axel's arm. He noticed her staring at him the whole time he was talking to Axel, but for some reason he felt if he looked back, it would cause trouble and he didn't want that. He was finally right where he wanted to be. Having dinner with Axel Smith talking about signing a contract. The only thing he hated was the fact that Lisa was here with him. He would've loved to be experiencing this moment alone. Lisa was very temporary. Now she would be hanging on to him like a leech. He was going to have to figure out a way to drop her. Logan knew it was both stupid and risky to sing a love song to her, but he was desperate. He had to get Axel's attention. If he couldn't hand him a demo, he would just showcase his talent; although being an artist wasn't his goal. He just wanted to get his foot through the door. Logan discreetly took in all of the broken beauty. He had never seen anyone as beautiful, but there was so much pain in her eyes. Normally looking at a girl like her, his mind would go straight to sex, but at that moment, all he wanted to do was hold her. She had on a black strapless cocktail dress. He looked at her bare arms. He could see fresh bruises on them. As if someone had grabbed her with a lot of force. Logan concluded that the bruises were probably not her only ones. This beautiful girl was being abused. Logan wanted to rescue her. Seems he had another mission in Axel's company other than making music. He had to be this girl's savior.

# CHAPTER FORTY-THREE

"Harmony, you need to just leave this whole thing alone. You knew what kind of man Axel was before you got engaged."

Harmony couldn't believe the words that were coming out of her father's mouth. Was this the same man that told her she needed to secure the bag.

"You told me to reach for the stars, well, I grabbed the sun, moon and stars with Axel."

"I know Harmony, but Axel is a real shady character and I just don't trust him. I never did."

"Then why did you sign on when he came to the house. After you guys talked, you were all but singing his paise."

"That's before I found out some more things about him." He didn't know what else to say. He couldn't tell his daughter that he was selling her out for a secret he was afraid would get out, but that was exactly what he was doing.

"Have you talked to your mom?"

"Yes, and she is singing the same song you are."

His eye brow raised. What did Axel have on his wife that would make her recoil. That usually wasn't her style. She was vicious if nothing else. He decided to keep this information in the back of his mind. He knew he needed to find out what her secret was just in case he would need it one day. It just might be the thing he needed to get from under Axel's thumb.

"So, what are you going to do?" He asked more interested now.

"I don't know. I know I have to go back. As humiliating as it might be, I'm going to have to go back and see if I can rejoin Autumn's dance team. That way, I'll have access to Axel. If nothing else I will make his life a living hell." A smile started to spread across Harmony's face. That was the nice version of the story that she could tell her dad. What she really wanted was to facilitate his personal tour of hell. She wanted him dead.

## CHAPTER

# FORTY-FOUR

Lisa walked up to the building where she worked on the third floor. "Well, you miserable prison. I won't be gracing your halls much longer."

She stepped inside and headed to the third floor. She opened the door and found Tiffany was already at her desk. She was always early. *I don't know if she's waiting on a promotion or what.* Lisa thought as she slid into her desk.

"Well, you seem to have a little bit more bounce in your step today." Tiffany turned to give her full attention to Lisa hoping for some juicy details.

"You would not believe how my night went! My days at this awful place are definitely numbered!"

"That good!"

"Better. You know that guy Logan I was telling you about? Turns out he can sing! He took me to Axel Smith's restaurant and he sang to me. So happens, Axel was walking by and he offered him a contract."

"Are you serious?"

"Would I lie?"

Tiffany shrugged.

"Anyway, I'm not lying. It's on YouTube. Check it out for yourself. But let me finish my story first. So, we got to have dinner with Axel and everything. Axel even personally invited me to the studio and called me Logan's girlfriend."

"So, is that what you are?"

"I am now."

"Is that what Logan is saying?"

"Logan doesn't have a choice. Wait a minute, who's side are you on?"

"Yours Lisa. I just don't want you to get hurt, that's all."

"Girl, believe me, I got this. I already have a plan."

"And what's that?"

"One of two things. First thing I'm going to either get him to solidify our relationship and fall deeply in love with me or I'm going to have to get pregnant and then he can't leave me."

"So, you haven't learned yet huh?"

"See this is why I'm going to stop telling you all my business! I can't believe you would even bring that up!"

"Lisa, I'm just saying, you already have..."

"You know what, just stop talking to me permanently. I know what I'm doing." Lisa went to her desk and began working on her schedule. She couldn't believe the nerve of Tiffany. Deep down she knew she was right, but she had to try anyway. She couldn't let this one get away.

## CHAPTER

# FORTY-FIVE

Autumn pulled the popcorn out of the microwave. It was another night at home alone. She didn't know if Phoenix had gone off to Paris or what. She had stopped asking. She didn't care. If she did what she really wanted to do, she would call Phoenix and tell him to come get all of his stuff and get out. She would be done with him. And this time she would never take him back. Ever. She grabbed a Coke Zero out of the fridge and headed to her favorite sofa and plopped down. This was her ritual "me time". She loved to watch movies and eat popcorn. She never went to theaters. She hated them. She loved to enjoy the movie by herself. Most film makers never had a problem sending her over an advance copy of their movie. That was one of the benefits of being famous. The down side; always having to be perfect, or your fans just might bail on you. But again, if Autumn did what she really wanted to do, she would throw caution to the wind and just enjoy life. She had made a lot of money and had invested well. She could not make another album for a minute. Go off the radar and just enjoy being Autumn. Not the Autumn Dance, but just enjoy being her. The girl who loved to dance and sing just for enjoyment. The girl who loved sweat pants and t-shirts. The girl who loved to curl up on the couch and read a good book or watch and an exciting movie. She didn't want to have to think about the pressures of her life. She didn't want to have to deal with Phoenix or Axel for that matter. She didn't want to have to deal with competing with Charlie or coming out with a new album. She just wanted to be Autumn. Autumn popped a couple of pieces of popcorn in her mouth. She didn't feel much like watching the movie anymore. She wanted to start planning her new make-believe life. Or did it have to be? Could this life that she was thinking about actually become a reality? Could she actually leave the music business? *What is in this popcorn? I am really losing it. There is no way Axel is going to let me out of my contract.* And then it hit her. Her contract was coming to an end. She remembered getting an email alert reminding her. She normally just hit renew and send it back but this time she hesitated. She had wanted to think about it. Something she had never done before. But here she was now and it was feeling like a real possibility. She felt trapped by her old life and she desperately wanted out. Then her mind fell on Michelle. She could imagine this was how Michelle felt. Trapped. She wished she could rescue Michelle from Axel and take her in and they could be roommates and they could enjoy life together. Autumn shook the thoughts from her head. She didn't want to disappoint herself by not achieving those goals. She wasn't ready to make those kinds of decisions. Or was she?

Autumn picked up the remote to start the movie when there was a knock at the door. She wondered who could be at her door. She wasn't expecting company. It can't be Phoenix. He has a key. Then she thought. *Axel. This better not be Axel. I don't have time for him tonight.* She got up and walked to the door. She was really going to have to update her security system. She never thought it was necessary but too many people were finding out where she lived and she didn't like it. She was going to have to get a gate with a camera and a passcode immediately.

She got up and walked to the door. She looked out the peephole and was surprised to see the figure on the other side of her door. She opened it.

"Harmony. What are you doing here?"

"Hey Autumn. I'm sorry to just show up at your house like this. I just didn't know where else to go."

"Oh my, come in. Is everything ok?"

"Yeah. I mean as good as it could be right?"

"I guess. How have you been?"

"Well, when Axel dumped me, I went to stay with my parents for a while. I was so hurt and upset."

"Understandably." Autumn tried to sympathize.

"I just needed some time to get my head together. Anyway, I realized I never told you I was leaving the team or anything and I'm sorry for that."

"It's cool. I completely understand."

"No, it was rude of me. To be honest, being on the dance team was the best part about my life. Look Autumn. I know we have not always seen eye to eye, but I respect who you are and what you do and I really would like to rejoin the dance team. I just don't have anything left good in my life."

"Well, I'm sure that's not true. You have your family and…" Autumn hesitated wondering if she was doing the right thing. "You always have your dance family. I would love for you to come back to the team. Right now, I can use all the help I can get."

Harmony's face lit up. "Thank you, Autumn! You won't regret this." Harmony picked up her purse and headed toward the door. "So, tomorrow then?"

"Yes, tomorrow at 8."

"See you then."

"Ok." Autumn closed the door and locked it before returning to her place on the sofa. "That was weird. I think I'm going to regret this." She said out loud. "Well, I might as well add to all the other things I regret in my life right now." Autumn leaned back on the sofa and pushed play; intent on drowning away all the stresses of her life, even if for one night.

Harmony returned to her vehicle. That was easier than I thought. She smiled satisfactory. Part one of her plan was now in play. She would get back on the team. Make Axel think that she was passed what he had done and then when he was most vulnerable, she would strike. I'm going to make you pay Axel Smith. Harmony recited for the millionth time. I'm going to make you pay big time. She pulled out of the Autumn's driveway feeling more hopeful than she did before she came.

# CHAPTER FORTY-SIX

"You know the routine right."

"Yes sir. I know the routine." Michelle hated being treated like a three-year-old before going into the grocery store.

"You know you got the smartest mouth I've ever seen. I guess that's why you interest me. You are the only one I know that has the nerve to talk to me like you do."

"I don't know what you mean."

"You will when we get back to the house."

Michelle's eyes got wide. She knew what that meant, and she was tired of him hitting on her all the time. She knew she should just keep quiet, but she couldn't. No matter how many times he hit her she just couldn't back down. She was just determined that nothing and no one would break her. Break her spirit. Break her hope. Her life may not have been much, but she was determined to break free and live the life that she planned to live and not the life that someone else had mapped out for her. She got free once. She would get free again.

Axel grabbed Michelle's arm and wrapped it around his. I guess he thought he was being gentlemen like. *It looks stupid to me.* Michelle thought to herself.

Axel and Michelle walked arm in arm to their usual table in the VIP section towards the back. They seemed like the perfect couple, but Michelle knew better. *Just because something glitters, doesn't mean it's gold.* Michelle thought to herself. Axel pulled the seat out for her.

"You okay babe, anything you need?" Axel asked as if he cared.

Michelle just looked at him. *You have got to be kidding me?* She thought. *You know exactly what you can do for me. Something like go find the deepest lake, jump in and drown. Then I would be great.* But Michelle knew not to let those words escape her lips, so she just shook her head instead.

"Good. I thought you were about to start getting testy before we even got our meal." Axel took his seat right next to hers. "You know things would be a lot easier for you if you would just stop fighting me. Don't I take good care of you? You have need for nothing. You have the best clothes and shoes. Your hair and nails stay done. Money is not a factor. What more do you want? Most women would take your place in a heartbeat, except they would know how to behave." Axel rolled his eyes at Michelle as he picked up the menu. "You are eating at the best restaurant in town right now. I don't know what your problem is?"

Michelle held her tongue once again. But she thought to herself. *Okay, let's do the math. I get to eat at the best restaurant and I also get beat at the best restaurant. No deal. I wear the best clothes, but I have to give up my body just to wear them. No deal. I keep my hair and nails done only because you constantly mess them both up when you knock me around, but I have to stay looking good for you. I may own a lot of clothes, shoes and plenty of material things; but you own me. NO DEAL!* Michelle was getting angrier by the minute. There was nothing about this life that she wanted. All the hell she went through was not worth being in the so-called, "perfect financial position". Not worth it at all when it cost you your mind, body and soul.

Michelle could feel hopelessness starting to set in. She tried to stay positive, she really did. But would she ever get out of this relationship? A relationship she was forced into. A relationship that she shouldn't be in. She remembered when she first got snatched up by Axel. He didn't care that she was only 17. Nowhere near legal. But he didn't care about any of that. If she could pass for 21, it didn't matter to him. And she did. Standing at 5'5 with a DDD rack and a rear end that made even the big booty video girls jealous. Michelle was every man's dream, but she considered it an absolute nightmare. When you have guys, who are willing to do anything to experience you, you would rather just be average. Michelle wished that a million times a day; to be average. Then maybe she wouldn't be in the position she's in now.

Michelle allowed her thoughts to come back to her present situation. Axel was rattling off his usual to the waitress all the while feeling her up, which the waitress was enjoying immensely. He then turned toward Michelle. "What would you like babe?"

Michelle was startled. This obviously was some kind of twisted joke, because he normally ordered for her. But what choice did she have but to play along. So, she did.

"I would like the grilled chicken, on rice, with steamed vegetables. With a sweet tea." Michelle looked up at the waitress with a smile. Michelle noticed that the waitress didn't smile back. All the women that came in contact with Michelle hated her. They all wanted to be in her position. Michelle knew she shouldn't get offended by it, but she did. It hurt like crazy. More than anything Michelle wanted a friend. And she hadn't been able to find one yet. Every female saw her as a threat and all she wanted to do was be their friend. If they so wanted to trade places with her, she would gladly oblige them. Axel never let her associate with anyone either, so that didn't help. If there was a girl that could overlook their desire to be with Axel and be her friend, he would never allow it. This was all a part of Axel's plan to keep her feeling hopeless. And to Michelle's dismay, it was wearing on her.

Axel looked at Michelle. "Is that what you really want? I mean really, really want?"

"Yes, I kind of have a taste for it." Michelle played along. She was sure the punch line was next in play.

"In that case, just give her a house salad with a water. Go ahead and add one lemon in there so she can feel special." Axel smiled at the waitress and handed her the menus along with a pat on her back side.

Michelle felt a pain grip her heart. She knew there was a catch and there it was. Find out what she really wanted and then strip it from her, further enforcing that he controlled her, and he can give and take at will.

Michelle tried not to let the tear that threatened to roll down her cheek escape, but it got through anyway. Axel saw it and as she expected, he capitalized on it.

"I know you're not sitting over here crying like a little girl. Every time I think you have matured a bit you go and do something childish like cry over some chicken you can't get. I'm getting real sick of you. But it's okay. You seem to like getting beat to sleep. That's fine with me. The exercise is good for me."

Michelle couldn't believe the foolishness that was coming out of this man's mouth. What he didn't realize is that she wasn't crying over the meal.

She was crying because he intentionally tried to rip her heart out every chance he got, and it hurt bad. She tried to numb herself to it, but who could get used to torment, day in and day out. It just wasn't in her makeup.

Just then Michelle heard a very familiar voice.

"Axel, my main man."

Michelle looked up to see Autumn Dance. She always enjoyed when she came around. Autumn was the only person Axel let talk to Michelle, but their encounters were very rare.

"Little Shelly, what's going on with you girl?"

"Nothing." Michelle beamed. She really wanted to be friends with Autumn but she was scared to get too close. She kept having flashbacks of what Axel did to Destiny and she didn't want the same thing to happen to Autumn.

"Stop treating her like a baby A. She already acts immature. I'm trying to get her to grow up." Axel teased Autumn.

"She is a baby Axel. And it's time you come to terms with that. You can't make her be something that she's not." Autumn shot back playfully.

"She's going to be whatever I want her to be and if she doesn't, she knows the consequences." Axel looked at Michelle to make sure she got the message.

"I'm not even going to comment on that because you already know how I feel about that. But that's your life." Autumn looked a bit defeated. She hated she agreed to come meet Axel. But she had to keep playing like everything was normal while she figured out what her next move would be. She also wanted to tell him about Harmony rejoining the team, but since he liked to throw surprises at her, she thought she might throw one at him.

"And you would be right to do so." Axel knocked Autumn from her thoughts. "So on to bigger and better things. I've got to get you in the studio with this dude I just signed. Logan Alexander. He is the real deal and I think he's going to be a real game changer."

"Yeah. I saw his video. It went viral. Signing people without talking to me again. It's cool tho."

"I know Autumn. I'm terrible but this dude is real slick. He only song to that girl to get my attention. Now he's trying to get rid of her. Man after my own heart. I had to sign him. But I'm going to help him out with his little dilemma. I got him."

"How are you going to do that?" Autumn wasn't sure she wanted to know the answer to that question.

"I'm going to pluck his girl's little flower. Give her some Axel VIP treatment. Get her away from my man and then send her on her way."

"You do know Michelle is sitting right there right?" Autumn felt embarrassed for her.

"And?" Axel responded without remorse.

"Anyway, that is wrong. But like I said, I'm out of it. I'm going to learn to stop asking you questions I don't want to know the answer to." Autumn turned to Michelle. "Michelle what do you think of the new artist?"

Michelle froze. She didn't know how to answer that question. She couldn't possibly tell Autumn that Logan made her tingle all over. She couldn't tell Autumn that Logan was the best singer she had ever heard, and she would love to make sweet music with him among other things. She looked up at Axel, who was staring at her intently. Autumn immediately regretted asking her.

"Don't worry about it, little Shelly. You don't have to answer." Autumn tried to save Michelle.

But Axel just wouldn't let her. "No, I want her to answer it."

Michelle could feel her stomach turning. This was sure to lead to a beat down and Michelle was still recovering from the last one when she accidentally yawned at one of his events and someone saw her. "He is a great singer."

"And..." Axel pushed.

"And I think that he will be a great asset to the company." Michelle tried to choose her words carefully.

"How?" Axel pushed further.

"That song he was singing seemed to be an original. So just as much as he can sing, he can probably write just as good."

Autumn was surprised at what Michelle knew. She smiled at her with pride.

"So, you think you know the business now?" Axel challenged.

"Well, when you're around the best producer in the business, you can't help but learn something." Michelle hoped to fan his flames.

"You think I'm stupid don't you? You think you can flatter me out of a beat down?"

"No. That's not what I'm trying to do. I..."

Before Michelle could finish her thought. He grabbed her leg under the table and squeezed it as hard as he possibly could until she couldn't help but respond to the pain. Michelle bent over and tapped the table, trying to get herself through the pain. Autumn looked on helplessly.

"Axel please." Autumn pleaded.

Axel held on for a couple of minutes more until he knew Michelle absolutely couldn't take anymore, then he let her go. Michelle began to sob as silently as she could. The pain was excruciating.

Autumn breathed a sigh of relief and realized she would have to choose her words more carefully. She didn't want to get Michelle in trouble.

Axel returned to his normal conversation like nothing ever happened. "So, are you going to do a song with Logan after he drops his first single or not? This could be just the answer you need for your little dilemma."

"Just might be. He seems to be very talented. I'm sure we could create some magic." Autumn was glad to move on from what had just transpired. But she could still see Michelle out of the corner of her eye, trying to regain her composure. She was just a baby. Autumn didn't know what to do but she desperately wanted to do something.

The drive home seemed like the longest ride ever. It always did when she knew what awaited her once they stepped behind closed doors. Michelle was already shaking like a leaf. She could already feel the pain from every blow of Axel's fist.

Michelle willed her legs to move as she stepped out of Axel's Escalade and walked up to the doorway. She entered in right in front of Axel as he kept his eye on her the entire time. She stood in the foyer and wondered where it was going to take place. Here or in his bedroom. Axel just stood there and stared at her. *Why did he have to make this so difficult?* Michelle thought to herself. *Why can't he just beat me and get it over with. I can't stand these psychological games he plays.* Michelle just stared back at him trying to figure out his next move. Axel grabbed her arm and led her to the bedroom. *I guess this is going down in the bedroom.* She didn't know what she preferred. Getting beat in any room was still getting beat. There were no consolation prizes.

Axel threw Michelle on the bed. She held her breath waiting for him to pounce on her, but he didn't. He began to take off his clothes. Michelle sat up on the bed, puzzled that he hadn't put his hands on her yet.

"I'm not even going to beat you, Michelle. You really ain't worth it." Axel continued to remove his clothing.

Michelle slowly breathed a sigh of relief. She was thankful for any and every break she could get.

"It seems like beating you isn't working. I only do it for my enjoyment, but I'm going to give you what you really need." Axel stood before Michelle fully exposed.

Michelle knew what this was. He was about to rape her. What way to make her feel even more worthless and empty than beating her is taking control of her body and soul in one fell swoop. He could look at her while he was violating her. She would see the evil in his eyes and the wicked smile on his face as he took what innocence and self-respect she had left. She now wished he had of just beat her and got it over with. This was bound to take longer and be way more awful than any beating could be.

Michelle closed her eyes as Axel climbed on the bed and began to violently rip her clothes from her body. Michelle just let it happen. She didn't want to fight. She wanted it over. That seemed to anger him more, because before she knew it, he hit her repeatedly. Then he still took his time and raped her.

"You're going to learn not to play with me Michelle. I promise you that." Axel pushed Michelle on the floor and there she slept all night.

Bloodied, bruised and naked. Shaking on the cold floor, Michelle cried herself to sleep.

CHAPTER

# FORTY-SEVEN

"Five, six, five, six, seven, eight." Autumn called out the count for her dancers. She hated having to come up with dance moves for an old song while Charlie had a hit single and was already in the studio working on the full album which she heard was going great. Autumn wanted to give up. She wanted to quit the music business altogether. But she knew if she did that Charlie would win and she couldn't possibly let that happen.

After going through the routine several more times, Autumn gave up.

"This is not working guys." Autumn plopped down on the floor. Her dancers followed suite.

"What's the problem Autumn? We are hitting all our marks."

"It's not you, it's me. You know what, lets pick this back up tomorrow. Same time. Same place." Autumn barely squeezed the words out between breaths.

Autumn sat with her head in her hands. What was she even doing? She couldn't vibe with her routine like she used to. It just didn't feel the same. *God what is wrong with me?*

She closed her eyes and begin to breathe deeply. In and out. In and out.

*I have more for you.*

Autumn cracked open one of her eyes and slowly surveyed the room. She didn't see anyone.

I have more for you.

She heard the still small voice again.

"Lord, is that you?"

*I have more for you Autumn. I always have.*

Autumn knew the Lord was speaking to her. "I know Lord, but I don't know what to do. I don't know how to transition out of this life and even if I did, what would I do? I just don't know what you want me to do Lord. You're going to have to give me some sort of sign."

Autumn stopped breathing. She thought she heard some music. Finally realizing it was her song. The one that everyone clearly hated. She made a note to herself to change it.

"Is the Lord calling me on my phone?" Autumn didn't think he would, but she ran to get her phone from her bag so she wouldn't miss the call, just in case.

"Hello." She answered hesitantly, not knowing what she would do if it was indeed the Lord calling her.

"Autumn, is that you?"

"Yeah, who is this?" Autumn thought it couldn't be the Lord. It was a female voice, but you never know.

"It's me, Destiny."

"Destiny! How are you girl? It has been a minute since I heard from you. You ready to ditch the pole and come dance for me like I've been asking you to for forever?"

"Autumn, you know I would love nothing more than to come dance for you, but I've been working on something here. Anyway, that's another story. I actually have been in the hospital, but I'm getting better and.."

"Wait a minute! Slow down. Did you say you were in the hospital? What happened?" By this time Autumn had taken a seat on the floor. She wanted to give Destiny her undivided attention.

"Axel happened."

"Destiny, no, why?" Autumn almost couldn't believe it. She really thought that Michelle was the only girl he had ever hit but it seemed like this was actually who he was. Autumn shook her head. She couldn't believe she was in love with someone who abused women. What was wrong with her?

"I got out of line. But I had to at least try, which leads to the reason I'm calling you. Have you met a girl named Michelle?"

"Little Shelly, yeah, she is such a sweet girl. How do you know Michelle?"

"I met Michelle when she applied to work at Axel's strip club."

"Really, she's like 17 right?"

"Yeah, maybe 18 by now, but she had a fake I.D. that said she was 21. And as you know she could pass."

"Yes, she could. She's pretty mature for her age if you know what I mean."

"Well, she came for her first day on the job and as soon as I saw her, I knew Axel would eat her alive. So, I got her out of there. But Demetrius had already told Axel about Michelle and he came to my house and got her. He didn't beat me that bad at that time, but I made the mistake of trying to go and bargain with Axel to let Michelle go and I really paid for it that time. It's just that, that girl has been through so much and I was just trying to help her Autumn. I think I have run out of ideas and that's why I called you.

I thought you could help her if you were in contact with her on a regular basis."

*So that's how he got Michelle.* Autumn thought back to the night Axel dropped Michelle off at her house. "I see her on and off when she's with Axel. He has pretty much made her his girl."

"She is only 17 or 18 Autumn. She doesn't need to be Axel's girl."

"I don't know what to do Destiny. What do you want me to do?"

"Michelle says she is really good at dancing. Maybe you can request her to be a dancer for you and keep her away from Axel. But you gotta do it in a way that he doesn't think that I contacted you or I may not survive the next encounter with Axel."

"A dancer. I think that would be great because I am stumped with this routine that I'm doing. I can't get the choreography right. But I think recruiting Michelle would be worth a try. I hope she is as good as she says. Why is saving this girl so important to you? I mean I've been thinking about it all the time too, but for you to contact me, it must mean a lot to you."

"Autumn, I never told anyone this, but if you are willing to help Michelle, I guess the least I could do is tell you. I have a sister. She was around Michelle's age when she went missing. I was only a couple of years older than she was so I wasn't thinking. But I got her to go with me to the strip club, got her a fake I.D., the whole nine. Anyway, she was really good at what she did and then one day, she up and disappeared. I think Axel had something to do with it but I have never been able to prove it. That's why I keep working there; to find out."

"Why haven't you ever said anything before?"

"I don't know, I feel so guilty about the whole thing. I should've never taken her to that strip club to begin with and now it's all my fault that she's missing."

"What do you think happened to her?"

"Well, she was pretty like Michelle; and of course Axel couldn't keep his eyes off of her. I think my sister was the first young girl Axel experimented with making his "girl", if you know what I mean. I think he had her hidden for a while, he never took her out in public and then I think he got spooked and sold her to the sex traffickers. He wanted to wash his hands of her. But I still have hope that she's alive and I'm not going to stop until I find her."

"Axel takes Michelle out from time to time."

"One thing Michelle has on my sister is that, she is mesmerizing; second, she actually looks a lot older than she is. My sister never did pass for older than 18. I don't' think Axel wanted to be seen walking around with a little girl. Now Michelle, she can hold her own. She can pass for at least 25."

"You're right about that. She could pass, but once you talk to her, you know she's just a baby."

"Autumn, I have to be honest with you, sometimes I don't think I'm going to find my sister alive. Michelle is like my one chance to redeem myself. If I can save Michelle, I feel like somehow, my sister will forgive me. That's why I need your help so badly."

"Destiny girl, I'm going to help you, but not just with Michelle. I'm going to help you find out what happened to your sister too."

"I am so grateful to you Autumn, truly."

"I just wish you had of told me sooner. By the way what's your sister's name?"

"Maxine, her name is Maxine."

"Destiny, we are going to save Michelle and get Maxine back and everything is gonna be okay, one way or the other."

"Thanks Autumn, keep me posted."

"Sure thing girl. Oh, and before I let you go. Autumn thought back to a statement Destiny had made. You said Michelle had been through a lot. What do you mean by that?"

"Well, I would hate to tell her business but just ask her about it."

"Ok. I will. You take care Destiny and let me take it from here. I don't need you getting yourself hurt anymore. Just relax and lay low. Can you do that for me?"

"Of course. Just please keep me posted so I won't go stir crazy."

"Will do. Talk to you soon."

Both girls hung up the phone with a lot on their minds. They hung up with very different feelings then they started the conversation out with. Destiny finally felt a little hope, while Autumn almost felt hopeless. How was she going to save Michelle, let alone find Maxine? At least she knew where Michelle was. She wondered how long Maxine had been missing. How long had Destiny been carrying this burden? She was glad that she could offer some hope, but just how much? Could she really pull this off?

"Lord, is this what you were talking about. Have you given me an assignment?"

Silence.

"Ok Lord, I trust you. But you gotta help me."

## CHAPTER
# FORTY-EIGHT

"Cuz, what's up? What you got for me?" Axel opened the door to let his crazy cousin through. He used to have second thoughts about letting him know where he lived, but his cousin was tried and true. He would never bring any trouble to his house. He would die before he did. This was an important meeting. When Axel heard about Autumn's engagement to Phoenix, he quickly called his cousin and had him find out what he might be up to.

"I got that info you wanted. It's like you thought. Phoenix is definitely into some funny business in Paris. And when I say funny, I mean of the homosexual kind."

"You're kidding me. Phoenix is gay?"

"From what I have gathered."

"What is he doing in Paris?"

"His man lives out there."

"Interesting. Autumn got engaged in Paris. I wonder how he worked that out?"

"Seems to me like he's been working out a plan this whole time."

"I knew that nigga wasn't up to no good. He must be trying to hit Autumn up for her money. He done finally gave me a reason. He can do whatever he wants, except come for Autumn. Now I'm coming for him. Cuz, you up for another pay day?"

"You know it."

"I got a little assignment for you. Hopefully this will be the last time. I want you to go into retirement after this. Take you a real long vacation and just enjoy yourself."

"You for real Ax."

"It's a done deal cuz."

"That's what's up man. Thanks. Mateo shook Axel's hand.

"Follow me. Let's talk finalities."

## CHAPTER
# FORTY-NINE

Autumn drove into Axel's circular driveway. She remembered living there when she first moved to L.A. She had never seen a house so big. It had so many different wings. There was no telling where Michelle could be in that house. Knowing Axel, he probably had a dungeon no one knew about where he kept all of his slave girls. Autumn took a moment to thank God for her singing and dancing abilities otherwise she could've been one of those girls who may or may not be locked in one of his dungeons.

"Thank you, Jesus, thank you, thank you, thank you Jesus." She said out loud. She couldn't believe how good it felt just to call on the name of Jesus. It sent a ray of hope all throughout her body. As she sat in her car, a single tear rolled down her right cheek.

"God, I know I've strayed, but if you could just use me to help save Michelle and hopefully Maxine and...." She hesitated not too certain of the words that wanted to come out of her mouth but she felt compelled. "God please save me too. I'm lost with this Phoenix situation and I don't know how to find my way back. Also, I know that I shouldn't be associated with the likes of Axel Smith, but like all these other girls we get caught up with money and fame, because we feel we don't have enough to offer on our own. Low self-esteem wins again. God, please help us break this spirit. Please God save us all."

Autumn pulled down the visor in her red jeep and touched up her make-up. She wanted to be on her game when dealing with Axel. She was sure he could smell a rat a mile away.

She stepped out of her jeep and walked up to the massive front door and rung the bell.

The maid came to the door.

"Hey Mrs. Barbara. How you doing?"

"Blessed as usual, blessed as usual."

Mrs. Barbara always had a smile on her face. Autumn wondered how she could stay so cheerful when Autumn herself had witness the evil that went on behind Axel's closed doors. And then for Mrs. Barbara to be saved. How could she work for a heathen like Axel? Maybe one day I'll have to ask her.

"You come to see Mr. Smith?"

"Yes, ma'am I did."

"Alright, just park your horses right there on that bench and I'll go retrieve him for ya. That sound alright."

"That'll do Mrs. Barbara."

Before she could sit down good, Michelle walked into the foyer where she was sitting.

"Shelly, it is so good to see you."

Michelle ran and wrapped her arms around Autumn as she always did.

"I'm so glad you're here. I saw you from the window and I just had to come down and see you. I might get in trouble, but it will be worth it."

"Please don't get yourself into trouble. I couldn't handle it."

"Don't worry about it. What brings you here?"

I came to talk to Axel about my video. I'm stuck, I hate to admit. I think I want to try out some new dancers. I normally use the same dancers all the time. I hate holding auditions. My dancers are like my sisters. And I am not too keen about adding to my family, especially when your family is crazy enough. But I'm desperate so I gotta do what I gotta do. I'm hoping to find a break out dancer that can change the game for me. You know get my creative juices flowing again."

"You looking for a specific person?" Michelle asked almost wanting to beg her to choose her. But how could she, Autumn had no idea she could dance. Michelle was going back and forth in her mind if she should say something or not.

"Well, not really, but I think I'll know when I see her or him. You never know." Autumn figured she might end up needing another male dancer if things keep going the way they are going with Phoenix. That might be the change she needed. Another male dancer. That would show him.

Autumn noticed how Michelle hung her head.

"What about you Michelle, do you dance?" She asked trying to bounce back from her rabbit trail of wounded emotions.

Michelle's head flew up in excitement. "I do, I really do. I was just fighting in my head about if I should say something or not. But I do dance and I think I could be that person you need to turn things around if you would just give me a chance. Please give me a chance?"

"What's going on in here?"

Both girls froze as Axel entered the room.

"I was just talking to Michelle. I think she might be the answer to my prayers."

What's that supposed to mean?" Axel cut Michelle a sharp look.

"I came over here to talk to you about the video for my song." Autumn exclaimed with a giggle.

Axel laughed back. He always enjoyed her company.

"And what does Michelle have to do with that?" He said ignoring her question.

"I wanted to hold auditions."

"Again?"

"I'm desperate Axel. But Michelle here has let me know that she can dance."

"Has she?"

Michelle felt fear hit her from the top of her head to bottom of her feet. She knew without a doubt she was going to pay for not only telling Autumn that she could dance, but that she had come down from her room in the first place. But something inside of Michelle told her that this was her way out and she was not going to give it up without a fight.

"Can you dance Michelle?"

"Yes." Michelle couldn't even believe that he was asking her.

"I'll tell you what, have your auditions and Michelle can try out, but I'll be there every step of the way and we'll see if Michelle can really dance."

Axel walked over to Michelle as she backed up against the wall.

"You better hope you can dance according to my standards. If not, you will wish you never even opened your mouth. I don't know what kind of game you are playing, but let me remind you, this is the big leagues baby. Don't cross me, Michelle."

Axel left the room.

Michelle finally exhaled. She didn't even realize she was holding her breath. She was sure this encounter was going to end badly. Anytime Axel backed her into a wall, his hands usually ended up around her throat and the next thing she would remember is waking up. But here she stood, getting ready to do something she only dreamed of. Auditioning to be a real dancer. Not a stripper, but a real back up dancer and then who knows; she could even end up being a choreographer. That was her ultimate dream. And Michelle could feel it within her reach.

"Thank you so much Autumn. You have no idea what this means to me."

"This means just as much to me Michelle, believe me. Just don't let me down. I need you on my dance team, so bring you're A game."

"Don't you worry, I will. I gotta go practice. It was good seeing you and you will let me know as soon as you know when auditions are, right?"

"I will. I'll be seeing you soon Shelly. You take care of yourself."

"I always do." Michelle said with a smile and she walked back to her room with her head held high.

# CHAPTER FIFTY

Autumn drove home with a fresh hope that things could actually change. She could not wait to get home and reflect on what happened. Her heart was beating a mile a minute. She knew she could reflect in the car, but there was something else that she wanted to do.

As she pulled into her garage, tears had already begun streaming down her face. She fidgeted with her keys as she tried to open her door. Once she made it in, she ran to her music room and fell to her knees and starting crying and shouting to the top of her lungs, "Help me Jesus, please help me Jesus, please." She lay curled up in a little ball on the floor and cried and cried until she got the release that she was so desperate for. After she contained herself, she got up and went into her CD closet. It was the place she kept all of her CD's, DVD's and she even had a whole collection of old records. Axel always made fun of her collection.

"You know no one has CDs and DVDs anymore, right?" He would say.

But she was old school. She loved going in there and listening to old music or watching an old concert. She loved the oldie goldies as they call them. But this time she was looking for something that she hadn't looked for in a very long time. She searched and searched. She couldn't remember how she had labeled these particular CDs. Finally, she found it. It was her Yolanda Adams, "Mountain High, Valley Low CD. She grabs it and she wanted to hug the CD, but she decided against it. She turned to her favorite song, "Fragile Heart."

God knew her heart was fragile right now. She wanted God to heal her. She was desperate for his healing; for his touch.

"God how did I get to this place? I used to sing for you all the time. You remember, don't you? Now, I'm just as horrible as Axel. Who am I?"

Autumn put the CD in the CD player that was hooked up to her surround sound system. The music filled the entire room and she turned it up as loud as it could go. She just let the sound take her back seven years ago, when she used to sing for God.

"Autumn, are you ready for church?" Ray Dance called to his daughter from the bottom of the stairs.

"Yes daddy, I'll be down in a minute, promise." Autumn did a final check in the mirror. She had to make sure her dress wasn't too short. Her hair style wasn't what her dad called too worldly. She also made the decision to wear flats every Sunday, because there wasn't a pair of heels that she put on that her dad didn't disapprove of. Better safe than sorry, she thought.

Autumn twirled around in the mirror humming as she did her last-minute check. She thought she might as well practice some of her dance and prepare her voice to sing. Autumn usually had to dance and sing on the same day. Luckily her father always gave her time to rest in between the two.

Autumn rushed downstairs to her waiting mother and father. She did a 360 spin around so her dad could either give her his blessing or send her back upstairs for another try.

"You look real nice pumpkin. Let's go."

Passed. Autumn was relieved she had finally got this dress code thing right.

The Dance family packed into the car and sang praises on the way to church as usual. Autumn was a PK, but she didn't have a problem with it. It didn't put any extra pressure on her to do right. She enjoyed living for God. She enjoyed doing what was right. She could do without the strict dress code, but as far as being at church every time the doors open, she was cool with that.

Service was going great once again. Pastor Dance was cutting up as usual.

"God wants us to live clean lives." Pastor Dance preached.

"Amen Daddy!" Autumn yelled back from the third row. But as she was settling in for her dad's next statement, a figure caught her eye as it passed her on the left. Autumn shifted her gaze toward the figure and realized it was a woman. She was heading to the front row. To everyone's amazement because the front row was normally reserved for special guest. Autumn stared at the woman. She didn't recognize her as being a special guest, unless that oversized belly of hers qualified as special. The woman had to be at least eight to nine months pregnant. She was definitely special because she caught everyone's attention. Most importantly as Autumn came back to herself, she realized that the woman had caught her dad's attention and evidently left him speechless. No one knew what to do. The message had stopped. Everyone was hanging on to Pastor's last words anticipating the next. But the woman that had caught the Pastor's attention stole the show. Autumn leaned over to see her mom where she was sitting on the pulpit. She had her special seat right next to the Pastor and she loved it there. She always said how special it made her feel by being right there next to her man, knowing she belonged to such an awesome Man of God. But at the moment she had a "what in the world is going on, don't make me take off my earrings" type a look going on.

Pastor Dance finally got back on track.

"We all need to clean up our lives. We need to deal with our own issues and stop trying to blame them on others" He preached with an attitude.

Autumn looked at her dad perplexed. She could have sworn he was talking straight to the woman with the big belly.

*This is getting crazier by the moment*, she thought to herself.

Pastor Dance preached about 10 more minutes before he retired back to his seat at which time the deacon came up and dismissed the congregation with a prayer.

Pastor Dance immediately tried to leave to go to his study.

"Don't you go anywhere." Mrs. Dance commanded her husband as she retreated from the pulpit straight to the woman with the big belly.

"Hello, I'm Mrs. Dance." She stated rather matter of factly. "How can I help you today?"

Autumn knew her mother so well. That was her, "I'm trying to be nice because I'm a Christian, but I will hurt you if need be" tone of voice.

"I'm not here to hurt you Mrs. Dance, but I am tired of your husband denying his child. I didn't know what to do."

The wind was knocked out of Mrs. Dance and Autumn, who had made her way to her mother's side.

"What's going on mom?" She said in her sweet little innocent voice.

Her mother didn't respond to her. She kept her eyes sharply on the woman. By this time the rest of the church stop fake ease dropping and just outright turned around and stared.

The woman turned and looked at Pastor Dance. "Are you going to keep denying our child Ray?"

At this point the rest of the congregation including Autumn and her mother turned to face the Pastor.

He stood up angrily. "I do not know this woman! She's crazy!"

Mrs. Dance looked turned toward the deacon who had dismissed the congregation who happened to be trying to escape.

"Deacon Fredricks, stop where you are, turn around and look at me."

Deacon Fredricks was Pastor Dance's right-hand man. He knew absolutely everything about him. The good, the bad and the ugly.

"Do you know this woman and don't lie to me; especially in the house of God?"

Deacon Fredricks turned to look at Pastor Dance and then he hung his head. Up until now Mrs. Dance had never asked him anything of Pastor's doings and he always hoped she never did. He knew when that day came, he would not be able to lie to her and to his dismay, that day had finally come.

"I'm so sorry." He said as he addressed his dear friend Pastor Dance.

He turned back to Mrs. Dance. "I do know this woman."

There were gasped all around the church. This was turning out to better than an episode from Maury, or worse depending how you look at it.

"Where do you know her from Deacon?"

Deacon Fredricks let out a long sigh. "She is one of Pastor's mistresses.

"One of." Mrs. Dance was in total shock. She was not expecting to find out there were more.

"My God Fredricks!" Pastor Dance screamed out furiously.

"I knew I shouldn't have trusted you with my business."

"That's what you're mad about Ray? That is what you have to say?" Mrs. Dance was getting more and more furious by the moment.

"What I have to say is I don't know that woman and I'm not going to stand here and let you all accuse me."

At that the Pastor retired to his study.

Mrs. Dance stood there for a moment. She didn't know if she wanted to interrogate this woman further, choke the life out of Ray and Deacon Fredricks or if she wanted to run out of the building in sheer humiliation. She hadn't quite figured it out yet until she happened to look down and see the horror on Autumn's face. So, she quickly readjusted herself and chose option D, which was wrap her arms around her daughter and gracefully exist the building.

She helped a stunned and speechless Autumn into the passenger seat and then she circled around and got into the driver's seat. As she drove off, she looked toward her daughter... "Are you alright Autumn?"

Autumn looked at her mom and immediately the tears just began to fall.

Mrs. Dance pulled the car over and embraced her daughter.

"How could he mom? He is always talking about living a clean life. How could he be doing this?"

"I don't know baby. I don't know. All I can tell you is that we will get through this."

"No mom, I won't." Autumn pulled away from her mom's embrace.

"Autumn, let's just go home and wait until your dad gets there and then we will talk this out."

"What's to talk about mom? He's already denying it. You think he's going to tell us the truth when we get home?"

"He might. He may have just been embarrassed to confess in front of the whole church." Mrs. Dance gave her a pat right before she started the car back up and pulled back on the road.

"Whatever you say mom. I'll see what he has to say and then make my decision."

What do you mean make your decision?

"I mean make my decision on if I should believe him or not and then what I'm going to do after that."

"What are you going to do if he says he's been cheating?"

"I don't know, maybe leave."

"Leave and go where?"

"Not back to that church, he has humiliated us!"

"First of all you need to calm your voice way down. You are not going anywhere. We are going to work this out. We are a very prestigious church, very popular and there are going to be plenty of people that are gonna want to take us down. I am not going to let that happen. We have been afforded a very good life and we are not gonna let this one incident destroy all of that."

"You seem to have already made up your mind. You are just going to accept it?"

"Are you really going to question me? Do you have any plans on how we are going to survive if we are on our own?"

"You mean you don't have a plan B?"

Mrs. Dance's eyes got really big. She couldn't believe that her daughter was back talking her. She had never acted like that before.

"Girl, you better be glad I'm driving. Do you have a plan B? Have you ever considered what you were going to do if we ever caught your father cheating? Did you ever think we would need a plan B? Girl, you don't know what you're talking about so don't sit over there and question me."

"I'm sorry mom. I'm just so upset and confused right now."

"Look, you better get it together and get it together quick. You are not gonna ruin this for us, so you better get it in your head to jump on board with whatever is going on."

"You mean pretend that everything is okay when it isn't?"

"Autumn, everything is okay, you'll see."

The car went silent and it remained that way the rest of the way home.

As Mrs. Dance drove up the long driveway to the Dance home, Autumn just looked the house over. It was a huge six bedroom, five bath home. It had a full basement complete with dance studio for Autumn to practice her dancing. It was a great big beautiful home, but it wasn't worth going along with what her father did. There was a time she loved her home. It made her feel so special. Of course, the house was way bigger than their three-person family needed, but it made her feel like she was on top of the world. Now it meant nothing. She dreaded even stepping foot inside. She was not prepared to deal with what was coming when her dad came home. Would they really talk about this sensibly? Would they just sweep everything under the rug? Would their family break up and go their separate ways? *Where would I live if that happened? Am I really ready to give up the luxuries that have been afforded me? What if mom was right?*

So many questions flooded Autumn's mind. She took a deep breath and just let it all go away. Every fear, every worry, every apprehensive thought.

I'm just not gonna worry about it. Autumn thought to herself and she closed her eyes until she felt the car come to a complete stop. She opened the door without uttering a word and went straight to her room and remained there until the dreadful moment finally arrived.

"Autumn! Autumn! Can you come downstairs please?" Autumn heard her mom calling up.

She reluctantly climbed out of her bed and proceeded to walk down the stairs. Her heart beating with a loud thud with each step she took.

Finally, she reached the bottom step and walked into the family room where both her parents were sitting on the love seat awaiting her arrival. How ironic, she thought. They are sitting on the love seat like they are in love. Like they are not going to deal with the problem. Autumn just sat down with no hope for where this conversation was headed.

"Autumn, I just want to tell you that nothing that you heard today was true. I have talked to your mom and reassured her that this is just a case of someone trying to take her place as first lady and I recently found out that Deacon Fredricks was after my position. Who knows, he probably came up with this scam himself. But I'm not gonna let these people win. I have worked too hard to let a couple of false accusations destroy it all. I just wanted to let you know as well and I hope that we can all be on the same page with this. I really need my family's support right now."

Autumn looked at her dad with a piercing look. She wanted to tell him how she didn't believe a word that was coming out of his mouth. She wanted to tell him how disgusted she was with him. How he had messed up their entire family. But she kept it all in because she knew it wouldn't help not one bit. So instead, she just nodded her head.

"You sure you're okay honey bun?" Her mother chimed in.

"I'm sure mom. Can I go now?"

Mrs. Dance glanced over at her husband. "Are we done babe?"

"Yeah, we're good. You can go."

Autumn stood up and returned to her room. She got back in her bed. She put on her headphones and turned on her radio, but for the first time, it wasn't gospel that she turned on. She searched for the first secular song she could find. Autumn had already made up in her mind that church was something she would do but it would not be who she would be. She started that day reinventing herself into a new Autumn. An Autumn that would take the secular music and dance world by storm and that is exactly what she did as soon as she graduated. She packed her things and headed straight to California. She never looked back.

Autumn lay on the floor still curled into a fetal position and Yolanda was still blessing her soul as she had put "Fragile Heart" on repeat. She eventually stood back up and lifted her hands toward the ceiling.

"God, I surrender to you. Forgive me for leaving you. Forgive me for turning my back on you. I know it has been a long time since we've talked, but I am so glad that we are. Thank you, God for embracing me back into your arms. Thank you, God for blessing me to have victory where Michelle is concerned and I pray that whatever is going on with Phoenix doesn't come back to haunt me."

Saying Michelle's name took her back to her upcoming auditions.

"God, I don't want to do this anymore. I want to dance and sing for you again. What am I supposed to do?"

# CHAPTER FIFTY-ONE

It was the first day of auditions. Michelle looked through her closet trying to figure out the perfect thing to wear. Maybe sweatpants and a T-shirt. Naw, not befitting for the sexy dancer that she was sure Autumn would be looking for. One thing she knew about the business was that appearance was everything. Axel would almost kill her if she walked out the house with anything less than perfection. On the other hand, she didn't want to show too much. She never wanted to be considered for a part based on her looks alone. She wanted to be chosen because she had talent as a dancer. She hated watching videos and seeing pretty faces with no rhythm. She wanted to be like Autumn. Beautiful and talented all in one and respected for what she did. Michelle continued to rummage through her closet. She couldn't wait to see what a real audition was like. All the other professional dancers and some amateurs that often better than the actual professionals. Michelle never got intimidated by other dancers. She enjoyed seeing the different talents, plus she knew she was good. Axel would be there though. She knew he would do everything in his power to make it hard on her. He would criticize her every move. Michelle knew she had to be above her A game in order to impress Axel. She had no doubt she would win over Autumn. Everyday Axel made a smart remark about her auditioning.

"If you know how to dance so well, I might consider letting you work in the club, on a real stage."

*That's not a real stage.* Michelle thought to herself.

She would never say that out loud though, she would remain quiet as usual. She wasn't about to do anything to mess up her opportunity of auditioning for Autumn. So far, Axel hadn't hit her since the initial beating he gave her for asking to audition. She thought she wasn't going to be able to make it to the audition, but Michelle was determined. She worked hard every day to get better so she could practice. As of lately he hadn't put his hands on her. Maybe he was trying to spare her since she was going out into the public. He wouldn't want her too scarred up. He didn't seem to mind beating her in his own establishments. The studios belonged to him as well, so why would he care if people saw bruises on her or not? It was all confusing. Michelle backed away from her closet and sat cautiously on the side of her bed, her mind scrambling trying to figure out why Axel hadn't been beating on her. He never went this long without at least putting her in a chokehold or something. As she continued to think about it, the only conclusion she could come up with was maybe he didn't want her to have any excuses if she failed. But Michelle was determined not to fail. She would show him she was made to dance and not to be his punching bag. But what if she did well and he decided to make good on his threats? Would he really make her dance as a stripper? At this point, she didn't put anything past Axel. He was as evil as they came. She couldn't allow herself to go there or she was sure to lose focus and destroy everything she had worked so hard for; dancing professionally for Autumn Dance. Michelle riddled with excitement at the possibility of dancing with Autumn. She remembered when Autumn came out with her first hit single entitled

"Dance." Michelle smiled at the curveball Autumn threw everyone with that song. You would think that it would be all about dancing, but it wasn't. It was about Autumn Dance and who she was. Michelle could feel a deep backdrop of pain in the song that Autumn was clearly trying to hide but Michelle picked it up. If there was one thing Michelle knew, it was pain. She had put it on paper many times. She wondered what Autumn could be going through. From where she stood, it seemed as if she had an amazing life. You can never tell what people are hiding by just looking at them. Michelle considered herself an expert in interpreting songs. She usually could tell what the person was feeling and if the song is a genuine reflection of who they are or something they were trying to be. One thing she hated were fake artists. People should just be themselves and write from their heart. You don't have to pretend to be something you're not. People wanted to go with what's hot now. But if someone would begin to pave the road for originality, people would eventually follow. Michelle was immediately drawn to Autumn's music. It was real, exciting and it had a hidden message of pain. She was also drawn to her skillful dance moves. She executed every move flawlessly. She always dreamed of dancing with Autumn. She thought back to the time she actually got to talk to Autumn. She nearly lost control, of course she paid for it later. Axel beat her unconscious for getting out of character. This was during her so-called "breaking period." Axel did everything in his power to break her spirit so she would feel worthless enough to comply with his every wish. But Michelle was a fighter. She was never going to allow Axel to break her beyond repair although he had come close many times. That's why she had to win this audition. It was her one chance to get away from Axel for good.

## CHAPTER
# FIFTY-TWO

Michelle walked into the dance room to find it completely empty. She couldn't believe she was in an actual dance studio. She walked around touching the walls and the mirrors. She imagined herself dancing in there. Starting a career. She couldn't help but smile. She spun around and she wrapped her arms around herself and fell to the floor sitting in perfect Indian style she couldn't wait for the auditions. *Guess I better stretch.* She thought to herself.

As Michelle was stretching the door opened. Michelle froze. It was her. Her new found friend Autumn Dance. She still couldn't believe she knew her and had talked to her. This was so amazing! It still gave Michelle butterflies in her stomach every time she was around Autumn.

"Hey Shelly. What's up?"

"Nothing, just excited about tryouts. Guess I'm early."

"Nope. Not early. You are right on time."

"Really. Then where is everyone else?"

Autumn took a couple of steps closer to Michelle. "I decided I didn't want a whole new team. I just want you."

"Me. why?"

"Cause I have a feeling you know how to dance and you can help me."

"I can. I really can."

"Ok. I have your first assignment. I want you to come up with a video idea and some choreography for one of my songs. And I know this sounds crazy, but I need this to be our little secret."

"Anything for you Autumn. I can do it. I promise. I won't let you down!"

"I'm sure you won't. So, you can practice here every day that we were supposed to have auditions. Cool?"

"Cool." Michelle beamed.

# CHAPTER FIFTY-THREE

Autumn paced back and forth. Phoenix was on his way home and she had had enough. She was ready to tell him where to go and how to get there. She hadn't had the time to confront him about Faith yet, but she would today.

Right on cue, Phoenix used his key to open the door. He froze when he saw Autumn standing in the doorway.

"Where have you been?"

"You know where I've been."

"Why are you always in Paris?"

"I have business there. I'm trying to start up a company."

"Why haven't you told me about this company?"

"Because you are always at the studio or up under Axel. I don't ever have any time with you."

"Is that why you're sleeping with my dancer?"

"What?" Phoenix tried to play innocent. "What are you talking about?"

"I saw you, Phoenix. At Charlie's party. I saw you and Faith."

Phoenix thought he could play it one of two ways. He could lie or be honest. Phoenix put his bags down and closed the door. He knew Autumn all too well. He decided to play the guilt trip instead.

"I have been seeing Faith, but what choice did you give me!" He snapped before Autumn could say anything. "You and Axel. I know you're sleeping together. You make me look like a fool because you won't announce our engagement, what was I supposed to do?"

Autumn was speechless. She was so angry, but was Phoenix right? Had she driven him to this?

"You're wrong!" Was the only thing that Autumn could think of.

"Am I? Axel has you, that Michelle girl and every other girl he wants. You stop your whole life for him. We could be happy, planning our wedding. But no, you have to make sure Axel is on board with everything first. And I'm guessing he's not, cause you still walk around here treating me like I'm just one of your dancers and not the man who asked you to marry him. And you wonder why I never show up. It's embarrassing. So yeah, Faith showed me some attention and I responded. So, are you kicking me out or what?"

Autumn didn't know if she should just let him go or fight for the relationship. Phoenix picked up his bags and walked back out the door. He had made the decision for her. Autumn fell to the floor, tears flowing uncontrollably. Was Phoenix right? Was Axel taking over her life, causing her to stop living even though he didn't want her either. Whether she decided to stay with Phoenix or not she knew she needed to get away from Axel.

# CHAPTER FIFTY-FOUR

Logan sat up on his bed. Lisa sat up next to him. He still hadn't found a way to get rid of her. She had pretty much upped her game since he signed. She was buying gifts, taking him out on dates and giving him all the sex he could handle. All the bells and whistles included. How could he say no? But he knew he would eventually have to. This was going to turn into a look at all I've done for you and you owe me type thing. Even though he was enjoying it, he was going to have to break it off soon and he knew just how to do it. He had just signed with Axel's label and already the women were all over him. He hadn't even released a song yet. Someone had caught him on camera singing in the restaurant and it had already gone viral. He would just start sleeping with as many as he could and blame it on hazards of the job. She would get jealous and he would have to end it with her. It would work out.

"Hey beautiful." Logan played along for the time being.

"Hey babe. Don't tell me our time is up and you have to go to the studio. I don't think I'm ready for that yet."

Logan held his tongue. *This girl is pushing it.* 'Naw, hand me the remote. This video looks pretty fye."

Logan took it off mute.

"That's Autumn Dance's new video. The dance moves are hot." Lisa informed Logan as she snuggled further under his arm. Logan embraced it because he didn't want her to see what he was really looking for.

"Have you met Autumn already?"

"Naw, not yet. I'm sure I'll meet her pretty soon."

"I can't wait to meet her too." Lisa beamed.

Logan again ignored Lisa's comment. His mind was too busy trying to locate someone more important than Autumn. He could have sworn he saw his broken beauty and just as clear as day the camera fell on her and stayed. Logan knew for sure it was her. She was in the front like she was the lead dancer and she deserved to be. She was amazing. Her body was equally amazing and she knew how to use it. He had no idea she danced. *I like it.* Logan thought to himself.

To Logan's dismay, Lisa had noticed her to. "Isn't that the girl that was with Axel? I didn't know she was a dancer."

"I don't know. I wasn't even paying any attention." Logan lied.

"Yeah, I'm pretty sure that was her."

It had worked. Lisa bought his lie. Logan continued to watch, hoping to see her once again.

"What's her name?"

Logan thought about it. He realized he didn't know.

"I don't know." Logan confessed.

"She is beautiful though."

Logan could agree with her on that.

When the video ended. Logan sat there amazed that there was more to his broken beauty and his desire for her grew even more. If I could just meet her and talk to her. No, I have to meet her. I have to talk to her and I can't have anyone around. I have to find out her story.

Logan's thought process was interrupted by Lisa nibbling on his ear. She jumped on top of him and continued kissing him all over. Logan almost forgot about what his plans were as Lisa headed south of the border. He made himself snap back to it. He knew he needed to save this girl. He wasn't sure from what or how, but he just knew he had to.

# CHAPTER FIFTY-FIVE

Logan walked around the massive label. Each artist had their own office. Not just a typical office. But each office was equipped with everything an artist would need to make musical magic. Axel had showed him inside on his first tour of the building. He walked through the doors and the first thing that caught his eye were the floor to ceiling windows. He walked straight to them and looked out. It was the most amazing view he had ever seen.

"I try to make sure my artist are properly inspired." Axel walked up behind Logan and placed a hand on his shoulder.

Logan still had not warmed up to Axel. He still wanted to find out the truth about his relationship with the broken beauty. He still didn't know her name. It is funny, he never heard Axel call her by her name. It was always babe or girl or the "B" word a time or two. Who would call their girl out her name? She could not mean that much to him. And based on those bruises he saw on her arms; he was putting his hands on her. Logan just did not know how in depth the abuse was. Was he just man handling her or was he hitting her? He really wanted to know.

Logan walked away from Axel; his intention was to remove his hand from his shoulder without showing him how disgusted he was with him. He turned to see a full sectional with a 65' inch TV hanging on the wall. Complete with PS5. No wonder his actual hit percentage was dropping.

Even though Axel was the biggest producer in California he was far from where he used to be. Axel was surviving based on his past reputation. People were too afraid or too star struck to tell him his music was not what it used to be. But Logan felt if he could at least get his foot in the door, he could change things. He really didn't want to be a singer, but who knows, the whole singer thing just might work out for him.

Axel continued exploring the office. "What's behind this door?"

"It is the restroom and bedroom."

"Are you serious?"

"Yeah. Why wouldn't I be?"

Logan opened the door and walked into a full bathroom with tub and separate shower. A huge shower. *Wonder what goes on in there?* Logan walked through the bathroom and into the bedroom. King sized bed; walk-in closet. "Why the bedroom?"

"Sometimes the artist work late and they need to crash here."

"And that's all?"

"Well, I told you, whatever my artists need to be inspired. Where do you think those amazing love songs come from?"

"Probably not these bedrooms. I think you can thank these bedrooms for a different kind of song."

Axel laughed. "I guess you're right."

Axel was pulled away before he could finish the tour, but Logan told him he just wanted to see his office and he would be fine. Now two months later here he was just now trying to finish the tour on his own.

He felt like all the halls were beginning to look alike, finally a door. The door. Something Logan wanted to see the moment he first entered the building. The recording studio.

Logan walked in. He had imagined himself sitting in this very studio directing an artist on how to sing his song. That is really all he wanted. Now he would be on the other side. Singing someone else's song. How was he going to get through this? He did not want to sing someone else's songs. If he was going to sing, he wanted to sing his own songs. But he was here. In the place he wanted to be, and he was willing to do anything to stay here.

Just as he was gearing up to tinker with a machine he probably should not be touching, the door opened and there stood his dream, well, the dream he never knew he had. The broken beauty stood before him, looking amazing as ever. She had on a pair of black high waist shorts with suspenders, accompanied by a black wide-rimed hat and black pumps. Logan could not help but stare. He knew he should probably say something but he was literally lost for words as he always seemed to be when he was in her presence.

"I apologize, I did not know anyone was in here. I'll leave you to it."

"No, please don't leave." Logan finally found his words. "I was just giving myself a private tour and I stumbled upon this room. I was actually about to touch something I probably shouldn't, so I guess I can say you saved me." Logan laughed nervously. "What about you? What brings you here?"

Michelle paused. Not knowing if she should trust Logan or not, but something about him made her feel safe enough to let her guard down. From the first time she heard him sing and she and Axel shared a table with him, she had been mesmerized by him. She longed to know more about him.

"I come in here sometimes to get away from the hustle and bustle of everything." Michelle finally decided to enter the room and let the door close behind her. Logan couldn't believe this moment had finally come. He could actually talk to this beautiful creature that filled his dreams night after night.

"So, I haven't been privileged to know your name."

"Michelle."

"Michelle." Logan repeated it, just to hear how it sounded on his own lips. Sweet as he thought it would.

"So, Michelle, you're not going to get into trouble for being in here with me are you?"

"I might."

"So, Axel does beat you?"

"Yeah. So. Everyone knows that. It is just better when no one brings it up."

"I apologize."

"It's cool."

"Can I ask you a question Michelle?" Logan was loving saying her name.

"You mean another question?"

"I guess."

"Sure."

"What is the real reason you come in here?" Logan began to feel a bit more comfortable talking to Michelle. After all, if he didn't capitalize on this moment, he would possibly not ever get it again. He had to say everything he wanted to say while he had a chance.

"What do you mean by that?"

"I meant I think there is more to you than what I see. And it has something to do with why you come in this room."

"The only thing that is different from what you don't see is the fact that I'm a dancer. I'm a backup dancer for Autumn."

"I know that. I've seen you dance."

"When?" Michelle was surprised. She didn't know he had seen her dance.

"Music video. I must say you are an expert when it comes to moving your body."

Michelle couldn't help but blush.

"But I still sense there is more. Is dancing your comfort zone?"

"Is singing yours?"

"Touché. What do you suggest? I step out of my comfort zone?"

"That song you were singing, in the restaurant; I've never heard of before. Had to be an original. Yet I haven't heard any originals from you in the two months you've been here."

"Axel didn't really sign me on to write. Just another handsome face, with a sexy voice."

"So, you say…"

"And you don't."

"Doesn't matter what I think. Besides you seem to like your womanizing position."

"Jealous?"

"Why would I be jealous? I'm with Axel."

"Are you?"

"I live in his house, don't I?"

"Whatever you tell yourself so you can sleep at night."

"You got a lot of nerve."

"I just call it like I see it. You never answered my initial question."

"What?"

"Is dancing your comfort zone?"

"What else do you think I can do?"

"Run this entire operation… in your sleep."

"How did you come up with that?"

"I've been watching you. Axel drags you along everywhere he goes. Every time I see you, I can see the wheels turning in your pretty little head. You know how to do it better. I think you know what this company needs to go to the next level, but I'm sure if you even think about opening your mouth, Axel will knock you off your feet."

"So, what's your point?"

"My point is that, he's going to beat you regardless, so you might as well make every blow count. I'm just saying."

"Well, it's not as easy as it sounds. You don't know how evil Axel's mind works. It's never going to be worth it and it's never going to work."

"Have you tried?"

"It took everything I had just to get up the courage to get him to let me try out to be Autumn's backup dancer, and yes, he beat me unconscious for that. I almost missed tryouts."

"But it worked right?"

"I guess it did."

"Look, I'm not trying to tell you to endanger your life. All I am saying is we have to start taking charge over our lives, our destiny."

"Did you say *we*?"

"Yes, we. If I'm going to ask you to take such a huge risk, I should be able to do the same."

"What do you have to lose? I could lose my life. Not the same thing."

"I could lose my contract. This is my one big chance. I have worked my whole life for this one chance. I may never get another opportunity like this ever. So, I know it's not my actual life but it's kind of close to it."

Michelle couldn't help but smile. She could tell Logan was trying to be sincere but all the while realizing how stupid he really sounded and silently hoping she didn't catch on, but she was way passed him.

"You have really tossed all your eggs in one basket huh?"

"I know it sounds stupid." Logan finally admitted. "But it is the truth. This is my dream and I ain't ready to let it go."

"Well, I will give it up in a heart-beat."

"The dream or the relationship with Axel, because they don't have to be one in the same."

Michelle stared at Logan. He had just repeated her hearts cry. Why did her life in the music industry have to be wrapped around Axel? She would love to do what she was doing without him to tie her down. She hated to admit it but Logan was right about there being more to her. She wanted to write, sing, choreograph, produce. The whole nine. But Axel would never let her do that. He would be afraid she was gaining too much independence and control. He couldn't allow that. He had to keep her under his thumb. Something that always puzzled Michelle. Axel could have any woman he wanted that would willing be his everything. Why did he want to force her to be his girl? It just didn't make sense.

"Earth to Michelle." Logan saw that Michelle had gone down a rabbit hole.

"Oh, I apologize. I was just thinking about what you said."

"What part?"

Just as Michelle was about to answer the door swung open. Axel walked into the studio. Michelle froze. She knew this would not end well. She thought she could be in and out before Axel came this way. Truth be told, she never expected Axel to come this way. He hardly ever went to the studio with the artists, but nevertheless, she should have known that he would eventually find her. She was not allowed to be out of his presence for long and she had exceeded her limit.

"What is this?" Axel asked walking up to Michelle. He could care less if Logan was in the room or not. He only held Michelle responsible.

"No... nothing." Michelle stammered

"What were you two talking about?"

Michelle looked at Logan. Was she really about to do this? Logan looked back at Michelle. The look in her eyes told him she was up to something.

"We were talking about writing a song together." The words fell out of Michelle's mouth before she knew it.

Logan couldn't believe what he was hearing.

"Writing a song?" Axel looked amused. "You, write a song? Since when did you become a songwriter?" Axel laughed.

Michelle could feel her heart sinking by the second. Could she really do this? Could she stand up to Axel and follow her dreams?

Michelle stood up straight and looked Axel directly in his eyes. "Yes, I can write. I have always known how to write. You've just never asked me what I could do. Logan can write too."

"So, you guys have something in common?"

"Only the fact that we both want to do our part for this label."

Axel didn't waste any time as he back handed Michelle to the ground.

"You expect me to believe that bull!"

Logan's fist balled up. He wanted to punch Axel in his arrogant face.

"Logan, what were you guys discussing?"

Logan tried to calm himself. He did not want to anger Axel any more than he had, for Michelle's sake.

"I came in here and I started talking to Michelle. I felt she had more to offer besides just being a dancer. So, I asked her to write a song with me to see if I was right."

Axel walked up real close to Logan to ensure he got his point across.

"I like you Logan. You're a real cool dude. But the quickest way to get on my bad side is to involve yourself with my girl. Michelle is my property. She belongs exclusively to me. I lend her out to no one. I know she's fine and you can't help yourself, believe me you ain't the first. But let me just tell you this; your ignorance and libido will only get her killed. So, from now on, you need to act like she don't exist."

Axel, walked over to where Michelle was still laying on the floor, reached down and yanked her up with one hand and dragged her out the door behind him.

Logan fell back in the chair. His assumptions had been correct. He had only one chance to talk to Michelle and get as much information as he could from her before Axel shut him down. But he felt he knew enough. He knew that she wanted more. He knew she dreamed of a life without Axel. And he was determined to give it to her. One way or the other. He just needed a plan. It's time I get close to Autumn and become besties with her. Over the two months he'd been there, she seemed to be the only one Axel will let get close to Michelle. That would have to be part A of his master plan. He would have to work through Autumn in order to communicate with

Michelle. Only thing… would Autumn be a friend or a foe? After all she was loyal to Axel. Would she ever turn on him to help Michelle? He had to find out, but without exposing Michelle or his plan.

CHAPTER

# FIFTY-SIX

Logan walked into the studio lounge where Axel was already waiting. *I hope I'm not late.* Beads of sweat had already begun to form on his forehead. He stopped abruptly at the door. Behind him Lisa bumped into him. Her eagerness was a bit irritating. He grabbed her hand behind him in hopes that it would get her to calm down. It didn't work. He could feel her raising up on her tip toes trying to see over his shoulder, while giving him quick nudges in the back. He knew he should have left her at home, but she was determined to come.

"Are you embarrassed by me Logan? Am I not what you think is acceptable in the music world?" Lisa's arms were folded and her foot was patting the floor a hundred miles a minute.

"Lisa, it's nothing like that. All I'm saying is that, when I'm at the studio, I'm working. You would probably be bored out of your mind." Logan did his best to try and dissuade Lisa from coming to the studio. Not because it was frowned upon but because he didn't want to solidify this relationship any more than he already had. He hadn't found a way to make a clean break yet, but taking her to the studio was definitely the opposite of what he was trying to accomplish.

"Just take me one time and at least you can say, 'I told you so', if I don't like it."

Logan couldn't believe he had allowed Lisa to persuade him yet again. *What is it about this girl that makes me bend to her will? I don't even like her like that. She's just fun in bed. I must be judging her with the wrong body part.* Logan eased through the door as if he was a burglar trying to make sure he entered a house undetected. But Axel was too keen for that.

"Come on in Logan." Axel didn't even bother to turn around. He kept right on messing around with the mixer board.

Logan stepped in with Lisa in tow.

Axel turned around at the sound of high heels hitting the marble floor. "I see you brought company?"

"Yes sir. I hope it's okay. She has been begging me to come down here."

Lisa playfully punched Logan in the arm.

"Naw, it's alright. A woman as beautiful as your girl is always welcome in my studio." Axel gave her a wink.

Logan figured he was flirting with her. But he couldn't care less. If he stole Lisa from him, he would only be doing him a favor. No harm. No foul. "What we got on the agenda today man?" Logan tried his best to change the awkward atmosphere in the room.

"The writers finally finished your first track. I like the song okay, but I wanted you to listen to it before I accept it or drop it."

"Okay. Cool." Logan walked behind Axel to the other side of the mixer. He didn't want to show his displeasure in the news he had just received. He wished Axel would just let him write his own music. He had told him several times that he just wanted to write, but Axel was determined to make him an artist. *Your voice man, it's a money maker. There's no way I can sign you and not let you get on the mic.* Logan replayed Axel's words in his mind. Logan even asked him about writing and singing, but Axel wouldn't hear of that either. He was a control freak. Everyone knew it, but on the flip side of that coin; everything Axel made turned to gold. People just ended up trusting his process, no matter how much they disapproved.

"You two love birds sit on down and listen to this track and tell me what you think." Logan took his seat first and Lisa followed suit making sure to scoot in real close to Logan. Logan wrapped his arm around her shoulder, just to piss Axel off. Logan noticed Axel hadn't taken his eyes off Lisa since they entered the room. The music started and it really did have a nice groove. It was also highly sexual. Even though Logan didn't have any problem in that area, it wasn't really what he had in mind for the direction of his music. Axel wanted to turn Logan into a sex symbol. Logan wanted to make love songs. He knew women would fall for a man who sung love songs so the same goal would be accomplished. Logan didn't like all his business in the streets. What he did in the bedroom, was his and the young lady he chose for the night's business only. He could see a lot of oil and taking off his shirt in his future.

He casually looked down at Lisa who was tucked securely under his arm. She seemed as if she was a little embarrassed herself. But another thing caught his eye as well. Axel had made it his business to mouth the lyrics as if he were grooving but his eyes were locked on Lisa's and hers were locked on Axel's. Logan couldn't believe the arrogance of them both, but it was okay. He wanted them to go as far as they wanted. He was determined to get himself out of this relationship and this was his open door.

"You ready to get into this man?" Axel asked when the track was over. "Or do you need to hear it again?"

Logan stood up. "I got this. It's a great song."

"Okay. Let's get it." Axel waved his hands and bowed as he ushered him towards the booth. As Logan stepped into the booth and put on the headset. Axel started the music. Logan gracefully took control over the song and Axel knew he had a hit.

Axel took a seat next to Lisa. He knew he had her by the way she blushed as he sat down. This was going to be easier than he thought.

"So, when you gonna let me get that?" Axel decided on the most direct approach. Lisa wasn't a challenge for him at all.

"What do you mean? I have a man. Logan."

"You think Logan ain't gonna drop you as soon as his star rises and all these girls start falling all over him?"

Lisa sighed and hung her head. She knew deep down Logan didn't really want her. He had dropped so many hints. She thought if she pushed hard enough, he would eventually fall in love with her.

"You don't need to try to solidify your place in this life with him. I got you." Axel responded almost as if he had read her mind.

Lisa gave it some thought. She would love to be Axel's girl, accompanying him to different restaurants and events. She thought back to the girl at the restaurant. She wondered what their relationship status was. Might as well ask.

"What about that girl you were with at the restaurant?"

"What girl?" Axel played dumb. That was always the best route to take with girls who asked too many questions.

"The girl you were with when you signed Logan." Lisa had been studying the girl ever since she seen her on Autumn's dance video. She watched that video more than she would like to admit trying to figure out what this girl had that made her appealing to Axel. And the list just kept getting longer. Lisa found herself hating her even though she didn't even know her.

"Oh her. She's a girl. What?" Axel wasn't about to entertain Lisa any further. Either she was gonna give it up or not. He just stared at her intently. Letting her know this was her last chance. Take it or leave it.

Lisa looked over at Logan at the booth. He was singing the song perfectly. Hitting every note like a pro. She so wanted him to love her, but she just couldn't pass up an opportunity to be with Axel. She submitted. "Your place or mine?"

"Mine of course." Axel smiled seeing the surprise on Lisa's face. He knew that she instantly felt special since he was inviting her to his place. Most girls thought that surely he would only invite the most special girls to his place, but Axel invited every girl to his place. He didn't care really. His security was tight. He didn't care who knew where he stayed. It wasn't a secret.

"Yeah. Okay." Lisa beamed.

"Give me your number and I'll text you the address. Can you get away from lover boy? I want you tonight."

Lisa blushed again. "Of course. It won't be a problem." She rattled off her phone number. Axel immediately sent her his info. Lisa checked her phone as it buzzed. There it was. Axel Smith's phone number. She had it. She could contact him at any time. If I play my cards right, this could be an even bigger score than Logan. She looked up at Logan as he completed the lyrics to his new single. She hadn't really heard much of it. She was too caught up with Axel. She hoped he didn't ask her how it was. But if he did, she would just lie and tell him it was great.

Logan placed the headphones back on the stand. Axel hadn't said anything to him the entire session. Although he knew there wasn't any reason to do so. He killed it. But Axel wouldn't know. He was too busy getting Lisa's digits. Logan played like he didn't see what was going on. He either kept his eyes closed enough so they thought he didn't see them or he looked to the side. But trust and believe, he saw everything. *It's cool Axel.* Logan thought to himself. *Have all the fun you want with my girl. Cause while you trying to take my girl. I'm going to be taking yours.* Logan's mind shifted to Michelle. His broken beauty. He couldn't wait to get her away from Axel and into his arms. He would show her what true love was really all about. *Yeah. I'm coming for you Axel. You won't get away with this for long. I'm coming for you.* Logan looked at Axel through the glass and met his gaze for the first time. Axel gave him the thumbs up. He had no idea of the thoughts that were running through his mind. But he would soon find out.

# CHAPTER FIFTY-SEVEN

Lisa walked around her living room anticipating her rendezvous with Axel. She went straight to the spa after leaving the studio with Logan. She wanted to make sure her wax was fresh. She wanted her body to be on point. After all, this was the multi-billion-dollar producer, Axel Smith. Whoever won Axel, pretty much wins it all. She just had to make this work. Lisa looked out the window to see if her car had pulled up yet. Before Lisa left the spa, Axel texted her to let her know he would send a car to pick her up instead. He said he didn't want his special girl having to drive all the way to his house and back. He wanted to make sure he took care of her. Lisa must have read the text a hundred times. Lisa fell deeper and deeper for Axel each time she read it.

"I got this in the bag. I can feel it." Lisa almost sang the words.

A knock on the door caused Lisa to almost jump out of her skin. She peeked out the window. A black Escalade was parked in her driveway. A man garnishing the traditional chauffer's attire complete with the black hat was standing at her door.

Lisa looked herself over in the full-length mirror she hung up in the living room. She had to make sure she looked perfect before she stepped out the door. *Best purchase ever.* She thought to herself as she kicked her left leg up behind her. Lisa took a deep breath before grabbing her handbag and opening the door.

Axel figured he would roll out the red carpet for Lisa. He didn't waste his time with his invitation, so he thought he would spoil her in the bedroom. Make her think she wasn't a hit and quit deal, but that is exactly what she was. He hadn't planned on dealing with her pass tonight. He took pleasure in playing with female's minds. He knew that Lisa would be hooked after tonight. Ringing his phone off the hook. He would just look at it and laugh as he had done so many times before with so many different girls. He just hoped hitting this particular girl wouldn't mess up his deal with Logan. Although he had him locked into an iron clad contract, he didn't want to affect his ability to make music by falling apart over this girl. To his knowledge, from the vibes he received at the restaurant when they first met, he didn't even like this girl. Maybe she grew on him. *Who knows what these dudes be thinking?* Axel thought to himself as he continued to spread rose petals all over the bedroom. These women come a dime a dozen. You can't just be falling in love and getting booed up. Every woman was replaceable. Except Michelle. Axel stopped in his tracks as he thought about Michelle. That girl was like no other. Axel couldn't really say he was in love with her. After all, he had done everything in his power to keep his emotions out of it. His fear was that the day he let her even remotely close to his heart, she would have him. Hook, line, and sinker. He couldn't be under some woman's thumb, but Michelle was not just some woman. She was perfect. Never before had he run across a woman who had no flaws, other than her weakness for being controlled. Axel knew Michelle was talented as well. He just couldn't let her know that. He had to keep her crippled so there would be nowhere that she could go. Axel tried to shake the thoughts of Michelle out of his head. He felt himself getting aroused just thinking about how perfect she was. How perfect her body was. Axel had finished laying down the last rose petal and headed toward the candles. He had candles leading from the front door to the bedroom. He intended to lead her to paradise and then escort out the next day. No one could stay. No girl had ever stayed passed one night with him. They may have come back on several occasions, but never did they stay passed one night, except Harmony. Axel shuddered at the thought of Harmony. But no one had ever lived with him. Until Michelle. Michelle had her own wing of the house. He wanted her to have freedom to go about as she pleased, but she couldn't leave the house, not without his permission. Which tonight she had. Axel allowed Michelle to go over to Autumn's house for a while, so Lisa wouldn't get suspicious. But she would be in for a rude awakening when she woke up in the morning and found Michelle sitting at the breakfast table. What a laugh that would be. It was always the icing on the cake after a night like this. The girl would be thinking she's his one and only. That they are the only ones that he would invite into his home. Until they see Michelle and realize, they are not her and never will be her. One thing he had to give Michelle credit for, she had that position on lock.

## CHAPTER
# FIFTY-EIGHT

Lisa lay in Axel's bed staring at the ceiling. The sun coming in from the bay windows in his bedroom had beckoned her from her sleep. She thought for sure he would send her home before the night was up, but instead he held her and kissed her and rocked her to sleep. She couldn't believe she had just spent the night with Axel! Lisa silently screamed. She turned to look at Axel, but he wasn't lying next to her. As she sat up, an aroma hit her nose. *Breakfast? Is my man really in there cooking me breakfast? This is it. He wants me. He wants me to be his one and only.* Lisa looked around the bedroom. She almost fainted last night when she walked in and saw all the rose petals and candles. There couldn't be anyone else living here for him to go all out like he had. That was the first thing she looked for when she entered; any signs of anyone living here besides Axel. She didn't see any. Lisa stepped out of the bed and walked over to the bathroom. Her own master bath could fit in his at least three times.

The shower was amazing. Lisa didn't want to get out, but she was anxious to see Axel and what he had prepared for her this morning. She looked in the mirror in his bedroom. Yes. She looked amazing. She was the perfect cross between dressed down and classy. She wanted a bit of a messy hair look, but sexy enough to make him want to come back to bed. After taking another deep breath, which seemed to be her thing now, she exited the room. The candles and rose petals were still aligned from the bedroom to the front door. Well, he didn't clean up, so I must still be the only one. Lisa followed the smell of eggs and bacon to the kitchen. She rounded the corner with a big smile on her face. She wanted to show her appreciation for his kindness. But her smile was suddenly wiped away. What she saw almost made her stop breathing. She didn't know what steps to take from here. But there was nothing she could do. She had been seen and this was really happening. Lisa walked over to the table, right across from the girl at the restaurant. She was sitting there eating like she did this on a regular basis. *What is she doing here? Does she live here? She is ruining my time.* So many thoughts flooded her mind as she stood there and stared at this girl she had been studying for the past month. The girl she hated. The girl she wanted to kill.

"You okay babe?" Axel asked as he watched the look on Lisa's face with pleasure.

"Yeah, I'm fine. I.. I just thought we were alone." Lisa managed to finally say without taking her eyes off Michelle.

"Well, Michelle lives here, so there's nothing I can do about that." Axel continued to amuse himself.

"You live here?" Lisa directed her question to Michelle almost daring her to say yes.

Michelle looked up from her plate for the first time. "Yes." She plainly stated. And went right back to eating her breakfast.

"Have a seat and have some breakfast. Then the car will take you home." Axel grabbed his plate from the counter after getting his breakfast just right and walked out onto the balcony leaving Michelle and Lisa to deal with the rest.

Michelle looked up at Lisa. She knew he had someone here. She noticed the rose petals and candles when she came home. She just didn't expect it to be Logan's girlfriend. She wondered if Logan knew that his girl had been confiscated. Probably not, but she wasn't about to tell him. She knew it was only a matter of time, but this had to be a new record. Michelle didn't even show her surprise. Nothing that happened in this house surprised her anymore. Although it never ceased to amaze her how these women get so caught up in Axel, thinking they are his one and only and then they wake up in the morning only to find her sitting at the breakfast table and their whole world comes crashing down on them. Michelle felt sorry for most of them, but not this one. She had a man. A good man. And she was dead wrong for betraying him. She deserved what she was getting.

"You might as well have a seat and eat before you leave. No reason to let this good food go to waste." Michelle tried to be civil with Lisa.

"What makes you think I want to sit here and eat with you?" Lisa snapped back.

"Because it's your only choice. Do you really think this is the first time this has happened? I have breakfast with all the one-night stands." Michelle continued to eat her breakfast.

"I'm not a one-night stand!" Lisa yelled a bit louder than she intended trying to hold her tears back.

"Okay. Maybe not. Maybe he'll invite you back. It has happened before."

"You didn't answer my question. Why are you here?"

"That's because Axel answered it for you. I live here."

"Why do you live here?"

"Because Axel wants me to live here. That's all I can tell you. I had my own place and then I met Axel and he moved me in. End of story."

"Why you?"

"I don't know. I really don't know. That's something you would have to ask Axel."

"How long have you lived here?"

"Why don't you have a seat first."

Lisa hesitated giving Michelle a look that could kill her if it was a weapon. But reluctantly sat down.

"Eat. Please."

Lisa picked up a piece of bacon. She wasn't hungry anymore at all. "My question? How long have you lived here?"

"A little over a year. What does it matter? Does Logan know you're here?"

Lisa almost choked on her bacon. "No and don't you tell him! I promise you Michelle if you tell him..."

"Calm down. I'm not going to tell him anything. What happens in this house, stays in this house. If he finds out. It won't be from me. I can promise you that." Michelle continued to eat her breakfast.

"Are you his girl?"

"I just live here. That's all I can tell you."

Lisa didn't know what to think. She wanted to be in Michelle's shoes so badly she could taste it. Michelle may not be his girl but she lived in his house and probably had his heart somehow. Whatever the case, Michelle had access to Axel in a way she didn't. How could she convince Axel she was better than Michelle? She didn't know how, but she would. With every fiber of her being, she would.

Michelle looked over at Lisa. She could tell she was not happy with her at all. But what she didn't know was, this is not what she wanted. Axel was a wolf in sheep's clothing. To the outside world he was the best man in the world, but to Michelle, he was her worst nightmare. If Lisa wanted him. She could have him. Michelle would not put up a fight at all. Lisa was mad at the wrong person. She wasn't the one keeping her from Axel. Axel just wasn't the settling type. Even though she lived at his house. She wasn't his girl, nor was he faithful to her and she was fine with that.

"Now since, you know why I'm here…"

"Actually, I still don't know."

"Anyway, why are you here?"

"Logan is great and all, but if you could go from good to great, wouldn't you upgrade?"

"Depends on your definition of upgrade?"

"You live in Axel Smith's house. You probably have access to all his money. I saw the dress you had on at the restaurant. You probably get things like that all the time. Do you also sleep in his bed?"

"Did you see me in his bed last night?"

"Are you always here when he entertains? How do you feel about that?" Lisa was trying her best to make Michelle upset.

"I'm here most of the time. Last night I was out. But I don't feel any kind of way about it. I have my own wing of this house and I'm good with that. Besides every girl that comes in eventually leaves. I will be here." Michelle said with a smile. She knew Lisa was testing her, but if she wanted to be that chick she could. She knew she had Axel. He couldn't live without her. So many women would love to be in that position. Michelle didn't want to be that chick because Michelle didn't want to be in that position. The price was too high.

"What if he gets married? What happens to you then?"

"I guess we'll find out when that day comes."

"Well, you better find out fast?"

"Oh really."

"Yes. Really."

Michelle finished the last section of omelet remaining on her plate and washed it down with her orange juice. "Well, let me know how that works out for you." Michelle got up from the table. "The driver will take you home when you're done, meanwhile, I'll be in my room."

Lisa folded her arms. She wanted Michelle gone. There was only one way to do it. Get Axel.

"I will have you, Axel. Bet on that."

# CHAPTER FIFTY-NINE

Autumn walked into the dance studio. Michelle was already there. Stretching and warming up.

"Hey girl! You're in her early." Autumn sat her dance bag down and walked over to where Michelle was sitting.

"Yeah. I have to stay on top of my game."

"Michelle, you are the best dancer I have. If anything, the rest of them should be in here with you or before you." Autumn took a seat next to Michelle and began stretching as well. "Michelle?" Autumn paused trying to see if she should ask Michelle what was on her mind.

"Yeah."

"I have been meaning to ask you something."

"Yes?" Michelle tensed up a bit not knowing what Autumn was going to say.

'Have you ever thought of being a real choreographer? You did great on that video. I thought you could become my own personal choreographer."

Michelle's eyes widened with surprise. "Of course, I have! I have always wanted to be a choreographer!"

"You serious?"

"Yes! You have no idea! When I lived with my grandmother, I would spend hours in my room coming up with different dances."

"You're grandmother? You have a grandmother?" This was the first time she had ever heard of Michelle having any family. She wondered if her grandmother knew what kind of life she was living.

"Umm... I used to have a grandmother. I don't anymore. Please Autumn, I really would rather not talk about it."

"Okay." Autumn didn't want to let it go. She saw how it was affecting Michelle so she thought she would table the discussion for another time. In the meantime, she might have to do some digging herself. "Well, anyway, I see it paid off. Do you know how many times I have watched my video just watching your moves? It's incredible. I even got the original footage before the editing and there are a whole lot more shots of you dancing and I'm amazed."

"Thanks. That means a lot coming from you. You are one of the best dancers I know."

"Not for long. Not when you really start doing your thing."

Michelle blushed. "You really think I'm that good?"

"I do Shelly. I really do. As a matter of fact, I would love for you to choregraph my next video."

"No! Stop playing with me!" Michell jumped to her feet. "Are you really serious?"

Autumn stood up next to her. "Of course, I'm serious."

"Oh my God! Autumn this is a dream come true! I promise I won't let you down. I promise." Michelle literally jumped into Autumn's arms.

"I don't doubt it, Shelly." Autumn returned Michelle's embrace. Autumn felt Michelle jump and instantly pull away from her. She looked at her and her head was hung down. The light in her eyes was gone. Her smile disappeared. There was only one person who could affect Michelle like that. Autumn turned around to see Axel walking through the door. Her smile faded as well. "Axel, what's up?"

"Just came to see what you guys were up too."

"We were just getting ready for a scheduled rehearsal." Autumn noticed Axel's eyes never left Michelle. His smirk made her stomach cringe. He knew he had affected Michelle and he was loving every minute of it.

"I see. Why isn't anyone else here?"

"Didn't invite anyone. Actually, I didn't invite Michelle but I figured she would be here. She is the hardest working dancer I have."

"I can see that." Axel still hadn't looked away from Michelle.

"But whatever the case, I'm glad you are here. I asked Michelle to choreograph my next video. What do you think about that?"

"You think she can choreograph an entire video by herself?"

"I do."

"Michelle?"

Michelle looked up for the first time.

"Do you think you can choreograph an entire video?" Axel's deep voice sent chills down Michelle's spine.

"Yes sir." Michelle answered softly.

"Well, I guess that would be a great idea Autumn, if you had a song."

Michelle looked over to Autumn. She didn't know Autumn didn't have a song yet. Her hopes fell to the bottom of her feet.

"I know, but I am working on that."

"Have you met with the writers?"

"Yeah, but they aren't giving me what I want. I was thinking Michelle and I could get together and write something ourselves."

Michelle eyes lit up once again, but this time it wasn't joyful. Her eyes were full of fear. She had crossed that writing bridge with Axel already and it got her knocked across the floor. *Why didn't Autumn run this by me first.* Michelle thought. *I would have told her not to bring it up.* Michelle's heart began to beat faster by the minute.

Axel's eyes turned to fire and brimstone. "So, you figured since Logan couldn't help you, you would come at me another way with this song writing business?"

Michelle was shaking by now. "No sir." Michelle wanted to burst into tears. She did not feel like getting beat today. "I had no idea she was going to ask me about writing a song. I only knew about the choreography part. I swear." Michelle was talking so fast it sounded like one long word.

"She's right Axel. I hadn't mentioned this to her before." Autumn hoped her words would save Michelle.

Axel stared intently at Michelle. Axel swung and Michelle hit the floor. The force of Axel's blow caused Autumn to hit the floor as well. Autumn looked over at Michelle. She was face down. When she looked over at Axel, she realized his fist was balled up.

"Oh my God! He punched her." Autumn's mouth fell open into a perfect "O." She looked back over at Michelle and realized she was not moving or crying or anything. She immediately scurried over to Michelle and began to shake her shoulder. No response. She turned her over. Nothing but dead weight. She put her hand on her stomach to make sure she was still breathing. She was.

"Oh, thank God. Axel, I think she is unconscious."

"I'll get my medical team to come in here and take care of this."

"Did you really just punch her?"

"Do you really think this is the first time I've punched her and laid her out? She'll be fine." Axel walked away and begin to dial someone on his phone.

Autumn had heard of Michelle getting beat and she knew it to be true. She had seen the bruises. But never had she seen it happen in person and she didn't think she ever wanted to again. She had to do something. What could she do? Who could she call? Autumn felt helpless. I promised I would help her, but I just don't know how. Autumn looked down at Michelle and began to cry. *God, how do I help her? Please show me.* Autumn silently prayed through a flood of tears and a heart that was slowly shattering like a piece of thin ice.

"Let's go Autumn." Axel beckoned between instructions to his crew.

Autumn didn't want to leave Michelle but when she looked up at Axel, she knew she had no other choice.

# CHAPTER SIXTY

Logan stood at the mixer listening to the final cut of his first single. It was cool, but Logan still thought he could do better.

"Man, I can hear that track jumping down the hall." Axel walked in bobbing his head to the beat. "That song is going to be a hit and all the ladies gonna be on you." Axel gave Logan a one-two punch combination on the arm.

"I guess that won't seem so bad since I'm going to need a new girl." Logan allowed his statement to hang in the air. He knew Axel was trying to figure out what to say.

"What do you mean?"

"We're both grown men. You can be straight with me. I didn't want her anyway. You gave me the reason I needed to get rid of her. I just need the facts. So, when did you smash?"

Axel respected Logan for coming at him straight. He was just relieved that his little escapade didn't run Logan off or interrupt his music making ability. "About a week ago." He finally confessed.

"After I brought her to the studio."

"Yeah. Same night. I got her number while you were in the booth. Sent a car to pick her. Sent her home the next morning. She's been ringing my phone off the hook ever since."

"You been answering?"

"Naw. I don't get down like that. There's only one constant in my world and that's Michelle. By the way, you should've seen her face when she saw Michelle that next morning. She had no idea she lived with me."

Logan could feel his blood beginning to boil. "How did Michelle take it?"

"Michelle is used to it. This ain't her first rodeo."

"If she's your constant, why don't you make her your only?"

"I don't do only. But I can do constant."

Logan had to get Michelle away from Axel and quick. Every time he opened his mouth about Michelle, it made him sick.

"I will get rid of her today." Logan tried to keep his cool.

"Who? Lisa?"

"Yeah. I gotta get ready to start making room for all this new booty."

"That's what I'm talking about man. Now we are on the same page. Worse thing you can be is booed up. Kill that man and get with this life. The life of a new girl every night. Or every hour. Just depends on how you get down."

"Either way sounds good to me." Logan decided to play the part. He would live the life, but he didn't mind being booed up. It just had to be the right person. It had to be Michelle.

"So, about this song. You ready to make it happen?" Axel stared at Logan.

"It's missing something."

"What do you mean?"

"Seems like it needs a female voice added to it. I know this is my debut single but I feel like a female voice would be perfect". Logan was already putting his plan to get to know Autumn in action.

Axel rubbed his chin with two fingers. "That ain't a bad idea. I wanted you and Autumn to do a song together after you dropped your first single, but this might work out better. I like the way you think my man."

Logan smiled. He had succeeded.

CHAPTER

# SIXTY-ONE

Lisa picked up her phone. She must have called Axel a million times over the last month and all she got was his voicemail. And to make matters worse, somehow Logan found out about her indiscretion with Axel and he broke it off with her. Lisa felt as if she couldn't breathe just thinking about it. She had no idea what she was going to do. She quit her job at the unemployment office, so she could be with Logan full time. Then the Axel thing came up. She was able to cipher enough money from Logan to take care of her for a couple of months. And by cipher she meant she sold or returned all the things he had bought her and a couple of things that Axel had bought her. She had two great dates. The first was ruined by Michelle but the second he had taken her shopping and bought her whatever she wanted. She felt like a kid in the candy store. Good thing she hadn't worn most of it and they still had the tags on it. She told him he shouldn't have and he gave her the receipts and told her she could do whatever she wanted with the stuff. He had just wanted to take his "special girl" out. His words. But now he had ghosted her and she didn't feel so special after all. He had used her.

She hit call. The phone rang once, twice.

"What do you want Lisa?"

Lisa almost dropped the phone. Her voice caught in her throat. She was not expecting Axel to actually answer, but he did. He finally did! She wanted to jump up and down and scream to the top of her lungs until she realized he was still on the phone and she had better say something before he hung up.

"Um, Axel, hey it's Lisa, I mean you know that already. I'm sorry. I'm just shocked you answered."

"Again. What do you want Lisa?" Axel repeated letting all the aggravation he felt linger through the phone.

"I just wanted to see how you were and you know see if we could get together sometime."

"I don't think this is going to work out. We had fun and now it's over. You cool with that?"

"I thought we had something special. You said I was your special girl."

"What's my name Lisa?"

"Axel."

"Axel what?"

"Axel Smith." She said sounding confused.

"Then you know I don't have any special girls. Girls come to me by the dozens. I wine them. I dine them and send them on their way. Now what I would like for you to do is be on your way."

Lisa could hardly hold back the tears that were threatening to roll down her face.

"Why are you saying these things? I... I left Logan for you. If you knew you didn't want me why would you..."

"Lisa, Lisa, calm down. I don't know if you're slow or what but newsflash... Logan didn't want you either. I was a very convenient reason to do what he wanted to do all along and that was get rid of you. So, I suggest you find something else to do with your life hun, cause if you are trying to bag you a millionaire, plastic surgery should be in your near future. Just a little friendly advice, from a friend."

The phone went silent.

Lisa stood there. Not knowing if what she just heard was real. Was this her life? Was this really happening? Had she been played so badly? What was she supposed to do now? All of a sudden she felt sick. She ran to the restroom and threw up. After pouring out her whole lunch, she sat by the toilet. *I can't let him just walk away. There has to be a way to get him back and I will find a way.*

# CHAPTER SIXTY-TWO

Autumn couldn't help but look at Logan. He sounded so good. She was so captured by his voice and the lyrics to this song she almost missed her cue to come in. Axel had done such a wonderful job writing this song. She rolled her eyes to herself. Why hadn't he put any effort into writing her a breakout song? She guessed she should just be thankful for the duet. She tried to push the thoughts plaguing her mind as she jumped in right on time with her verse.

Logan sensed Autumn looking at him. He looked over to the left and his eyes met hers. He continued to sing. As he continued to look at Autumn his intensity began to rise. He had never noticed how beautiful she was. He guessed he had been so caught up into Michelle, he hadn't even considered Autumn. He wondered if maybe there could be something there. He took a chance. He turned toward Autumn and grabbed her hand.

*What is he doing?* Autumn thought to herself. But she couldn't help but get drawn in. She turned toward Logan and allowed his words to take her to places she had ceased to allow anyone to take her in a very long time.

Logan saw the response he received from Autumn. *Is she really into me? She's Autumn Dance! I can't believe she would even entertain me.* Logan was sure she was going to pull away or at least playfully shove him, but she was really digging him.

It was time for the chorus and Autumn prepared to blend her voice with Logan's. She thought to herself. *I wonder what it would feel like wrapped in his arms?* She allowed that image to cause her voice to soar perfectly above his and a shiver went down her spine when his eyes lit up at the sensuality of her voice. She wondered if he was thinking the same thing she was thinking?

When the song was done, Autumn and Logan stood there staring in each other's eyes. They hadn't slept together but it sure felt like they had.

"So, you guys in love now?" Axel's voice caused them both to jump.

Autumn looked Logan over one last time. "It's just a song Axel." Autumn finally responded.

Autumn and Logan exited the sound booth feeling quite awkward.

"You two trying to hook up? I'm just asking." Axel asked.

Autumn looked over at Logan, butterflies were having a jam fest in her stomach. She wanted to see what his response would be.

Logan looked over at Autumn with the same sentiments in his head.

"I guess that's a yes. I'm going to leave that alone. I mean, as long as Logan ain't sniffing around Michelle, ya'll can do whatever ya'll want to do." Axel folded his arms across his chest.

Autumn looked surprised. "What do you mean by that?"

"Oh, you didn't know? Your boy got a thing for my girl. He just doesn't know he ain't the first and he surely won't be the last. The one thing that they always forget is that Michelle ain't going nowhere. All they doing is wasting time and effort." Axel said with a smirk.

Autumn looked over at Logan. She couldn't believe she was actually hurt by what Axel was saying. But it did hurt her. *Why does this keep happening to me. First it was Axel.* She thought. *Now Logan.* She thought for just a moment that they could possibly have something, but he wants Michelle. She would always have to compete with what Logan thought he could possibly have with Michelle. *What is it about this girl that makes guys fall all over her? I can't stand her. She can't keep doing this to me.* Autumn's blood began to boil. She shifted her weight back and forth. She wanted to run out of there as fast as her feet could take her. But she knew she had to play it cool. Axel wanted to rattle her and she couldn't let him know that he had succeeded.

"I have a man. So I'm not trying to fall in love with anyone else. Both of ya'll can have Michelle. Together." Autumn said matter of factly. "Look, I gotta go. I'll see ya'll later." Autumn grabbed her purse and bolted. The tears had already began to fall. She hoped Axel didn't see it. More so she hoped Logan didn't see the tears.

"Looks like you messed that up bruh." Axel shook his head at Logan.

"Wasn't nothing to mess up. It was a song. That's all. Besides, I already know what I want." Logan fired back without a smile. Staring Axel eye to eye.

Axel knew exactly what Logan wanted. He couldn't believe he was bold enough to put it out there like that. Logan's first single was bound to go platinum. He would be crazy to get rid of him right now. *I have to find out a way to hurt him.* Axel thought to himself. "Like I stated before, Michelle ain't going hv nowhere and I can promise you that." Axel refused to back down.

"You just make sure you stay on top of your game. Cause I'm coming for ya." Logan walked out the door and left Axel speechless. Logan exited the building and nearly ran to his car. *What was I thinking?* Logan thought as he laid his head back on the headrest. *Is saving Michelle really this important? Why am I so obsessed with this girl? What if she doesn't even want to be saved? Can I really go up against Axel?*

"It's Axel Smith! Are you crazy!" Logan yelled out.

"Get it together Logan. Get it together. Just do your job. Don't jeopardize everything for this girl. This girl that you know nothing about. Except she has a banging body. The most beautiful face I have ever seen in my life." Logan bit his bottom lip thinking about Michelle. "I gotta go make this right. I already messed up my Autumn connection. I don't know how I will ever get close to Michelle now." Logan took a deep breath. "I can't jeopardize my career. I can't make an enemy of Axel." Logan put his head in his hands. He knew what he had to do. Something he would almost rather die than do. Apologize to Axel.

Logan saw Axel sitting in the studio. He could tell he was working on some new beats. Logan stood there in amazement. That's why this guy is a multi-billion-dollar genius. I need to learn all I can from him instead of getting on his bad side over a female. I promised I wouldn't do that. Michelle got me acting crazy. Logan took a deep breath and stepped inside the studio.

Axel immediately turned around. When he saw it was Logan, he quickly cut the music and rose to his feet. Logan could tell he was expecting a fight by his stance and the way his fists were balled up. Logan couldn't believe Axel was willing to go toe to toe with him over Michelle. *I guess Michelle has some kind of hold on him too. But if he cares so much, why doesn't he just love her and cherish her instead of dogging her out. Maybe there's something I don't know. Maybe Michelle isn't as sweet an innocent as I think. Only one way to find out. I need to get close to Axel. Get on his good side. I need to find out his side of the story.* Logan swallowed harder than he expected to. He figured he better get him a large pack of chap-stick; a whole lot of butt kissing was in his immediate future.

"Axel..." Logan began as humble as he could. "I'm sorry man. I was out of line. I don't know what came over me. I think it's just Michelle. She just does something to me." *It was working.* Logan noticed Axel's fists un-ball. Logan sat on the couch. Hoping to cause Axel to relax even more. "I have never been like this with any woman. Just like Lisa. I use them and send them packing. So, it's got to be something dangerous about Michelle. I have had some of the finest, but it didn't faze me. I do know one thing. I ain't about to lose my career over no woman. I was standing outside and I heard you working. Pure genius. So, what I need to do instead of disrespecting you is learn from you. I'm sorry man. I really am. I just want to know what makes you great and team up with you so we can do something great together."

Axel squinted his eyes and folded his arms. He could smell bull from a mile away and he didn't smell any at the time. He could see the genuineness in Logan's eyes. He got caught up, just like any good man would. But he caught himself. Not only that, he came and apologized. Many men wouldn't do that. Even if they thought they were wrong; they wouldn't have apologized. Axel sat down in his seat. "Let's get to work," was all he said.

Logan was glad to hear those words. He could deal with that. That's all he needed to hear.

Axel looked at Logan and smiled. "I'm going to hook you up with a bunch of females. Just you watch and see."

Logan dabbed Axel up. "Now that's what I'm talking about."

"Fo sho."

# CHAPTER SIXTY-THREE

Charlie's hazel eyes glimmered as she peered around Single Ladies. She clutched her hand purse tighter than she meant to. Anticipation was overtaking her. Her eyes darted from target to target. People she knew she needed to mingle with to get to the top and stay on top. It was all about collaboration these days. She saw Autumn beat her to the punch. This must be her last ditch effort to beat me. Charlie thought. We'll see if this song is any good. Although she heard it was. She had to get ahead of the game. If she partnered with the right artist, she would be sure to blow Autumn out of the water. Her lips curled under at the thought of seeing Autumn's face as she witnessed Charlie taking over the music industry. Charlie's right foot dragged a bit as she began to step forward to one of her many targets of the night, but something caught her eye and she stopped mid stride. A beautiful red dress, filled with hips that spread it out just nicely. Just as Charlie was wondering what the back end looked like, the red boned beauty turned around with nervous energy filling every move she made. And there it was, a booty that jiggled just as much as the DDD's she was sporting in the fitted thigh length dress. Who was she and why had she never seen her before? Charlie made up her mind to make this her first stop.

She glided across the floor as not to startle the beauty that was already as jittery as a jitterbug. *What was her deal? Was she afraid of something or someone?* The closer she got to the beautiful sight the more she seemed to recognize her face. It was her. She had seen her before. But never like this. She was one of Autumn's dancers and Axel's girl. If that's what you wanted to call her. Charlie thought she was more like his punching bag. Charlie had never seen her all dressed up like this. She normally had on tights and a baggy shirt with her hair pulled back. So that's what she was hiding under those baggy clothes. Charlie would have never thought. Nevertheless, she wanted to see if she was exclusive to Axel or not.

"Hey." Charlie tried her best not to frighten Michelle.

Michelle turned like someone was about to attack her.

"Hey. Calm down. I'm not going to hurt you. Are you okay?"

Michelle let out a sigh of relief. "Yes, yes, I'm fine."

"You are so beautiful." Charlie's eyes roamed Michelle's body admiring every inch.

Michelle looked puzzled. She didn't really know how to respond.

"You don't know how to take a compliment?"

"Umm.. thanks."

"Do you know who I am?"

"Yes. Charlie, right?"

"Good girl. I'm impressed. Why don't you have a seat and let me buy you a drink?"

"I don't know." Michelle began to look around cautiously again.

Charlie motioned toward the bar stool.

*It's not a guy so maybe Axel won't mind.* Michelle thought as she took her seat.

"You look like a Martini kind of girl. Bartender let me get two Martini's on the rocks."

"Coming right up." The bartender mixed a couple of things and then returned to the bar with two fresh drinks.

"Drink up." Charlie grabbed her cup and began to sip without taking her eyes off Michelle.

Michelle's hands began to tremble as she raised her drink to her lips and begin to slowly sip. She wasn't sure if this was acceptable to Axel or not.

Charlie reached over and placed her hand on Michelle's thigh and gently began to rub it. "What's got you so shaken up sweet girl?"

Michelle's breathing began to speed up as she watched Charlie's hand find its way around her thigh. "I'm… I'm fine."

"You don't seem fine." Charlie pulled Michelle a little closer to her.

Michelle nearly fell out of the seat with fear.

"It's okay baby. I promise I'm not going to hurt you." Charlie caught Michelle's arm to steady her.

Michelle let out a sigh of relief. She was just glad that Charlie was no longer rubbing her thigh. She had never experienced this kind of attention and her head felt dizzy trying to wrap her mind around what was going on. Before Michelle could figure it out, Charlie's hand found its way back to her thigh but this time it had slid to the left, threatening to caress her hips and rear end.

"What's going on here?" The sound of Axel's voice nearly knocked Michelle out of her seat.

Charlie came to her rescue once again. "Baby girl, you are determined to hit this floor."

"What's up Axel?" Charlie pretty much sung her greeting. "I'm just chilling here with your girl."

"I can see that. It looks like you doing more than just chilling. It looks like you're doing some sampling."

"Oh, believe me, I have not even begun to start sampling yet." Charlie licked her lips as she looked back over Michelle.

"Interesting." Axel looked at Charlie and then looked at Michelle. Michelle could see the wheels in his head turning as a smile spread across his face.

Charlie picked up on Axel's interest and decided to capitalize on it.

"What's going through that brilliant mind of yours Axel?" Charlie asked hoping for the answer she desired.

"Tell me what's going through yours first?"

"You already know my angle player. I want a full fledge, long term affair with your girl here."

Michelle began to choke on her drink. Charlie and Axel couldn't help but laugh.

"Normally I would have back hand Michelle out of that chair, but I must admit that this intrigues me."

Charlie smiled. She just might get her wish after all. And every fiber of her being lit up with excitement at the thought of exploring and experiencing Michelle.

A single tear fell from Michelle's eye. Her stomach was queasy with the thought of sleeping with another woman. Where would Axel ever draw the line? Would he torment her forever? Was he ever going to let her go?

"Let's walk and talk." Axel reached out for Charlie's hand and she gladly obliged.

"I'll be back for you sexy. Believe that." Charlie leaned over and whispered to Michelle before disappearing with Axel.

Michelle sat at her bar stool contemplating another drink, but she knew better. She didn't want to give Axel any reason. She had already survived one encounter with him. She didn't want to risk another. Michelle twirled her straw around the remaining ice cubes in her glass. She locked eyes on a figure just across the bar. It was him. Logan. And he wasn't alone. Not by a long shot. As a matter of fact, he had several women crowded around him. There were regular girls and then there were the strippers. Michelle could barely tell the difference. It seemed like all the regular girls were trying to one up the strippers. Every time a stripper dropped an article of clothing, so did they. Michelle shook her head. *So desperate.* She thought to herself.

Michelle wanted to get up and walk away but for whatever reason she could not pull herself away. She just sat there. Twirling ice. Squinting her eyes trying to see everything that was going on. Until her eyes grew larger. Logan was looking right at her. Should she look away? She twitched in her chair pondering her next move, but there she sat frozen, unable to look away.

Logan noticed Michelle watching his every move. He decided to give her a show. He took off his shirt and began to serenade the women, grinding with every note he sang. His hands were like tentacles. They were everywhere he could think to put them. He would look up every so often and give Michelle a wink, until she obviously couldn't take any more because she got up and left.

Michelle couldn't take one more second of Logan's games. He was intentionally trying to make her jealous. Michelle was walking so fast she almost knocked a waiter over with a tray full of drinks. Michelle's heart stopped and so did her feet. She just imagined having collided with the waiter. The room would have grown quiet. All eyes would have been on her and then Axel would appear out of nowhere and backhand her clear across the floor in perfect view of all guest in attendance. Michelle trembled at the thought of it. She began to walk again. She moved as if she were walking through a volcano that was bound to erupt at any moment.

Michelle felt a small scream escape her throat. Someone had walked up behind her and grabbed her around her waist. Axel had finally caught up with her, She turned around to learn her fate.

"Logan. Not what she expected at all. Are you crazy!" She could have killed Logan.

"What's wrong with you?"

"You. You're trying to get me killed!"

"Never that pretty girl."

"If Axel had of seen..."

"I don't want to talk about Axel. I want to talk about you."

"What about me?"

"Why were you watching me?"

"I wasn't watching you." Michelle caught herself looking over him from head to toe. Feeling disappointed he had put his shirt back on.

Logan shook his head. "Go ahead and keep playing hard to get."

"I'm not playing anything."

"Ok then tell me why you left?"

"I wanted to go somewhere else."

"Why don't you just be honest and tell me you like me."

"What! I do not like you! Why would I like you!"

"Because you know I can love you like you need to be loved."

Michelle's voice caught in her throat. She couldn't believe what had just come out of Logan's mouth.

"What do you know about love Logan? You are no different from Axel."

"I haven't put my hands on any female." Logan responded defensively.

"You may not be putting your hands on anyone like Axel, put you are putting your hands on plenty of women if you catch my drift. I don't want a man who uses and abuses women because to me it's the same thing. Abuse is abuse whether you're hitting your woman or playing with her emotions. Sometimes I prefer the former. You can heal quicker from that." Michelle turned on her heals and walked away.

Logan stood there dumfounded. Michelle was right. He had taken Axel's advice and started running through women, but he couldn't really blame it all on Axel. This is what he did even before he was so-called rich and famous. He had tried to make Michelle jealous, but once again she had proved that she was not like other women. She wanted someone real, not someone who wanted to play games. He had to get himself together and really show her he was down for her and no one else.

# CHAPTER SIXTY-FOUR

Lisa sat at her table. Making sure she was facing the door. She knew Axel would be there tonight and she would make sure he talked to her. He wouldn't be able to ignore her phone calls or dismiss her. He would have to see her. He would have to explain to her why he was treating her the way that he was. They were supposed to be together forever. She had risked her relationship with Logan for him. Now he wanted to dump her and move on. Not in this lifetime. Lisa was getting angrier by the minute. She watched the door while she waited for her order to come. She ordered the tilapia on a bed of rice with asparagus on the side. Of course, she ordered the red wine to go with it. She needed a little extra motivation in case she had to act a fool in Axel's restaurant and she was fully prepared to do so.

*What is this?* The door opened and a familiar face walked in. Lisa shook her head. *I didn't expect this. I think I need to talk to her.* The girl seemed as if she was here for the same reason. Her eyes were darting all over the restaurant. Lisa was pretty sure she was looking for Axel. *I see she still hasn't let him go either.*

"I see you came looking for the same thing I did." Lisa got the attention of the woman when she came close enough to her table.

The woman looked confused. "What are you talking about?"

"Aren't you Harmony? Axel's ex-fiancé?"

"And what's it to you?"

"Let's just say Axel and I are currently in a relationship, but he seems to be acting strangely. Please have a seat. I would like to talk to you about it. Maybe we could help each other."

Harmony didn't really trust this girl but her interest had been peeked. Harmony sat down and picked up a menu. "Who are you and why do you think you can help me?"

"The name is Lisa and I came to confront Axel. Same as you. Maybe we can team up. Make a bigger impact."

"And if we do that, which one of us walks away with him."

"For all I care we both can. As long as I got him. We can pull and R. Kelly and we both can move in and be his girls. You know he's not a one-woman man. We can make it more appealing for him and get both our feet in the door. What do you say?"

Harmony couldn't believe what she was hearing. More so than that she couldn't believe that she was actually thinking about doing it.

"You mean being with him together but separate or are you talking about a three way?" Harmony asked genuinely confused.

"You're cute enough. I wouldn't mind a three-way with you every now and then." Lisa smiled and winked at Harmony.

Harmony couldn't believe that had just turned her on. She shook the feeling away. But as she sat there staring at Lisa, she allowed it to come back and just like that she was on board. "So, what's your plan?"

Before Lisa could answer, the waiter walked up with her meal. She asked if Harmony wanted anything, but she declined. Harmony was there for one reason and one reason only. To confront Axel. To make him see her.

Lisa took a sip of her wine. She allowed it to revive her being and then she took the rest of it to the head. Feeling better than she had before she walked in the restaurant. She knew for sure she could do what she came here to do, especially now with a new ally by her side. "We are going to wait until he's seated and then seat ourselves at his table. We will lay out our plan before him, not giving him any time to rebut us. I don't see him turning our offer down."

Harmony sat back in her seat. She hoped Lisa's plan worked, since all her plans seemed to be failing. Finding him and confronting him was her lame back up plan.

Lisa began to lay out all the details for Harmony so they could be on the same page and the ambush would be successful. As she finished putting on the final details, the door opened and her heart began to race. It was finally time.

Lisa watched him stroll in. "Let the games begin."

Harmony looked up to see Axel and to her surprise he had a girl with him. Who was this new girl? Where they engaged? Harmony had been out of the loop since she packed a bag and went to stay with her parents until this whole break-up with Axel could blow over. Then she visited Autumn and asked if she could come back and dance for her. Autumn being the sweetheart she is even to a fault let her back in. But seeing Axel with this new girl caused a fire to begin stirring in Harmony's chest like a volcano about to explode.

"We aren't making any kind of proposal to him. He is going to explain himself and he's going to do it tonight."

"Harmony, we have to stick to the plan."

Harmony watched Axel and his girl be seated.

"Are you listening to me Harmony?"

Harmony hadn't taken her eyes off of Axel and as soon as she saw her opportunity, she shot over to his table like lightening. Lisa couldn't do anything but run behind her. She wasn't about to miss out on this. Since this was her plan all along.

Harmony slid into the booth across from Axel and Lisa slipped in beside her. Their eyes stabbing daggers into him.

"Well, isn't this interesting." Axel was amused at their effort.

"Who is this, Axel?" Harmony was the first to speak, nodding her head toward the woman who was with him. Whom she also noticed had a scared look on her face. *She better be scared.* Harmony thought to herself.

"Who she is, is none of your concern."

"I know exactly who she is." Lisa stared at Michelle as if she could kill her. "Her name is Michelle and she lives with him."

"She lives with you! Like all the way with you!"

Axel smiled.

Lisa decided to answer for him. "All the way. All her things are there. She wakes up there. Eats breakfast there. Goes to sleep there. She seems to be wherever he is."

Harmony's blood was boiling. She was his fiancé and she was not allowed to fully move in with him. "Are you gonna explain yourself? Is it true?"

"It's true. She lives with me. Full time."

"Are you going to marry her?" Harmony was falling apart by the second.

"Maybe. Who knows?"

Harmony almost pushed Lisa out of the booth and ran out.

"This isn't over Axel." Lisa started to leave behind Harmony, but before she did, she decided to use plan B. She put her hand in her purse and pulled out a plastic bag containing a little stick and placed it in front of Axel. "By the way, looks like you're gonna be a daddy."

Michelle looked up for the first time, eyes stretched with shock.

Lisa winked at her knowing she had finally rattled her. Axel on the other hand, didn't seem bothered at all.

Lisa pushed. "You'll be hearing from me."

"Lisa..." Axel started as if he might be concerned.

Lisa walked off feeling satisfied with her results and decided to run and catch up to Harmony.

Axel looked over at Michelle. She was visibly shaken by what had occurred.

"What's wrong with you?"

"Just don't like to see people hurt. The girl that was your fiancé looked pretty hurt" Michelle thought it best not to share the fact that she felt like she was about to throw up at the thought of marrying Axel. She hoped he was just playing to mess with the women's heads. But she couldn't help the sick feeling in her stomach. She knew there was no limit to Axel's depravity. "Plus, the other girl said she was pregnant. That never happened before."

"Ha!" Axel was amused. "It's happened before, you just never heard of it because it never manifests. And just like the rest, neither will hers."

## CHAPTER
# SIXTY-FIVE

Michelle exited her room and headed toward the kitchen where she was met by the aroma of chicken and steak fajitas. She instinctively began to lick her lips. Her stomach growled in response to the amazing smoked deliciousness that was coming from the kitchen. She couldn't remember the last time she had eaten. She hoped Axel wouldn't give her a hard time about it. Axel wasn't above starving Michelle. She had gone to bed and awoken hungry more times than she could count. She slowed her pace. She could hear voices. Must be another one of his overnighters. Luckily for Michelle, Axel loved when she showed up and surprised his guest who had no idea that she lived there. Michelle could still see the look on Lisa's face when she showed up for breakfast. Lisa was one of the really naïve ones. She actually thought she would be Axel's one and only. As if Axel would ever settle down. Michelle thought that if Axel ever settled down, it would be with Autumn. Michelle loved the connection Axel and Autumn shared. She loved the way he looked at her and the way she blushed in response. But how could someone who treated her so terribly be capable of that type of love? Would Axel eventually start to treat Autumn the way he treated her? Or was she a special case. Was something wrong with her that men just loved to abuse her? Would anyone ever be capable of loving her? Would Logan? Michelle briefly allowed her mind to recall the words that escaped Logan's lips at the music release party. *No one could love you like I could.* Did Logan really love her or was he just another guy trying to get between her legs? She wasn't sure. So much had gone on with Logan and Lisa and now all of these other women. How could she trust him? Michelle couldn't believe what she was thinking. Axel would never let her go. She would never be free enough to ever consider finding out if Logan was for real or not. Michelle continued into the kitchen. Her heart suddenly stopped in her chest.

"Come on in sexy girl." Charlie stood at the counter watching Axel work his magic in the kitchen. She turned around giving her complete attention to Michelle." You are definitely wearing that dress too."

Michelle swallowed hard suddenly regretting her choice of clothes. Axel on the other hand wore a wicked grin on his face. Enjoying every minute of Michelle's misery.

Charlie began to slowly walk toward Michelle. Michelle couldn't help but notice the beautiful flowered floor length summer dress Charlie was wearing. She was so beautiful. Michelle would have never guessed that she was gay. She was pretty sure Charlie had disappointed plenty of men. Maybe even Axel.

"I would love to see what's under it. Even though those legs and thighs are keeping me quite satisfied all on their own." Charlie continued her ascent toward Michelle. Michelle wanted to back away and retreat to her bedroom, but fear had her feet cemented to the ground.

Charlie circled Michelle enjoying the fear that she saw in her eyes. She now knew why Axel treated Michelle the way he did. She was sure the fear that Michelle presented set his whole body on fire. Presently her body was about to explode in orgasmic satisfaction. And she hadn't even touched her yet. She could almost feel the softness of Michelle's body as she continued to circle around her, trying her best not to rub against her, fearing she wouldn't be able to control herself if she did. Axel had not yet given her the okay to experience Michelle yet. He called her over about 2 hours ago saying he wanted to talk to her. It took her a little over an hour and half to get ready and then drive over. She wanted to make sure she looked perfect. Not for Axel. For Michelle. Axel didn't specify what he wanted to talk to her about but she sat in her car shaking with nervous energy hoping he wanted to talk about Michelle. When she arrived at Axel's home, she stepped out of her Lexus convertible with her mouth hung open. She had never seen such a massive house up close and personal. She knew Axel was stacked in the money department but this just let her know how much so. Even tho her hit single continued to soar and bring in more money than she could have imagined, she was nowhere close to buying a house of this magnitude. She thought she had done something when she special ordered her Lexus convertible with the pink leather interior and paid cash for it. It was the biggest purchase she had made. She still rented her condo. Although it was a huge step up from where she was previously living. Before Charlie could ring the doorbell, his maid opened the door and welcomed her in calling her by name.

"Come in Ms. Charlie. Mr. Axel is waiting for you." The maid had said.

Charlie stepped in feeling like royalty. She sashayed into the dining room that was open to the kitchen. She found Axel standing over the counter with an apron on. Now this was something you didn't see every day. How could this man, that sent fear through everyone he encountered, be standing here with an apron on?

"What's up Charlie? Come on in. How's my number one artist doing?"

Charlie couldn't help but blush. She had worked relentlessly to put Autumn out of that number one spot and to hear Axel actually say it, was sheer victory. She continued on to the barstools that set right in front of the counter where she could now tell he was removing some chicken and steak. She was sure it had been marinating probably all night.

"Please tell me those are going to be fajitas?"

"They can be whatever you want them to be."

"I absolutely love fajitas. I might just sleep with you for those. That's how much I love them. Then I would surely vomit everywhere." Charlie busted out laughing.

"I can't stand you sometime Charlie, but who knows I still might use that against you one day. Getting in your pants or should I say under your dress would be well worth it." Axel responded while locking eyes with Charlie, hoping to see a bit of a crack in her hard, *I will never sleep with a guy,* mentality.

"So, you cook?" Charlie asked trying to change the subject.

"Of course. Why would I not?" Axel answered reluctantly knowing he was not going to get anywhere with sleeping with Charlie.

"I'm sure you have a whole chef team that does that for you."

"I do." Axel smiled. "But I like to cook myself from time to time. It relaxes me. Plus, I have a special guest that I want to impress."

"Do you mean moi?" Charlie placed her hand on her ample breast. Hoping he caught a fresh glimpse. He did. She didn't want to sleep with Axel, but she knew if she turned him on, it would definitely be a plus. A girl that he can't sleep with, must be driving him crazy.

"Of course. Who else would I be talking about?"

"Well, you know I thought your number one artist, the one to impress would be Autumn." Charlie stared at Axel wanting to see his full reaction to what she was saying.

Axel didn't even look up from what he was doing. "You already know what it is with Autumn."

"Actually, I don't." Charlie decided to push him to say what she wanted to hear. That she came and put Autumn out of her place. Instead, he wanted to play hard ball.

"Why are you so insistent on overshadowing Autumn? You both are amazing artist. If you all did a collab it would be amazing!"

"Never gonna happen. It's either me or her."

"But why? I don't understand."

"It doesn't matter. You already said I'm the number one artist, so that settles it." Charlie was trying to hide her frustration but was failing miserably. She couldn't understand why Axel kept defending Autumn.

"You are my number one female artist… as far as sales go, but I will warn you, if Autumn ever gets her head back in the game, you're going to have a fight on your hands."

Charlie stood up and walked away from the counter, she didn't want Axel to see how angry she had gotten. She walked around and looked at the pictures on the wall, hoping to calm herself. She could tell Axel was a totally different person at home than he was in the office. All of his paintings were peaceful and serene. Like he was the greatest person on Earth. But Charlie had already heard the stories. And actually seen him in action a few times. Mostly when he was beating the life out of Michelle. Either way, there was nothing peaceful or serene about him, typically.

"So, tell me about your girl Michelle." Charlie was desperate to change the subject, but she also didn't want to lose sight of the reason she came in the first place.

"What about her?"

"You gonna let me hit that or what?"

"You do know I don't normally lend Michelle out?"

"Well, there is always a first time for everything. You do want to keep your top artist happy; don't you?" Charlie turned toward Axel feeling his eyes roaming her body and they were. She gave him a sexy smile in satisfaction.

Axel gave a smile back. "Of course, I do. But there has got to be another way. I told you if you give me one chance. I will assuredly make you change your entire sexual preference."

"Assuredly?" Charlie couldn't help but laugh.

Charlie had heard it all before. It's like male egos couldn't except that a woman as fine as she, couldn't dare not be interested in them. There had to be something wrong with her. But there was nothing wrong with her, she liked women and that was that. She never went back to experiencing men after her first time with a woman. And she liked it like that. Women, she found, couldn't hurt you, well at least not sexually and Charlie was determined to never be hurt again.

"You look like you are ready to enjoy yourself." Axel joked with Charlie, bringing her thoughts back to the present.

"I'm hungrier for your girl than I am for those fajitas you're fixing and you know how I feel about those." Charlie responded without taking her eyes off Michelle.

"I tell you what; why don't you let Michelle take you back to her room and then, well… you can use your imagination when you get there." Axel looked up from where he had already began grilling the meat for his fajitas. He could see horror taking shape on Michelle's face. He still wasn't a hundred percent okay with sharing Michelle, but pawning her off on a girl, something he knew she would hate; he just couldn't pass up. So, he rolled with it.

Michelle stared at Axel; trying to plead with him with her eyes. But her silent cries went unnoticed. Instead, it was her that obeyed the command in his eyes that said keep your mouth shut and do exactly what you are told or there will be consequences. Michelle turned to face Charlie who stood smiling from ear to ear. She slowly began what felt like the longest journey to her room. Although it would never be quite long enough to put off permanently the unimaginable things she was about to experience. All the while she could feel Charlie close behind her; matching her every step.

Michelle could feel the rumbling in her stomach and realized she was definitely not about to eat lunch or dinner for that matter any time soon.

CHAPTER
# SIXTY-SIX

Michelle sat up in her bed. She couldn't believe she had fallen asleep. The last thing she remembered was lying in Charlie's arms as she whispered sweet nothings in her ear. She initially wanted to get up immediately and wash the memory of Charlie off of her, but Charlie seemed to not want to let her go. Michelle knew she had to oblige her or risk being punished by Axel. That was something she did not do willingly.

Michelle pulled back the covers and threw her feet over the side of the bed. She looked down realizing she was still naked. At least it would be that much easier to jump in the shower. Michelle scooted off the bed and headed towards the bathroom opting to leave her comfy slippers behind and bare the cold hardwood floors.

Michelle turned on the shower and looked around the massive bathroom while waiting on the water to warm up. She could still remember the day she first moved in with Axel. She knew for sure she would probably be staying in his room, but then he took her to her own room in a separate wing of the house and she could remember feeling relieved that as least she had her own space. Axel couldn't torture her continuously. That is exactly what it felt like any time she was in his presence. Torture. She relished the moments she was alone in her room or bathroom. It was the only place she had peace. The only place she was free from beatings, free from fear, and most of all free from Axel; for the most part. She detested his very presence. She thought about the dance studio. She often felt peace there. That was until Axel beat her unconscious there too. He came to almost every rehearsal checking up on her and now even the thing that she felt the most joy from was feeling like a place of torment and constant pressure.

Michelle felt pain in her hand. She hadn't realized her hands were balled up so tightly. She could feel the anger rising from the pits of her stomach. How could anyone be so evil? Michelle took a deep breath as she tried to clear her mind of all the negativity. She just wanted to wash her life away in the shower; especially the events of the past evening. She stepped into the shower slowly allowing the soothing stream to cover her body in its entirety. The water was as hot as she could handle. Michelle stood there hoping the hot water would wash away all of the humiliation and shame she had endured at the hands of Charlie. She threw her head back as she stepped further into the shower taking in the force of the water. Allowing it to fully caress her body. But instead of it washing all the grotesque feelings she felt, she found herself being reminded of Charlie's every touch as the water flowed over the different parts of her body. She could feel Charlie's breath breathing on her neck as the steam rose up all around her. As the water made it's way down her thighs, she remembered the touch of Charlie's hand caressing them ever so softly as she sat upon the bar stools at the club. She recalled the look in her eyes as she devoured her in her mind. She could hear Charlie's voice from last night, *Just relax baby girl. I got you.* Michelle was sure her words were meant to be comforting but Michelle felt anything but comfort. Her stomach felt as if she had just drunk sour milk from its container. Her head swam rapidly like fish in the sea. Except they were free. She was not. She felt violated as if she were being raped all over again. She allowed her tears to mix with the water as they flowed down her face. The same way they had done the day before. Except this time Charlie wasn't there to kiss them away. Michelle had hoped her tears would discourage her but they seemed to turn her on even the more. It was as if she was determined to make Michelle comfortable and accepting to what was happening to her. But how could she? She had never thought about being with another woman not one day in her entire life. She didn't like it. She didn't want it. Then she felt something. As she lay on her back, Charlie began to explore Michelle with both her tongue and her lips. From her neck to her breast. From her breast to her navel. From her navel to her thighs. She stayed in that region until she finally pulled Michelle's legs apart and went further. Michelle had experienced oral sex before, but never like this. This made every fiber of being quiver. Suddenly her tears ceased and soft melodic moans took over. Instinctively she began to crave the soft touch of Charlie's hands. And as if she read her mind, she began to touch her all over. From her thighs to her navel. From her navel to her breast where she remained until Michelle couldn't help but grab her hands and join in. She set Michelle on fire with every stroke of her tongue and she knew it. *How can I stop this?* Michelle remembered thinking. How could she be enjoying the very thing she hated just moments before? To Michelle's continual surprise, she could no longer hide her enjoyment. Her body began to shake as an orgasm threatened to take over her body. Why was her body betraying her? Why was she enjoying this instead of vomiting with every touch? Michelle couldn't wrap her head around it. Sadly, to say that wasn't the last orgasm she experienced during her time with Charlie. She was sure three more followed that one. Now Michelle felt a bit nauseated; but just like on yesterday the more she thought about it her nausea was replaced with a feeling of euphoria. The more she allowed the thoughts to run rapid in her mind the more her body continued to respond. Before her shower could even begin, she experienced yet another orgasm. How sick could she be? Was this part of who she was now? Would she begin to crave women? Or just Charlie? She didn't know and the dam that had been holding back her tears broke once again. Her tears began to flow just as rapidly as the water from her shower as she sunk to the shower floor. Michelle didn't know how to process what she was feeling. But she was determined to wash away the thought of yesterday's events even if just for a moment.

# CHAPTER SIXTY-SEVEN

Charlie drove down the highway with a belly full of fajitas and her loins filled with sexual satisfaction. The day couldn't have gone better. Axel had invited her to his personal sanctuary for the first time. Fixed her favorite dish himself. Called her his top female artist. And to put the icing on the cake he allowed her to finally experience Michelle, something she seemed to want more than the rest. Now she was hooked like a fish fighting for its life. It seemed as if she had spent hours with Michelle and with a glance at the clock on her dash, she knew it to be true. She had never been so thorough with a woman's body as she had been with Michelle's. She literally kissed her from her head to her feet and everything in between. She tried her best to devour every inch of Michelle's body. Michelle was the most beautiful, sexiest woman she ever had the pleasure of crossing paths with. And even though she had just left Michelle she could feel her body feigning for her all over again. Michelle was definitely a drug and she was an unintended addict. She normally had women falling all over her; obsessed after only one night. But with Michelle the tides had shifted. Charlie wanted Michelle more than she wanted anything in the world at this point. Not just sexually to her surprise. She wanted to make Michelle her one and only. She wanted to take care of her and love her like she knew Axel wasn't currently doing.

A devious thought began to rummage its way through Charlie's head. She decided she would take Michelle from Axel. Why stop there? The thought continued its destructive path. Why not take over his entire empire? Charlie shifted in her seat, overtaken with anticipation of living in a house like Axel's. Driving cars like Axel. Owning businesses all over LA like Axel. Last but certainly not least having the one woman Axel possessed exclusively. Michelle. Her life would be perfect. She would even take his so-called best friend Autumn. Except she would kill that whole best friend nonsense. Autumn would be to Charlie what Michelle was to Axel now. She would spend her days beating, emotionally abusing, and using Autumn as her personal sex slave. Unless Michelle didn't want her to. Knowing Michelle, she wouldn't. In the meantime, until the day Michelle became hers, she might as well try to get as much from Autumn as she could. Charlie pushed down on the gas causing the car to accelerate as the wind blew through her hair and fondled her breast. She was enjoying the very thought of her plan. She could only imagine how she would feel as it began to take shape. Charlie wasn't about to waste one minute carrying out her grand scheme. After all, everything else that she had wanted she had conquered. So why should her luck change now.

## CHAPTER
# SIXTY-EIGHT

Lisa walked around the baby store. She couldn't believe she was actually carrying Axel Smith's baby. She stopped taking her birth control right after Logan got signed hoping she would get pregnant by him, but it didn't happen that way. She lied to Axel and told him that she was on birth control. Of course, he believed her. She couldn't believe how trusting he was with things of that nature. Lisa rubbed her belly. She smiled anticipating the day her belly would swell with Axel's seed.

She hadn't heard from Axel or even tried to see him, but she had him. She told Michelle she would have him. Now what was she going to do? Axel may let her live there, but I'm sure he would never let her carry his child. But here she was in first place. She was so loving her life right now.

"Why did you ask me to meet you at a baby store?"

Lisa turned to see a clearly agitated Harmony. "Well, it's nice to see you too."

"Look, contrary to what you may think, we are not friends."

"Yet here you are."

"Let's just say I'm curious. Now what do you want?"

"Look. I want us to be friends. In a business like this, you need allies."

"I can be an ally without being your friend."

"Oh, so you don't want to be friends with the woman who's carrying Axel Smith's baby?"

"What? You're lying."

"Why do you think I asked you to meet me at a baby store. Gotta get prepared for the new arrival."

"Does Axel know?"

"Yes. I told him that day we saw him at the restaurant. Right after you ran out."

"What did he say?"

"There was nothing he could say. He knew I had him."

"I can't believe he's letting you have the baby."

"What do you mean by letting me?"

"Oh, you think you're the first one to get pregnant by Axel?"

Lisa could feel her heart sink to her stomach. "What, what did he do?"

"He made them have abortions. If you refuse, you can look forward to somehow miscarrying. That's why most women make sure they are on some type of birth control with Axel. He doesn't play about that kind of stuff."

"Well, he hasn't said anything to me since the restaurant so I think I'm good."

"All I'm saying is be careful."

"What am I supposed to do?"

"Tell him you lied. Get away from here so you can have your baby. Otherwise, you can put all this baby stuff back, cause you won't need it. Look, Lisa, I don't know what your game plan is, but you need to figure something out."

"Have you seen Michelle?" Lisa asked changing the subject.

"Yeah, she's still on the dance team. My first practice was yesterday."

"When's your next practice?"

"Tomorrow."

"Can I come?"

"You want to know if you affected Michelle?"

"Yeah, did she seem affected?"

"I don't know. I haven't paid her any attention."

"I bet. Anyway, text me the time of your practice and I'll meet you there."

"Ok. I would love to see this."

"Oh, you would love more to see this." Lisa patted her belly. "I'm trying to offer you a chance to be a part of it."

A smile began to form on Harmony's lips. She really did want to catch this Michelle girl without Axel. She had to know what her deal was. She also wanted to see if Axel would actually let Lisa carry his child to term. This was going to be quite interesting. "Look I'll text you Lisa, see you tomorrow."

Harmony rushed off. Deep down, she hated that Lisa was carrying Axel's baby, but she wanted to see him knocked off his throne more. Then a thought hit her. What if Lisa pulled this off and she got in good with her, who knew what this could lead to. She would be in Axel's life forever because of Lisa and her baby. I guess something's better than nothing she thought to herself.

## CHAPTER
# SIXTY-NINE

Charlie peered through the window of the dance studio. Autumn had arrived early as she always did. Charlie used to hate passing the studio and seeing Autumn in there coming up with the new hottest routines for her videos. But today it worked in her favor. Phase II of her plan was about to be put into motion.

She opened the door and relished in the shock that took over Autumn's face seeing her walk through the door.

"You look like you've seen a ghost." Charlie sneered as she closed the door behind her.

"Same thing." Autumn responded with a frown. "Neither of you possess a soul."

"Oh, she came out the gate swinging." Charlie sneered amused.

"What do you want Charlie? I don't have time for this."

"Just wanted to come see what Axel's top female artist was doing. Oh, my bad that would be me. My apologies." Charlie chuckled.

"As if." Autumn responded clearly irritated by Charlie.

"Well, I'm pretty sure that's what Axel said when he invited me over to his house on yesterday."

Autumn stop breathing. The air had been knocked clean out of her chest. Did Axel really tell this trick she was his top female artist?

"Oh, shocking isn't it. No return jab Autumn?" Charlie knew she had her. She walked closer to where Autumn was standing and she could tell she was becoming more uncomfortable the closer she got.

"Yep, I had an amazing time at Axel's place. He even cooked me my favorite dish."

Autumn was clearly turning red. Charlie was sure she wasn't aware, but she could see it clear as day. So, she continued.

"And you wouldn't believe the icing on the cake. An experience with his live-in plaything."

"What?"

Charlie knew that would get a response out of Autumn.

"What do you mean? What did you do to Michelle?"

"It's sad you knew exactly who I was referring to isn't it?"

"What did you do to Michelle?" Autumn asked a bit more forceful this time.

"Nothing she didn't want."

"Michelle would never agree to do anything with you."

"Not how I interpreted it. Seems like she was enjoying herself thoroughly."

"Did you really sleep with Michelle?" Autumn was near tears.

"Why, am I moving in on your territory?"

"Charlie don't play with me. Michelle has enough to deal with without you preying on her as well."

"Like I said, it was all consensual."

Just then the door opened and Michelle walked in. She stopped in her tracks once she lifted her head and saw Charlie. Michelle didn't know how to respond. She felt oddly attracted to Charlie but at the same time the fear she felt in Axel's presence she now felt in Charlie's.

"There's my beautiful girl." Charlie started toward Michelle. Michelle backed up towards the door until she couldn't go any further. She wasn't sure if her body would betray her or not and she definitely didn't want Autumn to know her humiliating secret. But something told her, she already did.

Autumn kissed Michelle on the lips. Michelle almost melted in her hands. Luckily the fear of Autumn seeing helped her keep her composure. Charlie went around Michelle and exited the room but not before giving her a pat on her round plump dairy Aire.

Autumn didn't really know what to say to Michelle. She could imagine she was embarrassed and she didn't want to make it worse. But she had to say something.

"Did Axel let Charlie violate you Shelly?" Autumn thought she should get straight to the point before the other dancers arrived.

Michelle immediately broke down. She fell to the ground and began to cry like no one was listening. Autumn ran over to her, embraced her while pressing her face softly into her shoulder hoping to muffle her cries. She didn't want anyone to hear her breakdown.

"It's going to be okay Shelly. I promise. Somehow, someway, it is going to be okay." She didn't know what else to say. This little charade had been going on for at least six months now and she hadn't been successful in stopping it as of yet. How would she be able to stop it now? What hope could she offer Michelle?

"Get up Shelly." Autumn pulled her to a standing position. "I don't want anyone to see you like this. We can go to my office and talk."

"Michelle what did Charlie do to you?" Autumn asked as soon as she shut the door to her office.

Michelle was still sobbing heavily.

"Michelle, we don't have that much time. You know Axel could be here any minute. You know I don't mean to rush you but I don't want to get you into trouble either."

Hearing those words seem to pull Michelle out of her despair. "Axel told me to take her to my room and let her use her imagination." Michelle said with disgust.

"Oh no Shelly." Autumn grabbed her and hugged her. "What are we going to do? We have got to get you away from Axel. I just don't know how. He will talk to me about everything else but he will not talk to me about you."

Michelle pulled back from Autumn's embrace. She looked up into her eyes and spoke so softly Autumn could barely make out her words. "Can't nobody help me but me Autumn."

Autumn stared at Michelle. She didn't know how to take what Michelle said. "What are you going to do Shelly? Please don't do anything crazy baby girl."

Michelle gave her a half smile. "Autumn, I don't know what I'm going to do, but I can't live my life like this anymore. If I don't do something different, I will get caught up in this life and totally lose myself. I can't do it. I won't do it."

"You know Michelle I have been thinking the same exact thing." Autumn sat in the chair beside Michelle. "I have gotten caught up in this stupid feud with Charlie and I don't even know why. But it's just driving me crazy because I'm actually afraid."

Michelle's eyes grew wide. "What do you mean afraid? Afraid of what?"

"Afraid she might actually be better than me." Autumn said just above a whisper.

Michelle stood up. "In what universe?"

Autumn couldn't help but laugh. "Shelly, you feel some type of way?"

"Autumn, you are the best artist and entertainer I know."

"Thanks Shelly. I've just been so stuck."

"What do you mean?"

"Shelly. I'm working on an old set list. Just making videos for the songs that don't have one. I need new music. Charlie is working on a full album and I heard iy was good. I need something new to knock Charlie off her throne."

Michelle returned to her seat. "What if I help you?"

"Help me?"

"Yeah. I can write you a song. You just can't tell Axel I wrote it. No one can know. I'm not going to let her outdo you. She's not going to win."

"Michelle, I don't want you trying to get involved because of what she did to you. I don't have anything to lose but you do."

"It's actually not that. It's something Logan said to me."

"Logan? When did you talk to Logan?"

"I ran into him in the recording studio. I go there sometime just to look around and he was in there."

"Wow. And you had a whole conversation with him?"

"Yeah. That is until Axel walked in."

"Oh wow, that couldn't have gone well."

"Naw. It didn't. He hit me and dragged me out the door by my hair. Pretty much threatened Logan."

"Sounds about right."

"Anyway, one thing he said before we were interrupted was that he thought there was more to me than just dancing. And I told him the same. Well more to him than just singing. He asked what is that and I told him about writing. That's when he said he thought I could be a writer too. Then he said something that hit me the hardest."

"What's that?"

"He said if Axel was going to beat me anyway, I might as well make it worth it, or something like that." Michelle giggled at herself.

Autumn smiled back. "I can't disagree Shelly. It's like you said, you are going to be the only person that can stop Axel from beating you. No one else."

"I know Autumn but the man nearly killed me trying to break me so I wouldn't fight him and he said if he had to, he would break me all over again and I just can't go through that anymore Autumn. I just can't!"

"Calm down Shelly. It's okay. Take a deep breath."

Michelle started to calm down. She couldn't believe she had gotten so worked up about it.

"Seems like he really hurt you."

"He nearly killed me. Autumn there were times I wished that he would because the pain and the torture was so unbearable."

"Michelle what did he do?"

Michelle shook her head. "I can't Autumn. I just can't. Not right now. I.."

"Shelly, it's okay, you don't have to tell me."

Michelle looked up at Autumn. "Can I ask you something?"

"Of course."

"The song, with you and Logan."

"Oh that. Girl, it's just a song. nothing to it." Autumn could see relief come over Michelle's face. "Michelle, do you like Logan?"

Michelle averted her eyes. She didn't want Autumn to see right through her.

"Michelle." Autumn grabbed her cheeks and turned her head to face her.

"I don't know. He makes me have these feelings, but I know I'm not supposed to be having any feelings because if Axel sees anything, he will kill me."

Autumn didn't really know what to say. She didn't want to reveal that she too had taken to Logan and was wondering if anything could be between them. She wondered if Logan felt the same way. She wondered if what Axel said in the studio was actually true. Michelle had already taken Axel away from her. Could she handle her taking Logan too? What was it about this girl that drove men crazy? The sad part was she was just a kid. Autumn stood up and walked off. She tried her best to shake those thoughts from her mind.

"You're not going to tell on me, are you?"

Autumn turned and faced Michelle with her puppy dog eyes. She looked and sounded as she was a little girl. Autumn wanted to say, yes, she was going to tell Axel. Maybe that would keep her away from Logan. She couldn't do that right now though, especially if Michelle was going to help her with her song. She wanted to outshine Charlie more than anything. Then it hit her. Even Charlie liked Michelle. Autumn wanted to scream to the top of her lungs. Why was this happening to her? Autumn took a deep breath and walked towards Michelle and sat in the seat next to her.

"Of course, I wouldn't tell Axel Shelly. I would never do that to you. I hate it when Axel beats you. I'm not going to help him."

"I don't even know why I asked. You just seemed different for a second."

"I was just thinking that's all. Look, tell you what. You work on that song and I will try to see what I can do to keep Charlie away from you. After all, she brought me in it when she came to my studio bragging about it, so I won't have to bring you up at all and you'll be safe."

"Thank you, Autumn. I really do appreciate you."

Michelle stood up to exit, but froze in her place. Autumn noticed Michelle became stiff as a board and she looked up to see what was going on. She saw that look of shear fear in her eyes and she knew. Axel must be at the door. Autumn turned around to have her assumptions confirmed. Axel was walking through the door.

"What's going on in here?" Axel asked as he entered Autumn's dance office.

Autumn started to answer, but Axel held up his hand to stop her.

"Michelle?" He stared at Michelle, thoroughly enjoying the fear in her eyes.

Michelle didn't know what to say. Tears began to roll down her face. She remained silent.

"No answer is always a bad answer Michelle."

"I asked her to come in here Axel." Autumn figured she owed Michelle to cover for her until she finished her song. "Charlie came to my office bragging about sleeping with Michelle and I just wanted to ask Michelle if it was true. That's all. I wanted her to be okay for rehearsals."

"She's fine. I don't care what she goes through or what happens to her, she will always be ok to do her job or she will answer to me and I don't think she wants that. Do you Michelle?"

"No sir. I'm… I'm fine. I was telling her that I was fine."

"You're also a terrible liar. Looks like you won't be making it to rehearsals today after all."

Michelle's eyes widened. She actually thought he was going to let her off. She couldn't believe it. She didn't want to be beat. Tears began to fall even faster from her eyes. "Please Axel. Please."

"Oh, now she begs."

Autumn looked at Axel. "I need her. Please."

Axel didn't take his eyes off of Michelle. Autumn stood directly in front of Axel to steal his gaze away from Michelle. "I need her."

Axel stared at Autumn. "Autumn…"

"Axel, please."

"Autumn, I'll let her go for now, but you and I will talk about this later." Axel turned to leave. He reached the door and turned back to the two shaken ladies. "By the way, did she tell you she enjoyed being with Charlie?" Axel laughed and left the room.

Autumn immediately turned toward Michelle. "What is he talking about?"

Michelle continued to cry. Her face began to turn a bright shade of red. "I don't know. It made me feel a way and I had an orgasm. More than one. I don't know what is wrong with me." Michelle managed to get out between sobs.

Autumn didn't know what to say either. She just grabbed Michelle and hugged her. She needed desperately to get away from Michelle. Her heart wasn't quite bleeding for her as it had in the past. She found herself just needing space. "Come on Shelly we gotta get back to work."

"Ok." Michelle grabbed a tissue and wiped her face. She stood there a minute after Autumn walked out wondering what she had done to make Autumn change towards her. Was she sickened by the fact that she liked what Charlie did to her? Did she feel like she had lied to her about the whole thing? Michelle wasn't quite sure what just happened but she knew something did and she knew Autumn did not feel the same way about her as she did when they first walked through her office door.

# CHAPTER SEVENTY

Michelle walked into the dance studio. As soon as she entered, she realized the air felt different. Something was wrong. She glanced around the room and spotted where the negative energy was coming from. Lisa and Harmony were both in the room. Michelle tried her best not to notice them too much. She walked over to the far side of the mirror where she always did her stretches. Because of who she was, no one really talked to her. Except Autumn. Michelle normally stayed to herself. Only time she bonded with the rest of the group is when they were dancing. After that they went their separate ways. Could you blame them? Who wanted to be friends with the weird girl that was always with Axel, whom he beat mercilessly in front of them? If she had a choice, she wouldn't associate with herself. Michelle closed her eyes and tried not to think about Harmony, Lisa or anyone else for that matter. She tried to shake all the negative thoughts from her mind and just think about dancing. Yes. Dancing. That was the one thing she did well.

"You think you're special, don't you?"

Michelle opened her eyes to see Harmony standing in front of her with their arms crossed. Lisa wasn't far behind. *Which one am I going to take down first?* Was the first thing that came to Michelle's mind. The way they were all up on her, she was sure she was going to have to fight her way out of there.

"Actually, I don't." Michelle responded without blinking.

"Good, cause you're not. Axel is going to eventually get tired of you like he does every other girl and you'll be yesterday's news." Lisa chimed in.

"You mean like you two." Michelle continued to stretch. She knew she shouldn't have said that. She couldn't resist.

"I know you didn't say what I thought you said. I could have Axel if I wanted him. Don't forget he asked me to marry him and not one time did he lay a finger on me. You may be in his house, but you ain't nothing to him but a punching bag and sex slave. Yeah, I asked around. I heard all about you, Michelle." She let her name roll off her lips in disgust.

Michelle felt like the room was closing in around her. People were talking about her. She figured they probably were but she never had proof. Until now. She wanted to hide somewhere. As a matter of fact, she wanted to disappear. That would be quicker. But instead, she did the only thing she could do: tuck tail and run. Harmony had hit her where it hurt. She knew exactly what she was to Axel but no one had ever said it to her face. Not even Axel.

"Whoa!" Michelle nearly bulldozed Autumn down leaving the room. "Shelly! Where are you going?" She wanted to run after her but it was too late. Michelle was gone. "What happened?" Autumn demanded as she slammed the door behind her. Her gaze was locked on Harmony and Lisa. "And why are you even in my studio?" She asked Lisa.

"I was just leaving." Lisa turned to leave.

Autumn stepped in front of her. "You're not going anywhere until I get some answers. Now what happened? Never mind don't tell me, cause right now I don't trust either of you."

Autumn turned toward Phoenix. "Phoenix what happened?"

"Do I look like a snitch to you?" Phoenix turned and walked away.

"Jaylah?" Autumn tried her other friend, trying not to show her annoyance with Phoenix.

"Your girls ganged up on Michelle. Told her she was just a punching bag and a sex slave."

Autumn turned back toward Harmony and Lisa. "Now you can leave. Both of you. And don't ever come back." Autumn walked closer and closer to the women with every word.

"Autumn. What are you saying? I'm still on the dance team, right?" Harmony's words were shaking coming out of her mouth.

"Wrong." Autumn responded through clenched teeth. "I would rather have Michelle here dancing than you any day. She has a better personality and she's a waaaaay better dancer than you are. So yes, I meant every word. Don't ever come back."

All the dancers jumped as the door swung open.

"What's going on in here?" Axel's deep voice echoed in the room as if he was talking through a bull horn. "Why did Michelle run out of here?"

Everyone was frozen with fear. Axel was angry. They didn't know if they had ever seen him this angry before.

Harmony was the first to speak up. "Why do you care anyway? All you do is beat on her."

Axel walked over to Harmony and got right into her face. "What I do with Michelle is my business and not yours. All you need to know is that Michelle belongs to me therefore she is under my protection. I can do what I please to her, but to anyone else she is off limits. If you ever forget that you will regret it." Axel's voice was elevating with each passing sentence.

Harmony's eyes were so big. She couldn't believe how Axel was responding. How could he treat Michelle like he does but still go hard to defend her? More than that how could he treat her like she was nobody? They were just engaged. Living together. Now he acted like he never knew her. Harmony was speechless. Now it was her turn to run out of the room and that is exactly what she did. Lisa was right on her heels. She didn't want to get caught in Axel's crosshairs. Maybe she had bitten off more than she could chew. She hadn't expected Axel to respond the way he did. But before she could walk out of the door, he caught her arm. Her eyes lit up with fear.

"We have some unfinished business. I'll be calling you." Axel released her arm.

Lisa flew out of the door. She didn't want to give him a chance to do anything else to her.

"Harmony is off the team." Axel turned toward Autumn.

"Already done." Autumn nodded her agreement.

Axel knew by Autumn's response and the look on her face she was just as angry as he was. He would talk to her about it later to make sure they were on the same page. That's if she would talk to him. This was actually the first time Axel had seen Autumn in a minute. She had been dodging him for a couple of months. And obviously adding people to the dance team he knew nothing about. He had no idea Harmony was even back in town let alone on Autumn's dance team. He would have to deal with that as well.

Axel watched Autumn as she walked over to the far side of the room and grabbed her phone. She put on some tunes and began to stretch like nothing had even happened, further more like he wasn't even standing there. What was her problem? He couldn't understand. She had been ignoring him for over a while now. And it was driving him insane. He glanced over at Phoenix who he now noticed was watching him watch Autumn. He had a scowl on his face that tried to come off as threatening. Axel gave a sly smile. Phoenix had no idea who he was messing with. Axel gave him a slight nod. *Your time is coming to an end buddy.* Axel thought to himself and then he gave Autumn one last glance before he turned and left the room.

CHAPTER

# SEVENTY-ONE

"Michelle, I swear, your body never disappoints." Charlie said as she slid off of Michelle. She lay back on the bed feeling satisfied and accomplished as she always did each time she slept with Michelle.

Michelle laid there with her soul torn to shreds as it had the many times Charlie violated her. She finally realized that her first experience did betray her actual feeling because she never felt the same way again. Instead, the feelings of euphoria that she felt the first time she slept with Charlie were easily replaced with disgust and shame each time afterward. Michelle didn't know how long she could keep this up. This was another level of torture that she didn't think that she could endure. She almost preferred the beatings over this. At least she would eventually be unconscious and the pain would subside, but this… this was unending and there was no relief, no escape from its torture even after it ended. The wounds unlike the beatings never healed. They remained open and infested.

Charlie sat up and stared at Michelle realizing she was not responding. She thought that she could get her to cross over, but it was proving difficult. Michelle had not responded like she had the first time they slept together and Charlie was growing more and more frustrated.

"What's wrong Michelle?" Charlie asked as she rubbed her fingers through her hair. "I thought this is what you wanted?"

Michelle turned toward Charlie. "It is." She replied expressionless.

"You can speak what's on your mind Michelle. I'm not Axel. I'm not going to beat you or tell on you."

Michelle thought for a moment and then felt as if she could trust Charlie. She took a deep breath. "I don't want to do this Charlie. I can't explain it. It felt good the first time, but maybe it was because it was something I had never felt before, but the past few times..." her voice trailed off. She didn't want to finish her sentence.

"The past few times what Michelle?" Charlie tried to contain the anger that she felt rising inside of her.

"I just haven't felt the same thing. I guess I really don't like it." Michelle confessed.

Charlie stared at Michelle with one of those Axel looks. Michelle knew immediately she had said the wrong thing. The next thing Michelle knew, Charlie had her hands around her throat.

"Look little girl! I am not playing with you. You will be mine whether you like it or not, but I promise you, you better start liking it or I can promise you a life worse than the one you have with Axel. If you act accordingly then you will be treated with all the love and respect that a queen deserves. No more beatings, no more hurt, no more pain. So, what's it going to be Michelle?"

Michelle couldn't breathe let alone respond. She just knew she was going to die right here at the hands of Charlie. Especially since she didn't believe Charlie knew how hard she was pressing against her throat.

"What the hell is going on in here?"

Charlie let go of Michelle as she gasped desperately for air. She had never been so happy to see Axel in all her life.

Charlie got up from the bed. Her intentions were to distract Axel with her body. The way his eyes moved over her she knew it was working. "We just had a slight disagreement baby. That's all. Your girl can be hard headed at times. But you know how that goes, now don't you?"

Axel hadn't looked away from Charlie's body yet; to her satisfaction of course. It wasn't until Michelle stood up, naked as well, that Axel's eyes diverted. Charlie folded her arms. She didn't want Axel sexually but she did want him to choose her over Michelle. But she could see that, that wasn't possible. She looked over at Michelle, who was still trying to catch her breath. Her body was flawless. She couldn't blame Axel. But Charlie was still upset. She wanted to be the Queen B and Michelle could be her chick. And of course, her chick had to be bad. Michelle was definitely bad.

Charlie walked towards the restroom. "You need to handle your girl. Get her to be a little more submissive the next time I come in here." She didn't wait to hear Axel's response.

Michelle looked at Axel, unsure of how he would respond. To her relief, he didn't. He just reached for the door handle and left. Michelle figured Axel knew whatever Charlie did to her would be punishment enough.

Charlie came back out of the restroom once she heard the door close. She was sure she would hear Axel beating Michelle, but it was unusually quiet. "Where's Axel?" She asked Michelle.

"He left."

"I see. I guess he left your well-being in my hands." Charlie rounded the bed to where Michelle was standing. "I wonder what I'm going to do about your little ungrateful, disrespectful..."

"Please Charlie, please." Michelle cried.

"Ohhh. I love it when you beg baby. I bet Axel loves it too." Charlie relished in Michelle's suffering.

"I'll do better next time. I promise. I'm so sorry. I promise I'll do better next time."

"That's what I like to hear." She walked to Michelle and kissed her on the lips. "I'll see you next time baby. Make sure you don't disappoint me like you did today."

"I won't. I promise."

"Say my name."

"I promise Charlie. I promise."

"I love it when you say my name." Charlie walked away from Michelle. Walked around the bed and began to slip her dress back on. Once she was fully dressed, she blew Michelle a kiss and exited the room.

Michelle fell to the bed. She was so relieved to be done with both Charlie and Axel. Then she thought about it. What if Axel came back to her room when Charlie leaves. She quickly jumped up and made her way to the shower. At least if Axel came back, he wouldn't find her sitting idle awaiting what terrible thing he would do to her. Too many ideas would probably flood his mind. Michelle turned on the shower. She stepped in once the temperature was to her liking. She thought back on the past few hours with Charlie and anger began to overcome her. She was determined now more than ever to take Charlie down. She was going to write a song for Autumn that would blow Charlie out of the water. Even if Autumn wasn't currently talking to her. Michelle thought back to her last rehearsal. Autumn didn't say a word to Michelle. Didn't acknowledge her in any way. Michelle allowed a single tear to fall from her face but she kept dancing. Kept participating. She didn't allow the hurt she felt to affect her performance. Everyone in the room felt the distance between them, but Autumn didn't seem to care nor did she address it in any way. At the end of rehearsal Autumn said that they were going to take a small hiatus from the project. Michelle knew that meant Axel probably finally pulled the plug on it and Autumn just didn't want to come out and say it. But she wouldn't have to worry too much longer. The wheels in Michelle's head were already turning. She would have her a hit song and dance in no time. She would prove to Axel and everyone else that she could not only be a choreographer, but a writer as well.

# CHAPTER SEVENTY-TWO

"So. I guess you made up your mind." Autumn sat up in her bed to see that Phoenix had returned home and was packing his things.

"You never gave me an answer so I figure you are still stuck on Axel and it's time for me to move on."

"I'm not stuck on Axel, but I do agree it is time for you to move on. This is clearly not working. I'm sorry for not fighting harder to make it work, but I'm just going through a lot right now and I don't have the energy."

"At least your honest." Phoenix continued to pack. Once he stuffed his last piece of clothing in his suitcase he turned and stared at Autumn. "I hope you get what you want one day, even though I'm pretty sure you won't but I will tell you this. This thing between me and you is over for life, so I hope that whatever Axel is giving you is worth it."

Autumn didn't reply. She didn't even feel like Phoenix was worthy of her words.

Phoenix picked up his bags and left.

CHAPTER
# SEVENTY-THREE

Michelle opened the door to Autumn's office. She had gotten there early with Axel. He had an early meeting and Michelle jumped on the opportunity to get to Autumn's office early. She had finally finished the song she wrote for Autumn complete with choreography.

Autumn looked up from her computer. "Don't you knock?"

Michelle had every mind to walk right back out of the door, but she decided she wanted to do this. Hopefully this would get her back on Autumn's good side; even though Michelle didn't know why she was on Autumn's bad side to begin with.

"I apologize." Michelle said after contemplating the right words. "I was just excited!" Michelle was now smiling from ear to ear.

"Excited about what?" Autumn sat back in her chair clearly aggravated.

Michelle shifted her weight back and forth. She was still considering whether she should give this song to Autumn or not. Part of her wanted to do an about face and head back out the door, down to Charlie's office and offer her the song. But she just couldn't. She needed to take Charlie down a notch. "I finished your song!" Michelle tried her best to maintain her enthusiasm.

"What song?" Autumn asked.

"The song I said I would write for you. Don't you remember?"

"Oh. You actually wrote it?"

"Yes. And I have choreography to go with it."

"Wow. I guess I could take a look at what you have."

Michelle opened her back pack and pulled out a small recorder. "When I know Axel's not at home, I explore my wing of the house. I recently came across a room that had some old instruments and recording equipment. So, I've been sneaking in there and working on your song and now I'm finished." Michelle beamed obviously proud that she had gotten away with putting together an entire song without Axel knowing it.

"Ok. Well, let's hear it."

Michelle turned on the recorder. Autumn listened to the song. She was amazed at how great the song was. But her mouth almost fell open upon hearing the quality of Michelle's voice. She looked up at Michelle, wondering if Axel knew his little plaything could actually sing. Scratch that she could be an actual artist. She went beyond just knowing how to sing. She was gifted. After Autumn finished listening to the song, she grabbed the recorder. "Let's go."

"Where are we going?" Michelle looked puzzled. She didn't want to get in trouble.

"The dance room; I want you to show me the choreography."

"Ok." Michelle smiled relieved she wasn't about to get into trouble. She didn't put it past Autumn to rat her out, especially how she had been treating her lately.

Once in the dance room Autumn played the song and sat Indian style on the floor. "Let's see what you got."

Michelle didn't need to hear anything further. From the first beat to the last Michelle danced like her life depended on it. And by all means, it did.

Once Michelle was done. Autumn just stared at her. Michelle stared back; eyebrows frowned. She didn't know if Autumn liked it or not.

Autumn didn't want to give Michelle any props. She didn't want to admit that Michelle might be better than she was. But through clenched teeth, she choked back her pride and smiled. "Michelle that was amazing. So how do you want to go about this?"

"What do you mean?" Michelle sat Indian style in front of Autumn.

"Do you want recognition for your song or what?"

"Of course not!" Michelle exclaimed. "Axel would kill me! You can take full credit. I just want you to crush Charlie." Michelle punched her fist into her hand.

"Why? I thought you liked her?"

Michelle hung her head. "My first time with Charlie was my first experience with a girl. I can't lie. It made me feel a way. My body enjoyed it and it responded." Michelle looked up at Autumn with a glare in her eyes. "But don't get me wrong. I was sickened by the entire experience and definitely every time since then. Actually, my body doesn't hardly respond anymore."

"What do you mean every time? How many times have you slept with her?"

"Too many."

"Shelly, did you want to or did Axel make you."

Michelle perked up at hearing Autumn's pet name for her. Hopefully they were getting back to their normal friendship. "Axel made me. Autumn, I swear I hate it. I hate it every time she comes over. I just die inside. I end up just lying there waiting on her to get done. I want it to stop so badly! I hate her!" The words were just pouring out of Michelle a mile a minute.

"Shelly, calm down." Autumn leaned forward and grabbed Michelle's arm.

"I'm sorry. That's why I wrote the song. I want you to crush Charlie! I want you to embarrass her!"

"Breathe Shelly please."

"I am. I'm fine. So anyway, you take full credit for the song and kill it."

"I'm going to have to keep your little recorder. Is that ok?"

"Yeah, just you know, don't let anyone get their hands on it, please."

"I got you, promise."

# CHAPTER SEVENTY-FOUR

Jaylah had decided today would be the day. She would tell Autumn that Phoenix was cheating on her, but with who surprised even her. She had spent nearly two months following him, tracking his every move. The places he went he tried to make sure no one knew. He would change vehicles and don a hat and sunglasses but Jaylah wasn't confused. She had been very proficient in the art of disguise.

Jaylah walked into rehearsal early. And as usual Autumn was there. With her. Michelle. Jaylah wanted to strangle her and watch the life drain from her eyes.

"Hey, how's it going?" She interrupted their little conversation. She could tell Michelle had been beat by Axel and was crying on Autumn's shoulder once again.

"We're good. How are you? You are early today."

*We're good?* She could care less if Michelle was ok or not. Jaylah tried not to let Autumn's response get under her skin. "I just wanted to talk to you privately."

"Oh okay. Um, is everything alright?"

"Yeah. Like I said just needed to talk to you about something."

"Okay. Do you think it could wait? I'm kinda in the middle of something."

Jaylah tried to compose herself. She was so hurt. She forced the tears not to fall. But maybe she could turn this for her good.

"Okay. That's fine. How about you come to my house later on? I would love for you to see my little abode."

"Oh okay. I'll call you and let you know."

"Cool." Jaylah turned around and left. Her heart was leaping out of her chest. This was her chance. She would finally have Autumn all to herself with no interruptions from Michelle.

# CHAPTER SEVENTY-FIVE

Autumn walked to the door of Axel's office. She had just finished recording the demo for the song that Michelle had written for her. To her dismay she had to have Michelle's help the whole way through. She had to give it to Michelle. She was a genius when it came to music. She didn't know if she could have perfected the song as Michelle did when she was working with her. Autumn recalled listening to Michelle sing the vocals live. Her heart melted. Michelle's voice was past amazing! She wondered why Michelle had never said anything to Axel about her vocal skills. Then she thought back to when Michelle told him she knew how to dance. He nearly killed her! And she was good! Autumn shook her head. Such talent gone to waste. *I guess I should be glad though.* Autumn thought to herself. Because if Michelle ever became an artist, she and Charlie would both be on the backburner.

Autumn took a deep breath and knocked on Axel's office door.

"Come in." She heard Axel say.

Autumn took another breath, readjusted herself, threw her head back in confidence and opened the door.

"There's my girl." Axel laid back in his chair with his hands behind his head.

"Axel. Hope I didn't disturb you." Autumn tried to be casual but not too friendly or familiar. She walked over to his desk and took a seat. She was tired of being used by Axel. If he wanted her, he was going to have to come correct, other than that he would not be getting any freebies from her.

"Well, for starters I was wondering why you knocked on my door. You know you can always just walk right in."

"You do remember the last time I just walked in your office you almost shot me."

"If I recall, you didn't just walk in. You came busting in like you were the police."

"I guess you're right. Anyway, the reason…"

Axel sat forward in his seat. "Hey. How are you?"

"Axel, I didn't come in here for niceties. I have business to discuss."

"Is that right?"

"Yes."

"And what has brought on this attitude?"

"I don't have an attitude. I just have a lot on my mind."

"You know you can talk to me about anything."

"It's nothing bad."

Axel leaned his head forward and down. He didn't believe anything that was coming out of Autumn's mouth.

"I want to show you something."

"Autumn, you know you're full of it right?"

"Whatever. I just know what I'm about to show you is going to make you happy."

"I like the way that sounds. What you got?" Axel figured he would ignore her obvious attitude.

She gave him the drive without saying a word. He plugged the drive into his computer and pulled up the file. He sat back in his chair and listened to Autumn's vocals. He listened to the beat. The song was incredible! He knew Autumn would come up with some great dance moves.

"This song is legit girl. What done got into you?"

"Nothing. Just been working hard." She lied.

"Well, whatever you're doing, keep it up. I can't wait to see the dance moves. When are you going to start working on a video?"

"Already done. Just need to start filming."

Axel's eyes grew wide. "You really on it, girl. All I can say is you are about to blow Charlie out the water. I hope you're ready for the backlash."

This time it was Autumn who leaned forward. "Oh, believe me, I welcome it."

"Then let the games begin." Axel sat back in his chair and placed his hands on the back of his head.

Autumn hated deceiving Axel, but she couldn't tell him that Michelle wrote the song and choregraphed it as well.

Maybe she could pull it off. She just had to keep him from asking so many questions.

## CHAPTER
# SEVENTY-SIX

"What do you want Axel?" Autumn answered her door wishing Axel would leave her alone. He had been stalking her for the past month. The more she tried to pull away from him the more he tried to get her attention. Although she had been doing a great job keeping away from him. Autumn was determined to show Phoenix that he was wrong about her relationship with Axel. She figured after she gave him the song, she wouldn't have to deal with him for a while, but leave it to Axel to try and make her life miserable. Or was she the one making her own life miserable? She would have to figure that part out later.

"I'm gonna keep popping up at your spot until you tell me why you are avoiding me." Axel stood at her door with his arms folded. "Are you going to let me in or what?"

Autumn once again stepped to the side and allowed Axel to pass her. She followed him to her den but didn't take her seat. She didn't want Axel to feel too comfortable around her.

"Really Autumn? Is this what we're doing? I thought we were BFF's?"

"Axel what do you want?" Autumn grew impatient.

"I want some answers and I'm not leaving until I get'em. So, you might as well have a seat and get real comfortable cause we might be her for a while." Axel pulled off his shoes and kicked his feet up on the sofa. He readjusted a pillow behind his head and let out a long sigh. "Man, I can get some real good sleep right here."

"You are not sleeping here." Autumn walked over to him and snatched the pillow from his head.

Axel grabbed her arm and pulled her down on his lap and kissed her. Autumn tried to struggle but Axel wouldn't let go. He held her until she submitted and kissed him back.

"What are you doing?" Autumn asked breathless. She had finally pushed herself free from Axel. Her heart was still racing from the passionate kiss. *Why do I feel this way?* She thought to herself*. I can't still have feelings for this man. Why did he kiss me? Does he still have feelings for me?* Autumn was so confused.

Axel allowed Autumn to slide off his lap. He knew kissing her probably wasn't the best thing to do but the way she was acting was turning him on something fierce.

"Autumn. I wanted you to take your mind off being mad at me and talk to me like you always do. What is going on with you and don't lie. You know I know you better than you know yourself and I will spot a lie in a heartbeat. So, what's up?"

Autumn allowed a tear to fall from her eye. She couldn't keep hiding this from Axel and she had to admit, she missed him. "It's Phoenix."

"I figured that. What, he don't want you talking to me?"

"He thinks that you want me all to yourself. He said you don't want me but you don't want anyone else to have me. And he said I let you do it. I give you all my time and avoid any man who tries to get close to me. That's why I'll never have a man."

"So ya'll broke up?"

He packed his bags and left.

"So what you gonna do?"

"I don't know. Maybe I haven't tried to make this work. Maybe I haven't given the relationship the time it needs to grow. I've been so busy trying to compete with Charlie until it seems like nothing else has mattered."

Axel just stared at Autumn until she looked his way.

"What?" She asked dumbfounded.

"Please tell me that's not really what you think?"

Autumn humped her shoulders.

Axel pulled Autumn closer to him on the couch. She let him.

"Let me tell you something. Phoenix ain't the man for you. I'm telling you that as my friend. I can promise you it's him, not you. To be honest I don't even know why you're doing this. I mean if it was to get me back for the whole Harmony thing then you won. I'm not with her anymore so can you please let this loser go."

Autumn's face scrunched together like she had just smelled something foul. "Really Axel. That's all you got?"

"Am I lying? Be for real. It's me. I know you're trying not to be vulnerable with me, but at least be real with yourself."

Autumn didn't know if she should come clean with Axel or not. She wanted to tell him everything that she felt, but would it help? She took a deep breath and hoped she wouldn't regret what she was about to say.

"Axel," she began cautiously. "I accepted Phoenix's proposal because I was hurt that you slept with me and then turned around and asked Harmony to marry you. I felt humiliated to say the least. But, you are right. Phoenix is not the one for me. I don't even know why I'm forcing it. I guess

I don't want to admit I have been made a fool of all over again. With you, I love you a lot. Probably more than I should. I love you as my friend, but I can't pretend like that night didn't happen. And now I'm just confused. Are we just friends or are we more than that? It hurts too much to think about it. I just want us to be one or the other. I can't handle the in between."

Autumn looked up at Axel fearing his response.

"Why can't we just be lovers and friends?"

"Really Axel, I can't with you!!" Autumn screamed in frustration. She stood up and started hurling pillows at him. He jumped up and began to hurl them back.

"See, we're already having pillow fights!"

"I hate you Axel!" Autumn screamed. Tears streaming down her face. "Just leave please."

Axel walked over to wear Autumn was standing and wrapped his arms around her waist and pulled her close to him.

"Look at me Autumn."

Autumn refused.

He repeated. "Autumn look at me. Please." He added.

Autumn slowly looked up and met his gaze.

"You are the woman that means the most to me in my life. And I'm going to be honest with you. Lately I just don't know what to do with you. You've always been like one of the guys, my homeboy, but one day, or I should say that day you walked in the Money Maker, it's like everything changed. You were no longer just one of the guys. You were someone I wanted to lay in the bed with and tell all my deepest darkest secrets. You were someone I wanted to be completely vulnerable with, but it scared me. Yes, I let my lust get the best of me, but I never meant to hurt you. I would never on purpose cause you any hurt or pain. I really do love you, Autumn. I respect the fact that you need boundaries and space and I'm going to give that to you. Only because I don't know if I'm ready to be the man you need or if I ever will, but I'm not going to make you feel like I'm dragging you along either. Is that ok with you?"

Autumn pushed away from Axel. "Doesn't look like I have much of a choice, but yes I do want my space."

"So, we cool? Or are you gonna keep giving me the stiff arm?"

"We're cool, I guess." Autumn sat back down on the sofa and Axel joined her. "It's just too much is going on right now."

"Who you telling? You got mad drama on your dance team. So, when were you going to tell me Harmony was back?"

"Ummm... Harmony is back." Autumn lifted both her arms like she was an emoji.

"Real funny Autumn."

"Well, I guess it doesn't matter since she's back off of it again."

"Yeah. I guess. Still not okay with you letting her back on the team without telling me."

"Anyway." Autumn ignored his comment. "Who was the other girl?"

"That was Lisa."

"Oh, you mean Logan's girlfriend?"

"Yep."

"Wow, how did they team up?"

"Somehow, they met and bonded over their hatred over me."

"Oh really. I should probably join their club."

Axel narrowed his eyes at Autumn.

She giggled uncontrollably.

"You done amusing yourself?"

"Ahhh, that was a good one. Sorry buddy, but you deserve every bit of it."

"Maybe. But I'll fix them."

"How?" Autumn turned toward Axel her expression turned serious.

"Don't worry about that."

"Axel just let it go, please for me. Don't do anything stupid. They are both gone. We won't have to deal with them anymore. Just please let it go."

Axel looked out the window. He didn't want to lie to Autumn but he had to protect her from his plans. "Ok, for you. I'll let it go."

"You promise."

Axel gritted his teeth. "I promise." He lied.

"I really don't believe you."

"I'm appalled."

"Whatever Axel."

"Look. Now that we are cool again, I need you to do me a favor."

"No."

"What?"

"Whatever it is no."

"You haven't even heard me out yet."

"What is it Ax?"

"I want you to go on tour."

Autumn's face lit up. Axel knew it would. That is until he told her the favor part.

"You really mean it Axel?"

"Yeah, your new song is a hit. Coupled with your other hits. It's going to be an awesome tour."

"Of course. Why did you think I would turn you down?"

"Because I want you to tour with Charlie."

"Absolutely not." Autumn was on her feet again. "Not gonna happen."

"See what I'm saying."

"Well, you were right. I'm not doing it. Not even as a favor."

"Autumn, you would be the main attraction, she is just headlining."

"Axel. You know we don't get along. This is not going to work."

"It will I promise. I will even give you separate tour buses. Come on Autumn. I already ran the numbers. With both of you, we are going to make bank. I'm serious Autumn. This is not an opportunity you want to give up."

"Fine I'll do it. I'm not gonna let Charlie stop me from doing something I've been wanting to do."

That's what I like to hear. Plus it's a done deal. Word went out this morning and venues are already filling up. You got two weeks."

"Now I really hate you."

"You and Charlie have already been practicing. It's a mini tour. Just a couple of venues. You'll be fine."

"Ok Axel. Now that you've gotten what you wanted can you please leave my house."

He grabbed her hand and pulled her back down on the couch. "Technically I haven't gotten what I wanted."

Autumn melted like a bag of ice in the sun. But she knew she had to stand her ground. "I don't think so. Leave."

"It's like that. I thought we were on good terms again?"

"I thought you were giving me space, remember that part of the conversation?"

"I am. After today. Now come cuddle your fine self up beside me so we can watch a movie."

Autumn shook her head but obliged him anyway. "Just a movie."

"Whatever you say." Axel smiled and gave her a wink.

## CHAPTER
# SEVENTY-SEVEN

"Michelle" sat across from Charlie at Axel's dining room table. She was relieved when Charlie said she wasn't interested in sleeping with her tonight. She just wanted to get this visit over with and watch Charlie walk out the front door.

"So, Autumn's new song?" Charlie looked up at Axel as she placed her fork back on the plate. "

What about it? It's hot, nuff said." Axel replied not even looking up from his plate.

"She didn't write it."

Michelle nearly choked on her steak.

"You ok?" Charlie asked her clearly startled.

"Yeah, I just can't believe you would think Autumn didn't write her own song. She's brilliant!"

"I don't remember asking you." If looks could kill, Michelle would have been dead at least five times by now.

Michelle dropped her head and continued her meal.

"I don't have any reason to believe that she didn't. Can't believe I'm actually saying this, but I actually agree with Michelle, Autumn is brilliant. She just hit a rough spot and now she's back in the game."

"So, am I still your favorite artist?" Charlie asked matter of factly.

Axel pressed his lips together. "This was definitely not a conversation he wanted to get into."

"Well?" Charlie had given Axel her full attention.

Axel realized she was not going to let this go without an answer. "You are an amazing artist and Autumn is an amazing artist, but to be totally honest..." Axel paused almost regretting his next words before they left his lips. "Autumn is a frontrunner right now."

Charlie stood up. Grabbed her purse. "I am going to prove that Autumn didn't write that song and those dance moves, if you were watching, are not Autumn's regular dance moves. Yeah, she comes up with things, but she has a signature and it ain't on any of those moves."

Michelle's heart began to race. She never thought about that. The truth was bound to come out. She just hoped it didn't make Axel too angry. She couldn't handle any new drama.

"That song, that choreography, belongs to someone else and I'm going to prove it."

"What if it is Charlie? What does it matter? All I care about is a hit song that's making me a lot of money. Nothing else matters."

Michelle felt a bit of relief. Maybe the outcome wouldn't be so bad after all.

"Well, it matters to me." Charlie huffed and stormed out the front door.

Michelle was left sitting at the table with a visibly frustrated Axel. His head was in his hands and he was rubbing it vigorously back and forth. Finally, after what seemed like forever, Axel lifted up his head. He looked at Michelle and she swallowed hard. She took a quick sip of her sweet tea fearing she wouldn't get another chance.

"Let's go." Axel stood up. "And get out of those clothes. I need to work off this frustration."

Michelle was actually glad to oblige this time. She'd rather be sleeping with him instead of being beat by him. She went quickly, quietly and obediently.

CHAPTER

# SEVENTY-EIGHT

Autumn pulled up to Jaylah's house, she had no idea what she wanted to talk about. She wasn't sure if she should have even agreed but she looked so sad. She normally took pleasure in hanging out with her dance team but this dance team was different. For some reason, she didn't trust them. Jaylah was a sweet girl. She seemed to have a better character than all the others. "Well, let's get this over with."

Autumn stepped up to the door and before she could knock, Jaylah opened the door.

"Hey Autumn. Come on in. I'm so glad you could make it."

"Well thanks for inviting me."

Autumn walked in and looked around. "The aroma was nice. Did you cook?"

"I did. Hope you're hungry."

"I actually am. Can't wait." Autumn was hoping she wasn't setting herself up to get poisoned.

After they sat down and began eating Autumn thought it best to just get right to it.

"So, what is it that you wanted to talk to me about?"

"Oh yeah that. I was hoping we could kind of talk and get to know each other before we got into that."

"Jaylah you are a very sweet girl and I like you a lot, but this is kinda a lot for me. I usually don't go to people's houses. But you're my dancer and I'm around you a lot, so I kinda trust you. I just really want to get to what you wanted to tell me."

Jaylah dropped her head. She considered not telling her behind what she had just said. But also based on what she just said this might be her last chance to get close to her.

"Autumn, I consider you a good friend, even if you don't see me that way. And I want you to know that I have your back. I have heard the other dancers talking about it and I didn't like them saying things behind your back so I suggested they say something to you about it. They would say it's not their problem but because I care about you, I made it my problem. I did research so I would have proof and not just hunches."

"Jaylah you're not making any sense. What are you talking about?" Autumn was clearly frustrated by this time.

Jaylah inhaled and then exhaled knowing there was no turning back. She decided to just rip the band-aid off. "Phoenix is cheating on you."

"What did you say? Autumn was not expecting to hear what Jaylah was saying and wasn't sure she heard her clearly.

"I said your boyfriend Phoenix is cheating on you."

Autumn didn't care much. Phoenix had already admitted he was cheating. Besides, her and Phoenix were already over, but she thought she would see the proof before she told this little heffa where she could go and how to get there.

"How do you know that?"

"I started suspecting it and then I decided to follow him."

"You have pictures?"

"Of course. I figured you wouldn't believe me without proof." Jaylah got up and grabbed an envelope off the counter. "Here, see for yourself."

Autumn opened the envelope. "She saw Phoenix with one of the twins in a very compromising position. No big deal. It was more so embarrassing. Especially learning all of this from a dancer.

"Which twin is this?" Autumn decided to keep the charade going

"Both."

"Both?" That was unexpected.

"Yeah. If you look closely, you can see it's two different houses."

The next picture bent Autumn over and she immediately began to vomit. "Is this some kind of sick joke?"

"No Autumn. It's proof and it's true. Your man likes men."

Autumn wanted to crawl in a hole and disappear? She had no idea. "Do you have copies of these?"

"No, those are the only ones. I don't have a hard drive or anything."

"You better not. And if these ever get out, I'm coming after you!"

"Me? I could have kept all this a secret and left you in the dark and this is the thanks that I get?"

"Jaylah we are not friends. You work for me. That's it. Now because you showed me this and I think you had my best interest at heart I'm not going to kick you off my team but you better not utter a word of this to anyone. Do you understand me?"

"I promise. I won't tell a soul."

Autumn stormed out of Jaylah's place, jumped in her car and sped off.

"Last time I try to help her, but at least I'll always have a place on the dance team, cause if she tries to get rid of me... all the secrets are coming out." Man, then she just barfed on my floor and left. Bet I won't be inviting her back." Jaylah slammed the door.

Autumn didn't know where else to turn to so she went to the only safe space she knew. She had already sent a 911 text so she wasn't surprised to see Axel standing in the driveway anticipating her arrival.

He opened the door for her and pulled her into his arms. "What happened? Who do I need to kill?"

Autumn looked up at Axel through tear filled eyes as a smile crossed her face. "I can't stand you. I don't want you to kill anybody."

"Come on in. I'll get you something to drink."

Ten minutes later they were sitting on his private balcony overlooking a beautiful lake. Autumn loved coming up here. It was the most peaceful place in the world. Not to mention Axel's company. That definitely couldn't be beat. Thanks for letting me use your bathroom to clean up. I threw up all on that girl's floor and left. Now that I think about it, I'm kinda embarrassed. Autumn let her head rest on the recliner.

"What are you talking about? You trying out women now?" Axel asked as he handed her a glass.

She took a sip and let the alcohol slide down her throat and revive her soul. "No stupid. I was given these today." She pulled the envelope Jaylah had given her out of her purse and handed them to Axel. "And I don't want to hear I told you so." She added before releasing her grip on the envelope.

"Ok. Ok." He responded snatching the envelope out of her hand. Already knowing what he might see.

"Oh wow. Is this the same twin?"

"Supposedly it's both."

"Oh dang."

"Oh yeah. You think that's crazy. Keep flipping."

Axel flipped the page and his mouth dropped open. "You have got to be kidding me. This nigga on the flip side?" Axel asked as if he didn't already know.

"Apparently."

"Who gave these to you?"

"My dancer Jaylah."

"Oh, that's cold."

"She said she was just looking out for me but for some reason I don't trust her."

"Then you shouldn't. What do I always tell you?"

"Go with my gut."

"Exactly. If you feel like there is more to this then her just being a friend, there probably is and you should watch your back. So, what you gonna do? You know I got people who can handle that for you."

"Axel. I don't want Phoenix to come up missing or dead. I just want him out of my life that's all. And I want a new dance team."

"I don't know about that one sweetheart."

"What do you mean?"

"It's almost time for you to go on tour. You need your team they know all the dances."

"I don't know if I can do it Axel."

"As your boss Autumn. You don't have a choice."

"Oh, you're pulling that card."

"I am. I mean I have to. Just get through the tour and then you can get rid of them if you still want to."

"Oh I'm still gonna want to."

CHAPTER

# SEVENTY-NINE

Phoenix pulled up at Cedric's apartment. He wanted to spend some time with him before he left. He was still debating if he should break it off with him for good or not. He didn't want Josiah finding out that he was still cheating on him, but he didn't really want to let Cedric go either. He weighed the pros and cons as he sat in the driveway. Moving to Paris gave him amenity. Josiah had way more money than Cedric. On the other hand, Josiah worked more often and Phoenix was mostly left alone. That's where he always got himself in trouble. Too much free time. Cedric always had time for Phoenix and time spent with him was fun. He also didn't have to be exclusive with Cedric because they were both still in the closet so Cedric didn't mind him playing around a bit. As long as it was understood that he belonged to him. Phoenix didn't mind keeping up the illusion. Phoenix didn't know what he was going to do, but he knew he couldn't sit in his car all day. He got out. Grabbed a bag from the back seat and used his key to go in.

"I'm in the kitchen." Phoenix heard Cedric yell from around the corner.

He placed his bags down in the living room and made his way into the kitchen.

"What's up you?" Cedric greeted him with a smile.

"I should ask you the same. What you doing cooking a gourmet meal up in here?"

"Well, you said you were headed back to Paris so I just wanted to make your last day here special. You know something to remember me by and something to make you wanna hurry back. I don't know what this business deal is you are working on in Paris but it must be a good one."

"It is. You might not ever have to work again in your life."

"No can do babe. I love my work. And I'll never quit, no matter how much money you make. But I'm not opposed to being spoiled."

"Spoiled it is then."

# CHAPTER EIGHTY

Mateo waited in the car. He had followed Phoenix from Faith's house to his guy friend's house. He shook his head. *This guy needs to make up his mind what team he's batting for.*

Mateo had been sitting outside Phoenix man's house for about five hours when he finally emerged with bag in hand. He had clearly changed. Mateo didn't even want to think of any reasons he would have had to change his clothes before heading to the airport. Axel had called him and told him he had two jobs for him. He upped the pay for the second job and Mateo was more than happy to oblige. First job. Phoenix. Second job. Lisa. And he planned on doing them both and heading into retirement. What Axel was paying, he never had to work again. He couldn't decide if he should stay stateside and just enjoy the good life or should he move abroad, just in case he ever needed to evade extradition. He thought about all the things he had done. So many of those things could come back and bite him and he wasn't about to spend the rest of his life in prison. Not with all the money he had just got his hands on.

Phoenix pulled out of the driveway and took off. Mateo gave him a minute and went behind him.

Phoenix was even more confused when he left Cedric's house. He almost didn't want to leave. But he knew he couldn't move in with Cedric like he could with Josiah and at present he needed somewhere to stay.

Phoenix looked in his rear mirror. He felt as if he was being followed. He needed to get off this street. It was too deserted. It would be a longer drive to the freeway, but he didn't feel safe where he was. Just as Phoenix was getting ready to turn, the car sped up and cut him off, forcing him off the road, down the embankment and into the river. Phoenix was momentarily out of it, but when he came to her realized his car was sinking.

"What is going on? What is happening?" Then he thought about it. Axel. *It's got to be Axel out for revenge.* He looked around. He didn't see anyone coming. He unbuckled his seat belt. He had to find a way to get out of there before whoever was behind him came to finish the job. Then it hit him. *My phone. I could call for help.* He looked all around. He couldn't find his phone. It would probably be useless anyway seeing how the majority of the car was over half full with water. "What am I going to do? I don't want to die. Please God don't let me die."

Mateo pulled his car over. Went to the back seat and pulled out a pair of gloves. He was sure Phoenix was in the car in full panic mode by now. But he needed to get to him before he managed to escape. "Time to finish this." Mateo smiled as he slipped the gloves on his hands and made his way down the embankment.

# CHAPTER EIGHTY-ONE

The tour was going excellent. Autumn had requested that Axel give her, her own space far from the dancers and Charlie. And he did. She knew he would oblige her since he was currently in the doghouse. Never had he allowed an artist to have her own room in a totally different hotel room from all of the rest of the artist, dancers, musicians and support staff. But here she was all alone and loving it. No one knew how to get in touch with her except Shannon and she had given Shannon a do not disturb order unless it was a life of death situation and so far Shannon had obeyed to a tee. Autumn was extremely thankful for Shannon. Shannon had been her stylist/assistant for about five years. She always knew what to pick her out for her performances. She even dressed her for the mood she was in. Autumn smiled at the thought. But even though Shannon was there for Autumn, they still didn't have a real friendship. You would think in this business friends would come a dime a dozen, but not for Autumn. She felt so alone. What in the world was changing? This was something that used to bring her so much joy. Now she didn't even know if she wanted to continue. She had been waiting for this tour for a while, but now she couldn't wait to get back home. Autumn needed to come to terms with the fact that she didn't want to do this anymore. Autumn laid on her bed with her hands behind her head and her eyes to the ceiling. She jumped up when she heard a small voice whisper. *Come back to me.*

"Hello. Someone there." No answer. Autumn shook her head. *I must be tripping.* She laid down once again. And the voice whispered once again. *Come back to me.*

This time autumn remained still and responded. "Is that you God?"

*It is me.* Came the whisper. *Come back to me.*

Autumn sat up on her bed. She walked over to the smallest of her suitcases. She opened the lock and there it was. Her Bible. She had asked Shannon to pack it off of a whim. That was the only thing she requested besides what was lying next to her Bible. A notepad and pen. She grabbed all three items and went over to the desk. *Where do I even begin? How do I find my way back?*

*John.* Came the whisper once again.

"John?" Autumn was puzzled. She looked down at her Bible. "Oh, the book of John." Autumn opened her Bible. She turned to the New Testament Gospel of St. John.

*"In the beginning the Word already existed. The Word was with God, and the Word was God. He existed in the beginning with God. God created everything through him, and nothing was created except through him. The Word gave life to everything that was created, and his life brought light to everyone. The light shines in darkness, and the darkness can never extinguish it."*

Autumn felt compelled to stop there." What are you saying to me God?"

And then she heard the still small voice once again. *I created you. I made you with my own hand. I breathed life into you to fulfill my purpose and my plan. That life that is in you will be a light to many, but you have to trust me. I know you see darkness everywhere you go and let me warn you now, it's going to get darker. But remember the darkness can never extinguish the light. Be the light.*

Autumn was in awe. Did God just speak to her? Did he just warn her that more craziness was coming? *Oh my, I believe he did.* Autumn couldn't believe what was happening. She immediately began to cry. She hadn't heard the voice of the Lord in a very long time. She felt like a traveler that had been wandering through the desert for years and finally came upon a well filled with water and took his first drink. It was beyond refreshing. She did wonder what else would happen though. But she knew whatever it was, God already had a solution to it and he would work it out. Autumn looked back down at her Bible. "The darkness can never extinguish it. The darkness can never extinguish the light." Autumn confessed out loud. That would make a great song. Autumn walked over to her keyboard. The one she kept up for private practice. She began to play with some chords and within the hour she had a brand-new song. An inspirational song. I wonder how Axel would feel if I closed out my last show on the tour with this song. She wasn't about to ask. She didn't care. It was settled. She was going to do the song.

CHAPTER

# EIGHTY-TWO

Lisa stood in the line at Starbucks. She had on a headwrap and sunglasses. She had been incognito for the past two weeks. She had even gone as far as staying at a hotel. Thankful she still had enough money. Which was quickly running out. She had to find something else to do. She looked up ahead as the person at the counter received their order and stepped out of line.

*Good.* Lisa thought to herself. Only two more people in front of her.

Lisa felt her hands begin to tremble. That seemed to be happening often. She realized Axel had her scared out of her mind. *What did he mean by we had unfinished business.* Lisa thought as she rubbed her trembling hand over her growing baby bump. Lisa thought about how angry Axel was at the dance studio. She did not want to feel his wrath. Lisa breathed another sigh of relief when the person at the counter received their order and left. One more person and she would be next. She couldn't wait to get her espresso, sit by the window and figure out what she needed to do.

As she continued to wait in the line, Lisa thought back to what Harmony said in the baby store. Would Axel actually try to make her get rid of the baby? Would he do something to her? She couldn't answer any of those questions for sure. Maybe she needed to get away. Maybe she would go home to her parents. She knew that would be a stretch. But she had to go somewhere. She couldn't very well wait and see what Axel had planned for her. A chill shimmied down her spine.

"Next." The lady at the register called out.

Lisa stared at her for second. *On second thought I might need to get this order to go.* She thought.

Twenty minutes later Lisa was at home packing as much as she could fit in her suitcases. She had stopped by the hotel first, grabbed her things and checked out. She realized she would have to go somewhere so she could have this baby. She wasn't quite sure where she was going, she just had to go somewhere. "I am going to have this baby and Axel isn't going to stop me." She said aloud.

Lisa almost jumped out of her skin at the sound of her phone ringing. Lisa reached over and grabbed her phone. Private number. Axel. She didn't know whether she should answer it or not. What did he want? Lisa reluctantly answered the phone. Her heart was beating a million miles a minute. Her hands felt clammy and cold. Her throat suddenly went dry. She formed the word hello in her mind but couldn't force it through her lips. Then she heard something she never expected to hear.

"Hey pretty girl. How are you?" Axel's deep voice sent tingles down her spine. She couldn't believe he wasn't upset.

"Hey." Lisa bit her lip. Her voice sounded as if it belonged to someone else. Who was this timid scared little girl? She had always been tough, fierce, did whatever she had to do. This was not like her at all.

"I was hoping you answered." Axel's voice was so calm, yet demanding. Lisa found herself melting at his every word.

"What do you want Axel?" Lisa sat up straight as she finally found her voice.

"I'm just trying to check on the beautiful mother of my child."

Lisa's heartbeat slowed. "I thought you didn't want me to have your baby?"

"Who told you that?"

Lisa didn't want to betray Harmony, but at this point she was willing to sell her own mama to get back with Axel. "Harmony." She said just above a whisper.

"I didn't want a baby with Harmony. You're different."

"Really?"

"You think a man like me will go around unknowingly getting females pregnant?"

"I don't know."

"I got too much to lose baby. I knew exactly what I was doing."

Lisa blushed, smiling from ear to ear.

"But a word of advice for the future. If you are going to be with me, you are going to have to stop listening to these other women, especially my ex-fiancé. You don't think they would do whatever it takes to get you out of the way?"

So many thoughts were rolling around her mind. *Did he just say be with me?*

"Lisa, you still there?"

Lisa jumped back to reality. "Yes, yes. I'm still here. I was just thinking."

"Thinking about what?"

"You really want to be with me?"

"I do. Do you want to be with me?"

"Of course I do."

"Ok then. I'll tell you what. I'm going to come pick you up so you can stay with me."

"Are you serious?"

"I'm very serious."

Lisa's eyebrows turned down into a frown. "What about Michelle?"

"You don't have to worry about Michelle. All I need to know is if you're moving in or not?"

"Yes. Yes. I'll move in." Lisa couldn't believe what she was hearing. "I'll start packing."

"No. Don't pack. Don't touch one single thing."

"Why not?"

"Don't you know that I upgrade all my women? When you get here you will have everything you need and whatever I missed. You'll have a black card for that."

Lisa jumped up and down. She had hit the jack pot after all. She quickly sat down and put her hand over her belly. She didn't want to do anything to jeopardize her pregnancy.

"Ok. Sure. I can do that. I won't touch anything. I'll just be sitting her waiting on you baby."

"Good. I'm on my way."

## CHAPTER
# EIGHTY-THREE

Axel sat on his black leather sofa. He had his popcorn, pizza and 2-liter Pepsi ready to watch Autumn's show which would be aired live. He had no plans of visiting Lisa, but he knew who would. He smiled thinking about how Lisa would no longer be a problem for him after tonight. He readjusted himself on the sofa and put everything out of his mind so he could focus on Autumn's performance. It was the final night of her tour and he couldn't wait for her to head back home. Axel couldn't believe how much he missed her. He thought about her every night since she'd been gone. *What is wrong with me? I have never let any girl get this close to me.* Axel shook the thoughts from his head. But with no progress. The thoughts came right back. *I should have gone on this tour with her? We could have spent more time together. More romantic time.* Axel thought about those words. He didn't want to play with Autumn's emotions but he wasn't ready to let her go either. He wanted her more than anything. Axel's mind shifted towards Michelle. Did he want her more than Michelle? He knew he would absolutely have to give her up in order to have Autumn. Axel looked down at his meal. He wasn't felling  hungry anymore. "I need to figure this out." He said aloud placing his food on the table in front of him.

Axel tried his best to relax and focus on the T.V. Charlie had opened up the show and Autumn would come and close it out. Axel sat up straight.

His eyes were now glued to the T.V. screen and all other distracting thoughts had vanished. It was finally time for Autumn to come on stage and did she ever. That outfit. She had worn different outfits throughout the tour but there was something different about this one. This was definitely something new. New but serene. It wasn't flashy but it was definitely sexy. Light. It fit her personality perfectly. Well, at least the personality of the Autumn he knew. She was the definition of two different people. She was fiery on stage, but humble and sweet off the stage. And speaking of new. Something was clearly brand new about Autumn. She was different. She was singing the same songs, but there was something completely different about her. Then she had the guitarist to play this banging solo as she disappeared off stage and then the guitarist finished. The crowd went wild and the stage went dark. Suddenly a single spotlight appeared and there she stood Autumn in a simple T-shirt dress that read "Let's Dance" with some killer heels. She had pinned her hair up and she looked amazing! What is she doing? This was not a part of the show. Is she improvising? Or is she trying to show up Charlie? If she is, she is killing it! And Charlie is going to hate her.

Autumn walked down a long staircase. She held a silver mic in her hand that sparkled with every word she spoke. "How you guys feeling tonight?" The crowd went wild. "Did we have some fun or did we have some fun?" The crowd responded with even more shouts and chorus of I love you's. "Well, I was sitting in my hotel room the other night and a thought came to me. So, I went over to my keyboard and I begin to write this song. I thought to myself, I should sing this for my friends." The crowd lost it once again. "Do you guys want to hear a new song? It's not on any album. No one has ever heard it, but I want you all to be the very first to hear it. What you think about that?" The crowd responded with shouts that could have blown the speakers. "Alright then, this song is for you guys." By this time Autumn had made her way over to the black baby grand piano that graced the stage. She sat down and placed her mic in the stand provided. She began to play the melody and the crowd responded with cheers. Autumn began to sing.

Axel was on the edge of his sofa by now. He couldn't believe Autumn was performing a song that she hadn't ran by him or anybody. *What is she doing?* Axel wanted to be upset, but the song was amazing. The audience loved it. Autumn sung from the depths of her heart. He could feel the pain in her soul. It made the beauty of the song resonate throughout the stadium. *Was this an inspirational song? Since when did Autumn do inspirational songs.* Axel didn't know what had gotten into Autumn but he knew the person that left on that tour was not going to be the same person that came back to him.

## CHAPTER
# EIGHTY-FOUR

Autumn returned to her room exhilarated by her performance. She had killed it! She twirled around as if she had on a poodle skirt from the 50s. She twirled until she lost her balance and fell to the bed. She couldn't believe she actually had the nerve to perform an inspirational song. Not only that, she didn't even run it by Axel. She wondered what he was thinking. He is probably going to be so mad. Autumn laughed to herself. She couldn't care less about what Axel thought. This was the new Autumn and she was loving it. Autumn sat up on her bed. "Social Media." She said out loud. "I wonder what they're saying about my performance."

Autumn jumped off her bed and ran to her closet. She pulled out her suitcase. The one with the Bible. She opened it and there laid her Bible and notepad. She picked them both up and held them to her chest. She fell to her knees and began to cry. "Thank you, Jesus. Thank you for speaking to me. Thank you for giving me such an amazing song." When Autumn finally opened her eyes, she saw her laptop. "Oh, social media." She laid her Bible and notepad beside her and booted up her computer.

"Hurry, Hurry." The suspense was literally tearing her apart. "I hoped they loved it. God please let them love it." Then Autumn heard that still small voice once again. *Didn't I give it to you?* By now Autumn knew who was speaking to her. She responded. "Yes, God, you did." *Then they'll love it.* The voice came again. Tears began to roll down Autumn's cheeks once again and she slowly calmed down. She pulled up her account and it was going wild.

*Autumn killed it.*

*I loved it.*

*Autumn never ceases to amaze!*

*Great show Autumn!*

She switched over to the labels account to see what people were saying about her compared to Charlie.

*Charlie was amazing, but Autumn took the show.*

*Autumn is so versatile. I am so glad I came to this show. This was epic!*

Autumn beamed. She saw a whole lot more praise for her than Charlie and it was beyond satisfying. "What am I saying? Why am I competing with Charlie? I am not about to get into this foolishness with Charlie. If she wants to compete with me then that's on her, but I'm not going to compete with her."

Autumn shut her computer down. She searched through the walk-in closet once again to find her purse. Once she located it, she rummaged through to find her phone. *There it is. I have got to get a smaller purse. I can never find anything in here.* She pulled out her phone and checked to see if she had any missed calls or messages. Twenty messages. Five missed calls. None from Axel. Autumn returned to her bed and fell face down.

"What is wrong with me? I just said I don't care about Axel thinks, but I at least expected him to contact me." Autumn peeled herself up off the bed and looked in the mirror. "I guess I should get ready for bed. It's a long flight home." And to make matters worse, she would have to leave her solitude and get on the bus with Charlie. Autumn stared at herself in the mirror for what seemed like an eternity.

"Why am I going through this God? Why does my heart hurt every day? I am living this amazing life. Doing what I love to do every day, but still I am hurting and unhappy. What is wrong with me God? What will it take for me to be happy?" Autumn listened for that still small voice. She waited and listened and listened and waited. But there was nothing. God wasn't talking to her anymore. Autumn felt lost. "I don't know what to do God. If you don't talk to me. I just don't know what to do." But still there was no answer.

# CHAPTER EIGHTY-FIVE

Harmony sat at her island sipping on a glass of red wine. She couldn't quite settle her mind. Did she give Lisa the best advice? What if she makes things worse for her. Harmony let her mind drift back to when she left Lisa at the baby store. She had been furious to learn Lisa was carrying Axel's baby. She wondered how Michelle felt about that? If only she could have seen her face when Lisa spilled the beans. Harmony tried to shake the thoughts from her head. Maybe Lisa didn't even take her seriously. She's probably out still baby shopping. Harmony took another sip of her wine. She couldn't take it anymore. She picked up her phone and dialed Lisa's number, it went straight to voicemail. She hung up and tried again. Same thing. Lisa always answered her phone. Harmony's pulse began to pick up a bit. She could feel her face flush. She was getting sick thinking maybe she was right, what if Axel had done something awful to her. Harmony couldn't stand the stress. She grabbed her purse off the table and headed to Lisa's house.

Harmony picked up the speed. With every minute her heart sunk in her stomach. She knew she should have just stayed with Lisa. She knew how awful Axel could be. She shouldn't have left her. Harmony remembered the first time Lisa invited her to her house. She didn't want to go. She felt stupid conspiring with someone to get back at Axel. Was it that deep? Why couldn't they just walk away and be done with it. Now look at us. Lisa could be hurt and here she was flying down the road trying to save someone who may or may not need saving.

Harmony's heart jumped to her throat. She could hear the clear pounding in her head as she saw the police lights up ahead. *Please don't let them be at Lisa's house.* But with all her hoping and praying, it wasn't enough to stop the reality that was taking place. She pulled to the police car that was blocking the road. She saw police tape around Lisa's door. *Please don't let her be dead. The baby.* Harmony thought. *Oh no, the baby!*

Harmony jumped out of the car and ran to the police car. She was stopped in her tracks. "My fri.. my friend, she lives there! Is she ok?"

"Ma'am. I need to ask you some questions?"

"Questions? I don't have time for your questions! Is my friend alright?"

"Ma'am, do you know a Lisa Campbell?"

"Yes, that's my friend. How is she? What happened? Why are you guys here?"

"We got a call saying that a lady was outside acting erratic. When we got to the scene there was no one outside. We checked the residence where they said the disturbance was coming from and noticed a female through the window who was bleeding."

Harmony almost collapsed. The officer asked her if she needed to be seated. She declined. "Just continue please."

"We broke down the door and when we entered..." the police voice trailed off.

"What.. what happened? What did you see?"

"You sure you want to hear this?"

"Yes I'm sure."

"You think you might want to have a seat?"

"Just tell me please."

"When we entered the residence, we saw the young lady with a knife in her hands stabbing at her stomach."

"No, not Lisa, she would never."

"Never what ma'am?"

"She was pregnant. She would have never hurt her baby. She was so excited."

"She was saying she didn't want the baby anymore as she was stabbing at her stomach."

"Oh my goodness. This can't be right. Is she ok?"

"She's at the hospital."

"Which one?"

"I still have some questions ma'am."

"You can question me later. My name is Harmony Ellis. My number is 555-0245. Right now I need to be with my friend just write down the name of the hospital on the back of your card, that way I'll know who you are." The officer obliged and Harmony was on her way.

So many questions flooded her mind. What would drive Lisa to hurt herself and the baby? Was the baby ok? If she stabbed herself in the stomach, the baby was more than likely not ok. Oh my, what is Axel going to think? Who cares what Axel thinks. He will probably be happy. Harmony was so angry that this was happening. She was more angry at herself. What if what she had said to Lisa caused her to harm the baby. She would never forgive herself. As a matter of fact, someone would have to put her on suicide watch. "Please Jesus don't let me had of driven this girl to kill this baby. Please don't let the baby be dead." At this point Harmony didn't know what to pray or what to say, she just needed to keep her mind busy until she knew the truth about everything.

Harmony was standing in the waiting room. Lisa was still in surgery. Harmony didn't even know if Lisa had any family. There was no one she could call to even let know Lisa was hurt. She thought about calling Axel but what would that help. He would just celebrate. She couldn't take that right now. She should have taken more time to get to know Lisa. For her, Lisa was just a means to an end. If she could help her exact revenge on Axel then that was all she cared about. She didn't want to be friends with Lisa or anyone else who had slept with Axel. She was still hurting from what he had done to her. She thought she had finally arrived. She was going to marry Axel Smith. But here she was two years later, still in the same exact place. She hated Axel for that and believe it or not even with everything that was going on. She still wanted revenge.

"Mrs. Ellis." Harmony jumped out of her sleep. She didn't even realize she had fallen asleep. She looked up to see a doctor in scrubs looking back at her.

"Is Lisa ok?"

"She's going to be fine. She has a long road ahead of her but she's alive and that was more than what we could have hoped for in her condition."

Harmony broke down crying. "Thank you Jesus for not letting my friend die." Harmony prayed silently. "Can I see her?"

"Absolutely. Although she isn't awake yet. It would be good for someone to be there when she wakes up."

"Thank you doctor."

"No thanks necessary. Follow me. I'll take you to her."

Harmony followed the doctor down the hall and through the doors that read intensive care. Tears fell down her face faster than she could wipe them. She didn't know what condition Lisa would be in. What she would look like. She just prepared for the worst.

They stopped in front of room 407.

Harmony paused.

"You can take your time if you need to. Just go through that door when you're ready." The doctor patted Harmony on the shoulder and walked off.

Harmony eased the door open like she was walking into a haunted house, halfway expecting to see someone jump out of a corner or a closet or something. She inched her way into the room and carefully walked up to the bed where Lisa was lying. She didn't look horrible. She looked like herself. Harmony was relieved. She didn't know what she was expecting. She pulled up a chair and just stared at her for a minute. Should she hold her hand. Pat her arm. Fix her hair. It was looking pretty terrible. Harmony thought she would do the latter. She opened her purse and found her brush. She gently brushed Lisa's hair. She had long pretty hair. It didn't take much to make it look decent. She sat the brush on the table and gently grabbed her hand. She felt cold. Harmony looked around the room until she spotted an extra blanket and pulled it over Lisa. She didn't want her to be cold. Harmony returned to her seat. Why she cared so much about the welfare of this girl was beyond her. She never even expected her to be in her life much longer let alone be taking care of her at a hospital, but she felt responsible somehow and she had to make it right. More than that, sadly to say, she really wanted to know what happened. The only person who could tell her was laying in the bed fast asleep. Harmony thought she should get some rest as well so she could be up when Lisa woke up. She moved over to the couch, laid down and was sleep before she knew it.

Harmony woke up to voices all around her.

"Welcome back to the world sleepy head."

Harmony heard Lisa's cheerful voice. She sat up on the couch. The nurses where attending to her, checking the machines and things of that nature. Harmony went to her bedside.

"Lisa, you ok?"

"As far as I can tell."

"What happened?"

"Honestly I don't know."

"Hi, I'm nurse Abby." She stook out her hand for Harmony to shake.

Harmony just looked at her.

The nurse lowered her hand. "Can I talk to you for a second outside?"

Harmony reluctantly followed the nurse outside.

"I just wanted to let you know before you start telling her stuff she doesn't need to hear."

"What do you mean by that?"

"I mean, Lisa doesn't know what happened. She thinks she's in the hospital because she was dehydrated and passed out. As least that is what we told her because we don't want to traumatize her any further. But she doesn't remember anything. Not the trauma. Not even the baby."

"The baby. I forgot. The baby. Is the baby.."

"The baby is deceased."

Harmony covered her mouth to keep from screaming.

"So, what now?"

"I don't know. She may be committed to a psych unit. It's up to the police. They are trying to figure out what to do."

"Will they charge her with something?"

"I don't know. My job is to take care of my patient and that means keeping her happy by not indulging such information. So, the story is she was dehydrated and passed out… for now. Got it."

Harmony nodded her head. "Got it."

They both entered the room.

"Bout time ya'll came back. I'm starving. When do we eat around here?"

"Can I get her something?"

"I'll bring her something. Would you like something as well?"

"Yeah, bring her something. I'm sure she hasn't eaten since she's been camped out here."

"Will do."

Harmony pulled up her chair and stared at Lisa. She didn't know what to say.

"I don't know what you are making a big deal about. It was just some dehydration. I'll make sure I stay hydrated and everything will be ok."

"Ok Lisa. Just make sure you do. Cause I don't want to be picking you up off the floor and rushing you to the hospital again."

"I got you. Promise. I'm just ready to go home."

"Yeah. I know." Then it hit her. Lisa's home was still a crime scene. It had blood all over it. She would know something happened. "Why don't you just come stay with me for a while."

"Harmony really, it's not that serious."

"Lisa. It kind of is."

"I'm not intruding on you so you can make sure I drink enough water. I'm going home."

Harmony didn't know what to do. Then she thought about the detective. She could call him and see if they had done anything to get her house clean.

"Ok. Let me just check on something. I'll be right back."

"Ok Harmony. But I'm fine really. You're doing too much."

Harmony pulled out the card that the police officer gave her. He answered on the first ring.

"Hello officer, this is Harmony Ellis."

"Hi, you ready for those questions?"

"Not yet. You know my friend has amnesia."

"I heard. Or she could be faking."

"I know her. She's not faking."

"What does her house look like because she wants to go home and if she sees the blood she will have questions?"

"Look, we might have to charge her, so she's going to have to deal with this."

"Charge her for what?"

"Your friend had a whole lot of drugs inside her. She was high and she murdered her baby."

Harmony was surprised at what the officer was saying. She never knew Lisa to take drugs. Something wasn't adding up. "Drugs? There is no way Lisa took drugs."

"The tox screen doesn't lie ma'am."

"Somethings not right sir. Lisa didn't take drugs." Harmony hung up the phone. She had to find out what happened.

Harmony sat down in the waiting room chair and now her mind began to wonder. She didn't want to think about where her mind was going but she couldn't help it. She was now for sure Axel had something to do with it. Could he actually kill his own child? And what did he do to Lisa? She knew Axel was involved but she didn't know how to prove it. She needed to call her dad. She had to prove that Axel was involved and also keep Lisa out of jail. She wouldn't rest until she did.

# CHAPTER EIGHTY-SIX

Autumn walked into the office after two weeks of being back from the tour. Axel hadn't tried to contact her, neither had he come by her place. So, she heard. She had been hiding out at a hotel since her return. She didn't want to answer any questions about her performance to the reporters that had swarmed her house for the first week of her return. They left after they realized she wasn't coming back anytime soon. That's what she was waiting on. She would return after another week. But she wanted to get back to work. See if she could write another inspirational song, but more importantly, she craved to see Axel. She wanted to know his thoughts on her new song, her performance. She knew she shouldn't be this attached to him, but she couldn't help herself. She walked down the hall as if she were in a horror movie. Almost tiptoeing. She didn't want to run into anyone or give anyone notice of her presence.

Yes! She had made it to her office without incident. Or so she thought. No sooner had she shut the door did it open again. She turned around and there stood Axel in all his 6'4 220lb chocolate glory. Instantly her knees became weak and she struggled to remain standing. The feelings that she felt when Axel's body was pressed against hers returned in full force as if they had just made love. *Why is this happening?* The feeling in Autumn's legs finally returned and she scampered around her desk and plopped down in her seat.

"What do you want Axel?" She said as if there wasn't a perpetual fire burning between her legs.

"I haven't seen or heard from you in a couple of months."

"I've been on tour."

"Not the entire time. But besides that, when have we ever not talked while you were on tour. We face-time all the time. So don't try that. What's your deal? I thought we got past all of our issues."

"We did."

"Doesn't seem like it."

"Axel." Autumn took a breath and gazed around her office as if what she had say was hard for her to say. In actuality she just didn't know if he would want to hear what she actually had to say. He had already turned her down once before, she didn't know if her heart could take another knife wound. So she decided to deflect.

"Axel." She began again. "I don't have any problems. I just needed my own space. Remember we talked about giving me space?"

Axel walked over to Autumn's desk and sat in the chair opposite hers.

"Autumn I can't do that. You're my best friend and I love you and I need you and I know don't deserve you but this is what it is."

Autumn wanted to throw up in her mouth. *If he referenced me as his best friend one more time, I'm going to kick him in his best friends.* Autumn just sighed.

"Axel, what I said stands. I can't deal with this. I don't want to do this anymore."

"So it's like that then."

Yeah, it's like that.

Axel stood and walked towards the door.

"What did you think about my song?" The words just seem to force themselves from her lips.

Axel's hand was just about to turn the knob. He dropped his head and turned around. He slowly walked back over to the desk were Autumn stood, with misty eyes.

"Autumn, I loved the song. I just can't believe you left me out the loop. That hurt more than anything. Like I said, I thought we were best friends." Then he turned and left the room.

Autumn stood there with her mouth forming a perfect O. *He loved it. He actually loved my song.* But then she recalled the sadness in his eyes. No matter what evil, stupid things Axel did. No matter how much he hurt her or got on her nerves. She believed that he actually did love her and cared about her and truly wanted to be a real friend to her. Autumn plopped back down in her seat. *Why do I keep messing things up with him? I hate him so much but I love him so much! I really need therapy.* Autumn couldn't help but snicker at her own insanity.

# CHAPTER EIGHTY-SEVEN

Autumn called an emergency meeting of the dance team. All five Michelle, Skye, Faith, Jaylah and River. Autumn had put chairs in a semi-circle in front of her and she put her and Michelle's chair next to each other facing the group.

"I know you guys were wondering why I called you all here and I promise you I'm not going to hold you long on your off day, but I wanted to let you all know face to face. I'm dismantling the team."

Gasp sounded off around the room.

"I know. I know. It's all so crazy to me as well. I just don't like the feel of this team and I am going to have another tryout. I do wish you all the best in your endeavors."

Jaylah could feel the blood boiling in her veins. And she just couldn't restrain herself any longer. "So, you're kicking us off the dance team just like you did Harmony? What about her?"

"Who Michelle? Michelle stays."

"Why does she get to stay? Is it because she's Axel's punching bag, cause it definitely ain't because she's the best dancer?"

"It's really none of your business Jaylah." Autumn stood up as well.

"It is my business. You're firing me from my job and I feel I have a right to speak my peace. Especially since you are firing everyone except her." She pointed violently at Michelle. "She is the only one that is putting a rift in this dance team. Her and the twins."

Skye and Faith's heads turned quicker than their eyes could blink.

"She's probably throwing us all of the team because you're sleeping with her fiancé."

"What?" They said in unison.

"Oh, don't play stupid. I have pictures and Autumn's already seen them."

Faith hung her head in shame, while Skye took another approach. "It is what it is, let's go Faith." She grabbed her sister by the hand and they rushed out of the room.

"Are you happy now?" Autumn shook her head at Jaylah.

"I didn't ask for this to happen." Jaylah said indignant.

"You should have never said anything. Everything I needed to know I would have found out for myself. I didn't need your help."

"You say that now, but wait til the truth comes out. You would have never been able to find that on your own."

"What do you mean? The truth is already out."

"Not talking about that truth Autumn Dance, not that truth."

"What are you talking about?"

"You'll find out soon. Bye Michelle. Just know this all your fault. I hate the day you ever joined this team."

Jaylah winked at Autumn and made her exit.

"What about me?"

Autumn had totally forgotten River was in the room.

"You know what River. You actually can remain on the team. I wasn't thinking clearly. You haven't been anything but a good dancer. I'm going to keep you. Come see me in the morning and we'll talk about future projects."

"Thank you, Autumn. I really appreciate you. River let a smile roll across her face as she turned to leave. Her plan was still in motion."

Autumn couldn't understand for the life of her what Jaylah was talking about and to second that why did she blame Michelle. Michelle was Axel's girl. There was no way she would be able to put her off the team even if she wanted to. But I guess anger and jealousy make you blind to the truth. Still autumn felt a bit uneasy about this other truth that Jaylah spoke of. *What was it that she didn't know about?* Had Phoenix gotten anyone pregnant? Well, even if he did, he no longer concerned her. Autumn finally let the thought drop. She turned around to Michelle and realized she had another problem on her hands. Michelle had plopped on the floor in true kid mode. She was Indian style with her head in her hands and she was sobbing like a whole toddler. Autumn was so caught up in what Jaylah said to her that she forgot how Michelle might feel about it; even though she hadn't been talking to her directly she imagined it hurt. Autumn stared at Michelle sitting on the floor. Could this girl go through anymore hurt and pain? It seemed as if everyone hated her. Axel, Lisa, Harmony, her dancers. It had to be too much. Autumn also knew how Michelle felt when it was brought up about how Axel beat her. That had to be the most hurtful and embarrassing. Axel was so public with his disrespect and abuse of Michelle, Autumn often wanted to crawl in a hole and die for her.

Autumn eventually sat on the floor. "Michelle. Hold your head up sweet girl."

Michelle obeyed.

"What's going through your mind?"

"Everyone hates me Autumn. I should have known not to try to be anything other than what I am and now all your dancers are gone. What do we do now?"

"Shelly they are only gone because I fired them. It had nothing to do with you. Please believe that. But yet and still I don't know what I'm going to do. You are the one with all the good ideas. You'll come up with something." She wiped a tear from Michelle's cheek as she watched a smile spread across her face. But that smile didn't last too long.

Axel walked through the door. "What's going on?"

"You said I could fire my whole team and so I did. Well, except River."

"You fired Michelle too?"

"No Axel."

"Then why is she crying."

"One of the dancers said some pretty hurtful things toward her. Blamed Michelle for the ruin of the team. Like how could she have done that?"

"Maybe she did. Maybe I should have never let her join the team."

"Axel, don't do that. You know exactly why I fired everyone. Plus, Michelle here is the best part of my team."

"I doubt that."

Autumn looked over at Michelle. She could tell Michelle had stopped breathing. She didn't know how Michelle was still alive as much as she stopped breathing whenever Axel entered a room.

"You just cause trouble everywhere you go don't you."

"It's not her fault…" Autumn started to say before Axel put up a finger to stop her.

Autumn was thrown aback. Did he just silence me? Why is he pushing the envelope? He knows this isn't Michelle's fault. Is he really this evil? Is he going to find a reason to beat this girl just for fun?

"Is that what you do Michelle?" Axel continued his attack against Michelle.

The tears had begun to fall from her face once again. She just knew she had a beating coming. She was still sore from the last one. How was her body ever going to fully heal if he kept beating on her without any breaks?

Michelle humped her shoulders and immediately she regretted it. She didn't have long to regret it though. Before her shoulders returned to their original position, Axel had grabbed her off the floor with both hands and threw her against the mirror that shattered on impact. Autumn jumped up to her feet and Axel turned towards her daring her to interfere. Autumn was his best friend but she knew not to interfere with his affairs. When he was handling business, especially of the nature that she didn't agree with, his only request had ever been for her not to interfere. She tried not to get involved, but how could she not. The day he brought Michelle to her house she was involved. The day Michelle became her dancer, she was involved and now as Michelle's only friend. She was definitely involved. But she wasn't stupid. Even though Autumn knew Axel would never lay a hand on her she didn't want him to take his anger out on Michelle any more than he already was. Autumn slowly took a step back to show him she was not about to interfere.

Axel turned back toward Michelle, picked her up off the ground with one hand and back handed her with the other. Michelle flew across the opposite end of the room. Michelle rolled over in pain, relieved he didn't hit her towards the broken glass. She didn't want to be all cut up.

Axel continued to take his fury out on Michelle as Autumn helplessly looked on. She prayed that he would stop but it seemed to go on forever. Finally, after being kicked repeatedly, Michelle became motionless. Axel reluctantly stopped his assault.

Why does Axel get so angry at Michelle over practically nothing? Autumn couldn't understand. Axel was the sweetest person to her, but to Michelle, he was this monster that she didn't even recognize. Autumn started to walk toward Michelle, hoping she was still alive, but Axel stopped her in her tracks.

"Leave her. She'll be fine. Let's go."

Autumn hesitated. She didn't feel right leaving Michelle all alone. But she knew she had no choice. She looked at Michelle one last time before submitting to Axel's authority once again. Tears streamed down her face as she walked past Axel not even allowing him to touch her as she breezed by him.

Axel smirked a bit. He knew Autumn was upset and he hated making her upset, but she would get over it. He would just sweet talk her like he always did. Buy her some expensive gifts and remind her how much her friendship meant to him. She'll come around. He thought to himself as he held the door open for Autumn. He pulled out his phone and put in a call to his clean-up crew. His crew would come and pick up Michelle, take her to a private doctor and clean up the mess. He loved being himself. One phone call, everything handled, no questions asked. He loved it.

CHAPTER

# EIGHTY-EIGHT

Michelle woke up with white walls surrounding her. She tried to move but she hurt all over. She felt like every bone in her body was broken. She tried to breathe deeply but her chest felt like a whole elephant was sitting on top of her. Her face. Something was on her face. She tried to move her hand to remove whatever was on her face but she couldn't. Her arms would not move. As a matter of fact, neither would her legs. Was she paralyzed? Tears began to stream down her face. *What is going on?* Michelle tried to call out for help but a silent scream was the only thing that escaped her lips. *It's finally happened.* Michelle thought to herself. *Axel has finally succeeded in ruining my life.* If she was paralyzed, her dancing career was over. Without her dancing career who would she be? What would she be? She had finally found a way out, so she thought, that didn't include her death. But here she lay, barely alive if you asked her. She might as well be dead.

Michelle heard someone moving around in her room, she darted her eyes from the right to the left, trying to figure out who had come in and if she could get their attention. God must've smiled on her because the nurse walked right up to her and asked if she was ok. A single tear after a river of many rolled down the side of her face as she shook her head from side to side. Grateful that she could at least do that.

"I know baby said the nurse. Have you tried to move yet?"

Michelle nodded her head.

"Do you remember being kicked in the back?"

Michelle closed her eyes. She thought back to Axel kicking her and she remembered rolling over, trying to get him to stop kicking her in the stomach. And then she saw it. Axel kicking her in the back until one of the kicks flipped her back over. And Axel continued to kick her.

Michelle opened her eyes and nodded her head.

"Well, that kicked injured your spinal cord. But don't worry. It's only temporary. You just have some swelling around your spinal cord but it will go down and you should be able to walk again. As a matter of fact, I heard you were a dancer. You will be back shaking your booty for the camera in no time." The nurse laughed and rubbed her hair. "I'm sorry for whoever is abusing you baby. I wish there was more I could do, but for now, I'm going to make sure I get you better."

Michelle nodded her head and began to cry even more. It was all she could do. Even though she had an oxygen mask on her face she felt as if she could breathe a bit more freely knowing this wasn't going to be her life.

## CHAPTER
# EIGHTY-NINE

"What are you doing here?" Logan opened the door shocked to see a disheveled Autumn standing on his doorstep. She always looked like she stepped off of the cover of a magazine, but not today. She had her hair tied back in a ponytail and a plain black hat pulled down low. She had a sweater on that was two sizes too big for her and a pair of leggings. Her ensemble was completed by a pair of tennis shoes. Brand unrecognizable. What is going on with this girl? And make-up? Did she know she wasn't wearing make-up. He had never seen Autumn without make-up. If it hadn't been for the defining features of her face, he wouldn't have known who she was.

"We need to talk." Autumn pushed past Logan and stepped inside his living room.

"Come on in." Logan said to no one in particular. Autumn seemed to have already made herself at home exploring everything in sight.

"Why do you still live in this small apartment. Our single just went platinum. Are you at least looking for a house to purchase?"

Well, aren't we judgmental today. I heard your new song. I thought you were on a different path, guess I was wrong."

Autumn jerked her head back as if Logan had just punched her in the face. He was right. "Sorry." Autumn took a seat on Logan's Walmart futon sofa. "I guess like you said, all of this is still new to me. I'm just going through a lot right now."

"You look like it. As a matter of fact, you look like you live here in this small mediocre apartment." Logan looked Autumn over again.

"Logan, can we talk, like for real talk?"

"You came all this way, unannounced I might add. You might as well get it all out."

"I think I messed up big time."

"What do you mean by that?" Logan took a seat on the futon adjacent to the one Autumn sat on. He figured he was getting a deal buying two.

"I think I might have inadvertently gotten Michelle in trouble."

"Wait, what do you mean got her into trouble?"

"I fired the whole team and Axel blamed it on her. I don't know how he figured it was her fault but he blames everything on Michelle. I think it's just a reason to beat her. I hate him so much right now."

"What is Axel going to do?"

He already beat her unconscious in front of my face. But he told me later on he had something else in store for her. I don't know what that is but I remember Michelle telling me that Axel took her through some type of boot camp when she first got to his house. His attempt to break her and train her to be the little obedient punching bag slash sex slave she is today. He told her that she had gotten out of hand and that round two of boot camp would need to commence. Michelle was horrified. I don't think her mind or body can take a round two and it's all my fault. The nurse had to sedate her when Axel told her. Michelle was literally shaking, she was so afraid of the possibility."

Logan was burning up on the inside. He had to get Michelle away from Axel one way or another.

Autumn dropped her head in her hands. "God what do you want me to do!" She screamed in frustration.

"God, huh?"

"Yeah, God. Know something about it?"

"I used to."

"Why not anymore?"

"Too much has happened."

"So you gave up on him?"

"Didn't you?"

Autumn just stared at Logan. She could let him put her off with his unbelief or she could win him over. She didn't feel much like being a witness but she knew she had to.

"Look Logan. I ran from God thinking it was his fault my family was so messed up. My dad was a preacher and he was sleeping with every woman in the church almost. Really messed me up. But lately I've been hearing God's still small voice speaking to me. The things he's been saying to me about my life has me really confused. Well, not necessarily confused more so I just don't know what to do. How do I leave this life I've built for myself and minister for God again? But I do know this, if we are going to save Michelle, we are going to definitely need God."

Logan dropped his head. He remembered singing songs to God. He remembered praying to God and feeling so hopeful. That was before his mom died. After she died, there was nothing left for him to feel hopeful about. But what if what Autumn was saying was true. He couldn't define his relationship with God based on something bad that happened. Maybe it was time he started listening to what God was saying to him. "Autumn, it's so crazy, when I first saw Michelle, I knew she was hurting. Then when we had dinner with her and Axel, I saw it much closer. The hurt, the pain and then the bruises. Then something deep inside me told me I had to rescue her. And I vowed to, but I haven't done a good job of it. To be honest I really don't know how."

"God told me the same thing. To help Michelle. Looks like we are both failing. So what are we going to do?"

"I don't know I'm even more new to this than you. You talked to God. What did he tell you besides come barge yourself into my house and insult it?"

Autumn couldn't help but laugh. "You are something else."

"I try to be. Let me ask you this though. What about Axel? What do we do with Axel? Do we save him? Cause if he takes Michelle through some stupid boot camp, he's definitely going to need a Savior and I can't help him."

"Logan." Autumn shook her head, then tilted it slightly to the right as if she was pondering something. "You know what. I never thought of that. What if Axel needs saving to? What if that is what we both came to this industry to do? You know, not just fit in, but to change the game. We need to be examples for Jesus. And that's why we are here!" Autumn stood up as if she knew exactly what to do.

"So what's the plan boss?"

Autumn sat back down. "I don't know Logan," she said barely above a whisper. "I wish I knew."

"I can't believe I'm saying this but maybe we should pray. Who knows it might work."

Autumn looked up at Logan. "I think that's a perfect idea." Autumn stood up and reached out her hand for Logan to grab.

"Ok. We're holding hands too. That's cool I guess."

"Just give me your hand."

Logan reluctantly connected his hands to Autumn's. He bowed his head and closed his eyes. Silence. He opened one eye and peered up at Autumn. Surely she wasn't waiting on him to pray. He saw Autumn with her head bowed and her eyes clothes breathing deeply. Maybe she was thinking about what to say. Logan thought he should give her a minute more. He bowed his head and closed his one eye back. Silently waiting.

"Dear Lord," Autumn finally began. "I don't know what it is that you want us to do, but you brought Logan and I together in your Name for a reason. And I trust you. I trust you to lead and guide us on the path you have destined for us to be on. Right now I pray for Michelle. Keep her and protect her from all hurt, harm or danger. Please God, don't let her get hurt because of me."

Logan peeked one eye open again a looked at Autumn. Tears had begun to fall down her face. Her hands were trembling inside of his.

"Lord, please, please keep her safe. And Lord, deliver Axel as well. I don't know why he hurts Michelle. I don't know why he has this mean streak when he really is a great person. You created him to be a great person. Why is he doing this? Only you know God and just the same only you can deliver him. Please deliver him God, please deliver him. Please, please, please."

Autumn was clearly falling apart at this point. Logan pulled her to his chest and embraced her before she hit the floor. He held her up and hugged her as she bellowed out deep sobs of pain.

Logan silently prayed. *God, please heal Autumn and help her fulfill her purpose. And help me to be a strong leader and a strong Godly man and a protector for these hurting women. Help me to stop hurting women and help me to start helping and healing them. Please God, we need you. We really, really need you.* Tears began to fall down his face as well. Eventually he and Autumn crumbled to the ground, falling on their knees. Logan never letting her go. He was determined to never let her go. He would help her be all she was called to be, no matter what.

## CHAPTER
# NINETY

Charlie sat in her office still fuming over Autumn's new decent to the top. She had to bring her down somehow, someway. She spun around in her chair. She paced her office. She couldn't stop obsessing over the situation. What am I going to do? I wonder if her office is open? She hadn't seen her come in today, maybe she could sneak in there and find something on her.

A few minutes later, Charlie found herself safely in Autumn's office. Stupid girl left the door unlocked. She is way too trusting. Charlie knew she had to hurry. Autumn could walk through those doors any minute. She went over to her desk and glanced around. Autumn kept her desk meticulously cleaned. There weren't even any papers on her desk. Not even any pictures. Autumn really didn't have a life outside this place. Maybe that's why she was hanging on to Phoenix. A man who was clearly going both ways. Charlie could tell a queer from a mile away and he was as queer as they came. *Poor girl, maybe she will find out eventually.*

Charlie carefully opened a drawer. She didn't want to disturb anything. In the bottom left drawer was an old school tape recorder. What was Autumn doing with this? Who uses these anymore? Charlie pulled it out rewound it and pushed play. It was Autumn's hit song. But Autumn wasn't singing it. Instead, it was the most beautiful voice she had ever heard. Charlie smiled knowing who the voice belonged to.

"Sweet little Michelle, so you wrote the song. You probably did the choreography for it too. Ohhh, little girl, you are talented." Charlie could feel her desire for Michelle grow even the more. This is some good stuff. "I know how I'm going to get Michelle and take over Axel's entire enterprise." Charlie smiled to herself. She tucked the recording into her pocket and headed out of Autumn's office.

# CHAPTER
# NINETY-ONE

Michelle sat on the floor in her room and went over the exercises her physical therapist gave her. She was already ready to start back dancing. Maybe today would be the day that she would give it a try.

Michelle got up. Put the disk into her radio and let the music fill her ears. She wanted to move but fear kept her feet glued to the floor. *Come on Michelle, you can do this.* Michelle began to two-step. A smile crept across her face, she had to start somewhere. She had to admit. It felt good to move her body even if just a little. *Here goes.* Slowly she tried a twist, a roll and then a pop. So good so far. She counted herself in and began her recent choreography. Like a fish being released back into the water, Michelle's body slipped right back into rhythm with the music. She grinned like she was performing on stage.

Michelle stopped abruptly at the bedroom door opening. Axel walked through. Michelle took a couple of steps back. She wasn't a month out of recovery and here he was, trying to send her back into the hospital. Why wouldn't he just leave her alone? Let her go. She stared at him. One of the few times she knew she was allowed to. It was his moment to deposit fear into her. And she always accepted. Her legs wanted to give way right then and there. Her heart wanted to stop. She wanted to give up and just kill herself.

"What are you doing?" Axel could tell Michelle was afraid. He loved it. The fear in her eyes. The quiver in her lips. He couldn't resist. His fist automatically balled up. He could tell Michelle noticed. The little color she did have drained right out of her. Axel didn't plan on hitting her though. It was the normal reaction he had when he was around Michelle. "I asked you a question." Axel let every syllable not only be heard but felt.

"I... I was... I was dancing." Michelle finally spit out.

"You know you ran off Autumn's entire crew, right?"

"I ... I didn't mean to. I... was only..." Michelle's voice trailed off. She couldn't believe he was back on this. He had already beat her for that.

"Only what. Only trying to end her music career."

"Of course... of course not. I would never do that. I promise."

Axel took two steps toward Michelle. He saw her look down, trying to see how much room she had before she hit the wall. She looked back up disappointed that there was no room left.

"The only thing you are good for is allowing me to let out my frustration. Whether through sex or with fist. Maybe I should let you continue doing what you do best and let all this dance stuff come to an end."

Michelle's eyes grew wide. He couldn't just take dancing away from her. She didn't know what she would do without dancing. "I can help. I promise. I can help." Michelle seemed to find her confidence.

"You really ain't even worth this conversation." Axel sputtered with as much disdain as he could muster up.

Michelle's chest caved in with pain. Sometimes Axel's words hit harder than his fists.

"Please Axel. Please don't do this. I can do better I promise."

Axel continued to advance towards Michelle. Michelle braced herself for impact.

Axel leaned over and whispered in Michelle's ear. "We will finish this at a later date." Axel turned to leave the room but before he could exit the room Michelle found a courage she had never imagined and she called out to him.

"Axel."

Axel stopped at the door. He didn't know if he was more shocked at her audacity to say something to him or the sound of her voice. He rarely ever gave her the opportunity to talk and when she did it was shaking with fear. But not this time. This time it was confident and beautiful and it was now his turn to be afraid. Because he always knew if Michelle ever found out the power she held, it would ruin him. Seemed as if that time had finally come. He just didn't' know what to do. He never dreamt of the day that Michelle would get to this place. He had done a pretty good job of breaking her, but it seems as if she couldn't be fully broken and now, here she was rising from the ashes, determined to be something she'd never been before.

Axel turned around hoping that Michelle would see the fire in his eyes and rethink her decision. But then again is that what she would see? He became unsure of himself as he turned to face this girl that had become a woman. Would she see the fire or would she see the fear and pounce like the strong, fierce lioness she truly was?

Axel saw Michelle take a deep breath and he could tell her heart was beating a mile a minute. She was unsure of herself as well. Could she really do this? Could she really say what she really wanted to say to him? They were both about to find out.

Michelle took three steps forward so she could make sure Axel heard and understood her every word.

"Axel." she repeated. "I can be the biggest help to this company and you know it. Autumn's song that Hit number one and is still at number one, well, Charlie was right. Someone else wrote it and choreographed it and that person was me. And that is just a sample of what I bring to the table. Now you can either keep me in the shadows or you can let me take this company to the next level. Both as an artist and a visionary. I have come to the conclusion that I have nothing to lose. If you keep beating me the way you do, you are going to eventually kill me, so right now I have nothing to lose. You can either use me to continue to make your star rise or you can kill me right now. Either way whether you know it or not. I win.

"You win? How do you win Michelle?" Was the only thing that came to Axel's mind.

"Because one road leads to me fulfilling my dream and the other leads me out of this life with you. Like I said, either way, I win."

Michelle stood up a bit straighter and held her head up a bit higher and gave him a matter of fact stare that could have burned a hole straight through his face.

Axel realized she was not backing down. He had two choices. Call her bluff and fail or he could make it seem like he was the one in control and is only thinking about the money. He thought about it for a moment. This might be just what he needed. His way out. He could still control Michelle through her employment at the label, move her into an apartment that he monitored and he could finally convince Autumn he was done with her. He loved the way his plan was coming together.

Axel took three steps closer and closed the gap between Michelle and himself. He could see the fear in her eyes, thinking she had failed.

"I'll tell you what Michelle. I'm going to take you up on your little offer. Only cause I'm all about the money. If you were the brains behind Autumn's song then I could definitely use some more of that. We'll sit down and talk tomorrow. Cause with Autumn's dance team situation and some other situations going on, we need to do some revamping any way. So, let's see if you can produce or not. You down with that?"

"Y... yes." Michelle couldn't believe what she was hearing. She didn't know if she wanted to jump for joy or pee herself. But what she did know is that her life was about to change.

CHAPTER

# NINETY-TWO

Axel stood outside of Autumn's office door. It was the last day before her contract expired. She never waited this late to renew her contract. Something was up. Axel ignored the sickening feeling that was swirling around in the pit of his stomach. Was it finally happening? Had Autumn finally had enough? He took a deep breath and opened the door.

Axel took a step back and his fist instantly balled up. The scene that played out before him had him wanting to tear the entire office to pieces.

There was Autmn, the love of his life, he had finally admitted to himself, wrapped in the arms of him. Logan. What was this guy's problem? First Michelle, now Autumn. This guy definitely had a death wish. If he wasn't in route to being Axel's top artist, he would show this guy the door quickly and violently, with plenty of prejudice.

"Am I interrupting something?" Axel asked not taking his eyes off Logan.

But it was Autumn who had spoken up. "We were just talking? Logan was helping me out with something."

"Something I couldn't help you out with." Axel didn't care how weak he sounded. He wasn't about to lose Autumn. He would kill Logan before he let him take Autumn from him. He came to her office with a purpose and he was determined to see it through.

"Sounds like jealousy Axel." Logan chimed in.

Axel returned his gaze to Logan. He had no idea how close he was to losing his life. "What did you say to me?"

Logan turned his full stature toward Axel. He wasn't about to back down. "I'm just trying to find out who I can talk to. First it was Michelle, now Autumn. Is every woman off limits?"

"Logan." Autumn chimed in before Axel had a chance to respond. "Thank you for everything. I need to talk to Axel. I'll call you later."

Logan kissed Autumn on the forehead. He enjoyed watching the veins popping out of Axel's neck. He had finally hit him where it hurt and he was determined to take him all the way down.

Logan walked past Axel without saying a word. It took everything in Axel not to punch Logan in the side of his head. That's not what he came in here for. He had to stay focused. He turned his gaze to the person he did come in here for. The one who standing beside her desk like she had stepped right out of heaven and into his heart.

"What's wrong? Why did you have to go to Logan? All of a sudden you no longer can talk to me?"

"It was about you. Well sorta." Autumn pushed a rogue curl behind her ear.

"Really." Axel nodded his head trying to process what he was hearing. He shoved his hands in his pockets and leaned against the wall. "It feels like our friendship is falling apart."

Autumn made her way over to where Axel was standing. She put her hand against his chest. "Our friendship is not falling apart Axel. It just needs to be redefined."

"Redefined. Is that the same as ending? Is that why you haven't signed your contract?" Axel placed his hand over Autumn's.

"Axel." Autumn looked deep into his eyes. "I want a different life. I love the music business but I feel like God is calling me to something different. I can't explain it. I just don't have the same passion I used to for what I'm doing. I think it's time for me to go in a different direction."

Axel stared into Autumn's sad but beautiful brown eyes. "The song. Is this about the song?"

"The song was inspired by the way I feel Axel. If I'm going to continue to do music, it has to be inspirational, but I also want to do mission work. Not like overseas or anything, but work with people like…" She hesitated not wanting to upset Axel.

"Like Michelle." Axel finished her thought.

"Yes. Like Michelle."

Axel grabbed the sides of Autumn's face. "Autumn whatever you want. I will support you one hundred percent. I just don't want to lose you."

Autumn couldn't help but let the tears that had been threatening to fall run down her cheeks. Which Axel caught and wiped away. "I just want a different life Axel. That's all."

"Does that life include me?"

"Not like this. I can't continue to love you and watch you with all these other women. With Michelle and all that comes with that."

"Did you say you love me?"

"I did, but I'm done Axel. I'm done."

"Then I'm done too."

"What do you mean?"

"I'm done with all the other women, Michellle and all that comes with that." He said sarcastically. "If you are done with this label then so am I. All I want is you."

"Axel. I don't have time..."

Before Autumn could finish her thought, Axel got down on one knee and pulled a small ring box from his jacket pocket.

"Axel what are you doing?" Autumn was trembling. She couldn't believe what she was seeing.

"Autumn, you have always been the one who has my heart. I will do anything for you. I just realized that means exactly that. Anything. All the women, the shady stuff, the music, Michelle. I'll do anything to have you, Autumn. I just want to share my life with you. I want to love you, hold you and make love to you whenever I want for the rest of my life. I can't live without you. I want you to be my constant, my one and only. Autumn, please tell me you will be my wife?"

Autumn fell to her knees along with Axel and began to kiss him passionately. After a few seconds Axel pulled back. Autumn's eyes popped open.

"What's wrong?"

"I just need an answer."

Autumn couldn't help but laugh. "Yes, silly. The answer is yes."

Axel slid the ring onto Autumn's finger. "Now you can get out of those clothes."

Autumn smiled while pulling her shirt over her head. Could God have answered her prayer so quickly? She didn't know but she was not about to turn down what she has wanted since she met Axel as an eighteen-year-old girl searching for a dream.

## CHAPTER NINETY-THREE

Axel lay in his bed. He turned to look over the side of the bed. Michelle lay on the floor. He clicked on the lamp next to the bed. He checked her out again. He could tell she was still breathing. She must've cried herself to sleep. That was the last thing she was doing before he dozed off. She had really worn him out tonight. He didn't beat her too bad this time, he mostly just wanted to release some sexual frustration he had pent up. And her body always satisfied him. He knew he was hurting her, giving her more than she could handle. After all she was only 18, maybe even 19. He had just realized he didn't know when her birthday was. Didn't much care either. He turned on his back and looked up at the ceiling. His mind shifted to Autumn. He finally had her. He had made a commitment. He told her to give him a week so he could settle things with Michelle. She reluctantly agreed. After the night he had with Michelle he was doubting if he could really give her up. He had some ideas but could he really keep such a secret from Autmn? She was bound to find out. Axel was knocked out of his thoughts by a buzzing on his bedside table. He picked it up and noticed he didn't recognize the number. It was a text message. Should he open it? It could be a virus? Axel's curiosity had gotten the best of him and he opened the message.

*Oh wow.* He thought to himself. It was a booty call from an unexpected source. But should he? Who was he kidding? Axel was always down to get into something he never had before and she was fine. Just like with Michelle, what Autumn doesn't know won't hurt her. Axel felt a bit tired, but he decided he would make the effort anyway. He got out of bed, stepped over Michelle's abused body and headed toward the shower.

Axel pulled up to the hotel where he had been summoned. He made his way inside and up to the 6th floor. He checked the signs to make sure he was headed the right way. Room 634 to the right. He reached the room and the door was already opened. He hesitated and then pushed it open. He didn't see anyone. He ventured around the corner into the bedroom. And there she stood in a pink lace negligée and three-inch stilettos. He was definitely ready to sample her.

"Well, it's about time you called. I knew you wanted this from the first day of auditions. You dance like you used to strip. I sure would like to find out if you can transfer those skills to the sheets."

River stood in front of Axel with her hands behind her back. She knew he couldn't turn down a booty call. "I'm afraid you won't be able to find out my love." River pulled the 9mm complete with silencer from behind her back and pointed it straight at Axel's heart.

Axel's eyes grew large. "What are you doing?"

"Just out for a little revenge."

"Revenge. What did I ever do to you River?"

"A life for a life Axel. That's all I want."

"Look I haven't killed anyone, so you can get somewhere with that."

"Of course not Axel. You're way too smart for that. You have people who will do it for you, except you failed." She raised the gun.

"What? River, stop playing!"

"Goodbye Axel." River smiled and pulled the trigger twice.

## ABOUT
# THE AUTHOR

**Angela M. Green** is a devoted mother of two incredible sons, Isaiah and Justin, who serve as her constant inspiration. Hailing from El Paso, TX, Angela now calls Hueytown, AL, her home. She is a proud graduate of Pleasant Grove High School and has dedicated eight years to nurturing young minds as a preschool teacher.

Beyond her roles within the community, Angela is fueled by a passion for creativity, literature, and innovation. Whether she's immersing herself in a good book, expressing herself through writing, or exploring new avenues of artistic expression, Angela consistently seeks to inspire and uplift those around her.

Printed in the USA
CPSIA information can be obtained
at www.ICGtesting.com
LVHW011348240724
786348LV00011B/401